# LOVE LESSONS

Before Agatha could stop him, Cooper's clever fingers removed the pins securing her coil. Her thick chestnut hair was released and came tumbling down her back in a burnished cascade.

"That's more like it," he said, eyes gleaming with approval. His fingers sifted through the silky mass of her hair. Fingers that were surprisingly sensitive in their touch. The sensation was incredibly soothing.

"An interesting demonstration," she managed to tell him. "But as you see, being sober on this occasion, I am still in control of myself."

That a challenge, Aggie? If so..." His fingers penetrated to her scalp, stroking downward in a long, slow caress that made her squirm with pleasure.

"I fail to see anything instructive in this experiment."

"You want schooling? I think we can manage some schooling."

"Regarding what area?" she whispered.

"Let's concentrate on something where your education is deficient. The subject of osculation comes to mind."

"Osculation. If I remember correctly, there is a more general term for the word."

"That would be kissing. Needs a knowledge of all its refinements, though, if you're going to practice it properly."

"Are you a qualified teacher?"

"Let's see if I am." His voice was husky, mesmerizing. He leaned into her until his mouth was a mere warm breath away from hers.

# JEAN BARRETT

# DELANEY'S CROSSING

LEISURE BOOKS　　NEW YORK CITY

*For Laura*
*Just Because*

A LEISURE BOOK®

March 1997

Published by

Dorchester Publishing Co., Inc.
276 Fifth Avenue
New York, NY 10001

# DELANEY'S CROSSING

# Prologue

. . . *Independence, Missouri, 1841*

It never occurred to Ezra Bottle that he might be in trouble. The small, dark mountain man was busy concentrating on a long soak in his favorite tub at Tibbet's Bathhouse. Eyes closed and in a dreamy state, he didn't hear the whisper of the curtain that screened the cubicle he occupied.

The next thing Ezra knew, a sharp, cold instrument was tickling the most vulnerable portion of his exposed anatomy. He gave a little yelp of alarm, and his eyes flew open to discover the wicked blade of a bowie knife pressed up against him. Damnation!

"Easy, Ezra," warned a silky voice. "You start squirmin' around in there and I'm apt to make a mistake and cut off somethin' you'd be real sorry about losin'."

Ezra went rigidly still. All that moved was his startled gaze which lifted to meet the face that leaned down at him through wisps of steam.

# Jean Barrett

It was a mean face with cunning eyes and an ugly, puckered scar that slashed diagonally down one cheek. The scar was so close to its owner's mouth that when he grinned, like he was doing now, it contorted his thin lips into something savagely menacing. Ezra had heard that the scar was the result of a knife fight with a Nez Percé Indian who had been reluctant to part with his cache of furs. The Nez Percé had lost the fight.

"Duke Salter," whispered Ezra, unable to help the tremor in his voice. "Whatcha want, Duke? I ain't done nothin'."

"That's the trouble, Ezra. You're supposed to be doin' something. You're supposed to be accepting that little gift one of my men wanted to give you last night. Hurt him real bad when you turned it down like that."

The bribe, the mountain man realized. Duke Salter had used a friend to try to bribe him not to guide that wagon train of Latter-day Saints out to the Oregon country where they'd figured to start a new colony.

Salter and his bunch were crazy. And so was the greedy Pacific Fur Company that employed him. Duke had spent the past several years in the Northwest using threats and bribery to coerce both Indians and white trappers into doing business with Pacific Fur over its hated rival, the Hudson's Bay Company. Whatever vileness had been necessary, Duke had executed it. There were stories about him that made rugged men shudder in the telling of them over campfires. Ezra didn't know if they were true, and he didn't aim to try to find out.

What he did know was that Pacific Fur, which had its headquarters in St. Louis, had recalled Duke to Independence to deal with another potential threat to its rich fur trade. Farmers wanting new lands. The company was ruthlessly determined to preserve Oregon as a wilderness. So far it had had its way. There were only a few settlers, and all men at that, in the fertile Willamette Valley. The handful of white women

8

scattered through Oregon were the wives of missionaries and posed no problem.

But Ezra knew that, if it should be successfully demonstrated that wives and children could survive the long crossing by wagon, the trains would come in hordes. Families always meant civilization, and when that happened, the valuable fur-bearing animals disappeared.

Ezra wondered how long Pacific Fur could expect to actually hold back the tide of immigration. But he wasn't about to argue the matter. Duke Salter was one chilling brute.

"Brought that gift with me," Duke informed him. "Now I'm gonna make the offer again, Ezra. Only this time I wanna hear gratitude, real gratitude. You understand me?"

Ezra felt the point of the knife press against the sensitive flesh of his male pride and joy. It was all he could do to keep himself from squealing in panic.

"Sure, Duke," the mountain man babbled. "Sure thing. Only it ain't necessary. These folks, see, they changed their minds. When I pointed out to 'em all the dangers and problems of tryin' to get a wagon train through that included females and younguns, they decided to settle right here in Missouri country. It's the truth, Duke."

Ezra sighed thankfully as the knife slowly retreated. Duke chuckled. "Well, now, that's smart of them. Real smart. Smart of you too, Ezra."

"Yeah, Duke. I aim to oblige."

"Let's keep it that way, Ezra."

The mountain man watched Duke turn and leave the cubicle. He sagged in relief in the tub and wondered if the rumor he had recently heard was true. That Duke had been promised generous shares in the Pacific Fur Company, what in fact amounted to membership in an exclusive club, if he and his mercenaries succeeded in discouraging an invasion of settlers. Because if it was true, without any law enforcement at all in the vast territory, it made him more dangerous than ever.

Hell, Ezra pitied anyone trying to get a wagon train through with Duke Salter guarding the Oregon Trail like a snake at a prairie dog's hole.

# *Chapter One*

The twenty-two women gathered around the open grave tried not to look confused and frightened. The man who had been their friend and protector was dead. They listened solemnly as Miss Agatha Pennington spoke their last reverent tribute to him in a voice that wobbled but refused to break.

"Hiram McMurdy, you were our salvation. We cherished you in life. Now we will keep you precious in our memories . . ."

From a safe distance away a pair of rawboned youths, hired from a nearby farm to dig the grave, leaned on their spades and idly watched the burial on the grassy knoll.

"Whatcha think?" drawled the lankier of the two. "Hoors?"

His carrot-topped companion snickered with excitement. "Yeah, hoors." Then his dull-witted face frowned. "But mebbe not. I mean, Jeb, some of 'em is sinfully ugly to be hoors."

11

Jeb spat tobacco juice in the swaggering manner of the bullwhackers he had seen in town and grinned. "Shows what you don't know. It's what they got under 'em skirts and how it works that counts."

"Well, Jeb, could be he was Mormon. I hear as how each one of 'em keeps a regular army of wives, and now he's in that box 'cause they plain wore him out."

"Naw. I say the ol' duck was a hoormaster headed west with his band of hoors so's all the trappers and traders could have their sport."

The two of them went on exchanging lewd speculations, none of which had a morsel of evidence to support it. There was only one certainty. The women were a thorough mystery and had been from the moment of their arrival in the oak grove days ago.

As the last jumping-off place on the frontier, Independence had seen every variety of mankind bound for the west, ranging from profane prospectors and wicked opportunists to devout healers and saintly missionaries. But this wagon train defied all belief. Composed entirely of females, it was downright unnatural. The community shunned it, even though curiosity gnawed at its inhabitants. The women offered no explanation for their existence. Aware of a general disapproval, they kept largely to themselves. But now that their leader was gone . . .

The two youths stopped talking, suddenly aware of the silence up around the grave. The women had finished paying their respects to the deceased. The starchy one they called Miss Agatha, the tallest woman Jeb and his gangly friend had ever seen, was gazing down at them in a direct manner that suggested she knew exactly what they had been discussing. Their faces flamed with embarrassment.

Her instruction to them was unemotional and quiet but reached their ears as clearly as a battle cry. "If you can trouble yourselves to manage it, gentlemen, you may climb off those shovels now and fill in the grave."

The women began filing down the slope in a long, sorrowful line, leaving the pair of humbled youths to cover the body. When they reached the leafy grove where their fifteen prairie schooners were parked, scattered under the oaks along with the grazing oxen intended to pull them, there was an awkward, helpless moment. None of them sat, except for a pregnant sixteen-year-old girl who lowered herself tiredly on an upturned flour barrel. They stood there forlornly, their mournful expressions registering their loss and their deep uncertainty about the future. All of them felt it, shared in the worry and wondered. What was to become of them now?

Agatha knew she had to reassure them. There had been no opportunity before this. Somehow she must convince them not to surrender the dream.

She was searching for the right words, the strongest possible argument, when Susan interrupted the long silence. Of all the women, Agatha was closest to Susan, possibly because she had been her first recruit. The small, plain Susan brusquely addressed an eight-year-old girl who had been waiting impatiently near her side. "Callie, you got something for Miss Agatha?"

Mystified, Agatha watched as the sturdy child raced toward one of the wagons, the riotous curls and grimy pinafore ribbons of a tomboy streaming behind her. She was back in seconds, soberly bearing across her outstretched arms a long hickory staff. She presented herself in front of Agatha, extending the staff toward her as she delivered her carefully rehearsed words.

"For you, Miss Agatha. We figger he'd of wanted you to have it. It's for takin' up the journey where he left off. And, uh—and we wish you will accept it."

In the pause that followed, Agatha could sense tension in the gathering, the anxious women wondering whether she would accept the offering or decline it.

Hiram McMurdy's staff. The cherub-faced little man had carried it everywhere. It had been a part of him. Agatha knew that the stout pole had aided their friend with his energetic, but aging, gait. Nothing else. It was not meant to be the symbolic staff of a prophet leading his flock to the Promised Land. Hiram would have been the first to scoff at such nonsense. But for the women it had meaning, perhaps to do with confidence and a perpetuation of the dream. Something they badly needed. She could not possibly reject it.

Agatha could almost hear a collective sigh of relief as she reached for the stick. The hickory was well worn, darkened with age and use. She weighed the crudely carved length of it, testing it. Yes, it felt right to her, already familiar in her hands.

"Thank you, Callie," she said simply. "That was very nicely done."

Her voice and manner bore every evidence of her innate dignity, but she favored the child with a private wink of approval. Callie squirmed in appreciation.

So, Agatha thought, planting the staff firmly upright in front of her, it was done. She had just accepted a challenge, and she knew it. She was touched by their faith in her but not surprised. Considering everything, it was only logical that she should try to replace Hiram for them. She prayed that she had skills enough to do exactly that. But even before Hiram's death the whole business had been complicated by problems of a seemingly insurmountable nature, and now, without his knowledge to guide them . . .

For a dreadful moment her courage failed her as she realized that she alone now was responsible for the welfare of these women. They were gazing at her trustingly, waiting for her direction. Where was she to begin? *How* was she to begin?

Her hand tightened on the staff, as if to extract confidence from it. But it wasn't in the tough hickory, polished with handling, that she found what she sought. What she needed came from the fabric of her own being. A well of fortitude had always been available to Agatha Pennington, even in the worst moments of her thirty-year-old existence, and she had certaintly known her share of those. She drew from that well now, straightening an already amazingly erect figure as she squarely faced them.

"Ladies, I suggest we follow Rebecca's example and seat ourselves. There are decisions to be reached." ·

The women arranged themselves on the grass, calico skirts bunched under them, or squeezed together on several logs placed there by earlier wagoners who had camped in the grove. Agatha perched on a stump, the staff placed at her feet. Callie squatted in the grass on one side of the stump. The dog, Roscoe, flopped down on the other side.

When they were all seated, Agatha continued. "I think there is no question that, before we can do anything, it must be settled whether we go on or whether we turn back."

The choice she offered them was met by an emotional clamor, twenty-one voices lifted all at once in a forceful decisiveness. Miss Agatha raised a hand to quell them.

"Not like that, ladies. Each of you must say separately what she wants. We must be certain when our very lives are at stake. But, naturally, it is unnecessary for me to tell you this. You all know that to undertake the journey unaccompanied by males is regarded by outsiders as an unthinkable madness, even a wickedness. When our friend was here to lead us, the venture involved incredible risks. We were all warned of that repeatedly. But now that he is gone the risks are staggering. So be careful of your decisions. What is it to be?"

She started with the woman she had known the longest. "Susan?"

There was no hesitation from Susan. "Oregon."

"Mavreen?"

"My Connemara was a fair land, and I was that sorry to leave it, but Oregon will be all the fairer, I'm thinking."

"May?"

15

"Nothin' waitin' back east for me but grief. I'm for Oregon."

"Renata?"

"Yah, Oregon, too, is where I go."

"Faye?"

"Ain't gonna be no turnin' back for me. Oregon, and I'll do what I have to to get me there."

"Lettice?"

"Hell, way I figure it, there's no man for me in the states 'cause I've looked. That must mean there's one out there somewhere in Oregon just waitin' to put his brand on me, and I aim to oblige him."

"Tessa?"

"I say Oregon. I say if we have to break our backs to reach it, we go to Oregon."

And so it went around the circle. Even eight-year-old Callie was offered a vote. Their choices were unanimous and definite. The women wanted Oregon.

So, Agatha thought, it would not be necessary, after all, for her to try to reaffirm the dream for them. She should have realized, even at their lowest, that they were capable of hope and direction. She should have remembered that they had committed themselves long ago to this trek with a stubborn determination born out of pure desperation.

Hiram's death had been a blow to them, and though it might be fearful to go on without him, there would be everything to lose if they stopped now before the journey even began. She understood this as well as any of them. They each had the will, of course. Only time could prove whether they also had the necessary stamina. Agatha was thoroughly confident that they did.

It was the young Rebecca from her place on the flour barrel who asked softly, "What about you, Miss Agatha? You haven't said what *you* choose."

Agatha smiled to herself. The women had put themselves in her temporary care. She had made promises to each of them long ago, both she and Hiram McMurdy, and she intended to satisfy those promises. Therefore, she had no choice. She wasn't in the least sorry about that.

"Oregon," she said. "Oregon without question."

There were no rousing cheers now that their purpose had been redefined, just quiet satisfaction on twenty-two faces.

In the end, however, the thin young woman called Rachel expressed in her nervous stutter the single doubt each of them had been silently entertaining. "M-M-Mr. McMurdy being the only one who knew the trail, h-h-how do we find the way w-without him?"

"Yes," Agatha agreed. "I feel we have already proved we are capable of all that is essential, but there is that one real need we cannot do without. We must have a pilot. To attempt crossing the continent without one would be suicidal."

She lowered her head, considering the problem. In the grass at her feet, where the staff now rested, violets had bloomed on the day of their arrival in the oak grove. There were no violets now. They were long gone.

Misfortune had delayed them. There had been that ugly episode on the way from St. Louis that none of them wanted to remember. It had resulted in the loss of precious days as Hiram struggled to train the women to replace the men originally hired to accompany them. Then more delay occurred when Hiram became fearfully ill.

Agatha knew the timing was crucial for any parties bound for the Northwest. The wagons couldn't head out on the trails until the spring prairies turned green to feed the livestock that pulled them. Anywhere from late April to mid-May was the rule.

It was now past mid-May. Too late to try to link up with any seasoned group that might be headed in their direction. Not that this would have been a serious consideration anyway, Agatha realized. Such a company was almost certain to be exclusively male and would have no part of them, even if the women were willing to trust a situation like that. Which, as experience had already taught them, they were not.

We are on our own then, she thought. No, not entirely on our own. There will be a pilot to guide us. There *has* to be a pilot.

Funds to hire one weren't a problem. Agatha was well provided with money in the strongbox hidden in her wagon. Available pilots were another matter. She remembered Hiram telling her that the few superior pilots in Independence were already committed and under way. Any remaining ones were second-rate.

"Who?" demanded one of the waiting women.

Agatha lifted her head. Yes, who? But she knew with a fatal certainty that there was only one choice.

Cooper J. Delaney.

That was his name. *Cooper J. Delaney.* She shuddered over the remembered image of him. Based on a brief glance, it wasn't much of an image. But it was more than she cared to see.

The sight had occurred last evening just before sundown. Hiram's condition had worsened, and Agatha had hurried into Independence to fetch the doctor. She was returning with him to their encampment off the western edge of the town when they passed a band of traders arriving from the Santa Fe Trail, their carts laden with furs, hides and Mexican silver.

Agatha had been too worried about Hiram to pay much attention to the freighters. But there was no way to overlook their leader as he stood in the middle of the road, employing his own brand of persuasion on a recalcitrant mule. She found herself gazing at a great hairy bear of a man cracking his fifteen-foot whip above the head of the impassive mule, cursing like a savage and looking as if he had most of the dirt of the southern trail caked on his sweat-stained buckskins. It was, at best, a fleeting and distinctly unencouraging impression.

Dr. Thaddeus Vine, a man of humor, had chuckled over

the startled expression on Agatha's face as they moved on. "You've just been privileged, ma'am, to view the fine sight of Cooper J. Delaney. And while I am sure," he added, "that this doesn't much appeal to you, there are certain ladies who will be delighted to learn Cooper J. is back in town."

Agatha didn't choose to imagine it.

"Not, of course," the doctor went on, "before he holes up at the Merchants Hotel for a solid twenty-four hours. Hibernation behind him, he'll celebrate for another twenty-four with a fair maiden on each arm, probably getting knee-slapping drunk before he heads back to the trail."

Agatha said nothing. She didn't have to. The doctor could easily read her disapproval, though she tried to tell herself it was not right of her to make judgments.

"Oh, it isn't all bad, Miss Pennington. Our legendary Cooper may be as ornery as one of his mules, and a hell-raiser in town, but out on the plains he's all sober business, and what he doesn't know about the trails west isn't worth knowing."

But Agatha, in her impatience to reach Hiram, hadn't cared to be reassured about Cooper J. Delaney. Not last evening anyway. This morning was another matter entirely.

Whether she liked it or not, it would seem that Cooper Delaney was their only candidate. Obviously, therefore, she must put her biases behind her and approach this flinty giant with their proposition. It wasn't a prospect she relished. She knew instinctively that the man was apt to be . . . well, rather difficult in this situation. But, having decided on her course of action, she didn't let this further trouble her.

"I believe," Agatha informed the women, picking up her staff and rising confidently to her feet, "there is a pilot for us. Dr. Vine and I passed him on the road last night. He assured me the man is a capable guide. Being the case, I see no point in any delay. I propose to locate him now and make the necessary arrangements for his services. Agreed?"

The women raised no objections.

Agatha was headed for her wagon to make her simple toilet when Susan joined her. As always, her speech was abbreviated and her manner devoted. "Oughtn't to try this on your own. Suppose you wouldn't like me to go with you?"

"I would, Susan, but it is important you remain with the women. I think they are skillful enough now with the wagons and oxen, but they must achieve accuracy with the rifles. You are the most able to direct target practice."

Susan accepted the charge, but her round face was knit with concern. "What if this man don't want no part of us?"

Agatha smiled. "You forget the strongbox. I am prepared to offer him any price."

"And what if it ain't enough?"

Agatha refused to consider the possibility. Why should she, when experience and Hiram McMurdy had taught her there was virtually nothing that couldn't be achieved? Providing, of course, one applied sufficient concentration and persistence. She was capable of both.

"Well, now, ain't that somethin'," Duke muttered to himself, his thin mouth quirking with amusement.

He stood at the second-floor window of his hotel room, his thumb lovingly stroking the edge of the knife that was always with him as he peered down into the street. Along with the rest of Independence, he was accustomed to eccentrics. They were common sights in a town that straddled the frontier as this one did. On almost any day of the week you could find weather-beaten mountain men mingling with the fashionable and the disreputable, burly rivermen up from the nearby Missouri to raise hell in the saloons, painted Kansas Indians on their shaggy ponies, fair skins and dark skins.

But at this moment even the hardened citizens of raw Independence were turning to stare at the regal figure of Miss Agatha Pennington passing beneath Duke's window. She was marching purposefully toward the town square, bearing her hickory staff like a scepter. Her head was high, as if drawn back by the weight of the thick chestnut hair coiled precisely at the nape of her long neck.

"Gawd a'mighty," Duke said, "she's got to be all of six feet. A real amazon."

He knew all about Agatha Pennington and her wagon train. His network in town had even informed him of the death of the old man last night. Laughable, he thought, that this new challenge to his promise to Pacific Fur should turn out to be something like this. Dirt farmers with their wives and brats he could expect, but not a troop of women who actually believed they stood a chance of making it to Oregon on their own. A joke all right. They wouldn't get any farther than Independence.

Even so, Duke had anticipated that with their leader gone, they would try to find a new guide. The Pennington bitch was probably on her way right now to hire a pilot. She wouldn't find one. He had made certain of that. Better safe than sorry, he always figured.

Duke had managed to reach all of the pilots left in town. All but Delaney, that is, who had arrived last night fresh off the Santa Fe. Even he had known better than to approach Delaney. The amazon would learn that for herself, if she was fool enough to attempt it.

Grinning sadistically, Duke lowered the knife and made a series of rapid, vicious chops along the window ledge, as though he were slicing up annoying insects.

"So much for you and your females, Agatha Pennington."

Agatha ignored the curious stares and snickers of the on-lookers in the street. She had been experiencing them most of her life, had often overheard the whispered references to her "altitude" or the coarse male jokes about "scaling her formidable peaks." She wasn't immune to the hurt of these cruel barbs. She had simply learned to handle them by hiding her vulnerability behind a barrier of pride.

21

Heartaches of the past had taught her other lessons as well, like the wisdom of softening her height and bold face in her choice of dress. She wore practical clothing, plain almost to a point of severity. Her garb this morning was an example— a narrow, black serge skirt with a matching jacket over a serviceable white blouse. She had convinced herself long ago that her robust figure would look ridiculous in fashionably wide skirts and beribboned bonnets, though at times she secretly longed for these feminine frills. But such desires must be controlled, along with other womanly yearnings that she could never realize. Oh, she knew what she was all right. She was an old maid. It was a state she tried to accept without the waste of regret.

There were plenty of idlers to observe her vigorous passage, and this did worry her. People hadn't been busy when only a week ago the thoroughfare had been heavy with traffic, the air brawling with the ring of anvils in blacksmith sheds, the incessant clang of the wheelwrights' hammers, the cries of horse dealers from their crowded pens as freighters were outfitted for the trails west. Another reminder to Agatha that the wagon trains had already departed while she and her friends were still here.

She planned to remedy that situation as she passed the handsome brick courthouse and crossed the square to the two-story edifice that was the Merchants Hotel. Avoiding a misplaced brass spittoon as she entered the deserted lobby, she presented herself at the front desk, tapping her staff on its polished surface to command the attention of the desk clerk.

He looked up from his ledger. The young man had a fancy waistcoat, an animated Adam's apple and a suspicious expression on his narrow face. She knew that unescorted ladies were not encouraged at the Merchants Hotel.

"Help you?" he asked lazily.

Agatha didn't appreciate his cavalier manner. "You may,"

she stated briskly. "I believe you have a Mr. Delaney staying with you."

The clerk's suspicion deepened. Cooper J. Delaney had an eyebrow-raising reputation where certain women were concerned. But he must see that she hardly qualified for that role.

"Well?" Agatha demanded, impatient with his inefficiency.

"Mr. Delaney is registered with us," he admitted reluctantly.

"It is imperative that I speak with him. Be so good as to send for him. I will wait in your parlor."

"No, ma'am, I'll not."

"You refuse to call him?"

"I do, ma'am." The Adam's apple above his standup collar did a stubborn dance. "Everybody knows that when Mr. Delaney comes off the trail the first thing he does is to sleep the clock around. And the next thing everybody knows is that to poke him awake before he's ready to be poked awake is as good as raising a hibernating grizzly. Probably worse."

Agatha stared at the clerk, taking his measure. The Adam's apple was still bobbing defiantly. It would be pointless to argue with him. "I see. In that case you may direct me to his room. I will risk your bad-tempered grizzly myself." It was hardly proper for a lady to approach a man in his hotel room, but she would talk to him out in the hallway. Yes, that would serve.

"Ma'am, if I did that I'd be begging to be skinned alive."

Agatha did not choose to be defeated. While it was against her principles to resort to a bribe, one did have to be flexible in an urgent situation. Slipping the old-fashioned reticule from her wrist, she placed it temptingly on the counter. "Perhaps for a consideration?"

The young clerk's reluctance promptly vanished. "Top of the stairs," he muttered, pocketing the coins she slid toward him. "Turn right, fourth door on the left, and you didn't learn it from me."

The Merchants Hotel, like the rest of Independence, had one foot in the civilized East and the other in the untamed West. Climbing the stairs, Agatha could plainly see this as she left behind the exaggerated elegance of the lobby and reached the upper floor with its cramped rooms and rough board walls.

Finding the door she needed, she raised her staff and rapped on its unpainted surface with every assurance that she would soon achieve her intention.

Three minutes later she was still standing alone out in the narrow hallway, her confidence reduced to supreme frustration. Repeated knocks on the locked door and insistent calls had raised no response except several curious and frowning faces poked out of other doors along the passage.

This was absurd! Not even a hibernating bear could be so immune to her noisy efforts. Apparently, Cooper J. Delaney was choosing to ignore her pleas. Either that or he had left the hotel without the desk clerk's knowledge. Unless, of course, he was dead in there.

How was she to reach him?

The answer to that dilemma arrived in the form of a little chambermaid scuttling timidly along the hallway with her bucket and broom. Agatha stopped her and explained what she wanted.

The maid's reply was a nervous, "Oh, miss, no. They'd have my job if I did something wicked like that. I couldn't consider it, not never."

Agatha sighed and reached for her reticule again. The chambermaid, for all her refusals, proved in the end no more resistant to a bribe than had the desk clerk. Seconds later the girl led her into an empty adjoining room, unlocked the connecting door and scurried away to avoid any possible consequences of her action.

Permitting herself no hesitation, Agatha slipped into the

room occupied by Cooper J. Delaney.

The place was in shadow, the blinds at the window adjusted to keep out the daylight. In the silent gloom rose an enormous bed whose elaborate rosewood headboard seemed out of character with the stark surroundings. A hulking form of intimidating proportions was stretched on his back along the length of the bed. Her target.

"Mr. Delaney."

She wasn't surprised when he failed to respond to her whispered call. Not after all her unanswered clamor out in the hall. She tried again, louder this time.

"Mr. Delaney!"

Never a stir. How could anyone sleep so profoundly?

Summoning her courage, she approached the bed and stood over him. He wasn't a pleasant sight. He still wore the filthy buckskins, not having bothered to wash or change before he dropped across the clean coverlet. Weeks on the trail had resulted in a long mane of unruly black hair and a bushy, dusty beard. There was something else. He smelled. Her nose wrinkled in disgust as she tried to identify the odor. Mules, she guessed. Or their manure. He must have slept with them.

"*Mr. Delaney,*" she insisted.

This time her proximity earned her a low grunt from the bed. Nothing beyond that, however. There was still the problem of rousing him. What was it the desk clerk had said about poking him awake?

Agatha glanced at the staff clutched in her hand.

Oh, surely not. Even a bear deserved to be awakened with something more gentle than a prodding stick. There was no helping it. She was not eager to touch him, but she had no choice.

Mouth set in a firm line, she leaned down over his supine bulk. Her hand closed on a shoulder as hard as stone.

"Mr. Delaney!" she demanded.

There was a soft moaning sound from him and a slight squirming movement under her fingers that she found oddly disturbing, but he never opened his eyes. She had a sudden survivor's urge to withdraw her hand, but this wouldn't win her purpose. Instead, she bent even closer, her fingers boldly squeezing unyielding muscle as she prepared to shake him into consciousness.

"Mr. Delaney, if you please—"

It all happened so swiftly that Agatha had time to issue nothing but a small, strangled cry. Then the breath was slammed out of her lungs as two great bear paws dragged her into an outrageous embrace.

She found herself tumbled along the length of him, held fast against a massive chest and unable to protect herself from the strange, rioting reactions of the powerful body clasping hers. A leg like a tree trunk wrapped possessively around her skirts, pinning her so intimately that she was unable to escape his startling, somnambulistic behavior. She heard dream-induced animal groans from the direction of his beard, tasted a hot, lusty breath against her face, smelled a pungent aroma. Not the reek of the mules but something male and earthy. Never had she been subjected to anything so utterly physical. It was shocking, mortifying and absolutely sensual.

She struggled, of course. Struggled violently against the strong hands splayed across her posterior. But that only seemed to make it worse. Now she could feel something swollen straining its heat against her abdomen. Actually, there were two somethings because there was another bulging hardness a bit higher. Baffling. Equally bewildering was the treacherous heat that flamed through her insides as she suffered this undignified sprawl atop a strange, very aroused masculine body.

Agatha had no experience with the carnal, but she had enough sense to be genuinely alarmed. The situation was raging out of control and needed a strong, immediate action to terminate it. What?

She was still gripping the hickory staff in her free hand.

Obviously useful in more ways than one. She managed with some effort to wedge the stick between them and to thrust it against vulnerable flesh. An armpit, she guessed.

Success!

Her instant release, on the heels of an angry oath, was followed by a rush of movement. The two tangled bodies couldn't get away from each other fast enough. Agatha scrambled from the bed and regained the solid security of the floor. Cooper Delaney, fully sensible now and equally stunned, shot up against the headboard and stared at her in horror. The roar that issued from him was less like a bear's and more like a bull's.

*"Who in sweet hell are you?"*

Striving to regain her composure, Agatha hastily straightened her skirts while managing a somewhat shaky, "After that—that appalling exhibition, I am left wondering exactly *who* you did think I was."

His scowl, involving a pair of thick eyebrows, was as black as his beard. "How should I know? I was dreaming that I *wasn't* out on the trail for weeks on end without a willing woman to—"

He broke off as another realization apparently occurred to him. Agatha had no time to question it. The next thing she knew, his hand whipped under the pillow, and she found herself confronting a long-barreled Colt pistol.

His demand, as he leaned toward her menacingly, came in the form of a lethal growl. "What are you doing in my room, and how did you get in here? You have five seconds to answer before I put a hole in that long, aristocratic nose."

Intolerable! She was prepared to forgive him the humiliating tussle on the bed. After all, it was a mistake. He hadn't actually been awake and was presumably responding to a dream that didn't bear thinking about. But there was no excuse for *this* performance.

"Was I misinformed," she challenged him rigidly, "when I was told that Westerners, no matter how mean their dispositions, are never in the habit of threatening ladies with firearms?''

The pistol leveled at her never wavered in his large hand. ''When they invade my room uninvited, maybe they aren't ladies. Maybe they're something else.''

''I assure you, sir—''

''That you weren't after this?'' His free hand slapped at his waistline, where Agatha was now able to detect a certain thickness under the buckskin. The other, mysterious hard bulge she had experienced on the bed was suddenly explained. He was undoubtedly wearing a money belt. A heavy one.

''I am no robber, Mr. Delaney.''

He wasn't impressed by her stiff-spined righteousness. The predatory green eyes above his hawkish nose went on regarding her suspiciously. ''Female or not,'' he informed her in a voice as deep as river gravel, ''you wouldn't be the first customer who tried to relieve me of my belt. Some of them even lived long enough to regret it.''

''I am *not* interested in your bank.''

''Then maybe you'd care to tell me just what you are after.''

''If,'' she requested matter-of-factly, ''you will put down that weapon I will be happy to explain.''

''You first.''

''I beg your pardon.''

''The club you whopped me with.''

The barrel of the Colt gestured toward the staff she was still tightly clutching. Agatha glanced down at it in surprise. It never occurred to her that he might regard it as a threat. She obliged him by dropping the long walking stick. It clattered to the floor at her feet.

The pistol in his hand relaxed. He lowered it against his side, but he didn't release it.

''Now,'' he instructed her in that deceptively lazy voice,

"suppose we move on to the particulars of how you managed to sneak into my room."

"Nothing so furtive, Mr. Delaney. I made every effort to rouse you from the hall. That failing, I simply came through the unlocked adjoining room." She nodded toward the connecting door but offered no further details, hoping to protect the chambermaid. He seemed to accept her explanation. For the moment anyway.

He nodded slowly as he settled back against the towering headboard, his buckskin-clad legs crossed negligently at the ankles. "Very good. Now let's move on to names and just why you're so eager to make my acquaintance. Soliciting donations for a favorite charity, are you? You look the type." A white and lecherous grin blazed out of the shaggy black beard. "Or am I to hope you maybe had, uh, pleasure in mind when you tiptoed to my bed?"

He was reminding her of that shameful embrace, something a gentleman of sensitivity would have forgotten. Cooper J. Delaney was not a gentleman. He was a thorough scoundrel. But he was a scoundrel she needed, so she made every effort to curb a tongue that longed to lash him severely.

"I am Miss Agatha Pennington," she informed him calmly, "and the services I require of you are *not* of an illicit nature."

"That so?"

Cooper considered her. His eyes, less blurred now with sleep, were better able to define her. He wasn't about to tell her so, but he had to admire her for standing up to him like this so coolly. Few enough men did that, and no woman in his memory ever had.

"Agatha Pennington, huh?" He leaned against the headboard and languidly appraised her. He noticed her height, of course. There was no way not to notice. But since he was far above average himself, he found no reason to dwell on this.

It was her face that he found remarkable. It certainly

wasn't conventionally attractive. Maybe it wasn't attractive at all, in fact. But, like the rest of her, there was nothing indecisive about it. It was all clearly, proudly there—an arrangement of strong, dark eyebrows, a nose that could possibly be termed unfortunate in its length, a wide mouth, a firm, stubborn chin and a pair of intelligent, alert blue eyes that waited for him to finish judging her.

"So, Agatha Pennington," he drawled, "what services are we talking about?"

"The Oregon Trail. I was given to understand you are familiar with it."

"That and every other trail west," he admitted. "Can't imagine why it should interest you, though. Or are you looking for material? Maybe you're one of those ladies scribbling a romance about a wilderness she's too delicate to visit for herself."

One of his thick black eyebrows elevated with amusement. Agatha noticed that the eyebrow was divided by a diagonal white scar, like a blaze on a tree trunk. She wondered how he had received it. Not that it mattered. It was, however, evidence of a battered, but tough, warrior, reminding her again of what she was dealing with.

"I am not going to write about it," she said. "I am going to live in it, along with the twenty-one friends and companions I represent. We are going to the Willamette Valley in the Oregon Territory where land has been secured for us, and we need an experienced pilot to conduct us there."

Realization flared like lightning in that pair of compelling green eyes. He hiked himself up so sharply that he banged his head against the headboard. "Holy Lucifer!" he thundered. "You're one of those crazy females the whole town is yapping about, that sect camping out at Oak Grove."

"We are not a sect," she insisted. "There is nothing in any manner religious about our purpose."

"Then I'm damned if I can imagine why twenty-two women without husbands should be headed for what a lot of fools are beginning to think is the Promised Land.''

Agatha was expecting this. Of course, he would want an explanation, was entitled to one. She was prepared to offer what she hoped was a credible motive for their journey without disclosing any compromising details.

She never got the opportunity. He silenced her with a grim, ''I don't want to hear it. Whatever it is, it can't be sane. You have to be out of your heads to believe that a flock of women and one old coot, all on their own, stand any chance of hauling a wagon train two thousand miles to Oregon.''

He was referring to Hiram. He didn't know. ''Mr. McMurdy is no longer with us,'' she told him quietly.

''Got smart and walked out on you, did he?''

''No, Mr. Delaney,'' she corrected him, ''he did not leave us in that fashion. Hiram McMurdy died last evening of pneumonia and was buried this morning.''

We forgot, Agatha remembered painfully. Hiram was so full of life that all of us forgot he was no longer young, that he couldn't go on forever. We failed to see how overworked and worried he was about us after what happened on the road from St. Louis.

''Yeah?'' Cooper mumbled. ''Well, I'm real sorry about that.'' He had the decency to look contrite. It lasted no more than ten seconds before he demanded roughly, ''That still doesn't explain why there are no men with you.''

''There were experienced men hired in St. Louis to escort us.''

''Where are they?''

''There were . . . well, problems,'' she said reluctantly. ''It was necessary to let them go.'' Unless it was absolutely essential, Agatha didn't care to share with him that cruel episode on the way from St. Louis or why, afterwards, they had deemed it wiser not to try to replace the men. There were enough biases against them without telling him this.

She stood there watching him, hands clasped together at her waist while he shifted restlessly against the headboard.

31

He was wearing that ferocious scowl again.

"So you come to me. You've got a lunatic notion that I'm supposed to guide you to Oregon. Well, you can—" He caught himself. With a full understanding now of her errand, he had been about to thicken the air with some of his choicer curses. Swearing was as natural to Cooper as rainwater. But he supposed, after all, that she was a lady, so he traded the curses for an emphatic, "Oh, no, Agatha Pennington, not me. Not if you were to bind me with hemp and mount me on the lead wagon."

"I do not believe that will be necessary. I am prepared to offer you a substantial sum. In fact, whatever you ask."

"I've just come off the Santa Fe," he said flatly. "That was my last trail for hire."

"But surely—"

"At *any* price." He poked the heavy pistol in the direction of his money belt. "The haul was a profitable one. I've got all the gold I want right here."

And all the gold he needed, he thought. He had been slaving for years to accumulate the necessary amount, and the contents of the money belt finally made it a reality. Most of his savings were waiting for him in California where he had sent them to a friend he trusted. Now he could begin fighting to recover what had been taken from him. It was all that mattered, all that had *ever* mattered, and no one was going to interfere with his aim. Certainly not this obstinate female. He told her so.

"The gold is going to California to join the rest of my earnings, and this time I'm going to be attached to it. Understand?"

She looked thoughtful for a few seconds, then nodded slowly. "Yes, I think I do. You wish to go to California, and we wish to go to Oregon. I believe they lie in the same direction. How fortunate."

"Yep, real handy," he said with sweet sarcasm. "And

Oregon would put me—oh, let's say just a few short miles off my destination.''

"But is it not? Fortunate, that is.''

"Lady, I don't think you're hearing me. Even if I was available for hire, eager for hire, there is no chance in this world, or the one hereafter, that I would consider taking you and your females to Oregon.''

"Whyever not?''

She might be built like a mastiff, he thought, but she had the tenacity of a rat terrier. She didn't know when to give up. Damn, but he needed to let loose with some favorite cuss words. Instead, he blew out his cheeks in exasperation, trying not to explode, trying to be reasonable.

"Because, for one thing, you can't make it without men.'' Why did she have to wear her hair like that, parted in the middle and drawn back in a tight bun?

"Male strength, you mean? I wonder, Mr. Delaney, if you realize just how much strength is required in childbearing?'' His shoulders were braced against the headboard. It annoyed her that she should notice, or care about, the breadth of those shoulders.

"How about the little matter of endurance? Four or five long months of endurance.'' He wondered what that thick chestnut mass would look like turned loose and cascading wildly down her back.

"Endurance is simply a degree of commitment. The women will not quit. They have sacrificed everything to come this far. They proved that on the road from St. Louis.'' What did his face look like under all those untamed whiskers? Brash? Rugged? He would have a pugnacious jaw. She was certain of that. She dared not try to picture the shape of his mouth.

"The road from St. Louis is a romp. The Oregon Trail happens to be something just this side of hell, and that's only when a wagon train gets lucky. When it doesn't, it's even worse.'' Her wide mouth ought to be thin-lipped to suit her prim image. It wasn't. It was full-lipped. Lush really, now that he came to think about it.

"We will manage. We will do what has to be done." The soft buckskin was stretched tightly over his long legs, revealing the thick muscles on his huge thighs. She tried not to look at his legs. Or his shoulders.

"It's past mid-May. A risky start for a wagon train." He wondered if that mouth had ever been on a man before.

"Yes. That much is regrettable." A deep chest, narrow hips. Really, she must not notice any more.

"A lot more regrettable if you meet snow in the Blues." What were her legs like under those skirts? He wished he could tell.

"Blues?" She made an effort to concentrate on his face. Nothing lower than that.

"Mountains, Aggie. *Bad* mountains." The hell with this. He was going to stop imagining what was inside her skirts. He had been on the trail too long, or he'd never be thinking about a female like Agatha Pennington.

"I see. Then we must make every effort to get through the Blues before the first snowfall." *Aggie?* He had called her *Aggie*. No one had ever called her *Aggie* before, not even in her childhood. She told herself she resented the familiarity, that it hadn't given her a silly, warm glow deep inside when he had said her name so carelessly like that.

"You do that. Only before you try it, you'd better acquire all the skills you lost when you let those men go. Or didn't you reckon they might be useful?"

"I assume you are referring to such essentials as hitching and driving heavy wagons, managing livestock, handling repairs under extreme conditions and knowing how to load and fire flintlock rifles should circumstances demand it. We have those skills, Mr. Delaney."

"You do, huh?"

"Yes, we do. Some of the women already had a fair knowledge of them, and the rest learned them from Mr. McMurdy when the hired men were turned away."

"Well, that's just real fine."

"It will be when we have the pilot we need."

Cooper felt himself sliding down the headboard in defeat. What was the use? He was talking, and she wasn't listening. Didn't *want* to listen. Was too blind and stubborn to understand that he wasn't going to have any part of her insanity, not at any price. All right, leave it at that.

"Then I hope you find one," he said mildly.

"Mr. Delaney, before you refuse me, would you do me the favor of riding out to the encampment to meet the women? I think if you talked to them you would begin to appreciate their earnest need to reach Oregon."

"Afraid I'm going to be too busy for that with answering a few needs of my own. Starting with about two more hours of uninterrupted sleep just as soon as you take yourself out of here the way you came in."

"Come to the grove," she persisted. "See for yourself that I do not exaggerate about those skills."

"Then when I get me all the sleep I want, I'm going to soak the prairie out of my hide over at Tibbet's Bathhouse where, if I'm lucky, that buxom girl of theirs will scrub my back."

"Will you not at least consider my offer?"

"After that I'm calling on the barber for the first shave and haircut I've had in weeks. That's before I buy myself the biggest and tastiest meal in town."

"Mr. Delaney, I beg of you—"

"Should be after sundown by then. Time to head for the Cattail Saloon around the corner and a bottle of their smoothest whiskey."

Useless, she thought. She should have known better than to try to appeal to him on any level of decency, to win him with a nobility of purpose. Cooper J. Delaney didn't want to understand about such things because he had only one cause. Himself.

Cooper watched her, waiting for her to move toward the door. But the fool woman continued to stand there, staring

35

at him reproachfully. Well, hell, what did it take to get her out of here?

"And then, Aggie," he went on slowly, his voice husky, deliberately suggestive as he deepened his effort to provoke her into flight, "I'm going to hunt up the saloon's prettiest, most willing fancy girl. Care to imagine what that fancy girl and I are going to do together?"

Agatha gazed at him as he lounged there on the bed, the pistol dangling between his parted legs. He was despicable. She wanted no part of him now. Somewhere in Independence there had to be at least one other man knowledgeable about the Oregon Trail and willing to be enlisted for their purpose. She would find that man.

She still wasn't moving, Cooper realized. He'd have to get blatant about it. "Oh, that fancy girl is going to do the sweetest things to me, Aggie," he taunted her in his drowsy voice. He demonstrated by stroking the long barrel of the Colt slowly and seductively along the inside of his leg.

Agatha refused to let him see her disarmed by his obscene performance. With an easy, graceful movement, she retrieved the staff from the floor, lifted her chin and serenely promised him, "We will prevail, Mr. Delaney. With or without you, we *will* prevail."

He was still rubbing the barrel of the Colt along his loins, an unconscious action by now as she reached the door and looked over her shoulder. Brazen of her or not, she couldn't resist sending a parting shot into his swollen male ego.

"Take care with that pistol," she cautioned him bluntly, "before you shoot off something you may want later on."

The Colt froze in his hand. She was smiling with satisfaction as she left the room. Cooper glared fiercely at the door closing behind her, and then a slow, wolfish grin parted his beard.

Maybe, he thought, just maybe she had potential under all that whalebone, after all. But not for him. He liked his women sane.

# Chapter Two

Susan had only to glance at her face to read the discouragement written there. "Refused us, I suppose," she observed tartly.

"Both promptly and eloquently," Agatha admitted.

"Then where you been all this while?"

"Ah, yes, that." Agatha smiled at her wryly. "Everywhere in Independence, dear friend, learning just how terribly mistaken I was."

"About what?"

"My smugness when I parted from Mr. Delaney at his hotel. I told myself there had to be at least one other qualified pilot still available to us and that I was sure to find him. There is no pilot. The few who are left, even the inexperienced ones, are already spoken for. Or so they insist."

"Leaving only Delaney."

"Yes, Cooper J. Delaney is the only one not committed."

"What now?"

"The same question I asked myself all the way back from town."

Agatha feared the answer. Cooper Delaney was a mistake. Apart from all the other difficulties involved, he worried her on a personal level. She rarely lost control of her emotions, even in stressed circumstances. But this man had a talent for provoking her without effort. How was she supposed to survive such a rascal?

"What's the answer?" Susan demanded.

Personal choice had nothing to do with it, Agatha reluctantly decided. In the end, Cooper Delaney was all they had.

"Whether he wishes it or not, Mr. Delaney must be secured. He is completely opposed to us, of course, so we must be determined and resourceful."

"How?"

Agatha shook her head. "I must sort through the possibilities."

"Don't suppose a cup of tea would help?"

"I would welcome one." Agatha looked around, noticing that she and Susan were alone in the silent grove. "Where are the others?"

"Some down at the creek doing laundry. Others out in the pastures seeing to the oxen. I stayed back to clean rifles."

Just as well, Agatha thought. She had dreaded being eagerly welcomed by the women and then having to report her dismal failure. Now she had the opportunity to correct that.

Susan left her to stir up the fire and fill the kettle on the tripod. The sun wove dappled patterns on the trampled grass under the oaks as Agatha settled on the broad stump to attack the problem of winning Cooper Delaney.

She began by examining the things he had so carelessly revealed to her in his room, finding them useful ammunition. Out of that information a scheme began to take shape, but it was so daring and unprincipled that she resisted it.

*Desperate needs call for desperate measures, Agatha.*

No, it was wrong, shamefully wrong.

*You made the women a promise, you and Hiram. A clean start, you told them, new lives. Are you going to rob them of that chance just to protect yourself from quilt?*

It would be blackmail, clearly a form of blackmail.

*It is a necessity. There is no other way. You know there is not.*

But to be so deceptive . . .

*You will make it up to him. Before it is all finished, you will see to it that he benefits handsomely.*

In the end her resolute half won the argument over her regretful half. With the matter now settled, she thrust aside any lingering squeamishness and rose to her feet. "Forget that," she called excitedly to Susan. "I have a plan, and I want you to hear it."

But Susan had already prepared the tea. She returned to the stump, bearing the steaming brew in a tin cup. "I'm listening."

Agatha quickly outlined her intention, ending her explanation with a concerned, "It is an outrageous stratagem, I fear, but is it a workable one?"

"Risky, but oughta work with the right girl."

"Which would you recommend?"

Susan was thoughtful for a second. "Kitty," she decided. "Knows how to keep cool in a tight spot."

"I think you are right. Where is Kitty? I must know if she is willing."

"Stay here, drink your tea," Susan ordered her, thrusting the cup into her hand. "Had enough running. I'll bring Kitty."

Agatha didn't argue. Susan departed, and she perched on the stump again and sipped the bracing liquid. It was strong and sweet, just the way she liked it. While she waited for the women, she reexamined her plan, testing it for flaws and trying not to think of Cooper J. Delaney in any emotional connection with herself. This was impossible.

She couldn't seem to shake the image of that brief, but wanton, embrace on the bed in his room. The encounter should have been utterly revolting to her, the persistent memory of it humiliating. Instead, having had virtually no physical experience with men, there was a curiosity inside her that regarded the contact as instructive, even fascinating. And on a deeper, less detached level . . . well, her feeling could only be described as a breathless confusion prompted by a strange, soft yearning she wasn't prepared to define.

Absurd, of course, these tugging sensations deep down inside her. The great brute had practically assaulted her, though his action hadn't exactly been a conscious one. Had he been in a sensible state, she, of all people, would never have been the target of his lust. Still, Cooper Delaney was a man not to be trusted near any decent woman, and the thought of bearing his potent closeness for long months on the trail . . .

Well, he was a necessity. She would just have to manage him. And her own emotions as well.

She was draining the cup of tea when Susan returned to the campsite. Kitty was beside her. Agatha studied the young woman as they approached the stump where she waited. Kitty was a radiant blonde with the face of an angel and the alluring body of a voluptuary. The perfect device.

Agatha came to her feet as the two women joined her. She described her intrigue to Kitty, ending her explanation with an anxious, "I regret asking you to resume a practice you detested and which I promised you would never have to resort to again when you and Polly escaped it, so you must not hesitate to refuse me."

Kitty's response was a demure, "No need to fret, Miss Agatha. I know you wouldn't be asking this if there was any other way. Anyhow, it's not as if I'll have to . . . well, you know, go all the way."

"No, but will you be able to handle him?"

Kitty laughed, and she was suddenly no longer demure. It was the low, sultry laugh of a confident professional. "I guarantee it. By the time I'm finished with him, Mr. Cooper

J. Delaney will be just where we want him, and he won't even know how he got there.''

The Cattail Saloon was crowded with celebrating bull-whackers fresh off the Santa Fe Trail, its air harsh with to-bacco smoke and hoots of drunken laughter. At the bar a brawl threatened to erupt between a burly wagon freighter and his natural enemy, a riverman. The saloonkeeper swore to evict both of them. Someone was wailing on a mouth organ.

Cooper had appropriated a corner table for himself away from the worst of the noise. The fancy girl, whose name he couldn't remember—and what did it matter?—had joined him there without the least urging. Even better, she was snug-gled on his lap like a loving kitten, all silver-blond and built for pleasure. The choicest female in the place. Cooper, in a whiskey-induced haze, was immensely pleased. That's what he kept telling himself anyway.

"Soft," he whispered into her shapely ear. "All soft and sweet, aren't you?"

"You like me, sugar, don't you?" she purred, exaggerat-ing her Carolina drawl.

"Damn right I do. Real perfection," he said, stroking the seductive swell of her hip.

He fought away the persistent memory of another feminine bottom he had handled earlier today. A luscious bottom along with an old-fashioned, but provocative, fragrance he couldn't seem to get out of his nostrils. The memory couldn't be right. Had to be the result of his dream and not reality. Reality had been waking up to find himself trapped on his bed with an angular, outraged spinster pleading her crazy mission. Bony old maid like that just couldn't have a luscious bottom. All wrong.

"Nothing hard and mean about *you*," he said angrily to the girl on his lap, needing to convince himself. "Not like some willful females sneaking into a man's room with their wild-assed proposals." Damn it, he wasn't going to feel guilty about Agatha Pennington. He wasn't going to feel anything about her. He was going to California. *Directly* to California.

"That's right, sugar. I'm real agreeable." Kitty squeezed herself against his solid chest, assuring herself with a series of subtle caresses that he was still wearing the money belt.

"You sure are," he said, catching his breath on a sharp hiss as her skillful hands aroused him.

"I know how to make a man feel *real* good," she promised him.

"Can't deny that." He chuckled. Then he frowned, sidetracking himself again. "I tell you I'm heading for California? Leaving this crazy town behind with all the crazy females that've invaded it. Riding out for good."

"That so, sugar?"

He went on rambling about California, and Kitty made appropriate responses, all the inane junk customers liked to hear. She was a practiced and sympathetic listener when it came to masculine, drunken nonsense. Except this mister wasn't exactly drunk on whiskey, though he didn't know that. She prayed no one else in the room would realize it either.

From her first glimpse of him, Kitty had realized that the strapping great devil had the kind of head that could hold liquor all night without passing out. And she needed him in a stupor. It had been a risky business introducing the drops into his drink. When she'd paid the customary fee to ply her trade in the bar tonight, the saloonkeeper had warned her he would tolerate no crookedness in his place. She'd had to be very careful.

The necessity of the drops was something Kitty planned to keep strictly to herself. Miss Agatha would never condone such a measure. She had urged Kitty to be as gentle as possible with Cooper Delaney. Miss Agatha was a woman of propriety, already laden with guilt by the whole setup. She didn't understand about survival's more sordid demands. Kitty did.

But the nubile blonde was worried now. The drops were working all right—she could see that—but what if he collapsed on her before she got him safely back to his room? Of course, rushing things might have made him suspicious. Only now it was time to get him out of here before it was too late. He was still going on about California.

Kitty interrupted him, crooning into his ear a teasing, "Like to take me to California with you, sugar?"

Cooper grinned foolishly. "That's an idea."

"But not before you take me back to your place first, huh?" she coaxed. She blew seductively into his ear and then began to describe in breathy, lurid detail the kind of exciting things she planned to do to him once they were alone together in the privacy of his room. She could feel him growing heavy and full, and to guarantee his total arousal she wriggled slowly against his loins.

He laughed low in his throat, his voice husky with a painful heat. "Careful, sweetheart, before you destroy me right here."

He was suddenly impatient to have her. He needed to sink himself deep inside her, to lose himself in her ripe body where he could wipe out any other intrusive female image.

She must have sensed his readiness. She slid off his lap and waited for him. Fists planted on the table, Cooper levered himself to his feet. Once he was standing, his head began to spin. What was happening to him? He never lost control with his liquor. Hell, he was getting old, even if he had just turned thirty. The result of too many years on too many trails. No more, though. He was finished with trails.

The girl wrapped an eager arm around his waist. "This way, sugar."

They slipped out the back, ignoring the lewd remarks that followed them. Cooper didn't clearly remember stumbling through the dark alleyway and up a rear stairway of the Merchants Hotel, the girl half supporting him. The next thing he knew, they were in his room, and she was lighting a lamp and he was weaving on his feet next to the bed and thinking how much he wanted her. He started to tell her so, but somehow the words never got out of his mouth. What did emerge was his favorite song, "Comin' Thro' the Rye." He whistled it happily as he sank on the bed, flopping back against the mattress.

Kitty placed the lamp near the bed and then stood over him, a small smile of satisfaction on her painted mouth. In the end he had dropped abruptly without a fuss and lay sprawled on his back, as helpless as a log. The whistling turned into a snore. She had timed it perfectly. She watched him for a moment, needing to be certain he was completely under. He never stirred.

"Sweet dreams, mister," she murmured. Then she crossed the room and unlatched the connecting door to the adjoining room, calling a placid, "It's safe."

Agatha emerged from the shadows where she had been waiting, having gained access to her hiding place with another generous bribe to the little chambermaid. She joined Kitty in Cooper's bedroom. They spoke in conspiratorial whispers, though nothing would disturb the man on the bed for many hours.

"Was there any difficulty?"

Kitty chuckled. "Only for him. He wants to go to California."

"He will. Unfortunately, his destination involves a certain detour."

The two women moved toward the bed.

"Are you sure he will not wake up?"

"It would take a cannon going off in his ear. Maybe not even then."

Agatha stood close over the bed, inspecting the brawny length of Cooper Delaney. He went on snoring softly.

"He looks considerably different, not at all the bear of this morning."

Undoubtedly, she decided, the result of the shave, haircut and bath he had promised himself. She could see his full face now. It was the rugged, imperfect face she had expected, all hard planes and angles in the lamplight. There, too, were the square, pugnacious jaw she'd anticipated, the sharp blade of a nose and the wide, sensual mouth. But there was a surprise in all that bold virility. It lacked the harshness she had also expected and was—in this state of repose anyway—dismayingly vulnerable. Agatha felt her courage falter on her.

"He—he does look rather helpless like that. I suppose he must have drunk a good deal to get himself like this. Will he be all right?"

"He'll have a head as big as a melon when he wakes up, but that's all. Miss Agatha, you don't need to be here for this. No reason I couldn't have removed the belt on my own."

Kitty gazed sideways at her, sensing her reluctance and concerned by the moral dilemma that triggered it. Miss Agatha was plainly out of her element here and suffering for it. Kitty had no compunctions whatever about lifting the money belt. It was simply necessary.

"Absolutely not," Agatha insisted. "Should anything go wrong, I will not have you accused of taking his property. We must be able to honestly say *I* stole the belt."

"*Borrowing*, Miss Agatha. You said it yourself. We're just borrowing it for a spell."

"By our reckoning we are, but I am rather afraid neither Mr. Delaney nor the sheriff will wish to look at it that way. Well . . ."

She glanced again at the sleeping face below her. Even oddly divided as it was—pale on the lower half where the heavy growth of whiskers had blocked out the sun and deeply tanned on the upper half—it was not an unpleasing face. She had a sudden, inexplicable urge to drop a cloth over his head

45

so she wouldn't have to see that unexpectedly appealing countenance while she relieved him of the belt.

Agatha sniffed with impatience over her own foolishness. All this hesitation was dangerous. She must remove the money belt so they could leave the hotel before they were discovered.

Conquering her uneasiness, she leaned down over his sinewy form, prepared to lighten him of his burden. Her closeness, however, presented another small problem. The body that had reeked of mules this morning now offered a clean and very distracting male aroma.

"Like my help?" Kitty offered.

Agatha shook her head, renewed her resolve and attacked the waistline in front of her. To get at the belt, it was necessary to raise his fringed buckskin shirt and unbutton the top of his trousers. She managed this task with fumbling fingers. Male anatomy was an alien affair to her, and the hair-roughened flesh exposed by her effort produced a series of mysterious flutters in her nether region.

The money belt itself caused a further aggravation. It was not designed to be easily unclasped. The work of separating it from its owner involved her hands coming in repeated contact with that same disturbing flesh. Heat radiated from the bare skin she touched, searing her fingertips. Agatha found it difficult to breathe, and the more she hurried to loosen the belt and slide it free, the more awkward and delayed was her struggle.

"Miss Agatha, wouldn't you like me to—"

"No, I will prevail on my own, thank you. I almost have— *Oh, dear!*"

Kitty, baffled by the choked exclamation, followed her friend's startled gaze and found it riveted on the sizable, rigid bulge in Cooper Delaney's trousers. Miss Agatha's cheeks were stained with embarrassment.

"I seem to have caused a—a—"

"An erection," Kitty supplied nonchalantly.

Agatha swallowed painfully. "I was about to say a *reaction*. But as he is unconscious, I do not see how it is possible that—"

"He could swell?" Kitty hid her amusement and tried to delicately explain. "It's like that with men, Miss Agatha. Some men especially are easily stimulated, and you were— well, touching him a real lot."

"Yes. Yes, I see." She went on staring at his involuntary arousal, awed that she had the power to cause such a remarkable thing. She remembered that same hardness strained against her this morning and how she had failed to properly explain it to herself. It was understandable now. Of course. How could she have been so stupid not to realize?

Kitty glanced at her companion's slim hands hovering helplessly over the money belt and was sympathetic to her flushed anguish. "Should I finish getting the belt for you, Miss Agatha?" she offered gently.

"I think," Agatha said faintly, "that might be very wise."

Feeling a trifle weak in the knees, she backed gratefully away from the bed. Kitty, taking her place, stripped the belt from him with ease and passed it to her triumphantly. Its stout canvas pockets were heavy with gold pieces. Hefting the burden in her hands, Agatha gazed at the still figure on the bed, attacked by sudden pangs of remorse.

"We'd better go now," Kitty urged, blowing out the lamp.

Agatha nodded. With a last glance of regret in the direction of the bed, she followed Kitty out of the room and down the back stairway to the street.

No one noticed them leaving the hotel, and the roadway to the oak grove was deserted as they trudged back toward their camp. They had a lantern with them, but it wasn't necessary to light it. A gibbous moon in a cloudless sky showed them the way.

The two women didn't speak. There was silence except for the familiar sounds of nighttime insects and the sharp bark of a coyote off in the distance.

Agatha tried to preserve the secure silence, to resist what she suddenly longed to know from her experienced companion. In the end she couldn't stand it. She had to ask.

"Kitty," she said softly, "what is it like being with a man in that—*that* way?"

"Sex, you mean?" Kitty said bluntly, a little astonished that *their* Miss Agatha would ask such a thing.

"Yes."

"Then you've never—"

"No," Agatha said quickly. "I have no personal knowledge of it."

"Oh." The alluring blonde was thoughtful for a moment. "Well, maybe I'm the wrong one for you to be asking that question. I know that sounds peculiar, Miss Agatha, seeing as how that's the way I lived. But feeling about it like I did, could be I'm no fair judge. All I can tell you is that with some of them it wasn't too unpleasant, and with others it was just something to get through, and not with one of them did it mean anything."

"I see."

"The thing is—"

"Yes?"

"Well, there have been girls who've told me that with the right man, a really special man, it can be the most blissful thing in the world."

There was a wistful note in Kitty's voice, and Agatha was shocked at how strongly she related to it.

"Thank you, Kitty. I—I do hope you find that man for yourself in Oregon."

Kitty, suddenly suspicious, glanced up at the woman beside her. She wore a carefully controlled expression, her eyes on the road. "Miss Agatha," she asked worriedly, "you're not wondering how it would be with—"

"I think we had better hasten on to the wagons," Agatha said, cutting her off and thereby denying the unthinkable speculation both to Kitty and herself. She quickened her pace, patting the money belt looped over her arm. "We will need to find the perfect hiding place for this and then gird ourselves for the morning."

"He's going to be pretty mad all right."

"Like Chinese fireworks, I imagine. I expect it to be quite a stimulating challenge."

# Chapter Three

The roar that issued from Cooper's room shortly after day-break roused most of the guests at the Merchants Hotel. He didn't care. Nor was he in any mood to regret the terrified expression on the face of the little chambermaid as he charged out into the hallway, his trousers still undone.

Backed against the wall, the maid defended herself with a babbling, "Oh, no, sir! I never saw anything, sir! Never heard anything! I promise you I don't know a thing about it, sir!"

When Cooper blasted through the lobby five minutes later, the desk clerk, his Adam's apple bobbing furiously, promised to correct the disturbance he was creating by sending for the sheriff. Cooper informed him what he could do with that promise and slammed out of the hotel. Excited, half-dressed guests followed him into the street and around the corner to the Cattail Saloon.

Ignoring the pop-eyed bystanders congregated behind him, he banged on the saloon's locked door with his fists, de-manding in a booming voice that the proprietor let him in.

The saloonkeeper, who had living quarters over his establishment and who had been asleep for less than two hours, finally crawled from his bed and came down to unbar the door.

"Go away!" he shouted. "Ain't my business if she pinched your money belt over to the hotel. Didn't pinch it in here, did she?"

The saloonkeeper prided himself on being a tough man in a rough business. He failed to realize he was no match for Cooper Delaney in a vile temper. In the end, Cooper seized the resistant saloonkeeper, bodily lifted him off his feet and thrust his nose menacingly into his startled face.

"Talk!"

The saloonkeeper, helpless as he dangled in midair, finally recognized the error of his resistance. He complied with a resentful, "All right, all right, I'll tell you what I know about the girl. Name of Kitty. Said she was almost broke. Said she was eager to return to a trade she knew. Said she was fed up with all those pious females out at Oak Grove and wanted to get free of them. All I know. Now put me down, you blundering buffalo!"

Oak Grove?

Understanding exploded inside Cooper's head as he released the hapless saloonkeeper. *That woman.* Agatha Pennington. She was behind the theft of his belt. Last night had been a trap, and he had been sucker enough to fall into it. She had gone and arranged a little conspiracy to coerce him into piloting their damn wagon train. He knew this was the explanation just as plainly as he knew his skull was throbbing from the effects of whatever had been slipped into his whiskey.

Pivoting on his heel, Cooper headed in the direction of Oak Grove, a striding thunderstorm guaranteed to flatten anything that got in its path.

An emaciated codger, scurrying behind him, squealed happily, "Where you goin', Coop?"

"To recover my money belt."

The old fellow was delighted by the promise of another entertaining scene. So were the rest of the onlookers trooping behind him. The word spread like a Kansas prairie fire, and the crowd swelled as they moved toward the encampment to watch the fun.

Cooper paid no attention to the mob following him at a safe distance. He was too busy dealing with his blinding headache and his savage anger. He thought about his weeks of backbreaking labor on the Santa Fe Trail, all the risks he had endured to earn the gold pieces in that belt. He thought about how broke he was without the contents of that belt, stranded here in Independence because every other penny he had sweated for through the years had gone to California. He thought about Agatha Pennington and how he'd see her roasted live on a slowly turning spit before she got away with what she was trying to do to him. He thought about how he'd *enjoy* seeing her cooked on that slow spit.

Cooper's long legs delivered him to the clearing among the oaks ahead of the eager witnesses behind him. Several campfires smoked between the wagons as the women prepared breakfast. They halted their chores to stare at him with silent, impassive faces. He paid no attention to them after a sweeping glance informed him that Agatha was not among them. She wouldn't be far away, though. He was certain she was expecting him.

Taking up a stance in the center of the clearing, head back and legs apart, a warrior braced for battle, he issued his challenge in a volume that could have moved rocks.

"I'm here, Agatha Pennington! Are you coming out, or do I have to dismember every wagon until I find you?"

There was a brief stillness in the grove. Even the smoke from the fires seemed reluctant to stir. Then the curtain at the back of one of the covered wagons parted, and Agatha emerged. She had been checking the contents of the medical kit, intending to purchase remedies they might need before they left Independence. Descending from the tailboard with an easy grace, she dusted off her skirts, straightened to her fullest height and headed serenely toward the man waiting for her in the center of the clearing.

By this time the skinny octogenarian, leading the pack, loped into the grove, calling over his shoulder an eager, "Catched me a sight of that amazon in town yesterday. Ought to be a rare good battle here, folks."

Spectators began streaming into the clearing. Agatha paid no attention to them as she faced the volatile figure looming in front of her. Not many men looked down on Miss Pennington. This one did. He was nearly a head taller than she. Having dealt with him in nothing but reclining positions until now, she hadn't actually realized this. Nor had she appreciated how impressive he could be.

Cooper J. Delaney, in full rage, was an intimidating sight, glaring at her from those stormy green eyes with a look that would have chilled any other woman to the marrow. Agatha, with an effort he must never guess, preserved her composure and offered him the delighted smile of a welcoming hostess.

"Mr. Delaney, you are answering my invitation of yesterday, I see. Very good of you, I am sure, but I must ask you to explain all this mysterious clamor."

"No games," he warned her. "I want my money belt."

Her blue eyes widened in surprise. "Have you lost your money belt, Mr. Delaney? I am sorry."

"Why you larcenous—You get that belt. We both know you're holding it hostage and why. I want it back with every gold eagle accounted for, and if I don't get it back in five—"

"Make way here! What's the matter, Junior Hunsaker, you deef or something? I say make way for the law!"

Cooper's tirade was interrupted by a thick-waisted figure slapping his wide-brimmed hat at any spectator who got in his path as he waded through the crowd. Sheriff Cornelius Mullin had appeared on the scene.

Jowls quivering like gelatin, the sheriff reached the center of the clearing, demanding a loud, "What in dadblame is goin' on here?"

Cooper eyed him coldly. "I don't need you to mediate this, Sheriff. I can handle it on my own."

"Well, dadblame it, Cooper J., ain't I the official peace officer in this place? Next I know you'll try usin' that mule whip of yours on these ladies."

"Not until I have to," Cooper grimly promised.

"Mr. Delaney is under the impression that we have purloined his money belt," Agatha informed Sheriff Mullin mildly.

"Did you?"

She spread her hands in a gesture of cooperation. "You are welcome to search our wagons as thoroughly as you like, Sheriff. Search us as well, if you must. There is a strongbox, but you will discover that it contains silver dollars only, no gold."

Cooper's eyes narrowed on her. So, he thought, she's playing it that way. No outright lies, no denials, just a lot of clever evasions and his money belt where no one was going to find it. He wished suddenly he *had* brought his mule whip.

"Now that's just dandy," he fumed. "And where are you hiding the girl?"

"Girl, Mr. Delaney?"

"That cheating little baggage you used to rob me last night. Where is she?"

"Cooper J.," the sheriff warned him, "you watch that sinful tongue of yours. Who is this gal you're referrin' to anyway?"

It was Junior Hunsaker, the cadaverous old fellow in the front ranks of the crowd, who identified her. "There!" he crowed gleefully, pointing a bony finger. "Right there she is! I seed the siren myself last night over t' the Cattail Saloon enticin' Cooper!"

The spectators parted again to permit the arrival of a slim, radiant blonde bearing a wooden bucket in either hand. She had been down to the creek to fetch water for the coffee pots. Looking startled by the conflict in progress, she lowered the buckets. Agatha moved protectively to her side.

"This supposed to be your painted hussy?" the sheriff wondered dryly.

The gathering stared at the girl, finding it difficult to believe that the angelic beauty could be capable of anything more wrongful than a naughty smile. She looked demure, anxious and altogether innocent.

Cooper smiled cynically. "Amazing, isn't it, how a woman can switch overnight from virgin to trollop and back to virgin again."

Agatha slid a reassuring arm around the girl's waist. "This is absurd. I can promise you, Sheriff—under oath, if you like—that the young lady here at my side was nowhere near the Cattail Saloon last night."

Sheriff Mullin, perplexed by the aggravating affair, scratched under his arm, tugged at his ear and shifted his considerable weight from one foot to the other. "Well, I suppose we got to prove this one way or the other. Must be plenty of witnesses from the Cattail last night we can look up."

"That won't be necessary, Sheriff," came another interruption from the crowd. "*I* can attest to the whereabouts of the young woman last evening."

Sheriff Mullin swung his head, searching the ranks. "That you, Parson? Come out here and state yourself."

The Reverend Mr. Deal from the Church of the United Brethren struggled through the gathering, presenting himself to the participants.

"Parson couldna seed the girl," objected an indignant Junior Hunsaker. "He weren't at the Cattail last night. Told you *I* was there, and *I* seed her plain enough."

"Junior, shut that dadblame trap of yours," the sheriff ordered. "Everybody knows you're half blind when you're sober and all the way blind when you're drunk. Parson, where did you see the girl last evening?"

The beetle-browed, earnest Mr. Deal gazed for a moment at the young woman beside Agatha, as though needing to be certain of his identification. "In my church," he said quietly.

The crowd buzzed over his declaration. Sheriff Mullin frowned. "You certain about that, Parson?"

"No question of it, Sheriff. The choir was practicing, and this young lady appeared and asked if she might listen. As you know, we don't condone the encampment here, but we had no good reason to deny her request. She sat there quietly in a front pew all evening."

Several devout parishioners, also present at the Church of the United Brethren's choir practice, murmured their assents from the crowd. Junior Hunsaker shook his fists and sputtered.

"Lord's witnesses or not, this here's got to be a trick! Coop, you ain't gonna let 'em get away with this, are ya?"

But Cooper, much to the old man's disappointment, remained strangely silent. He was staring at Agatha with hard green eyes that made the closest spectators squirm with discomfort.

*I should have known,* he thought. *I should have realized it wasn't going to be any easy, straightforward recovery.* Under all that refinement, Agatha Pennington was a crafty adversary, and she had been ready for him. He didn't know how she had managed to flimflam him. He just knew that for the moment he was defeated. He also knew that, before he was finished with her, she was going to be extremely sorry she had ever messed with him.

Sheriff Mullin made a decision. "Don't see how we can doubt the parson and his congregation. If they swear the accused was with them in church all last evening, then that there is where she had to be. Looks like some other vixen made off with your belt, Cooper, and is probably halfway to

St. Louis by now. That bein' the case, best make your peace with these ladies here.''

Cooper had no response. The sheriff turned to the crowd. ''Entertainment's over, folks. That way back to town.'' He pointed down the road. ''And, dadblame it, that goes for you too, Junior Hunsaker.''

When he'd satisfied himself that the gathering had scattered and was in retreat, he checked on Cooper again. He hadn't stirred, hadn't taken his eyes off Agatha Pennington's face. The sheriff, uneasy, cleared his throat.

''Hope you ain't figurin' on any more trouble here, Cooper J.''

It was Agatha who answered for him. ''I think you may trust the situation to be settled amicably between Mr. Delaney and myself, Sheriff.''

Her promise was delivered with a confidence strained by the potent eyes drilling into hers. She noticed how the scar slashing his eyebrow seemed whiter than ever, betraying a vein that throbbed there in evidence of his dangerous mood. She rather thought she preferred him gruff and thundering as compared to this rigid silence. Yes, most definitely.

Reassured, Sheriff Mullin departed with the others. Agatha felt he left them in a state of deep relief. The women, too, seemed to have melted off, as though instinctively realizing that the moment had arrived when she could be counted on to deal with Cooper Delaney on her own. She didn't deceive herself. The difficult part wasn't ended. It was just beginning.

Steeling herself, she offered him a bright but risky, ''Can I interest you in Oregon, Mr. Delaney?''

Oh, she was going to pay all right, Cooper promised himself. Sooner or later, one way or another, she was going to pay, and he was going to take the sweetest pleasure in his revenge. But in the meantime he had no choice. She had his money belt concealed somewhere on this wagon train, and he was penniless without it. He would have to join them on the trail. It was the only way he could seize opportunities to search for his property. He'd find it all right, and once he had it back . . .

He surprised her with a pleasant, "I reckon you can, Miss Pennington." And then he worried her by following his affirmative with a deadly grin.

Agatha maintained her self-control. "Then perhaps you will join me in my office where we might comfortably settle the terms of our agreement."

Office? The scarred eyebrow went up. "What now?"

"This way," she invited without explaining.

She turned and started toward the prairie schooner from which she had earlier emerged. He followed. There was a small woman with a sour expression hovering near the back of the wagon. Cooper could feel ill will in the gaze she directed at him. She didn't trust him.

"It is all right, Susan," Agatha assured her. "You may leave us alone."

The protective Susan nodded without comment and slipped away to join the others. Cooper watched her go, then leaned on the tailboard of the wagon. His offensive grin was still in place.

"Plan to invite me into the cozy privacy of your vehicle, Aggie?" he baited her.

"I keep my office outside, Mr. Delaney. Around here, please."

She beckoned him to the other side of the covered wagon where he discovered planks laid over a pair of sawhorses. Two camp stools faced each other across the makeshift table. He scowled at her arrangement.

"Pretty sure of yourself, weren't you?" And why not, he thought, when she had taken pains to hold the winning hand in this little setup. He was trapped, and there was nothing he could do about it. Not yet anyway.

"Let us just say I had expectations."

"Uh-huh."

"Please be seated."

She settled herself on one of the stools and waited for him. He continued to stand, continued to scowl his resentment. Outwitted by a woman, and the worst of it was there was a part of him—a *reluctant* part—that couldn't help respecting her for it. He was a fool.

Cooper shrugged and swung his long frame into the seat opposite her. That was when he noticed the document resting on the planks in front of him. It was written in a precise hand and pinned down with a small stone serving as a paper-weight. He swept aside the rock and snatched up the document.

"What's this?" he demanded.

"A contract to be signed by both of us. I have my own copy here."

"Like hell you say! A handshake. That's what's customary between a trail guide and his wagoners, and all that's ever been necessary to bind an agreement."

"Perhaps, but since the circumstances in this particular situation are, shall we say, exceptional, I felt a written contract would be judicious."

His scowl deepened.

"Of course," she said offhandedly, "you may choose not to sign the contract." Then she added an equally casual, "Just as you may choose not to go to Oregon."

*No contract, no money belt.* That's what she was really telling him. Whichever way he turned she had him hog-tied and ready for slaughter, damn her cunning hide.

Agatha sighed. "If you continue to glower at me like that, Mr. Delaney, we shall get nowhere in our transaction."

Why not? he thought. It was only paper. What was she going to do about it if he failed to honor the thing? Chase him all the way to California? Come to think of it, Agatha Pennington would probably do just that. But a lot could happen between here and Oregon. He planned to see that it did.

"I suggest, Mr. Delaney, that you read the contract."

"Damn right I will."

Cooper scanned the document in his hand. He wasn't surprised by its formal language. It sounded just like her. He wondered how legal it was. Knowing her, probably very legal. She would have made certain of that.

"You will notice," she pointed out, "that I have left blanks wherever your name is to occur. If you will tell me what the J stands for in Cooper J. Delaney, I will fill in those places now."

He looked across the planks at her, his gaze suddenly wary. "You got a middle initial, Aggie?"

"Yes."

"What is it?"

"T."

His finger tapped the contract. "It doesn't appear here where your own name occurs."

"But that is different. I never use my middle initial as you regularly use yours."

"What's the T stand for, Aggie? You tell me yours, and I'll tell you mine."

She hesitated and then said hastily, "Well, perhaps full names won't be necessary, after all."

He smiled as she reached for pen and ink. He had just won a victory, small though it was. He wondered what that T did stand for? Probably something as embarrassing as his own well-concealed middle name, or she wouldn't have surrendered like that.

He handed her his copy of the contract and then watched as, head bent, she scratched in his name. The sun, lancing through the canopy of oaks, drew golden lights from the fragrant mass of her chestnut hair. It was a beguiling sight. He didn't want to notice it. He decided to try for another victory.

"While you're at it, you can add a clause to that thing specifying that my money belt is to be returned to me when we reach Oregon."

She looked up from the contract, her expression as virtuous as a nun's. "I was under the impression that the question of the missing money belt in connection with this wagon train was already determined by Sheriff Mullin. However—" She held up a hand to forestall another outburst from him. "—I will be happy to state in writing—just as a matter of form, you understand—that any property belonging to you, and unwittingly in our custody, will naturally be returned to you intact at the satisfactory conclusion of the journey."

*Oh, neatly done, Aggie. Lets you wriggle off the hook without admitting anything.* Well, it didn't matter. He intended to have his money belt back in his possession long before Oregon. But there was something that did matter, and he bluntly told her about it.

"There's another thing you'd better put down, since you're so dead set on seeing it all on paper."

"And that is?"

"Out on the trail I'm the boss. What I say goes. That's just the way it works, Aggie."

"We do expect to obey your instructions, Mr. Delaney," she assured him. Then she added a nonchalant, "Within reason, that is."

His frown was instantly back in place. "What's that mean?"

"Merely that we will defer to your experienced judgment in all circumstances pertaining to the trail, but in personal matters—"

"No exceptions," he insisted. "We're talking about survival, and I don't intend to argue about it."

She didn't argue. She nodded and went back to the contract, writing rapidly. But he had the suspicion he had somehow been outmaneuvered again.

Cooper's headache seemed to have retreated, but now his jaw ached. The result of teeth clenching and grinding in frustration, he supposed. He suddenly felt that the long trail ahead of him would be the toughest he'd ever undertaken, probably something he would regret for the rest of his days.

# Jean Barrett

The additions in place, Agatha's pen poised over the contract. "And now what sum for your services?"

She seemed to have plenty of money to throw around. Cooper unhesitatingly named a price that he knew was ridiculously excessive. "Five hundred dollars. In gold."

She also realized it was excessive and just as promptly rejected the amount. "Out of the question."

Prepared to bargain with her, he assumed a lazy posture, long legs stretched out under the planks, arms locked across his chest. "Thought I heard you tell me the other morning you were willing to pay any price." Maybe he was going to enjoy this.

She put down the pen. In counterpoint to him, her own posture became stiffly erect, hands folded neatly on the table's surface. "That was yesterday, Mr. Delaney."

"Meaning that today I'm in no position to haggle about it, is that it?" He rocked slowly on the stool and pretended to consider. "All right, I'll be generous about it. Four hundred dollars."

"Two hundred dollars. And no gold. Silver."

He shook his head. "I won't settle for less than three-seventy-five."

"You will accept two-fifty, and that is unreasonable."

His grin was slow and wolfish. "You're a mean negotiator, Aggie. Two-fifty then."

"To be paid to you at the completion of the journey in Oregon."

"To be paid to me in full amount," he insisted, "wherever the trek ends. Trains have been known to turn back when they decide they've had enough."

"We will not turn back."

"No," he said cynically, "we'll just all expire out there, twenty-two mule-headed women and one man crazier than the females he's trying to bring through."

She smiled with her habitual unconcern. "In that case I will have saved two hundred and fifty dollars."

She reached for the pen and ink again, efficiently completing the details and then signing both copies of the contract before sliding them across the table. Cooper added his own signatures without further pause. If he stopped to think about it, he'd probably abandon his money belt and beg his way to California. He'd certainly be a wiser man if he did just that.

It didn't help his pride at this point, but there was one last request he couldn't avoid. "I'll need an advance. I have a hotel bill to settle and a horse to claim from the stables."

"Yes, I rather expected you might require funds." She produced the old-fashioned reticule from somewhere near her feet, extracting several coins from it and passing them across the table.

Cooper pocketed the money and unfolded his long frame from the camp stool. He came around the table, hand extended as Agatha rose to her feet. She gazed at the offered hand, as distrustful as an unbroken mare.

"Come on, Aggie," he coaxed lightly. "You aren't going to deny me that customary handshake to seal the bargain, not after I signed your contract."

"Very well," she said.

But she went on hesitating, and he suddenly understood her reluctance. Well, well, he thought gleefully, so the immovable Miss Agatha was bothered by his physical nearness, fearful of his touch. He considered it a useful observation.

Cooper reached out, seizing her hand and placing it in his. "There, Aggie. Just a handshake."

But it was more than an ordinary handshake, Agatha realized breathlessly as that big, rough hand wrapped possessively around hers. His warm flesh pressed against hers had all the impact of an intimate embrace. Long fingers shocked the pulse point in her wrist while the heel of his palm slid sensually against her sensitive skin.

"Good luck to both of us," he said.

His wish for the journey was spoken seriously enough, but

63

when her gaze collided with his she read mischief in those intriguing green eyes. She didn't dare to try a response. The words would surely catch in her throat. Then he would know her sudden, emotional agitation. Defensive silence was much safer.

"Guess I don't need to tell you just how tough this is going to be," he said.

"Yes."

"The trail, that is."

"Yes."

"Course," he said, his voice turning deep and drowsy, "it has its pleasanter aspects, too. The long nights out there can be real magic. Ever slept out under the prairie stars, Aggie?"

"No."

"You're in for something special then. Nature in the raw. Nothing like it."

The huskiness in his promise conjured up forbidden images that made shivers run up her spine. She couldn't help it, even though she knew he was testing her with this performance, probing her in order to find a weakness. He would try to repay her for taking his money belt. She knew he would.

All the while he went on clinging to her, prolonging the handshake. His fingers subtly stroked and fondled, making a slow, hot caress. The strong hand squeezed around hers exerted just enough pressure to prevent her escape. She could have struggled or simply asked him to withdraw the contact. He would have released her. But she didn't want him to realize how susceptible she was to his brazen animal magnetism. She didn't want to hear him chuckling over another victory. So she went on enduring the lingering clasp of his hand, the low, smoky drawl of his voice seducing her senses.

"Tell me something, Aggie."

"Yes?"

"How did you manage it?"

What was he talking about now?

"The alluring little blonde couldn't have been in two places at the same time. So how did you manage it? Did you buy witnesses? A large donation to the Church of the United Brethren maybe?"

She tried to snatch her hand away. He held onto it.

"What I told the sheriff was the truth," she informed him frigidly. "The young lady you accused did not rob you last night."

"Then who did?"

Agatha didn't answer.

He used the handshake now to drag her toward him, exercising his latent power to draw her so close to the solid wall of his chest that she could feel his body heat.

"Who did, Aggie?" he persisted, his breath fanning her cheeks.

She began to resist then, struggling against his grip. He paid no attention to her silent efforts. The mesmerizing green eyes burned into hers. A realization began to awaken in them.

"You took the belt yourself, didn't you?" he said slowly. "You were waiting there when she brought me back to the hotel."

She refused to implore him to let her go.

"You helped yourself to the belt. That's what happened because you aren't denying it."

Agatha went very still. She stopped fighting him and used her strength to withstand his challenging gaze locked inexorably into hers.

"My trousers were undone," he taunted her softly. "You had to open them to get at the money belt. Did you enjoy the experience, Aggie? Tell me what you saw, what you touched while I was lying there unconscious. Hell, I should have been awake. I should have been enjoying the whole thing myself."

Panic surged through Agatha, sudden and relentless. Dear Lord, she had just gone and committed herself to long months with this man in the wilderness. An unprincipled man without a shred of respect for women. A man who wanted revenge and wouldn't hesitate to use his virility to extract it from her. A devil capable of putting her very soul in jeopardy.

There was only one way to survive him. She must rigorously oppose the temptation of him. At all times and at every turn she must resist. Starting now.

"Release me, Mr. Delaney," she commanded him emphatically. "*At once.*"

Cooper immediately dropped her hand. Not because she ordered it but because he suddenly found that he liked touching her. And that was dangerous, a risk he couldn't afford. There was a long hell waiting out there on the trail, and the only way to beat it was to remain emotionally detached.

Time to lighten the mood.

"I've just decided something, Aggie."

"Yes?" she questioned warily, drawing away from him.

"About your middle name. I think I've figured out what that T stands for. I considered Temptress, but that didn't quite fit. No, I'm sure it's T for Tormentor."

She didn't react.

"See you this afternoon, Aggie." He lifted his hand in a little salute and started away from the wagon.

His swaggering stride carried him only a short distance in the direction of the road to Independence before she called after him.

"Mr. Delaney."

He stopped and swung around. "Forget something?"

"I believe I have deciphered *your* middle initial."

He favored her with a cocky grin. "Think so?"

"Yes, Mr. Delaney. J for Jackass."

Duke turned away from the door he had just closed behind one of his paid informers. He had learned from his departed visitor the outcome of the scene in the oak grove. He no longer found the situation amusing.

"Hell, Duke," drawled the man lounging on the bed across the room, "you could have bribed Delaney like you bribed the other pilots and saved yourself this grief. Why didn't you?"

It was the wrong moment to challenge Duke. With the frustrated rage of a wild beast, he whipped the knife out of the sheaf strapped to his leg and launched it with deadly accuracy in the direction of the bed. The weapon buried itself in the wood of the headboard where it quivered like a tuning fork.

Without the least concern, the man on the bed regarded the bowie knife that had missed him by mere inches. Then he reached up and withdrew the knife and calmly began to pare his nails with the razor-sharp blade.

In control of himself now, Duke considered the lean form stretched out on his bed. The man hadn't bothered to drop his boots or change his garments, filthy from the trail. The bedclothes were suffering from his negligence. It was a familiarity Duke wouldn't have tolerated in any other individual. But his nomadic brother, recently arrived from the west, was his one weakness. Other than himself, Jack Salter was the only being he cared about. Physically, the brothers were as unalike as Beauty and the Beast. Jack had inherited all the good looks of their wayward father, but it was Duke who had gotten Will Salter's cunning.

At the moment, however, Duke was in no mood to be patient with anyone, even the brother he had been looking out for since they were youngsters. "Because," he answered Jack's challenge with a growl, "I got a head on me, and I use it. Delaney ain't no Puritan, but he's got a code that's basically a clean one. Sure he wants to see this trek fail, maybe as bad as I do, but bribery ain't his style."

Duke couldn't bring himself to add that Cooper Delaney was too tough an opponent to attack openly, that he might have to defeat this female expedition by more devious methods. In fact, Pacific Fur had recently warned him against his usual blatant tactics. The company wanted results, but they were nervous about unfavorable attention.

"Okay," Jack said, "so you didn't want to tip your hand. What are you going to do?"

"I'm gonna wait, little brother. Just wait."

"Until?"

"They give up. They're all women, ain't they? By the time Delaney puts them through their paces, they'll be beggin' to quit. That wagon train ain't goin' nowheres."

"But what if it does leave Independence?" Jack persisted as he went on carefully trimming his nails.

"Leavin' Independence is one thing," Duke said. "Reachin' Oregon is another."

And he would never let that happen. He couldn't forget how he and Jack had lived like animals for most of their lives, eking out an existence in the wilderness, surviving by corruption and terrorizing. Now Duke had a chance to put the miserable years behind him. He wanted those rich company shares that Pacific Fur had promised him if he was successful in keeping their territory unsettled. He would do whatever was necessary to get them.

# Chapter Four

"Welcome to purgatory, ladies."

Cooper smiled at them. An intentionally grim smile. They gazed back at him without comment or expression. He hadn't alarmed them. Not yet.

Diabolical grin still in place, he nodded slowly. Then he went on, "Because that's just where you're going, and you might as well learn the worst of it right now."

His first command as their guide had been to assemble them this morning here in the clearing. Twenty-two assorted females were perched on logs, stools and kegs as he addressed them, his arms folded across the knee of his buckskin-clad leg propped up on the oak stump that served him as a speaker's platform. They were strangers to him. After long weeks of the conditions he was about to promise them, they would be anything but strangers. Providing they lasted that long. He was prepared to think they wouldn't.

Right now they were huddled in shawls against the chill of the early morning air. He knew it would be sultry by midday. Unpleasant weather but nothing compared to the extremes that awaited them out on the open trail. He was ready to warn them about that, and all the rest as well, hoping they would give up and return his money belt to him. Then he could go away and forget this bad dream Agatha Pennington had imposed on him.

"Purgatory, ladies," he insisted. And Agatha, standing quietly nearby, thought that the scoundrel looked like he was enjoying the dire threats he was about to catalog for them.

"And not the purgatory you've heard about either," he continued. "Forget the Indians and the rattlesnakes. They won't bother you if you don't bother them. Everything else you don't have a choice about. I'm talking about weather that can be blistering in one minute and turn to sleet and hail in the next. Wind on the prairies that never quits and can drive you mad. Rivers so bad they defy you to cross them. Plagues of insects that bite and sting and chew. Alkali dust so caustic it inflames your eyes and splits your lips wide open. And maybe, if we're unlucky, cholera that can have you feeling fine in the morning and dead by night.

"Course, that's all before you even reach the mountains. Mountains so mean that, if they don't break you, they'll probably break your wagons. Or your tired oxen, which just lay down and die. By then you'll be marking your progress with the graves of others before you who didn't make it. Still interested in the Oregon Trail, ladies? If you are, there's plenty more on the subject."

The women were silent, and for one satisfying minute Cooper thought he had them. That was before Agatha, maddeningly pragmatic and sounding just a trifle bored, informed him crisply, "Fascinating, Mr. Delaney, but scarcely necessary. There is nothing you can tell us, you see, that Hiram McMurdy did not already share with us. I believe I did mention, too, did I not, that whatever the hazards, we will prevail. Now, is there anything else you wish us to know?"

Their eyes challenged each other across the clearing, and he thought: Blasted woman! Whatever he tried, she was onto him. And why did he have to keep wondering what was under those drab spinster skirts?

And she thought: He is not to be trusted. And why must he look so . . . well, so very male with his hard body leaning into his knee like that?

"Yeah, there is something else. Men. We need to hire at least a half dozen to accompany us. That is, if I can find six men crazy enough to sign on with us."

That brought a reaction all right. Cries of objection from every side. Once again, Agatha spoke for the women.

"Whatever your arguments, Mr. Delaney, there will be no men other than yourself. We are insistent about that, I am afraid. As I have said, on our own we—"

"I know. *You will prevail.*"

Right into oblivion, he thought. And I'm the lucky son-ofabitch who gets to join you. Well, fine. He'd forget about hiring those men who, for some wild reason, they refused to consider. Probably better this way. A few days out on the trail, lacking any male assistance when they faced those first tough obstacles, they'd be ready to give up and turn back.

"That being settled," demanded an impatient, gravelly voice from the ranks, "just when do we get under way?"

He was already learning their names. This one was May. A sagging-breasted woman with a mop of badly dyed red hair and clothes as outrageous as Agatha's were conservative.

Cooper leveled a forceful gaze in her direction, a look meant for all of them. "We don't roll until I say you're ready to roll. And I don't say you're ready until I'm satisfied you can manage wagons, livestock and firearms under any and all conditions."

There was another storm of opposition, their emotional voices assaulting him all at once.

"But we already know how—"

"Hiram taught us everything that—"

"We've been practicing for days and—"

Let them complain, he thought. It wasn't going to do them

any good. He wasn't going to change his mind on this one. Whatever their training, he was going to make sure that they had the skills to handle all the grueling demands of the trail. Anyway, if he couldn't scare them into being reasonable, there was always the chance, just maybe, that he could exhaust them into being reasonable.

To his surprise, Agatha supported him. All she had to do was lift her hand, and they were immediately quiet, ready to listen to her. It didn't take brilliance to realize that the women, without exception, were devoted to her. Amazing, Cooper thought. He wondered what she had done for them to earn such unquestioning trust and loyalty.

"Mr. Delaney is correct," she said, and she had their attention without raising her voice. "His experience is much broader than was Hiram's, and we can all benefit from it. This makes a further delay, and that is unfortunate, but his personal training may mean the difference between success and failure. Do you not agree?"

There were no more objections. Cooper had the feeling, however, that it might be a long time before Agatha Pennington sided with him again on any issue.

He removed his foot from the stump, crammed his hat on his head and issued his invitation with a deceptive politeness. "All right, ladies, let's go to work."

"Think you're a sweet pea? That what you think you are? Well, I'll tell you what I think. I think you're a lowdown, ornery . . ."

Agatha, hearing the language from across the grove, shuddered. Its content was bad enough. Its bellowed manner, which was a faithful imitation of Cooper Delaney's, was worse. Even Callie's swaggering gait was an alarmingly close version of the original.

She watched in concern as the eight-year-old in grubby pinafore and wild curls strutted around the trees, the mongrel Roscoe trotting happily at her side.

"In line, I say! Keep in line!"

Agatha had removed the tomboy from the blistering scene down by the creek, lecturing her about her demeanor, but she feared it was too late. Cooper had spent the morning bullying everyone, including the oxen, losing his temper at the slightest provocation and cursing like a pirate. Callie thought he was wonderful.

"It's a fact, Miss Agatha. You look as limp as day-old collards."

Agatha, turning her attention from Callie, smiled at the freckled, good-natured young woman whose speech carried the strong dialect of the Southern hills. She finished dressing Emmie Jo's ankle, which had been scraped by one of the heavy logs dragged by chains behind each of the wagons to slow its precarious descent to the creek bottom. They had been practicing there on the slope all morning.

"We are all of us exhausted, Emmie Jo."

"It's a fact."

Agatha didn't bother to explain it was her nerves that were tired, not her body. That Cooper was capable of driving them without mercy, even with a relentlessness amounting to a fiendish delight, she was prepared to suffer. His impatience was another matter. She had spent the sweltering hours at the creek arbitrating one dispute after another. Calmly arbitrating them, when what she had longed to do was wallop him with her hickory staff.

A constant awareness of his masculinity contributed to her tension. But that was something she preferred not to examine.

"How is the leg now, Emmie Jo?"

"Most good as new, I reckon."

Callie was still blasting her dog with choice oaths. Agatha braced herself to talk to the girl again about her unfortunate choice of a hero. Then she must return to the activity at the creek. It was going to be a very long five months indeed.

\* \* \*

73

Cooper could have shared her opinion, though he would never admit it. Hell, he was having trouble with the length of this first day, and he was responsible for the making of it. He might have felt better about his own fatigue if the women had begged for relief or evidenced any signs of surrender. They didn't. They accepted everything he threw at them and bore it all, including what he demanded late in the afternoon when the wagons returned to camp. They had all been looking forward to collapsing around the cooking fires. Cooper had other plans.

"I want each of you standing by your wagons while I go through them. If I find anything not in order, you need to be there to hear it. Think of it as the officer inspecting the barracks," he added with a sadistic grin.

He should have inspected the contents of each wagon the first thing this morning, but he had saved this necessity for the last, hoping it would be a kind of final straw.

There were scattered groans but no serious complaints. Only Agatha raised a cool, "Could this not wait until tomorrow, Mr. Delaney?"

"No, it could not, Miss Pennington. Because if the wagons aren't carrying what I think they should be carrying, we'll need all of tomorrow to correct the situation."

It was a tedious process as, wagon by wagon, he checked supplies, gear and the condition of each vehicle. He found no flaws. It was all there, sufficient stores of dried and salted foods, carpentry and blacksmith tools, essential household wares and farm equipment for Oregon, even spare parts for the wagons against any possible breakdowns. There was no indication of the frivolous, those goods he associated with impractical feminine sentiment.

They had been well instructed, Cooper thought. The work of Hiram McMurdy probably. He admired the old man's thoroughness while damning him for convincing these women they could make it on their own. Madness. It had only recently been proved that a wagon could make it all the way to Oregon without falling apart, and that was with the support of brawny men.

In each carefully packed wagon he kept a sharp eye out for the possible whereabouts of his money belt. It could be anywhere, but none of the women seemed nervous by anything he got near or examined. Even the strongbox concealed inside an iron stove was opened for him. Agatha insisted on it. It contained stacks of silver dollars, reputable bank notes and what looked like deeds. No gold. Obviously, his money belt had been well hidden. Locating it would take time, something that would have to wait.

Right now all he really wanted was his supper, followed by a long, uninterrupted night wrapped in his blanket. And he wanted both his supper and his sleep out of earshot of the women whose unceasing chatter laid siege to his nerves. Cooper was used to the company of rough bullwhackers who, for the most part, talked only when they needed to communicate. He couldn't imagine how he was going to endure unending weeks of female prattle. Although, to be perfectly fair about it, he had known a few men out on the trails whose jabber had made him itch to reach for his whip.

Just to be sure that didn't happen this evening, he took his cup of coffee and his plate of beans and rice and removed himself from the area of the cooking fires where the women were congregated. He found a stump at the edge of the grove and perched on it, long legs stretched out in front of him. The twilight was peaceful, and he enjoyed his solitude. Until Callie joined him at the stump. Flopping down on the grass in front of him, she gazed at him with an unnerving adoration.

Cooper tried to ignore her. He wasn't used to children, and this little urchin was forever underfoot, threatening to attach herself like a burr. He didn't know how to deal with that.

The dog was with her, a homely, ginger-colored mutt with floppy ears and stubby tail. He could relate to animals anyway. When the dog came to him, long nose poked into his lap, he set aside his tin plate and cup and fondled its ears.

"What's the dog's name?" he asked.

"Roscoe," Callie said, in no way sensitive to Cooper's awkwardness with her.

"Roscoe, huh?"

He went on stroking the dog who, delighted with the attention, raised up to place forepaws against his chest. Cooper chuckled as Roscoe squirmed against him, trying to lick his face. He decided he had found a friend of his own kind.

"Well, ol' son," he informed the animal companionably, "it looks like it's going to be just you and me all alone against this army of perverse females. Two men of the world, huh?"

Callie, with fists squeezed against her mouth, began to giggle uncontrollably. Cooper, freezing, shot her a long, questioning look. Callie went on tittering behind her fists. Suspicion awakened, he ducked his head and searched under the dog's hindquarters. The equipment he had assumed would be there was not there. Roscoe was plainly misnamed.

"Holy Lucifer!" he thundered in disgust, pushing the animal away. "Even the goldanged mutt is female!"

Callie, convulsed with outright laughter now, tipped over into the grass. But under her mirth an exciting idea began to take shape. Something guaranteed to please her fascinating idol.

Cooper's mood was in no better state the following morning when he rolled out of his blanket and realized that he had to face it all over again. Target practice with women who claimed to know which end of a rifle to aim and which to pull and often didn't, wagon drill under conditions that were supposed to simulate those on the trail and didn't come nearly close enough to the harsh realities of the plains and mountains, and Agatha ready to challenge his authority at every turn. Agatha, completely unaware of her own sexuality and troubling him on more than one level.

He was in this frame of mind when he was offered a basin of water to wash himself before breakfast. The women ignored him then and went about their morning activities in the clearing. He was grateful for that much.

He stripped to the waist and leaned over a bench, soaking himself liberally before he scrubbed his face and chest with a ball of soap, working up a healthy lather. Inadequate as it was, the bath lifted his spirits. That was before, streaming with water after dousing himself with a bucket of fresh rinse water, he groped blindly for the towel on a line over his head.

He was in the act of rubbing his face dry with the soft cotton when he realized that the cloth was already damp. What the—

Cooper held the article away from him, examining it in horror. Someone had replaced the towel with her laundry. Drawers! His nose had been buried in female drawers! The largest undergarment he'd ever seen, leaving no doubt as to the identity of its owner. The one they called Dolly had a monumental girth.

This kind of intimacy was just the beginning, he realized dismally. There would be months of it. Long months where he would be subjected to one embarrassment after another.

Wondering if his mortification had been witnessed, he pivoted away from the bench. Callie chose that moment, when his nerves were at their rawest, to make her startling appearance. He stared at her in disbelief as she came sauntering toward him across the clearing.

It was Callie all right, though she was barely recognizable. She had hacked off her long curls, making a bad job of it since her remaining hair was poked up in uneven tufts across the top of her head. She had somehow managed to acquire a boy's outfit consisting of a homespun shirt and corduroy trousers that were a size too big for her. The trousers would have been in a heap around her ankles if it hadn't been for a pair of bright red suspenders.

Her thumbs were hooked behind those suspenders with an air of satisfaction as she planted her bare feet in front of him.

"Yup, it's me, Coop," she informed him with a confident familiarity. "Bet you couldn't be more surprised."

"What in the name of all that's holy have you gone and done, little girl?"

"Cal," she insisted. "I'm Cal now. Turned myself into a feller, see, so you wouldn't have to be the only one on the trek."

"Where did you get them? The britches and the shirt. Where did they come from?"

"Traded for 'em with that boy from the farm down the road."

"Traded what?"

"Mama's banjo. Was my banjo now, and I didn't have no use for it no more." Her lower lip went out in a sign of mutiny. She was beginning to perceive that he might not be as pleased by her metamorphosis as she had assumed he would be. "You—you like it, don't you, Coop?"

"Stop calling me that," he growled. "And don't ask me for my approval because I think you look God-awful. That hair would scare a witch."

He didn't see the rebellious lip wobbling now with hurt and embarrassment. He noticed nothing but the expression of defiance in her eyes.

"What's more," he blundered, "if I was your mama you'd be over my knee for a memorable licking. Hey, get back here, little girl. This issue isn't settled yet."

But Callie was already halfway across the grove, fleeing in the direction of the creek as fast as her bare feet could carry her. She streaked without pause past an astonished Agatha who had just emerged from the rear of her wagon.

One of the women had overheard the scene and explained it now to Agatha. Drawing a steadying breath, Agatha marched across the clearing to confront Cooper, firing at him a curt, "Has no one ever told you, Mr. Delaney, that you have a very thick skull on that insensitive head of yours?''

"Why? Just because I was ready to discipline the little urchin? She should be disciplined. She's running wild."

"If she is, it is all because of you. What she did was simply to please you. You did not, of course, stop to think of that before you humiliated her."

"All right, so she caught me in a wrong mood. I'll make it up to her later."

"How can you when you do not begin to understand?"

A mistake, she suddenly realized. She had made a mistake in cornering him when he was half unclad like this. She should have waited. The situation was too dangerously provocative.

Agatha had never seen a man this exposed before. His chest, still damp from his wash, was layered with slabs of hard muscle and a wedge of dark, curling hair that enriched his blatant masculinity. The sight was riveting. She wanted to ask him to cover himself, but it would be admitting a weakness he would only use against her.

Too late. Without realizing how it happened, she found herself backed against the tailboard of the wagon just behind her. His outstretched arms, braced on the tailboard, were on either side of her, fencing her in. Trapped!

She fought for air as he leaned toward her, his tone deliberately seductive now, a hint of laughter under the husky surface. "So make me understand, Aggie. I'm listening."

He didn't try to touch her. He didn't have to. The close heat of his daunting sexuality was weapon enough in their ongoing battle of wills. He was prepared to use that weapon shamelessly, knowing full well how his nearness unsettled her.

"What's the matter, Aggie?" he drawled. "Lost your tongue? That's not like you."

She struggled to keep her gaze on his face and not on his compelling, half-naked body. Not a very successful effort. His rugged face was bristly with a morning beard he had yet to shave. It shouldn't have been an appealing sight. But it was. She couldn't breathe.

"Stand away from me," she ordered him.

"Or what? Physical force, Aggie? Would you resort to physical force?"

Oh, he would welcome that, wouldn't he? She refused him the satisfaction of losing her control. "If necessary," she conceded with a complacent smile. "As I have already told you about us, Mr. Delaney, what men can do, we can do."

His vivid green eyes gleamed wickedly. "Oh, not quite, Aggie. Not quite."

Another mistake. He was taunting her, of course. Using every opportunity to deliberately taunt the old maid, either as a form of revenge or as some underhanded method for recovering his gold. Probably both.

"We were discussing Callie, Mr. Delaney," she reminded him. "And your unfortunate influence on her."

Her accusation gained her a temporary advantage. He dropped his arms and pulled back. He was wearing his familiar scowl. "You care to clarify that?"

"I am speaking of your offensive language. Hopeless, I suppose, to ask you to refrain altogether from your explosive oaths in our presence. Might I suggest less objectionable substitutes? Surely not too difficult for someone whose vocabulary is so highly creative."

"Yeah, I might do that." He recovered himself, his brash grin back in place. "Should be a useful exercise for this book I've promised myself I'm going to write one day. All about my life-threatening experiences in the wilderness. That is, if I survive them. Think I'll be devoting a whole chapter to you, Aggie."

"Admirable, Mr. Delaney. However, there is one essential word for the composition of such a book that your vocabulary does lack. It is called *patience*. You will no doubt have to consult a dictionary for its definition."

"I'll be sure to do that."

He shifted his weight from one leg to another, drawing her attention to the way his tight buckskin trousers rode low on his narrow hips.

"But no dictionary is going to provide me with that middle name of yours. Ought to have it for the chapter on you."

His altered position revealed his navel shadowed by whorls of dark hair. She had never realized that this portion of a man's anatomy could actually be enticing.

"Let's see. T, isn't it? T for Tease maybe."

Agatha caught her breath as his big hand drifted to the area of his navel and began to scratch himself languidly. In spite of her best efforts to resist, she couldn't keep herself from being mesmerized by the slow, tantalizing rhythm of his fingers raking across his belly. He was doing his best to disarm her and succeeding on every level.

He'd had no chance to dry himself yet. Beads of water clung to his skin, forming little rivulets along his ribcage. Before she could prevent it, she experienced an outrageous urge to taste that moisture on his sleek flesh, to delicately lap up the droplets with her tongue. Like a kitten licking up sweet milk. The impulse stunned her. No man had ever induced such a wanton arousal in her. In view of the crisis with Callie, it was worse than shocking. It was nothing less than obscene.

Mortified by her indecency, she dragged her gaze away from his body. The young Rebecca was approaching the water bench. Agatha saw her opportunity to rescue the situation, even though it meant turning Cooper in another stormy direction. Anyway, it was inevitable that he should learn about Rebecca.

"Rebecca, I wonder if you can find a towel for Mr. Delaney. He seems to have misplaced his."

There was a stack of clean towels in plain sight below the bench. The willing sixteen-year-old girl bent over to select one of them as they watched. Agatha knew what would happen when Rebecca straightened again. She proceeded to arch herself like a bow to relieve her back. It was a position which clearly revealed what, until now, had been in no way apparent to Cooper under a shawl and loose calico skirts.

The expression on his chiseled face would have been comical if Agatha hadn't realized what it heralded. He at least had the sense to wait until Rebecca cheerfully presented the fresh towel to him and retreated from the scene before he erupted.

"Holy Lucifer! She's—well, she's—"

"In the family way. Yes, Mr. Delaney."

"She can't have a baby!"

"I am afraid it is rather late to avoid the condition. And will you please lower your voice before you embarrass Rebecca? We are all quite happy for her."

"You are all quite out of your minds, is what you are. Do you realize what this means?"

"I do, but I am certain you will tell me all the same."

"She'll deliver out on the trail, hundreds of miles away from any doctor and under the worst possible circumstances."

"Nonsense. Rebecca will not be the first woman, nor the last, to deliver her child in the wilderness. She is young and healthy, and at least two of our ladies are experienced midwives. It will all be capably handled when the time comes. You need have no concern over the matter."

"She can't go. She'll have to be left behind."

"Not even discussable, Mr. Delaney. We would never consider abandoning Rebecca, nor any of our party. Now, unless there is anything of further consequence in connection with this matter, I suggest we return to the subject of Callie."

Much to her relief, she had managed to defuse him. Muttering something about manipulative, obstinate women digging their own graves, he rubbed himself dry and dragged on his shirt.

She found she could breathe easier now, even when he faced her with a fuming, "And just why are we making the little urchin my problem? Why isn't she her mama's problem?''

"Her mother," Agatha informed him quietly, "is dead. Dorothy was killed less than two weeks ago. *Brutally* killed. And contrary to appearance, Callie is still dealing with her loss."

His eyebrow, the one broken by the white scar, lifted in surprise. "What happened?"

It was a cruel episode, and she wished she could avoid telling him. But if there was any chance of his understanding about Callie, he had to know. She related the story as briefly and unemotionally as possible.

"We were on the road from St. Louis where our wagons and supplies had been purchased. Hiram deemed it expedient for the women to accustom themselves to travel by wagon train before we reached the frontier. It was also a method for testing the value of the men who had been hired to accompany us since after Independence it would have been impossible to replace them."

Cooper had been wondering why they hadn't journeyed by steamboat up the Missouri, which was the customary route to Independence. This explained it.

"It was a sensible decision with unfortunate results," she continued. "The eight men had been carefully chosen. What we failed to take into account were the—shall we say, the appetites of several of them."

Cooper understood her. "Uh-huh. They figured the women could be persuaded to accommodate them."

"Yes."

He could see how this would have easily happened when there was alluring female flesh like Kitty on the train. "And the women didn't appreciate their interest."

"They did not. Hiram warned the men, and all of them were insolent about his authority. There remained no alternative but to discharge every one of them. An effort was made to obtain replacements from the town near which we

83

were camped, but the men had already talked against us. There was a rather ugly scene as we were invited to leave the area.''

Agatha saw no point in explaining that the women were familiar with such intolerant attitudes, that a small town in Missouri hadn't been the first community to drive them away.

''Their sheriff made the poorest of efforts to control the mob. No one seemed to know, or perhaps cared to know, who fired the wild shot that killed Dorothy as she tried to hurry Callie out of the street. And that, Mr. Delaney, is why we are opposed to hiring any further men to accompany us on the trail.''

She could have added that the women had suffered too much male abuse in their lives. In some cases it had been excessive beyond imagination. But she could see that he had heard enough and was already struggling with a guilt that was probably alien to him.

''The urchin's father,'' he demanded.

''Callie has no knowledge of her father. Dorothy never talked about that, and we did not ask.'' He would come to learn that past existences were not something the women easily discussed.

''So the child goes to Oregon with you.''

''Naturally. We are her family now.'' She paused, then nudged him with a hopeful, ''It was foolish of her to turn herself into a boy so you need not be a solitary male in a company of females. Totally unacceptable behavior, even if it was simply to please you. But then you agree with that.''

She was being cunning again, Cooper thought resentfully. He knew what she was really telling him. Well, she could forget it. It was bad enough that he was playing nursemaid to a bunch of green women. He wasn't going to have a kid shadowing him. He didn't want to be drawn into any of their lives, bound to them in any personal way. He wouldn't let himself forget that he was getting out just as soon as opportunity permitted. So that was it. No involvements. Final.

Well, hell.

"You any idea where she went?" he muttered.

"The creek, Mr. Delaney. I imagine you will find her down at the creek. She likes to watch the polliwogs there in the pool just below the ford."

He swung away without another word. She watched his imposing figure stride off through the trees, and she thought how easy it would be to let weakness overcome her. But whatever his appeal of the moment, she must not forget that in essence he was a sardonic devil. And, like the devil, he offered up a feast of temptations capable of a woman's destruction. She did not intend to be that woman.

The urchin was crouched at the edge of the creek, poking a stick into a pool of wriggling tadpoles. Roscoe was stretched out on a flat boulder close by, panting from a run through a meadow thick with milkweed.

Callie ignored Cooper as he hunkered down beside her. He regarded her for a moment, feeling ridiculously clumsy. What was he supposed to say to her? He had no idea how to talk to a child, especially one he had hurt.

"I've come to apologize," he said gruffly.

She didn't look at him. She went on jabbing with the stick.

He tried again. "I shouldn't have said what I did. I guess it was because I didn't understand."

"You told me I look awful."

"Well . . ." He cleared his throat and pretended to gravely study her, his head angled to one side. "As a little girl, you're in trouble. But as a boy . . . maybe you're not too bad."

The stick went still in her hand. She glanced up at him. "Mean it?"

"Sure I do." He gestured toward her badly shorn head. "Considering that when you had the curls, most of the time your hair looked like a rat's as—uh, not so good—this is definitely an improvement.''

"Then can I keep my hair this way? And the britches?''

"Why not?'' he promised recklessly.

"And be called Cal?''

"I don't mind, if the women don't.''

"They won't. Not if you say so. You're the boss now.''

Cooper smiled wryly. "I don't think Miss Agatha knows that.''

Callie thought about this seriously for a few seconds. ''Miss Agatha is different.''

He wouldn't argue with that.

She dropped the stick and stuck out a grubby hand. ''Shake on it?''

His big hand closed around her small one. "It's a deal. You can copy my haircut, and you can copy my britches. But, ol' son,'' he warned her severely, "if I ever catch you trying to copy my language, I will personally wash out your mouth with lye soap.''

"Not even pisspot? It's my favorite.''

"Especially not that one.''

"Then I won't.''

They started back to the camp together, the dog ambling behind them. Cooper was satisfied that the problem had been so easily resolved and that the urchin was cheerful again. He was also worried. He didn't want Callie too close, thinking he was going to be there for her. Because whenever he could manage it, the day would come when he would pull out. He didn't want to have to look back. Not for anyone.

And that included Agatha Pennington, no matter what primitive thoughts he had entertained about her when she'd stared at his naked chest like that.

There was nothing more he could do for them.

Cooper came to this decision when the weary company returned to the grove late that afternoon. They had spent another long day submitting to his training under the broiling sun. He had hollered, pleaded, threatened. They had struggled to please him. The progress of their skills had been slow but noticeable. They weren't real teamsters yet or crack marksmen. Probably would never be. But this was as close as most of them were going to get. So it was now or never.

Cooper signaled them to gather around after the wagons and teams were secured. When he had their full attention, he delivered his simple announcement.

"We roll tomorrow at sunup, ladies. I suggest you make your last night in civilization count because it's going to be a long while before you see it again."

He intended to make certain that his own last evening in Independence was an agreeable one. He didn't know how long it was going to take him to recover his gold, but he suspected it would be some time before he enjoyed either liquor or an obliging woman again.

He slipped away after supper and rode to town. The women were too excited about tomorrow to notice his departure. All but Agatha who glimpsed him leaving the camp. Never missed anything, did she? She neither objected nor asked for an explanation, though he sensed she understood his intention. Too bad. He wasn't going to feel any guilt about it, which was exactly what he did feel all the way to town.

An order of the Cattail Saloon's best malt whiskey took care of that. He was feeling much better after a couple of deep swallows. He went easy on the stuff, though. Not smart getting drunk the night before you took a train out. But there was no reason to restrain himself with the fancy girl who took him eagerly to her room.

She was exactly what he needed, totally voluptuous and without a single inhibition. He was convinced that her knowledge of the exotic was the envy of every whore this side of the Mississippi. When he performed for her lustfully, she begged for more and, he could swear, actually meant it.

Cooper spent himself in a prolonged orgy of sexual pleasure and wondered afterwards how he could possibly feel hollow and unfulfilled. Fair or not, he blamed Agatha Pennington for his illogical dissatisfaction. He didn't try to analyze it. Maybe he was afraid to. He just sourly knew that this was something more he owed that woman.

He had planned to spend the whole evening with the fancy girl. Now he was no longer interested. He paid her handsomely and rode back to the sleeping camp, where he endured a bad night wrapped in his blanket.

The dark thing he never talked about, that unknown demon from his dimly remembered early childhood, haunted his sleep. He woke up in the blackness of the night shaken and sweating. He never understood it, didn't want to. Fear was a weakness. He'd learned that the hard way in his miserable adolescence.

It didn't come often, but he knew how to deal with it. Push it away, forget it. It would happen again, of course. It always did. But he could handle it. Just had to be tough. Never let anything, or anyone, get the better of you.

The sky was lightly overcast by morning. Nothing to worry about, he decided as he directed the first turnout. The fires were doused for the last time in the oak grove, the wagons loaded, the oxen pinned to their yokes. Cooper, mounted on his big roan, Bucephalus, his Hawken rifle strapped to his saddlebags, gave the signal to start.

"All right, ladies, stretch 'em out!"

It was always a moving experience for him to yell that order and then to watch the wagons roll for the first time. He should have known that with this deranged caravan even that simple joy would be denied him. Because nothing happened. The women stationed beside their teams gaped at him.

Cooper groaned.

Agatha called out a cheerful, "Does your instruction mean for us to be under way, Mr. Delaney? You have not used the expression before, I believe."

Grunting in exasperation, he tried again. "That's just what it means, Miss Pennington. Fall into line with your wagons. An orderly line. A sensibly spaced line. In other words, *move*."

And they did. All at the same time. Half of them shouted "gee" to teams which swung obediently to the right. Half of them screamed "haw" to oxen which tried to turn left and got in the way of the other teams. Excited, overeager, they forgot everything he had taught them.

Somewhere in all the confusion a gun went off. Whether intentionally or accidentally didn't matter. The oxen, already panicked, became uncontrollable.

Roscoe, persuaded that it was all a wonderful sport, charged in and out of the tangled ranks, barking up a frenzy. The oxen didn't like that either. They went crazy.

Cooper, observing the mess from the back of his mount, decided it was not an encouraging beginning. Eyes turned heavenward, he pleaded a pitiful, "A bolt of lightning. That's all it would take. Just send down one quick bolt of lightning, and I'll be out of my misery."

His maker must have determined that he was entitled to, if not that request, some form of mercy. The turmoil did get sorted out, Cooper did get his line of wagons. They were on their way.

It was going to be all right, he thought gratefully. Looking good. Everything turning out just fine.

That was when it began to rain.

# Chapter Five

And it didn't stop raining.

In those first days as they pushed toward the unmarked boundary between Missouri and Kansas, it drizzled. A thin, persistent, cheerless drizzle.

Cooper, huddled in his poncho, water dripping from the brim of his hat, watched Agatha slogging gallantly through the mud. Even drenched, she was a regal figure with that eternal hickory staff of hers.

Leaning over the bullwhip coiled on the pommel of his saddle, he called down to her caustically, "Are we still prevailing here, Miss Agatha?"

She flashed him a confident smile. "The weather will change, Mr. Delaney."

She was right about that. As they left the frontier behind them, and any established law and order with it, it no longer drizzled. It poured. Poured without letup as storms struck them day after day. The women had never experienced weather as fearful as this. Hadn't realized that out on the swelling, limitless prairies, without the protection of woodlands or hills, that lightning and thunder and wind could be so violent.

Cooper, riding to the head of the train where Agatha was still marching relentlessly beside her oxen team, spoke to her through the driving rain from the back of his roan.

"Tell you something, Aggie."

"What is that, Mr. Delaney?"

"Someday, providing I'm ever dry again, there's this educational museum I'm going to open. A collection of real Western curiosities."

"Along with that book you are planning to write?"

"That's right. And prominently featured in my museum, Aggie, right up front—"

"Oh, I think I can guess, Mr. Delaney. I will be in your museum, mounted and stuffed by you personally."

His scarred eyebrow climbed to a devilish altitude. "Uh, Aggie, I think you have those steps in reverse order."

Her face went the color of a desert sunset as she understood the spin he had put on her innocent banter. He boomed with laughter over her mortification. A rich, resonant laughter that startled her. His pure, unrestrained mirth added another dimension to his potent appeal.

White teeth still gleaming, he doffed his soaked hat in her direction and dashed away through the slop on Bucephalus.

Putting the fork of the Santa Fe Trail behind them, they turned northwest. By the time the train crossed the Kansas River, not without considerable difficulty, there was no more light drizzle, no more ferocious thunderstorms. There was just rain. Mean, unending rain.

Cooper challenged her again on the morning he struggled to lever a wagon wheel out of the mire.

"I'm enjoying myself here, Aggie. You enjoying yourself?"

"Immensely, Mr. Delaney."

Matching his grinning sarcasm with serenity wasn't easy. He was a formidable sight stripped to the waist, the rain slashing his slick skin, his muscles bulging as he strained to free the wheel.

There were more quagmires to battle, more streams to cross, sometimes with banks so steep the wagons had to be lowered by rope. The women amazed Cooper. They were far from being seasoned veterans, but they had survived the worst awkwardness of Independence. Just as Agatha insisted, they were prevailing.

There was something else about the women that won his grudging respect. When the ordeals were the most demanding, they overcame a lack of male strength by combining their efforts. The teams worked smoothly and without quarreling. Seldom was there any complaint and never a suggestion of turning back.

Cooper realized that, if he weren't careful, he would end up admiring them. Even worse, be proud of them. He prevented that fatal possibility by systematically searching the wagons for his gold. No easy job considering the foul weather, the constant presence of the women and his own exhausting duties.

In the middle of the nights, when it was his turn at watch and the women were asleep in their tents, was when he snatched his opportunities to look. He never located any sign of his gold. But it had to be here somewhere on the train. He wouldn't give up until he found it.

None of Duke Salter's band of mercenaries had the nerve to question him on the subject of the wagon train that had left Independence. Only his brother, Jack, dared to confront him in his hotel room.

"You can rage at me all you want, Duke, but it's the truth. They're gone, on their way. You were dead wrong about that pack of women never gettin' out of town."

Duke kept his familiar bowie knife so sharp that, among other things, it served him as a razor. Leaning into the mirror on the wall, he applied the blade to the lathered whiskers on his narrow, bony face. He was too busy carefully scraping around the puckered scar on his cheek to offer any comment to his brother.

"You ain't ragin'. Must be a good reason for that."

Duke paused after a moment, eyeing Jack's handsome reflection in the glass. "It's like I told you, little brother. Heading out on the trail don't mean a thing. They can't last. They're all women except for Delaney, ain't they? And there's every hell out there to turn 'em back."

"Yeah, but there's always the chance . . ."

Duke went on calmly with his shaving. Inwardly, however, he was seething. He was still confident that the women didn't stand a prayer of surviving the rigors of the long trail. But even the slight possibility of their success made him sick with alarm. He would look like a fool if they reached Oregon. Worse, their accomplishment would be an invitation to every dirt farmer in the country. Potential settlers who would decide, "Look, if those females made it practically on their own, then anyone can make it."

If that ever happened, Duke would have failed Pacific Fur. It couldn't happen. The women had to be stopped.

He laid the knife on the washstand and dried himself with a towel. Jack continued to watch him, his suspicion deepening.

"You're bein' too easy about this. You got something up your sleeve."

Duke turned to face his brother. "They'll give up, but I figure to help 'em along in that direction."

"How?"

"It's time to place Magpie on that wagon train."

Jack's dark eyes glinted with understanding. "I get you. Think she'll agree to do it?"

"You forget what I got to hold over her. Besides"—his mouth curled in a brutal smile, his hands tightening into a pair of meaty fists—"there's other ways to persuade her."

\* \* \*

There was a reason why Agatha had placed her wagon at the rear of the train today. Her oxen needed little supervision in this position, plodding willingly in the wake of the teams ahead of them. That left her free to work on her journal from her perch at the front of the wagon.

There had been few opportunities since Independence to attend to the record she was keeping of their journey. The vile weather had prevented anything but the constant grind of survival.

But this morning . . . ah, this morning was altogether different. The rain was finally behind them. There was the blessed relief of a clear blue sky and a kind sun.

There was only one problem in that, Agatha thought with a faint sigh. The canvas top had been folded back on its bows to air the contents of the wagon, and neither the invasive sun nor the vast scene it lighted permitted her to concentrate on the journal. Her attention kept wandering to the views on all sides.

They were wrong, she decided. All those people who damned the western prairies for their monotony were wrong. There was an infinite variety in the grandeur of these immense spaces rolling to the horizons on every hand. She found it in the majesty of the buzzards circling overhead, in the sweet song of the wind in the grass that glistened after the rain, in the field daisies and black-eyed Susans that brightened the undulating green. Awesome. All of it was truly awesome.

"Like what you see?"

Agatha swung her head around, startled by the deep voice. He was suddenly, unexpectedly there, his mount level with the left side of her wagon. Earlier, he had ridden off ahead of the train, either to scout the country or to hunt for fresh meat. Perhaps both. He must have circled around, arriving so quietly from behind her wagon that she hadn't heard him. Cooper Delaney never failed to surprise her.

Or to disarm her with his presence, she thought nervously.

Cooper watched her. She had an unconscious habit, whenever he appeared, of lifting her hand and smoothing it up the nape of her neck under the coil of her thick hair. As if she were tidying herself before battle. He liked seeing her do that.

"Yes, I do, Mr. Delaney. It is glorious country."

"You feel that good about it, Aggie, then why don't we pick a spot right here for you to settle? I'll even help you to build your first shelters before I mosey off to California. What do you say?"

She eyed him, judging his mood as his horse ambled beside the wagon. She detected no real mischief in his lazy smile, but with Cooper Delaney one never knew.

"No sparring today, Aggie," he assured her. "Hell, I'm too grateful for the sun to be anything but sweet and easy."

"Then I must disappoint you with my answer, Mr. Delaney. Oregon remains our destination. Only there can it all begin for us."

"Whatever *it* is. But then you like keeping that a big mystery, don't you, Aggie?"

"Not at all. There was simply no purpose in explaining the need for this journey until you cared to hear it."

He looked away, gazing off into the stretching grasslands. She knew he was fighting the curiosity that was gnawing at him. And she understood his resistance. He feared any knowledge of the women and their objective. Knowledge demanded some form of emotional involvement, and that was dangerous for a man who wanted to do nothing but run and leave no commitments behind him.

He glanced back at her finally, his voice harsh with surrender. "Yeah, well, don't think I'm interested now because I'm not. I'm crazier than the rest of you. Must be, since here I am, one man piloting a flock of females on a two-thousand-mile trek that would make Hades look like a church social. It's just that the way I figure it, I'm entitled to understand why I'm committing suicide."

"To save women who need saving, Mr. Delaney," she informed him solemnly.

"From what?"

"A variety of abuses." She shut the journal on her lap and folded her hands on top of it. "I will try to be as concise as possible. Two years ago I found myself alone in the world equipped with two powerful advantages. A classic education, for which I must thank progressive parents, and a great deal of money that had come to me unexpectedly. No need for you to hear the details of this or why I resolved never to marry."

Agatha felt much too vulnerable with Cooper to trust him with that cruel story.

"It is sufficient for you to know," she continued, "that I determined, if I were to be an old maid for the rest of my days, I would be an old maid with a meaningful direction. Just what my use would be eluded me until the evening I met an exceptional man."

"Let me guess," he said dryly. "The late, lamented Hiram McMurdy, huh?"

"That is correct, Mr. Delaney. I stumbled over Hiram quite by chance when returning from a temperance meeting. *Literally* stumbled over him. He was lying in the gutter, and since I was much inspired by the lecture I had just heard, I stopped to help this poor drunken creature."

"Saved his soul, did you?"

"No, Mr. Delaney, he saved mine. Hiram was not drunk. He had been badly beaten and thrown out of a saloon where he had been trying to rescue a girl much too young to be there."

Cooper smiled cynically. "I know what's coming. Mc-Murdy turns out to be another harebrained savior who takes you by the hand and leads you into a shining revelation. And with his mission and your money . . ."

"Your reaction is typical," Agatha informed him coolly. "The result of a male-dominated society which views its women as mere chattel. Hiram was genuine, enlightened to the needs of degraded women by the remorse he suffered following the death of his own daughter. He had turned away from her in the shame of her unwed pregnancy. It changed him forever."

"Yeah, well, some of us find faith tougher than others, Aggie."

"Yes, it involves a certain amount of trust, Mr. Delaney." Something he sorely lacked.

"So your faith had you joining up with McMurdy, the benefactor. To do what exactly?"

"To help women unable to help themselves, of course. Women battered by the injustices of life. Money will buy a great deal, Mr. Delaney, even freedom from unspeakable bondages. Oh, we had our failures. Regrettable failures. But we also had wonderful successes. They are here on this wagon train with as many different stories as there are women."

Cooper knew what was coming. She was going to reveal the identities and personal histories of her women. He didn't want to know them like that. Didn't want them to emerge as distinct individuals demanding his sympathy. He had no sympathy to give them. But there was no stopping Agatha.

"Susan," she said. "Susan was the first."

The sour one with the abbreviated speech, he remembered. She didn't like him.

"The jury who judged Susan, all male, naturally, was unable to believe that a delicate female could be driven to such action unless she was insane. Susan was shut away in a horrible place, suffered for years and was shunned to such a degree when she got out that she lost the ability to communicate. Only recently has she fought to recover it."

He couldn't help it. He had to ask. "What was she tried for?"

"Murder, Mr. Delaney. Her husband was a hideous brute who beat her unmercifully. She killed him in self-defense."

"Jesus," he whispered. There was something else he remembered about Susan that made him gulp. Of all the women on the train, she was the best shot.

"Tessa," Agatha continued. "Have you observed Tessa, Mr. Delaney? An outcast because of a crooked body and a birthmark. Her family was ashamed of her. They never troubled to see the beauty that is inside her. Rachel was also mistreated by her family. A father and brothers who molested her regularly."

She went on telling him about the women.

There was Henrietta, the black slave whose freedom Agatha had purchased.

Dorcas, sold by her father to a despicable old man.

Willow, the Oriental a seaman had brought from China and then abandoned to starve in the streets.

And the others. She told him about the others, too.

Their pasts were varied, but all of them shared the common need to escape from the cruelties fortune had dealt them. All of them wanted the same thing. New lives.

Cooper began to understand the desperation that drove them. But he didn't want to understand. And he damn well didn't want to hear any more disturbing details about the women.

"Fine," he said, with a caustic abruptness that was a buffer against the risk of sentiment. "Life is hard, and you're giving them second chances. But what the hell has Oregon got to do with it? What's wrong with back east somewhere?"

She turned those vivid blue eyes on him. "Intolerance, Mr. Delaney. The ignorant intolerance that resulted when we tried to establish a community of our own. The women were viewed as degraded, unfit to be the neighbors of those who drove us out."

"Oregon," he said.

"Yes, Oregon, where we will be judged by nothing but the wilderness. Hiram went there months ago to secure tracts for us in the fertile Willamette Valley. The funds you saw in the strongbox are to pay the men he hired to hold the land for us, along with the documents they signed agreeing to turn those acres over to us when we arrive.''

"An Amazon utopia." He chuckled over the image. ''That your version of redemption for these women, Aggie?''

"Certainly not. There will be husbands, and with females in short supply in the West and land in their possession . . . well, the women will be able to marry on *their* terms.''

"Ah. And what terms would those be?''

"Equal partnerships in which the women are not subjugated and where there is love and nurturing on both sides. It is not too much to expect for deserving women who are risking everything to have them.''

Hell, she had fortitude. Cooper didn't deny her that. She just didn't have sense. Not on this subject. This new-age Canaan they were promising one another sounded as practical and realistic as a fairy tale. Well, it was their funeral.

"That takes care of your friends, Aggie. Now where do you fit in this scheme?''

"There will be children eventually. They will need to be educated. I will build a school and teach them.''

Agatha had another important ambition, but she didn't share it with him. She knew he already thought her dream for the women was an impossible one. But that didn't matter just as long as he got them to Oregon. And if he didn't get them to Oregon . . . well, her secret ambition would have no meaning then, anyway.

"No husband and children of your own, huh?''

"The women are my family now, Mr. Delaney.''

"Why is that, Aggie?''

"I told you—''

"Yeah, I remember. The vow never to marry. Old maid with a meaningful direction. It went something like that, didn't it?''

The green eyes watching her were gleaming wickedly. His mood had altered again. She didn't like it.

"Who convinced you you weren't mating material, Aggie? That you didn't have what it takes to please a man?"

"You are talking about lust, Mr. Delaney. I suppose it should not suprise me that this is your definition of marriage."

"Nothing wrong with a little healthy lust."

His husky voice stroked the words seductively. She stirred uncomfortably on her perch. He chuckled. It delighted him whenever the perpetually composed Agatha threatened to lose her self-control with him.

"I think this is a subject we will not pursue, Mr. Delaney."

But he did pursue it. "Maybe you just don't know what you're missing. How about I show you? A sample. Just a small sample."

He had pressed his big roan closer to the side of her wagon, so close that mere inches separated them.

"You are interfering with my wagon, Mr. Delaney. I must ask you to remove—Ooof!"

It happened so swiftly, and with such incredible ease, that the breath was squeezed out of her before she could prevent it. In one instant she had been seated safely on her perch. In the next instant his strong arm had shot out and scooped her off that perch.

Agatha found herself deposited in front of him. He had slid back onto the bare rump of his horse to make room for her on the saddle. But the cantle of the saddle was no barrier between them. He was squeezed tightly against her, his arm snugly around her waist to hold her in place. The intimacy of their position was both sudden and shocking.

"There," he whispered, his breath tickling her ear. "Now isn't this nice?"

Agatha immediately panicked. She began to buck and squirm against him, fighting to be released.

"Ooo, that feels good, Aggie. Reeeal good."

She felt a ridge of hard flesh thrust against her backside.

After her appalling experience with him in his hotel room back in Independence, she had an alarming idea just what that hardness represented.

"You keep that up," he cautioned softly, "and with Bucephalus bouncing along here under us, something satisfying is bound to develop."

Recognizing her mistake, she made an effort to remain still. Under the circumstances, her restraint was anything but easy.

"This is absurd, Mr. Delaney. Put me back on the wagon."

"You're squirming again."

"You fail to understand." She hesitated, hating to admit a weakness. Better that, however, than having him think her anxiety was all because of him. "I—I do not ride. Horses make me nervous. Have done since childhood."

"You're safe with me, Aggie. Just relax and enjoy it."

"I do not enjoy it. I insist—"

"Why don't I sing to you, Aggie? Used to sing to the longhorns when I rode herd on them as a kid back in California. Always soothed them."

"Please, I—"

"Sweet and gentle, Aggie. This is my favorite." Mouth close to her ear, he sang to her softly in a rich, true baritone. "If a body meet a body, Comin' thro' the rye . . . If a body kiss a body, Need a body cry? . . ."

The lyrics of the old song were anything but innocent in this situation. They were definitely suggestive, lewd even. They were also absolutely mesmerizing with his warm, arousing breath on her cheek, the masculine aroma of him in her nostrils, the heat of his solid body as it strained against hers. She could barely breathe, much less find her voice to object.

He was taking his revenge on her because of the gold, she thought. That was what this whole performance was about. And that was all it was. He wouldn't be interested in her otherwise. Couldn't be. Not like this. Then why did she . . . ?

"You like that, Aggie? I think you like it."

The song. He must mean the song. But he had stopped singing. His lips were nuzzling her ear.

She found her voice then. *Had* to find her voice, shaky though it was. "Mr. Delaney—"

"Time you used my Christian name. Cooper. It's Cooper, remember?"

"I think—"

"*Cooper*, Aggie. I'm Cooper."

"Very well. Cooper. But only for now because—"

"That's good, Aggie. I like hearing you say my name."

He wondered how she would sound saying it in a different mood. One, for instance, in which both of them were hot and wild and naked. Would she plead for him in a low, sultry voice? Was she capable of that?

Cooper wondered a lot of things about her. Reckless, wanton things. Like what this statuesque body of hers would look like stripped of its prim clothes. He had an idea it might be magnificent. With her fantastic height, her legs were bound to be endless. And her bottom . . . well, he didn't want to just look at her lush bottom. He wanted the sensation of it rubbing against him erotically.

The images in his head made him tighten his arm around her waist, made him push his aching hardness against her longingly.

Agatha knew the situation was out of control. Why couldn't she correct it? Why must she feel so blindly, senselessly helpless?

Thank God for Susan. It was Susan who came to her rescue.

One of the women had neglected to wear her bonnet. The sun on this first brilliant day was too strong for her, blistering her sensitive skin. Susan was on her way to Agatha's wagon to fetch salve from the medicine chest. One glance at the

102

conflict in progress on the horse made her understand the need for immediate action.

Susan was not imaginative, but she recalled how Agatha had used the pregnant Rebecca to distract this devil in similar circumstances back in Independence. The memory was an inspiration. Kitty and Polly. She needed Kitty and Polly.

Cooper was still entertaining sensual thoughts about his captive when he was jolted out of his sweet fantasy by the sight of the two young women who came sauntering toward them hand in hand like a pair of schoolgirls. Blondes. Gorgeous blondes. *Identical* blondes.

Realization exploded inside his head. "Twins!" he roared. "Holy Lucifer, they're twins!"

This was how he had been tricked out of his gold, how half of Independence had been deceived along with him. What's more, they had managed to go on keeping the ruse a secret from him. Probably without much difficulty either. He had resisted seeing the women as individuals anyway, and as long as the twins remained apart, probably taking turns hiding in their wagon, there would have been no reason for him to guess. Not with torrents of rain keeping him constantly occupied and everyone under cover much of the time.

Cooper couldn't get rid of Agatha fast enough.

It would be an exaggeration, Agatha thought, to say he flung her out of the saddle. However, she was so rudely and abruptly released that she came slithering like a rag doll down the side of the roan. Managing to find her balance before she landed in a heap on the ground, she hastily lowered her skirts. They had been bunched up to an indecent level while she had been pinned on the horse.

Cooper, meanwhile, was circling her on his mount.

"What are you doing?" she demanded.

"Just trying to see if you're as sneaky from the back side as you are from the front. Cunning, Aggie. One of them sits there all night in church creating an alibi while her sister's busy fleecing me in the saloon."

He kept circling around her, his outrage all too evident.

"If you are going to shout at me," she requested, "will you please do so from a standstill? You are making me dizzy."

He obliged her, drawing Bucephalus to a halt in front of her. By now the whole wagon train had drifted to a stop several yards up the track where the women were gathering in silent curiosity.

There was fire in Cooper's eyes as he leaned toward Agatha from the saddle. "I ought to abandon the lot of you out here. Leave you on your own and head straight back to Independence."

"But you will not do that," she said calmly.

"Don't count on it," he warned her. "Don't count on that gold being enough to keep me just where you want me."

With a crude oath, he wheeled around, dug his heels into the horse's flanks and tore off across the prairies. A round-eyed, worried Callie appeared at Agatha's side as Cooper and his mount vanished over a rise.

"What's the matter with Coop? Where's he goin'?"

"He will return," she assured the child. "You and Roscoe go along now and help the women to get the wagons under way again."

Susan joined her as Callie ran off with the dog. "Sorry about Kitty and Polly. All I could think of to shake that rascal to his senses."

"No need for an apology, Susan. I am grateful for your action. We could not have kept the twins a secret from him much longer in any case."

"Know he's searching the wagons most every night for his gold, don't you?"

"Yes, just as we anticipated."

"Doesn't find it, what's to prevent him from taking the strongbox and clearing out for good?"

"Never, Susan. That would never satisfy him. Cooper Delaney will settle for nothing less than his own gold. I think we can rely on that.''

Agatha wished she could be as certain of her own self-restraint. It had been rather severely battered on top of that horse with Cooper's body clamped to hers.

Cooper lowered himself onto the lid of a flour barrel at the back of the wagon. He sat there, legs apart, head in his hands in an attitude of defeat. He was drained, disgusted and as frustrated as a man who had combed fifteen wagons from end to end could get.

Nothing. Not a sign of his money belt. And he had looked everywhere. Carefully looked both inside and outside of each wagon. Not like all those inadequate forages after dark either. This afternoon the perfect opportunity for a thorough search had finally presented itself, and it was the women themselves who'd made it possible.

Days on the trail, many of them spent in muddy conditions, had dirtied nearly every garment on the train. The women had demanded a half day's halt to launder their clothes. This was one occasion when Cooper had readily obliged them.

All of them, including the urchin, had trooped off to the banks of a nearby stream, leaving him alone in the camp. He had promptly and gleefully attacked the contents of each wagon, certain that this time he would find his belt.

Only now, several hours later and with no result whatever, did he realize that he'd been outmatched again. They wouldn't have left him all by himself with the wagons unless they had taken his belt with them, or— Or, he thought grimly, it was so cleverly hidden they were absolutely confident he could never locate it.

He sat there on the barrel fuming over the situation.

He wanted that belt. Was more determined than ever, since learning about Kitty and Polly, to have it back. He had been a fool. He had weakened the other day when Agatha had told him all about the women. Had almost gone soft on her and her damn mission. That was before he'd been reminded how they had tricked him. How they were using him.

Well, he didn't owe them anything. Certainly no loyalty. They owed him. Owed him his gold. He needed it to get away from here. Far away from the women and their threat to his independence. Far away from Agatha Pennington.

Cooper shifted around angrily on the lid, his impatient movement disturbing the contents of the barrel. Flour puffed through the staves, powdering the floor between his legs. He knew it was flour. He had raised the lid earlier, making certain that was what the barrel contained.

Nothing but flour, he thought as his boot stirred through the dust. Nothing that could—

Wait a minute. There was something here he was overlooking. The barrel. Why a barrel for the flour when it was customary to store all meals in sacks? Sacks took up less of the valuable space in wagons, were much lighter than barrels to handle.

Unless . . .

What if this barrel contained more than just flour? What if the flour inside it concealed something? Something buried down in the depths of the flour itself. The perfect hiding place, right?

Cooper surged to his feet in excitement. Something told him he was about to locate his money belt.

The space in the wagon was too cramped. He wanted the barrel outside, down on the ground where he could really get at it. It was loaded and cumbersome. He tugged at it, levering it off the tail board of the wagon. And all the while he wrestled with the barrel, he quivered with anticipation.

He could already feel that money belt in his hands. And once he had it back, he would be in control again. Would offer them his ultimatum. Either they agreed to return to Independence where he would safely lead them, or he would leave them out here on their own. Ride off to California with his gold. And he wouldn't look back.

He had the barrel off the wagon now, the lid pried off. He considered turning it over and dumping the whole thing on the ground. But food was too valuable on the trail to waste like that. He would do it the hard way.

Cooper was grinning with eagerness when he plunged his hands into the barrel. He began with the top layer, sifting his fingers carefully through the flour. Nothing. He dug deeper. No belt. Only flour. He went on burrowing.

His grin faded along with his cocky conviction. His action was no longer controlled and confident. He was raking wildly through the stuff now, buried up to his elbows in white while muttering black curses.

Flour flew recklessly in every direction, spilling on the ground, coating his clothes until he looked like a ghost. There was a cloud of it in the air around him, the powder sneaking up his nostrils. He sneezed violently. Then he began to swear again.

His fingernails scraped wood. The bottom of the barrel. He was at the bottom of the barrel. No money belt. No gold. He wanted to heave what was left of the flour into the nearest buffalo wallow.

"What a delightful surprise!"

Cooper jerked up from the barrel. Agatha had entered the circle of wagons. She was smiling as she came briskly toward him, bearing a basket of freshly laundered clothes.

"When you maneuvered to stay alone in camp, I told the ladies you had to be planning something special. What is it to be? Buns? Or a cake perhaps?"

She rid herself of the basket when she reached him, placing it on the lowered tail board. He glowered at her as she moved around him, considering him from several close angles.

"Oh, dear, you do seem to have been carried away with your sudden enthusiasm for pastries."

"The only thing I'd like to bake right now," he growled, "is—"

"Yes, I know. My tongue." She leaned toward him, extending a finger in the direction of his nose. "There is a very interesting smudge right here on the tip of—"

She never finished. His hand shot out, capturing her by the wrist. In the next second he had hauled her against his flour-dusted length, his mouth so close to her own that she was lashed by his warm breath.

"And maybe you could find an interesting way to remove it, Aggie. What do you think?"

For a moment she couldn't think. All she could do was feel the hardness of his chest and thighs against which she was tightly pinned.

"I think, Mr. Delaney," she finally managed to tell him in a strangled voice, "that after our recent encounter on the horse, this position is one I do not care to repeat."

"A big difference this time, Aggie. I'm not after you. I'm after my money belt. Nowhere in the wagons. Not in the flour barrel. Maybe you're wearing it. I need to satisfy myself you're not wearing it."

The powerful arms clasping her shifted as his hands left her back and descended toward her waist.

"Told myself none of you could be wearing it. Would have showed under your dresses. That belt's much too heavy and bulky for a woman anyway. But then you're not an ordinary woman, are you, Aggie?"

She went rigid, prepared to suffer a brief examination of her waistline. But his big hands skimmed her waist with scarcely a pause before they drifted on to a lower area. Agatha gasped as those brazen hands cupped her backside in a firm grip that kept her locked against him. Even more outrageous was the shameless pleasure she experienced when his thumbs began to caress her pliant flesh.

He was a fool, Cooper thought. The worst kind of fool for caring about anything under her skirts but his money belt, which plainly wasn't there. He couldn't help it. Ever since their first collision in his hotel room, he had been longing to know whether her luscious bottom was real or whether he'd dreamt it.

He knew now. She was as soft and full in that region as any man could hope for. He felt himself go hard. A painful hardness that could only be eased by sinking—

"Release me," she demanded harshly.

He chuckled, his cheek brushing hers. "Not yet, Aggie. I'm still searching."

His hands began to roam again, this time stroking up her sides, moving in the direction of her breasts.

"Tell me where the gold is, Aggie," he whispered alluringly. "Just tell me where the gold is, and I'll stop."

His hands tested the sides of her breasts, his thumbs circling slowly. To her dismay, her nipples hardened.

"Otherwise," he warned her, "otherwise, I'll be tempted to . . ."

His lips went to her ear, mouthing the indecent things he would do to her. Agatha shuddered over his promises.

He lifted his mouth from her ear, angled his head to consider her speculatively. There was an intense expression in his green eyes.

"Know something, Aggie? I've never met a woman almost as tall as me. Makes us a good match. Convenient for things like kissing and . . . well, other activities."

Why was she bearing this coarse assault? All she had to do was summon the will to—

"More soap, Miss Agatha! They sent us back to fetch more soap!"

The excited young voice behind them was as effective as a shrill alarm. Agatha and Cooper leaped apart as Callie came trotting into camp, accompanied by Henrietta and Mavreen.

The evidence of the flour, along with Agatha's deep flush of embarrassment, was enough to make the two women understand the situation at a glance. They were tactful enough not to pursue it beyond an exchange of knowing looks. Callie was not so easily satisfied.

"Holy Lucifer!" she cried in her best imitation of Cooper. "Did that ol' flour barrel explode on you?"

Cooper made a choking sound. Agatha looked desperate. Callie danced around them, inspecting them from all sides.

"Heck, you got flour everywhere. On your hands, on your faces, on your—Well, double heck. Miss Agatha, there's great big handprints right smack on your rump. That sure is a funny place for—"

Roscoe, on the edge of the circle of wagons, began to bark in a frenzy. The occupants of the camp turned their attention in the direction of the dog's interest. The flour was no longer a subject of concern. A band of Indians was approaching across the prairie.

# *Chapter Six*

Agatha's grip tightened on the rifle as she peered around the corner of the wagon. She prayed she would have no reason to raise the weapon and fire it. She was one of the poorest shots on the train. Probably because the prospect of harming anyone, even an enemy, made her ill.

Susan, she thought. It should be Susan crouched here behind this wheel. Her friend knew exactly what to do with a rifle. But Susan was with the others at the stream where Henrietta, slipping away from camp in a safe direction, had gone to warn them. Mavreen was hiding in one of the wagons, guarding Callie who didn't want to be there. That left Agatha to cover Cooper as he went out to meet the Indians.

She kept her anxious gaze fastened on his tall figure moving with a loose-limbed, unhurried gait in the direction of their visitors. The band had stopped a few hundred yards away from the wagons. They stood watching Cooper advance on them, his arms lifted in a greeting that showed he was unarmed.

Agatha couldn't understand his extreme caution. He had

assured them that the Indians never bothered wagons passing peacefully through their lands. But he'd looked grim from the moment they spotted this party. His stone-faced concern worried her.

She held her breath as he reached the band. A long dialogue was exchanged. Impossible to hear any of it at this distance. She continued to watch them. There were perhaps twenty in the party. One of the figures stood apart from the others, head lowered in an attitude of weary despair. Agatha's eyes narrowed with interest.

Seconds later she breathed in relief as Cooper started back to camp. She was there to meet him when he entered the circle of wagons.

"The scum of the trail," he pronounced in disgust.

She gazed at him in disappointment. "Why did I think you had regard for the Indian people?"

"I do, but not this lot. They're renegades with a code of their own. The respectable tribes don't like them any better than the traders."

"You knew that when you went out there."

"Suspected it. There were a couple of them I thought I recognized."

She glanced toward the prairie where the band was settling down on the grass. "But if they are not to be trusted—"

"We'll be all right. Just have to guard our stock. I don't think they plan to camp out there. I think they'll move on."

"Then what, pray, are they waiting for?"

"Presents. We give them gifts, and they leave us alone." With any luck, he thought to himself.

"I understand. All that extra coffee and sugar you insisted we purchase in Independence suddenly has meaning."

"Indians are crazy for coffee and sugar, Aggie. Come on, help me load up a few sacks."

They gathered what was needed from the supplies.

"You carry the sugar," she directed him, "and I will manage the coffee."

He glared at her. "And just when did we decide you were coming with me?"

"I insist." Agatha was determined to learn about that one figure in the band who seemed unwilling to be there, and she didn't trust Cooper to secure the information for her.

"It's too risky."

"Nonsense. We are bearing gifts, not weapons."

She gave him no opportunity to argue with her decision. Armed with two sacks of coffee, she marched out from the camp. Cooper caught up with her, growling an irritated, "You never listen, do you?"

"Only when it is instructive, Mr. Delaney."

"Well, you're being instructed. You hang back when we get there, and you keep your mouth closed."

She obliged him but only because it suited her. It wasn't conversation she sought but a close look at the band, that one member in particular.

The Indians, seated on the grass while their ponies grazed behind them, watched with stoic expressions on their faces as Agatha and Cooper neared them.

She was fascinated by the sight of them. They were a motley collection, some with shaved and painted heads, others with locks of hair thick with bear grease. Their garb was just as varied, ranging from traditional shoulder blankets and leggings to the shirts, trousers and hats worn by white men. There were adornments everywhere—clumps of eagle feathers, brass earrings, claw necklaces, beads and porcupine quills.

The band rose to their feet as they arrived. Cooper relieved Agatha of the coffee and went forward to present the gifts. She stood back as he had commanded, seizing the opportunity to inspect the figure who dared to do nothing but wait with downcast eyes a subservient distance from the others.

She was young and slim. A half-breed, Agatha guessed. She might have been pretty if she had been wearing something other than ragged, filthy buckskin. And if, Agatha thought furiously, she hadn't been mistreated. She recognized all the signs. A body that was undernourished, a swelling on her jaw from a recent blow, a mark on her arm that was probably the result of a burn.

The young woman felt her gaze and glanced up. Their eyes met briefly before she looked away. Agatha, turning her head, saw that the leader of the band had noticed her interest.

She couldn't wait to question Cooper on their way back to the wagons. "The girl with them is a captive, is she not?"

"Could be. Or they might have traded for her. It's common."

"It is obscene."

Cooper groaned. "I might have known that's why you wanted to come out here. That nose of yours went and sniffed out another female victim. Well, you don't stand a prayer of rescuing this one, so just forget about her."

Which was exactly what Agatha chose not to do. In the next half hour her mind seethed with possibilities.

The other women were back in camp by now and nervous over the presence of the Indians on the prairie. Why hadn't the band moved on as Cooper had predicted? they wondered. What was keeping them out there? Cooper wasn't easy about their existence either. Agatha alone was unworried.

Having finally settled on a solution, she approached Cooper. He was keeping a vigil on the renegades from behind one of the wagons. She came straight to the point.

"I mean to buy the young woman who is with them. I would be grateful if you would aid me in the negotiations."

He stared at her in silence for long seconds. Then he laughed. There was no humor in his laughter. "Why didn't I think this was exactly what you would propose to do?"

"I am not interested in your judgments, only your assistance."

"Uh-huh." He leaned back against the wagon, his rifle hanging loosely in his arms as he regarded her. "And just supposing I'm blockhead enough to help you, what do you intend to do with this girl when and if you get her?''

"Free her, of course. After which I will invite her to join us on our trek to Oregon.''

"What makes you think she'll want to be traded away from them?''

"You forget my experience on this subject, Mr. Delaney. Trust me, she will welcome her release. It was all there in her eyes.''

"So you say.''

"Yes, I do say,'' she told him heatedly. "No woman should be made to tolerate abuse, whatever her culture.''

"Maybe you ought to tell them that.'' He jerked his thumb in the direction of the band. "Maybe they won't mind your interference, probably love to strike a bargain with you. Oh, wait a minute, I forgot. This isn't Boston or Phildelphia, is it?''

She smiled at his sarcasm. "Yes, they will strike a bargain with me. That is exactly what they are waiting for out there.''

His eyes widened.

She nodded slowly. "Their leader did not miss my interest in the woman. I am certain they are hoping for an offer.''

"You just couldn't stand it, could you, Aggie?''

"The thought of leaving her with them? No, I could not.''

"What do you plan to offer them? They already have the sugar and coffee. And they're sure as hell not going to be interested in a handful of silver dollars from your strongbox. Or maybe you want to give them Bucephalus.''

"It will not be necessary to sacrifice your horse. There is something else.''

"What?''

"Jewelry. I observed their fondness for adornment. Our women have very few pieces, and nothing of any real value, but I believe all of us would be willing to contribute something we cherish in order to free that girl.''

She was right. The women didn't hesitate to part with necklaces, earrings and bracelets from their meager belongings. Agatha surrendered her only treasure, an heirloom brooch which she added to the bonnet containing the offerings.

There were few precious metals in the small collection, and any gems were artificial. But Agatha, bearing the bonnet as she accompanied Cooper out to the band, was confident that there was enough to entice the Indians into a trade.

"You stay behind me, and don't get involved in the bargaining," he instructed her. "They have no respect for women."

Agatha, anxious to release the girl, didn't argue with him, though this contempt for her sex was maddening.

There was no welcome from the renegades when they arrived, but she noticed the gleam in their eyes when Cooper squatted in front of them, spilling the trinkets on the ground.

He had told her their leader was called Bull Bear. Agatha thought the name was appropriate for the burly figure. Cooper's lengthy exchange with him was in Pawnee. She couldn't understand a word. She didn't need to in order to realize that Bull Bear was a canny individual. He regarded the offerings with supreme indifference.

Agatha, unable to bear the thought of failure, thrust herself forward. Crouching beside Cooper, she snatched up a necklace from the pile, dangling it temptingly in front of the leader. Cooper twisted around, his eyes blazing.

"I thought we agreed—"

"My silence was not a promise, and you are a poor salesman."

"And you're going to show me how to be a better one."

"Yes." The necklace was composed of a web of chains studded with garnets. She demonstrated the piece for Bull Bear, turning it so that the paste stones caught the sunlight. "There. Pretty, is it not? And so very versatile. Observe." She displayed the necklace at her throat, then draped it over her forehead. "You see? You can use it in both areas."

"Understands every word you're saying, Aggie."

**116**

"The language of mime is universal. Now, this bracelet
. . . this bracelet here—"

She was interrupted by a bark of laughter from Bull Bear,
followed by his rapid dialogue with Cooper.

"What does he say?" she demanded.

Cooper grinned at her. "He's intrigued by your height.
He's given you a name."

"What name?"

"Uh, don't think you'll like it."

"Tell me."

"Woman Who Is Like a Lodgepole."

She thought about it for a moment. "Tell him Woman
Like a Lodgepole is grateful for her new name. She would
be even more grateful if he accepted her offers for the girl."

"Oh, he's impressed by your negotiating skills, Aggie.
Hell, I'm amazed, too."

She experienced a warm glow of pleasure over his casual
praise. "But am I achieving success?"

"You're getting there."

She proceeded with her enthusiastic pitch, modeling the
cheap trinkets for them until she was loaded with earrings,
bracelets, the necklace and waving a painted fan under their
noses.

There was a long minute of silence. Bull Bear spoke to
Cooper, who turned to her with a sober, "There's one last
article he wants before he accepts your bargain."

"Yes?"

"The ring you're wearing."

Agatha glanced at her hand. She had never considered
parting with the simple jade ring. It had been her father's
wedding gift to her mother.

Cooper, sensing the significance of such a loss, murmured
softly, "You don't need to sacrifice the ring. I think I can
talk him out of it."

"Better not risk it." The dignity of a human life was far
more important than the sentiment of a ring. She tugged it

from her finger and resolutely added it to the other jewelry she removed from herself.

There were grunts of approval from the band as Bull Bear reached for the pile of trinkets. Agatha turned her head, permitting herself for the first time to consider the young woman she had just purchased. Throughout the transaction, she had remained apart, head lowered, making no sign she understood anything of it. Agatha tried to smile at her reassuringly. There was no response.

Cooper and Bull Bear were arguing again in Pawnee. Agatha turned her attention back to the men. One of the band had handed a lighted peace pipe to his leader, who was pressing it on Cooper.

"What now?" she asked anxiously.

"He says the pipe has to be shared to seal the bargain."

"We must not offend them. Smoke the pipe with him," she urged.

"Oh, I've got no objection to his pipe." He grinned at her again. "But I'm not the one he's demanding."

She stared at him. "Surely, you cannot mean—"

"Uh-huh. He wants to puff a few clouds with the chief negotiator. That would be you, Woman Who Is Like a Lodgepole."

Agatha hesitated while Bull Bear watched her. There was a stubborn challenge in his dark eyes. "Very well," she agreed.

Cooper took pity on her. "Look, this is no situation calling for a peace pipe. He's just having fun at your expense. Let me change his mind."

"No. He might give the jewelry back, refuse to part with the girl. Tell him Woman Like a Lodgepole is happy to comply."

Cooper shrugged and translated her decision.

Bull Bear nodded, sucked on the pipe in satisfaction, belched out a stream of smoke and then passed the instrument to her. Agatha accepted the long-stemmed, ornamental calumet, gingerly regarding the glowing bowl. It emitted a foul odor.

"What—what exactly is it?"

"*Shongsasha*," Cooper explained. "A mixture of tobacco and red willow bark."

Bull Bear was waiting. They were all waiting. Agatha braced herself, inserted the stem in her mouth and dragged in the fumes. The result was disastrous. She was instantly seized by a fit of uncontrollable coughing.

"Hell, Aggie, you're not supposed to swallow the smoke."

Regaining a measure of self-control, she tried again. Even worse this time. She gagged on the stuff. It was vile, absolutely vile.

"That's enough," Cooper warned.

"Yes, I believe—that is, I am afraid—" She returned the pipe and scrambled hastily to her feet. "Please excuse me, gentlemen."

There was a stand of wild cherry trees a dozen yards away. Agatha fled toward the spot, ignoring the peals of laughter behind her. She reached the cover of the squat trees with no seconds to spare. Dropping to her knees, she was immediately, violently sick.

She was still vomiting when Cooper arrived on the scene. Mortified by his presence, she started to tell him to go away. Her effort cost her another bout of painful heaving. Suddenly, surprisingly, he was on the grass beside her and silently held her head while she continued to be ill.

What should have been a deeply embarrassing experience became something unbelievably tender. His big, calloused hands were gentle as he cradled her head, waiting patiently for her retching to subside.

When she was finally empty and no longer gripped by seizures, he pressed his bandanna on her. Agatha hesitated.

"It's clean," he said gruffly.

That wasn't her concern. She was simply reluctant to validate a situation that was already too personal. Disturbingly so. But she accepted the bandanna with a quiet, "Thank you."

When she had cleaned her mouth, she turned her head, gazing at him in wonder. There was an expression of rough concern on his face. She remembered how he had held her head with a quality of warmth and caring. This was a new and unexpected dimension to Cooper J. Delaney. She found it touching, but she wasn't sure she liked it. It was decidedly unsettling.

Uncomfortable under her gaze, he smiled at her with a touch of his old cynicism. "So, Woman Like a Lodgepole, was it worth it?"

"It was disgusting and humiliating, and I would go back out there and smoke that peace pipe all over again, and a dozen others like it, if it is what they required to free . . ."

She broke off, realizing that there was absolute silence beyond the screen of the cherry trees. The silence of desertion. Alarmed, Agatha surged to her feet. The renegades! Had they departed, taking both the jewelry and their captive with them?

Cooper was close behind her as she raced out onto the prairie. Gone, just as she had feared! The Indians had slipped away on their ponies without a sound and were already out of sight. But to Agatha's relief, they had left the girl behind. She sat there on the grass with her bundle of pitiful belongings, calmly waiting for them.

Agatha turned to Cooper. "She must be absolutely bewildered, frightened even. Explain the situation to her, please. Assure her that—"

"Not needed, missis," the young woman said with soft dignity as she rose to her feet. "I speak English, and I understand what you have done."

"Excellent!"

"It is an excellent thing, missis."

She approached, and before Agatha could stop her, she

dropped to her knees and grasped her hand. She started to kiss her emancipator's fingers in earnest gratitude.

Cooper, watching the performance, chuckled over the hot flush that rose on Agatha's face. She snatched her hand away and lifted the girl to her feet.

"Unless you are praying to a higher authority, you must not ever kneel again. Certainly not to me, nor to anyone . . ." Agatha paused. "What is your name, please? Tell me your name, and we will discuss your future. Because, as of this moment, your past is unimportant."

The young woman nodded solemnly. "Missis, I am called Magpie."

The night guards on the wagon train were vigilant. But Magpie had observed that the man called Cooper and the woman who never smiled, the one known as Susan, were particularly alert for trouble. She was careful, therefore, to time her departure from the sleeping camp when neither of these individuals was taking their turn at watch.

It was the darkest hour of the night. Charlotte, who chattered like the bird for which Magpie was named, was on sentinel duty. She was not chattering now. She was nodding over her rifle when Magpie crept silently away from the circle of wagons.

She had been with the train for five days now. They had been five days of interesting and disturbing discovery. But only to Magpie. She had learned nothing of use to those who waited for her first report. But she dared not fail to appear as arranged.

Once safely away from the wagons, she made her way quickly along the trail they had traveled that afternoon. A mile or so down the track, with a rise between her and the camp, she halted and listened. There was no sound. Even the insects were still. But she knew she was not alone on the prairie.

Head back, she made her signal. From her mouth issued

the perfect call of a magpie. Within seconds, she was surrounded by several members of the renegade band. Bull Bear himself was with them. He spoke rapidly to her in Pawnee.

"What words do you have for us to pass back to our friend Salter?"

She tried to offer something worthwhile, informing him of the collection of weapons the women carried on the train and how surprisingly well prepared they were against any possible attack. She knew by Bull Bear's single grunt that he wasn't satisfied.

"And mischief?" he demanded. "Has there been no mischief these five days?"

She knew he was referring to her orders to sabotage the train in some manner. Anything to hinder the trek, even cause the women to turn back if possible. Duke wanted that. *Expected* it from her. He asked too much.

"I have found no opportunity yet," Magpie defended herself. "I must be careful or risk their suspicions."

Bull Bear digested her words in silence for a moment. Then his hand came up to catch her by the ear. "I will twist this from your head if you fail us. Then I will send what is left of you back to Salter, who will show you no mercy."

Magpie shuddered over his threat. The loss of an ear was nothing. She could bear any physical pain. She had been doing so most of her life. But Duke Salter was another matter. He had a powerful weapon to control her, and it was this alone that she feared and why she had no choice but to obey him and his mercenaries.

"When the time is right, there will be results," she promised Bull Bear.

"Make certain there are." His thumb and forefinger cruelly pinched the lobe of her ear before he released her. "In five more nights you come out to meet us again."

She knew that until then the band would shadow the wagon train, keeping a safe distance behind them on the trail, waiting to relay some word of success to Duke and his brother back in Independence.

Magpie parted from the renegades, hurrying back toward the camp before she was missed. She thought of how kindly she had been treated by its occupants and how much she hated her treachery. But it was necessary.

There was the rumble of thunder as she neared the wagons. Storm clouds were gathering over the prairie, signaling the end of the dry interval. It was going to rain again.

Agatha stood on the banks of the Big Blue, thinking how much she hated this river as she gazed longingly at the wooded shore on the other side. That desirable objective couldn't be more than several hundred feet away, but it was as unreachable as the moon.

The Big Blue was in spate, swollen from weeks of rain. The ford at which they were camped near Alcove Spring was too deeply buried beneath the rushing waters to permit their wagons to roll across. They had spent three days, three intolerable days, waiting for the river to subside. But there was no sign of the waters easing.

Precious time lost, Agatha thought. Time they could not afford, considering their late start from Independence. And with the likelihood of further delays on the trail ahead of them . . .

Enough, she determined stubbornly. We have waited long enough. There had to be a means of crossing this barrier now, and she meant to find it.

Wheeling, she marched back to the corral of wagons. She found Cooper where she had left him. His big body was hunkered down on the ground as he slathered grease from a tar bucket over the hub bearings of a wheel.

"Not a very useful occupation," she observed, "considering the wagon is going nowhere."

He turned his head, cocking that scarred eyebrow in her direction. "A bit short-tempered today, are we, Aggie?"

"I am frustrated, Mr. Delaney."

His green eyes wore a lascivious gleam. "I could suggest a cure for that."

"Yes, I am certain you could, but the only suggestion I care to hear from you is a method for crossing this wretched river."

"I thought we agreed—"

"Patience may be a virtue, Mr. Delaney, but my supply of it has been exhausted. There must be a means of reaching the other side. What do the freight trains do in a situation like ours?"

He shoved the tar bucket aside and rose to his feet, hooking his thumbs in the waistband of his trousers as he regarded her. "Rafts. They build stout rafts and pole the wagons across. Plenty of timber along the shore. Even got the right tools in your stores. Only one thing we lack." He leaned back against the wheel he had been greasing. "Manpower. Even you have to admit we don't have enough combined muscle for a job like that."

She was reluctantly forced to agree with him. "Is there no other way?"

His massive shoulders lifted in a small shrug. "Always the cordelle."

"Cor—No, I am not familiar with the term. Explain it to me, please."

"Nothing to it, Aggie. All it involves is sealing the bed of every wagon with pitch until they're watertight, jacking up each of the fifteen wagons in turn, removing the running gear, which gets heaved into the beds along with the replaced stores and passengers, and floating the wagon boxes over one by one along a cordelle line."

"Which is?"

"Strong rope passed through the open bows of the wagons. One end is wrapped around a tree on this side. Then some poor bastard—and we all know who that would be if we tried it—gets to lash the other end to a trunk on the opposite shore. Of course, he can only do that after he swims his mount across. Probably with the rope between his teeth. Easy as pie after that. Just requires hauling each wagon hand by hand along the line.''

''I see. And, of course, if Bucephalus is able to survive the current, there is nothing to prevent the stock from being driven across.'' She frowned, considering the plan. ''A complicated procedure, I suppose, but I am certain we can manage it. Yes, Mr. Delaney, the cordelle is our solution. I am rather surprised you neglected to mention it before now.''

''Oh, you are, huh? Don't suppose it's occurred to you that I didn't mention it because it's a damn risky operation in waters like these.''

''Possibly, but I am confident of its success.''

''I don't think so.''

''Is there a choice really? It may be days before the river goes down, even weeks perhaps. And if we are delayed like that, what worse risk do we face later on when we reach the mountains? Snow in the passes. You warned of that yourself. Therefore, Mr. Delaney . . .''

How did she do it? Cooper wondered hours later as he stood on the opposite bank of the Big Blue, ready to wave the first floated wagon on its way. Not only had Agatha talked him into this laborious operation, she had also managed to convince him, and everyone else on the train, that she alone would sail the first wagon box over the stretched line.

Her argument had gone something like: ''Of course, this will be as safe as a bridge, but it would be wise to test the first craft without stores or passengers aboard. A navigator is all that is necessary. Only logical it should be me since I had every faith in this plan from the start. Yes, I insist on it.''

And, naturally, they had all surrendered to her will. Blasted woman had even refused his suggestion to swim her across on Bucephalus or one of the other mounts. No, horses made her nervous, remember? She'd rather risk her stubborn neck in a bouncing wagon bed on a river that was a holy terror.

"I am hooked into the line and ready, Mr. Delaney," she called to him from the opposite bank. "May I proceed?"

Look at her, Cooper grumbled to himself. Perched on that thing like a captain at the wheel of his clipper.

He didn't want to admit that there was something gallant in the sight of her tall, proud figure waiting for his signal. He glanced around, making sure of the situation.

The rope on this end was snugged securely around the thick trunk of a sycamore. Half of the oxen had already been swum to this side without a single loss. Several of the brave women had mounted the wagon train's few horses and helped him to do this, difficult though the current was. Those oxen waited now, along with their drivers, to drag the arriving wagons to solid ground while the teams waiting on the opposite shore hauled them down to the line. Cooper was satisfied.

"Anchors aweigh, Miss Pennington."

"What, Mr. Delaney?"

"Launch her!" *Just don't go down with the damn ship, Aggie.*

He watched tensely as the wagon box, stripped of its canvas cover, was shoved from the bank. There wasn't much effort required from Agatha to pass it along the rope looped through the bows. Cooper had angled the taut line so that the swift current did most of the work, driving the craft at a downstream diagonal.

That's it, he thought, pleased as he followed the progress of the rocking wagon, which was nearly midstream now in its crossing. No problems. It's working. Gonna be just . . .

God almighty!

The line had snapped. The towline had snapped without warning. And the wagon, without its restraint, spun madly and then was swept away, bearing Agatha with it on the

126

vicious current of the Big Blue.

Cooper ignored the shrieks of the women on both banks. He was too busy hurtling himself into the saddle, urging Bucephalus into a race along the bank of the river as he chased the runaway wagon. It had already vanished around a bend in the stream.

He was sick over Agatha's plight. And he was puzzled. He had checked every foot of that thick rope himself to make sure it was strong and solid. It shouldn't have snapped.

# Chapter Seven

Agatha was so stunned by her predicament that a full thirty seconds passed before she recovered her senses. Then, aware that she was not only adrift but catapulting like a log down the furious river, she rapidly examined her situation.

The lifeline was gone. Snipped in two as though it had been no stronger than a thread. The stress on it must have been greater than any of them had calculated. Also gone was the comfort of familiar faces on either shore. She had been carried around a bend, and all of them were out of sight. She was alone on the river.

The wagon was tossing wildly, threatening to pitch her into the muddy waters. Common sense dictated a safer position. Gripping the side of the wagon, she lowered herself to the floorboards. Dry. No sign of the wagon taking on water. The women had performed a thorough job of sealing the cracks. A small blessing. Other than that . . . well, her peril was very real, and only a fool wouldn't be frightened. She was not a fool.

"You have been gifted with a very good brain, Agatha

Pennington. I advise you to use it.''

Ah, that was better. She was employing a technique she had acquired in childhood.

She couldn't have been more than five or six when someone had mounted her on a neighbor's pony. Ponies were supposed to be sweet, gentle creatures. This one had proved to be mean and devious, promptly running away with her. Its owner had yelled to her to speak reassuringly to the animal. She'd done so and somehow survived the terrifying experience. Not because the pony had listened to her—it hadn't—but because she had ultimately listened to herself and clung to its back like a burr. Never mind that the result had been a lifelong mistrust of any beast that resembled a horse. She still found audible self-encouragement highly beneficial.

"You can either sit here and suffer or you can help yourself. Which?"

No choice really. It was just a question then of method. A pity she had never learned to swim. An oar? If she could manage to paddle her way to the riverbank, ground the wagon on shore . . .

"Now what do we have on board that might serve as an oar?"

Unfortunately, nothing. There was only the running gear with its wheels and the wagon's canvas cover folded in a neat square. The knobby head of a familiar stick peeped out from one corner. She had placed it there for safekeeping. Hiram's hickory staff. Her staff now.

"It would never satisfy the purpose, Agatha. Much too thin."

But the staff did have promise as a pole. If she could shove her way to the riverbank . . .

Seizing the staff, she lifted herself on her knees and braced herself against the sideboards. She lowered the point of the staff into the churning waters and searched for the bottom.

Hopeless. The stick was too short for the river's present

129

depth. But she kept poking as the wagon rushed onward, hoping she would encounter something solid. A gravel bar perhaps, a snag even. Nothing.

Seconds later, and without warning, the wagon was dragged into a whirlpool. The rocking and twisting were so sudden and ferocious that, in steadying herself, Agatha lost her grasp on the pole. She watched in dismay as the cherished staff bobbed away on the current and disappeared from view.

For a moment she could do nothing but gaze after the staff, mourning its loss. It had been an important symbol, representing the faith the women had placed in her.

"Nonsense, Agatha. It is a regrettable sacrifice and nothing more than that. The human spirit is all that matters, not a piece of wood."

Unhappily, her spirit was at a rather depressed level. No sensible solution to her problem appeared to be offering itself.

The wagon, escaping the whirlpool, was carried onward with the tearing waters. It remained maddeningly in the center of the river, never drifting toward either shore. There were islands, and she would have welcomed landing on one of them. But the wagon, seemingly with a mind of its own, avoided them.

She sank back against the side of the box, wondering how far the torrent had borne her. A mile? Several miles? Difficult to tell. What was happening with the others back at the submerged ford?

Absurd to mind her aloneness so much when all that should matter was her safety. She made an effort to renew her courage by talking to herself again out loud. The tactic seemed to fail her this time.

At some point, however, she became aware of a voice other than her own. A male voice, loud, deep and wonderfully exasperated.

Twisting around on the floorboards, she eagerly searched

the shoreline. The thick belt of trees had thinned, affording her glimpses of the prairie. Happy relief! She wasn't alone. Cooper Delaney was out there on a charging Bucephalus, keeping abreast of her drifting wagon as he wove through the trees, seeking the solid ground.

She realized that he must have been close by all the while, chasing the wagon as he waited for an opportunity to intercept it. The riverbank was open here, permitting him to hug the edge as his mount surged forward. Only the waters separated them now. She had never been so pleased by the sight and sound of anyone.

"Damn it, Aggie," he bellowed at her, "if you'd just stay in one place out there for five seconds, maybe I could rescue you."

"Sorry, Mr. Delaney," she yelled back. "Had I a choice, I would remain fixed beside the dragon until you slayed it. I fear I make a poor damsel in distress."

"Yeah, well, I'm no shining knight either. How you doing?"

"Thank you for inquiring. I remain dry and reasonably calm, though rather giddy at this point from the prolonged turbulence. Have you a suggestion to remedy my circumstance?"

"Blast it, Aggie, only you would get yourself in a scrape like this."

"That is an observation, not a suggestion."

He managed to keep abreast of the rushing wagon as they called out to each other. "Just hang on, because at the first opportunity I'm going to—Sweet mother! This is real trouble!"

He'd been scanning the river ahead of them from the elevation of his swift horse during their exchanges. Alerted by his sudden alarm, Agatha dragged herself up on her knees, turning her eyes downriver. She could now see for herself the fearsome sight that had grabbed his attention.

Rocks directly ahead! Rocks like rows of wicked teeth

waiting to grind the wagon into tiny morsels as it sped toward the foaming mouth of the rapids! Her situation had just become critical.

Cooper, his gaze sweeping the river, desperately seeking an answer, shouted, "Deadhead just up to your right! Catch it, Aggie!"

"Dead—I fail to understand, Mr. Delaney!"

"Tree trunk trapped on the bottom! If you can manage to snag the wagon against it—"

"Yes, I spy it!"

She could make out the mass of twisted roots from an uprooted tree where they broke the surface of the river, creating a V in the parted current. Agatha, already on her feet, began rocking the wagon in a fierce effort to maneuver it against the snag.

If she missed this opportunity, slammed into those rocks beyond . . .

Whether in the end it was her concentrated jockeying of the wagon, or just sheer luck, didn't matter. The result was the same. To her immense relief, the wagon bumped, lurched, then ground to a standstill against the barrier. But Agatha, clutching at the gnarled roots, knew that her anchor was not a dependable one. She could feel the powerful current tugging at both the wagon and the tree, threatening to tear them away.

"Mr. Delaney!"

"I'm here, Aggie, right here."

Not precisely the case, she realized when she looked toward the shore, but near enough. He had driven Bucephalus down the bank and into the waters as far as he dared. The current at that point in the Big Blue was too swift and deadly to permit a close approach. A good twenty feet still separated them.

"How good are you at being lassoed, Aggie?"

Cooper had produced a lariat and was already swinging its loop over his head.

"How accurate are you at delivering it, Mr. Delaney? And I advise you to hurry. I can feel us coming loose here."

His first shot missed, landing in the water.

"Perhaps I should go over the side, try wading it. The distance from here is not so—"

"No! Too deep, and you'd never survive that current. Just hold on. Stand still and try to keep as straight as possible."

She did as he commanded. He tried a second toss of the line. And missed again. Despite her frantic grip on the roots, the wagon was beginning to swing slowly away from its berth. Another thirty seconds and it would be too late.

Once more the rope came winging through the air. This time his aim was true. The loop descended over her head and settled around her shoulders. His whoop of triumph was that of a herdsman who has just snared an ornery steer.

The similarity was something Agatha was too busy, and too grateful, to mind. She rapidly secured the line under her arms, an action which required her to release her precarious hold on the roots. The loop tightened around her, and she was lifted off her feet just as the wagon slid away from its perch.

The next thing she knew, she was in the river and spitting up a mouthful of water as she was dragged toward the shore against a belligerent current fighting to haul her in the opposite direction.

Somewhere over her head, she heard Cooper threatening her with an angry, "Damn it, Aggie, if you drown on me now I'll never forgive you."

"Why is that, Mr. Delaney?" she managed to gasp while struggling to find a footing that wasn't there.

"Because," he said, bracing himself as he reeled her in like a prize catch, "you might be the only one on the wagon train who knows where my gold is."

"Then I refuse to disappoint you."

And she didn't. Seconds later she stumbled through the shallows. Cooper, sliding from his mount, splashed toward

133

## Jean Barrett

her. She didn't object when he scooped her up in his arms, staggered with her to the riverbank and deposited her on a flat boulder.

"You all right?" he asked, crouching beside her.

She didn't immediately answer him. She gazed toward the river where the rapids had already swallowed the wagon. "How unfortunate. We have lost one of the wagons."

He stared at her disbelievingly. Then he sank back on the grass, hooting with laughter. "Almost lands herself inside the pearly gates, and all she can think about is a wagon gone to hell. Aggie, you are something else."

"It is a legitimate concern now that I"—she paused to untangle herself from the lariat that was still binding her— "am perfectly safe, thank you for that. And once I am reasonably dry again—"

"Wouldn't count on that anytime soon."

She eyed him questioningly. He nodded, jerking a thumb in the direction of the horizon behind her. She turned on the boulder. Storm clouds were racing up from the west.

"Looks like we're both in for another soaking, Aggie."

"Is there no hope of regaining the camp before the storm breaks?"

He climbed to his feet. "Let me point out three things to you. We're probably three, four miles downstream from the ford. Bucephalus is too blown from that race to do anything but rest. And in case you haven't noticed it, we're less than an hour now from sundown. Gonna get dark real fast with those clouds."

He was right, and there was no point in arguing with him about it. "Then, since we cannot hope to either ride or walk back to camp before nightfall, what do you propose? Surely we cannot—"

"Spend the night out here? That's exactly what we're going to do."

"But—"

"Not to worry, Aggie. I've already found us a shelter. Or

134

what's left of one. I passed an abandoned soddy about a quarter of a mile back.''

"Definition, Mr. Delaney."

"A hut made of slabs of sod dug from the prairie. Probably the work of a trapper. You're gonna love it.''

The prospect of spending the night alone with Cooper Delaney was a daunting one. He didn't fail to sense her discomfort.

"What's the matter, Aggie?" he challenged her. ''Afraid to play house with me?''

She rose decisively to her feet. ''If we hurry, we may reach your soddy before the storm breaks.''

They weren't that fortunate. The rain, sweeping in from the open prairie, drenched them as they raced the last yards to the earth-walled hut.

Miserable in her sodden clothes, but refusing to complain about it, Agatha stood in the doorless entrance to the shelter and gazed out at the slashing rain. Or what she could see of it in the rapidly dwindling light.

Cooper was on the earthen floor behind her, having settled himself at the end of the tiny hut where the low ceiling of rough timbers was still intact. The roof had caved in on the other side. He had secured Bucephalus behind the structure before dragging his saddlebags and rifle into the soddy. She could feel him watching her. She wished he would say something. He was making her nervous.

In the end, when she could no longer stand the silence between them, she expressed a concerned, ''What will the others think when we fail to return?''

"Probably that the Big Blue got us," he responded casually. ''Or maybe that we used our heads and found someplace to shelter for the night. And since nobody can reassure anybody about anything until morning, why worry about it?''

She glanced at him over her shoulder. *He* certainly wasn't worried. She could just make him out in the thick shadows,

135

long legs drawn up toward his chest, arms folded across his knees. He was totally relaxed.

"It's going to be a long night, Aggie. You plan on spending it there in the doorway?"

She didn't answer him.

"A lot more comfortable over here in the corner," he urged.

"Perhaps later," she murmured.

"Uh-huh."

His teeth gleamed whitely in a grin that expressed his amusement. He knew what she was thinking. That his body was much too big, the hut much too small. He began softly whistling "Comin' Thro' the Rye" under his breath.

Agatha turned her head away, watching the rain again. The whistling behind her stopped. There was another long, disquieting silence before he broke it with a startling, "You know, Aggie, sooner or later you'll have to do it."

She faced him, afraid to ask for a clarification. He was nodding slowly in the thickening gloom.

"No fire," he said. "Not a stick of dry wood in the place for a fire. Can't warm ourselves, and it's getting cold. We'll both have to do it."

She stared at him.

"Wet clothes, Aggie. We'll have to get out of our wet clothes."

"I think not, Mr. Delaney."

He didn't argue with her. He began unpacking a saddlebag. He removed an oilcloth which he spread open on the ground as a shield against the dampness. She didn't need an explanation to know that he was making a bed for the night. One bed.

He produced a blanket from the bag, displaying it for her inspection. "Too bad I don't have another blanket. But this one is real generous. Wide enough so that each of us can tuck an end around ourself and still have a layer between us. Now that's safe, isn't it, Aggie?"

"Let me see if I understand you correctly, Mr. Delaney. You are proposing that we cast off our clothing, wrap ourselves in one blanket and lie down together for the night."

"Perfectly innocent, Aggie. A real tradition, in fact. Isn't bundling an old respected custom back east where you come from?"

"I have not personally practiced it, but I believe the participants remain fully dressed."

"You don't say. Even when their clothes are wet? Even when they're standing there shivering hard enough to bring on a fever? Even then?"

"I am not shivering." But she was, and had been for a good five minutes now.

"My mistake. Thought you were." He slipped his hand inside the saddlebag, extracting an article which he held toward her. "Do me a favor, though. Get a nip of this inside you."

"What is it?" She stared suspiciously at the object, unable to make it out properly in the fading light.

"Something to warm you. Go on, take it."

She moved toward him, gingerly accepting his offering. She found herself holding a dented metal flask. Uncapping it, she sniffed the contents. "Spirits."

"French brandy. Guaranteed to put a fire inside you."

"I am not in the habit of—"

"Hell, Aggie, it's not liquor in this situation. It's medicine."

She hesitated. She *was* very cold. "Well, perhaps just a small dose."

Head back, she swallowed a generous measure of the brandy. It went down like liquid flame. The impact was so unexpected that for a moment she couldn't breathe.

"Hey, take it easy. You're supposed to sip the stuff, not gulp it."

The first burning shock eased, leaving a pleasant glow inside her.

"You all right?"

"Splendid. I do think, however, that I will . . ." She broke off to lower herself to a seat on the other saddlebag. "Ah, an improvement." She was still clutching the flask. She helped herself to another taste of the brandy. "Quite effective. I do feel warmer."

"Careful," he warned. "No supper, remember? On an empty stomach, it'll go straight to your head."

"Nonsense. I have a very strong head."

"I noticed."

She was thoughtful for a minute as she perched on the bag, cradling the flask against her breasts. "It occurs to me, Mr. Delaney . . ."

"What?"

"The thought occurs to me that, if I were made tipsy, I might shamelessly agree to remove my clothes. Has that thought occurred to you?"

The light was almost gone now. The only thing she could see was the whiteness of his teeth as he flashed another diabolical grin.

"Can't fool you, Aggie. I suppose you've gone and figured out the rest, too. That the only reason I want you to strip for me is so I can check for sure whether you're wearing my money belt under those wet skirts. No chance of any interruption this time either. But wouldn't you think I'd be smarter than that?"

"I would, Mr. Delaney. I most definitely would. The thing is . . ." She paused to lift the flask to her lips. "The thing is, my state of undress would be of no value to you. No money belt. Gone. Much too cumbersome for any of us. It was destroyed after its contents were placed—Ooo, careful with your tongue, Agatha. Enough to say the gold is perfectly safe."

"Sure glad of that."

"Yes."

"Aggie, are you at that flask again?"

"Certainly not." She hiccuped softly. "Beg pardon."

"You've had enough."

She didn't resist when he removed the flask from her hand. She couldn't see him in the dark, but she could hear him moving about. She listened to his activity for a few seconds.

"Mr. Delaney?"

"Yep?"

"Are you taking off your clothes?"

"Yep. Sure you won't join me?"

She thought about it. The brandy had made her all cozy, without her usual restraints. "Perhaps ... perhaps I will. Since my garments *are* uncomfortably damp, and since it is dark now, and since you promise that a layer of blanket will remain between us ... Yes, I think I might risk it."

"That's good, Aggie. Sensible of you. Need any help?"

"Thank you, no. I—" She dragged herself to her feet. Her limbs felt slightly numb, but pleasantly so. "—can manage."

Ridding herself of shoes and stockings, she started to undo the buttons down the bodice of her figured muslin dress. But they were tiny buttons and there were so many of them. It was difficult.

"Besides," she said, "there is no longer a reason not to trust you. As it has been established I am not wearing your money belt, you have no motive for examining my exposed body."

"You think so?"

"I do. Men are not interested in me in that way."

"You're certain of that?"

"Oh, very," she assured him solemnly. "Experience taught me—"

"What experience?" he demanded.

"Not a very nice one, Mr. Delaney." She succeeded with the buttons, began to squirm out of the dress. "I was betrothed, you know. In Philadelphia."

"What were you doing in Philadelphia?"

"Keeping house for my widowed uncle and his son after

139

Mama and Papa died in a typhus epidemic. They were teachers, you see.''

''Your uncle and his son?''

''My parents. Superb teachers.''

''No money?''

''Absolutely none. And that was why I was so grateful for Henry.''

''Uncle or cousin?''

''Neither. Henry was the personable young lawyer who courted me. He persuaded me to believe that my physical shortcomings didn't matter to him in the least, which was a considerable achievement since they had always mattered to me.''

Dress out of the way, Agatha removed her pantalettes.

''Henry had the power to charm, did he?''

''He did. I earnestly believed he wanted me for myself. Why else should he ask to marry me when I was a woman without property or expectations?''

''Your uncle—''

''Oh, yes, he was very rich, but everything was to go to his son. Henry knew that.''

Agatha started to work on the tape that secured her petticoat. It was wet and stubborn, and her fingers didn't want to obey her.

''What else did Henry know?'' Cooper prompted her.

''A great deal, I am afraid. All secretly learned from a friend of his in the firm that served my uncle. That I was to inherit, should I survive my cousin, which I did not know. That my uncle did not trust Henry and was thinking of changing his will.''

''Something else you didn't know, huh?''

''Not until after the boating accident on the Delaware that killed my uncle and my cousin. Which, as an investigation eventually disclosed, was not an accident at all.''

''Henry?''

"Astonishing, is it not? That he should be so greedy, so foolish."

The tape loosened. Agatha freed herself of the petticoat. No corset, thank goodness. She was in no state to struggle with a wet corset. She hadn't worn one since Independence, convincing herself it was an impractical garment for the trail.

"I was also foolish," she went on. "Even after all the evidence, I wanted to believe in Henry's innocence. That is, until I confronted him in his cell. Until I saw his smile and listened to him inform me that, aside from being an heiress, there was absolutely nothing desirable about me."

Cooper muttered something that sounded like one of his more savage obscenities.

"What is it, Mr. Delaney? Did you—"

"Never mind. What's taking you so long?"

"A moment, please."

It was black inside the hut now. She couldn't have cast off her linen chemise otherwise. It was her last defense. She stood naked and anxious.

"Mr. Delaney, where are you?"

"Right here."

"I am ready for the blanket."

"All right, here's how it works. I take my half over and under. You take your half under and then over. And if we're careful, nobody gets embarrassed. Understand?"

"Yes. May we begin? I am uncomfortably cold."

"Anytime, Aggie."

She groped her way down to the pallet, aware of him already settled on his end. Obeying his instructions, she covered herself with her half of the blanket. The wool was scratchy against her bare skin but blessedly warm.

Snug as a cocoon, she thought. And very puzzling. His hard, naked bulk was right there, separated from her by nothing but a single layer of blanket. She had never been this intimate with a male body. She should be shocked by the situation, alarmed even. She was not alarmed.

141

The brandy, she decided. It had left her with a mellow feeling. Without the brandy, she wouldn't have taken off her clothes, wouldn't have agreed to share a bed with Cooper Delaney. Well . . .

"He was wrong."

His deep voice in the darkness startled her. He had been so still she had convinced herself he was asleep.

"The bastard was wrong," he repeated. "He never really looked at you. All he saw was the money."

Henry. He was talking about Henry.

"Oh, no," she insisted, "Henry was right. In that one respect, he was very right. I have no physical charms to recommend me. It was absurd of me to permit myself to think . . ."

A wistful note had crept into her voice. She controlled it, continuing with a brisk, "But I no longer have any illusions on that subject. And, really, the shameful episode with Henry was beneficial in one vital respect. It taught me how to relate to the humiliations suffered by women. Yes, I am grateful for that anyway."

He growled something unintelligible. She didn't question him. There was silence again in the soddy. She interrupted it a moment later.

"Mr. Delaney?"

"Still here, Aggie."

"It has stopped raining."

"I noticed."

"The clouds have cleared away. I can see the sky up there where the roof is gone. I do not believe I have ever experienced a sky like this before."

Her voice was soft with wonder.

"A prairie sky after a storm. There's nothing like it, Aggie. Spangled with a million stars so close you feel you can reach right out and touch every one of them."

"Yes," she whispered, sharing the awesome magic with him.

Seconds passed. He stirred restlessly under his half of the blanket and then demanded roughly, "So, exactly what is it that's wrong with you?"

He confused her with his abrupt change of mood. "Are we discussing—"

"*You*. I want to know what these fatal physical flaws are."

"You have eyes, Mr. Delaney. Surely—"

"Tell me. I want to hear you tell me."

She laughed. The combination of the brandy and the splendor of the night sky made her laugh. Made her willing to play this ridiculous game with him. "Shall we begin with the obvious? My proud, unfeminine height."

"Doesn't count. I can still look down on you."

"Barely," she conceded. "Very well, let us move on to other particulars. My face. My face is a definite problem."

"Is it? How so?"

"My features are much too bold. A nose too long, a mouth too wide. *Unfashionably* wide."

"Hmm, I don't remember that. Can't judge it now either. I'm blind here in the dark. Maybe . . ."

She heard him shifting around. He must have raised himself and was looming over her. She sensed his closeness. No, more than sensed it. She could feel the animal heat of his powerful body, could scent his masculine aroma.

"Tell you what, Aggie," he murmured. "Why don't I feel that mouth? Just sort of skim over it, so to speak. Then I could tell for myself whether it's a real problem for you."

"Trace the shape of it, you mean?"

"Yeah, so to speak."

She considered his suggestion. "I suppose there is no harm in such a contact. It would be strictly for the purpose of enlightenment."

"That's right."

"Very well, Mr. Delaney. You may touch my mouth."

She was aware of him dipping lower. She prepared herself for the sensation of his fingers stroking her lips. It was not his fingers, however, that investigated this region. It was the tip of his tongue that licked lightly, experimentally, over the contours of her lips.

Her mouth opened in shock. He must have read her re-action as an invitation. That exploring tongue didn't hesitate to probe into the recesses of her mouth itself. Now there was more than just his heat and scent for her to experience. There was the taste of him, earthy and elemental.

Was this really happening? Was she *permitting* it to hap-pen?

He deepened their joining, his plundering tongue invoking the most wanton images imaginable. Henry had kissed her. Nothing like this. Nothing all wild and lusty.

There was a roaring in her ears when his mouth finally released hers. She heard his voice far away utter an ordinary, "There, you see, Aggie, your mouth is just fine. Now, what are these other areas you object to?"

"Angular," she informed him in a hoarse whisper, know-ing she was beyond all resistance and not caring. "I am much too angular. Legs too long, bosom too flat. Hopeless, Mr. Delaney."

"Oh, I don't think they can be that bad," he drawled. "Why don't I just check on them?"

He proceeded to do so. She caught her breath as his hand, sliding up under her side of the blanket, began to caress her breasts, his fingers making slow, enticing patterns against her sensitive flesh. Her nipples went as rigid as pebbles.

"A little hard to tell," he said. "Maybe . . ."

She felt a brief rush of cool air as he folded the blanket back from her breasts. It was followed immediately by heat. The wet, incredible heat of his mouth inhaling first one of her breasts, then the other. His sleek tongue wrapped around each of her buds in turn, tugging with a gentle forcefulness. Agatha had never known that pleasure could be so raw and powerfully sensual.

"I'd say your bosom is no problem either," he reported

finally, his voice low and raspy. "No problem at all. What was that other concern? Legs, wasn't it?"

His hand trailed downward, passing over her belly with agonizing slowness, stopping at the juncture of her legs. His fingers began to stir lazily through the nest of curls that framed her womanhood. Agatha gasped.

"Good," he whispered. "Real good."

"This is not my legs."

"No, it isn't, is it?"

His fingers went on searching, moving inward between her thighs, carefully parting the petals of her secret place.

"Mr. Delaney—Cooper," she pleaded.

"We'll get there, Aggie," he promised. "We'll get there."

But he had lost interest in her legs. And she lost all awareness of reality as his skillful fingers began to torment the small, slick nub that was suddenly the total core of her being.

"What is happening?" she implored as waves of primal heat coursed through her. "I don't—Oh!"

"Let go, Aggie. Just let yourself go for me."

She couldn't do otherwise. His compelling fingers had robbed her of all control. There was nothing but this raging urgency that mounted, mounted. And finally peaked in a searing, fantastic incandescence.

She was rocked by disbelief when the spasms finally subsided. "I have never known anything to compare to it," she confessed weakly. "It was as though I were soaring."

"Aggie," he muttered. There was a sudden note of anguish in his voice, but she was oblivious to it.

"The brandy," she decided. "It must have been the effect of the brandy."

"Yeah, that's just what it was."

"But—"

"Don't think about it," he commanded, his voice still strangely thick. "Go to sleep."

She was aware of him settling down again under the blanket.

"Are you angry with me, Mr. Delaney? Have I done something wrong?"

"Shh," he hushed her.

His hand, which had withdrawn after she peaked, found her again in the darkness. His magic fingers slipped beneath her heavy coil of hair and lightly massaged the nape of her neck. He began to sing to her, this time treating the old song as though it were a lullaby.

" 'Every lassie has her laddie, nane, they say, ha'e I; Yet a' the lads they smile on me, When comin' thro' the rye . . . ' "

It was soothing. Soothing and irresistible. She couldn't keep her eyes open.

Cooper stopped singing when her breathing became slow and even. She was asleep. And he was awake. Miserably awake and aware of his frustrated, throbbing hardness under the blanket.

He could have had her. When she'd climaxed for him like that, all wild and wonderful, she had been ready to accept him. He had even pictured it. Ripping the blanket away from both of them. Straining his body against her nakedness. Her long legs wrapping around his hips while he drove into her. The remembered image now made him groan aloud.

He hadn't taken her. Instead, he had exercised a massive restraint. Why? He was still trying to understand it. She was a virgin, of course. Had to be. And not an entirely sober one after the brandy. Was that it? Had he been reluctant to take advantage of her? But since when had he ever let an opportunity like that get by him?

Cooper stirred restlessly inside the blanket.

Why did she have to be so damn innocent and vulnerable? Telling him that story about the bastard who had used her. She had been casual about it, but she must have been devastated at the time. The snake had inflicted on her a cruelty that made it impossible for her to see herself as anything but an unattractive old maid. No telling what other hurts she had experienced before that, all of them raising defensive barriers. All of them contributing to the image of the prim spinster. But Cooper had revealed another Agatha tonight. And wished now he hadn't. Because this one gnawed at his gut.

He shouldn't have touched her. He shouldn't have verified that lush bottom of hers. He didn't need this aching hardness. All he needed was what was waiting for him in California. No other longing, no other involvement. Just California, remember?

"Mr. Delaney! *Mr. Delaney!*"

The voice was shrill, penetrating. It was accompanied by a hand clutching at him insistently.

Cooper jerked up from the pallet, striking out blindly at his attacker.

"Stop!" she cried out, catching his fist in the darkness.

He knew then where he was and who he was struggling with. He went suddenly limp, his voice gruff. "I hurt you?"

"No, of course not." But she sounded scared as she released him. "You were having a bad dream. I fear I awakened you too abruptly."

The nightmare, he thought, trembling like an infant over the memory of it. His damn recurring nightmare with all its nameless demons he never understood.

"Are you all right, Mr. Delaney? You seemed to be fighting a rather nasty battle in your sleep."

"What did you hear?" he demanded, fearing her discovery of his weakness.

"Only your very agitated muttering. And perhaps . . . yes, I do think you mentioned California."

"Forget it. It was just a dream. It didn't mean anything."

There was a silence between them, and then she asked softly, "Why do you need so earnestly to get to California, Mr. Delaney?"

"Business," he said, refusing to explain.

"I see." She paused again, then offered him an apologetic, "I am sorry it is necessary for us to delay you in reaching your destination."

There was genuine regret in her voice and a forlorn quality that tugged at his insides. He didn't answer her.

"Mr. Delaney?"

"Yeah?"

"It hardly seems fair."

"What are you talking about?"

"You have considerable knowledge of my own history now, while yours remains a mystery to me. I do wonder . . ." Her voice had taken on a thoughtful, dreamy tone that told him she was still under the influence of the brandy. "Well, I do wonder what makes you such a contradiction. I believe that would be the correct term to describe your character. All rough on one side, you see, and on the other not, I am convinced, uneducated."

"You're gibbering, Aggie. That liquor's still got you by the tongue."

She paid no attention to him. "There are clues," she persisted. "For example, your horse. Only a learned man would know that Bucephalus was the name of Alexander the Great's noble steed. Yes, I do feel this indicates that somewhere in your past you enjoyed the advantage of an education."

"Aggie?"

"Yes?"

"Go back to sleep."

She was sober enough not to press him. He was grateful for that much, because he had no intention of sharing his past with her. His secrets were his own.

He heard her settling down again on the pallet. He lowered himself beside her, taking care that the layer of blanket remained between them. He'd had enough temptation for one night.

There was silence again inside the soddy. He thought she

148

was asleep until her voice floated to him out of the darkness. "I cannot rest. Not while I am still worried."

Cooper sighed. "What is it now?"

She hesitated before telling him in a faint, breathless rush, "What happened between us earlier . . . well, I did enjoy it. Do you suppose this means I am a shameless wanton?"

He chuckled dryly. "I'd say it means you're perfectly normal."

"That would be reassuring, except there is more to it. Because afterwards, you see," she confessed shyly, "afterwards, I had this wicked longing to touch your body in the same manner that you touched mine."

Cooper dragged in a mouthful of air. Oh, Lord, he thought, she sure wasn't making this night any easier on him. Or on herself either. Because he had the feeling that when tomorrow came, and she was no longer lightheaded, she was going to have a hell of a job forgiving herself.

"Believe me, Aggie, when I tell you there's nothing wrong with you. Now will you go to sleep?"

"Yes."

And she did, almost immediately. But Cooper couldn't manage to join her. Not after the nightmare, not after her unsettling confession. He lay there, staring up at the patch of starry sky through the gap in the turf-covered roof.

Sometime before dawn he drifted off again. When he awakened, there was sunlight streaming through the broken roof. It revealed the long muzzle of a Kentucky rifle directed in the vicinity of his nose.

# *Chapter Eight*

This is not good, Cooper figured. Not good at all.

There were three of them. He wasn't worried about Rose, who'd once been a pickpocket on the streets of New York. Rose must have seen everything in her career, although the expression on her face told him she was still capable of being shocked. And he didn't mind the crooked grin on the sassy mouth of—What was her name? Yeah, Lettice, the one whose tough humor defied a cruel upbringing at the hands of a fanatic father.

It was the woman who had the rifle shoved in his face that was making Cooper unhappy. Susan was neither smiling nor registering shock. She was simply looking grim. He remembered Agatha telling him that her protective friend had shot her husband.

This situation is probably going to be a little hard to explain, he thought. The two of them huddled stark naked under a single blanket was one thing. But Aggie, half sprawled over him and clasped in his arms (and when the hell had that happened?), was something else.

Cooper decided to do the smart thing and let Aggie handle the explanations.

"Uh, Aggie, company."

She didn't stir, not until he practically flipped her back over onto her side of the pallet. Then her eyes opened, focusing on him in puzzlement. He jerked his head in the direction of their visitors. Her gaze turned and lifted, discovering the three women looming over them. Cooper knew she had to be entirely sober this morning. Otherwise her face wouldn't have taken on such a ripe shade of mortification.

"Before this gets too unfriendly," he suggested, "I'd like you to urge your friend here to back off with her cannon."

The rifle was still leveled at him, and it was making him increasingly nervous.

"You all right?" a worried Susan asked Agatha while she kept the weapon pinned on him.

Agatha, struggling for composure, offered a hasty assurance. "Susan, you may lower the rifle. My virtue, along with the rest of me, is still intact."

Clutching the slipping blanket, she tried to sit up. The abrupt action contorted her face with pain.

"What is it?" Rose demanded.

"Hammers," Agatha muttered. "There seem to be tiny creatures inside my skull equipped with large hammers."

Lettice, chuckling, nudged the brandy flask beside the pallet with her toe. "Interesting thing about those hammers. They got a way of turning up after swigging down something that ain't water. Maybe you *were* taken advantage of, Miss Agatha."

"The gold," Susan said, eyeing him with sudden suspicion. "He get you to tell him where the gold is?"

"No, I believe . . ." Agatha broke off, pressing a hand to her splitting head.

Cooper no longer found the situation amusing. "If I'm gonna be accused of deceit, along with lechery, I intend to

151

have my clothes on. Give us some privacy so we can get dressed. And take that damn thing out of my face.'' He swiped angrily at the barrel of the rifle.

Susan grudgingly removed the rifle, but neither she nor her companions were willing to leave the soddy. They ended up clustered tightly around Agatha, shielding her from his view while they helped her to dress. Snatching up his own clothes, and not caring what glimpses they had of his own exposed anatomy, Cooper stormed out of the hut.

He was out back seeing to Bucephalus when Agatha joined him minutes later. They were both fully clothed now, but there was a very real tension between them. He could see she was still suffering from the effects of the brandy. There was a stiffness in her gait, as if it were an effort for her to move. There was a stiffness in her tone, too, when she addressed him.

''I have explained to the women how you rescued me and how afterwards it was necessary for us to . . .'' She broke off to draw a steadying breath. ''Well, let us just say I made clear to them that appearances were deceiving and that perhaps they were being presumptuous.''

''That was real generous of you, Aggie. Denied the whole cozy scene, did you?''

His resentment was too plain for her to miss. ''You are not making this easy for either of us, Cooper.''

''Cooper? *Now* you call me Cooper? That's pretty funny considering how I was Mr. Delaney the whole time we were being intimate last night.''

He watched the color drain from her face. ''We were not intimate,'' she informed him rigidly.

''Yeah, I see. It's the cold light of day, and you couldn't live with your shame if you admitted you got too friendly with the lout you had to spend the night with. Well, trust me, we did get friendly, and what's more you enjoyed every bit of it.''

''I—I am not altogether clear about last night,'' she confessed. "And that is why I am here. Not because of any familiarities we might have engaged in but because of my concern that I might have betrayed the women."

"Meaning what?"

"About the gold . . ."

"Uh-huh, I understand. You're asking me if last night was really all about the gold. Was I just using you, like old Henry used you back in Philadelphia for the sake of profit?"

She winced over the cruel reminder of her fatal mistake with Henry. Cooper knew he had hurt her, and he was too angry to care.

"Hell, Aggie," he went on recklessly, "that isn't what last night was all about. It was about revenge. Pure revenge. I swore back in Independence I'd get even, and I did. But you knew that all along, didn't you? Probably even laughed about it. I know I did. See, nothing to worry about. We never got around to the location of my gold pieces."

He had Bucephalus saddled and ready. He swung onto the horse's back. "I'll see you and your friends back in camp."

He left her standing there and rode away. He was furious with himself. His appreciation of her as a woman last night had been real and honest, without a thought for himself or his gold. And this morning she had turned it into something mercenary with her suspicions and mistrust, making him feel like a fool.

No more weakness like that, he promised himself. No more surrenders to temptation that could lead to nothing but grief.

It was in this state of determination that he regained the fording place. He was hungry, but he delayed the breakfast the waiting women offered him. There was something else he had to do first.

He went in search of the rope that had snapped yesterday during Agatha's crossing. He wanted to examine that line. It shouldn't have separated like that. But there was no sign of the broken rope, and none of the women he questioned on either bank knew what had happened to it. It had somehow disappeared in the river during the night.

The mosquitoes were vicious, the weather unbearably sultry. Agatha refused to let either of them prevent her from completing the history lesson she was preparing for Callie.

Seated at the makeshift table of sawhorses and planks, she was aware that summer had sneaked up on them. It was a concern. They should have been farther along the trail by now, but they had lost all that precious time back at the Big Blue.

The terrain, too, had somehow crept up on them. The lush Kansas prairies had given way to the drier plains of Nebraska. A barren land of sand hills and coarse buffalo grass, broken only by the meandering Platte River. Except for scattered cottonwoods, trees were nonexistent in the region. That was why the women were out collecting buffalo chips, which made an excellent fuel for the evening cooking fires that would soon be lighted.

And in the meanwhile . . .

Agatha rose from the camp stool, knowing it was time to summon her pupil. Howls of laughter led her across the clearing. She stopped just outside the circle of wagons, reluctant to interrupt the game in progress on the site of an abandoned prairie dog colony.

The man was outrageous, and watching him as he frolicked with the child in her boy's outfit brought an unwanted lump to her throat.

"Golf," Cooper had informed the eager Callie shortly after they made camp. "That's what the old Scot I met down in Santa Fe called it. Said it was an ancient game in his country, played by kings and queens. All we need is clubs and balls."

Perhaps not exactly what the kings and queens of Scotland had in mind, Agatha thought with a smile as she observed the two of them pursuing golf with a pair of spare plow

154

handles and a supply of walnuts. There was more enthusiasm than accuracy in their efforts as they took turns whacking the walnuts toward designated prairie dog holes.

"That one," Callie challenged the big man, pointing toward a hole they had flagged with a red bandanna tied to a stick.

"That one, huh?"

"Yeah. Bet you can't sink it. Too far."

"Watch me."

Taking careful aim with the upended plow handle, Cooper smacked the walnut in the direction of the next hole. It didn't seem to matter that the two players had no real knowledge of the game. They were thoroughly enjoying themselves.

Poor Roscoe didn't understand the rules either. Unable to resist the temptation of the flying walnut, the dog streaked after it, caught it between her teeth and headed triumphantly in Agatha's direction.

Callie screamed with laughter. Cooper chased the dog, bellowing his outrage.

"You cursed mutt! That's another perfect shot you've spoiled!"

Roscoe delivered the walnut at Agatha's feet, tail wagging happily. Cooper arrived behind the dog, and Agatha held her breath over their sudden awareness of each other.

The day was steamy, and the heat of his exertions had resulted in a sheen of perspiration on his upper chest exposed by his open shirt. Beads of sweat glistened on the dark, curling hairs and trickled down inside his shirt. She could see a pulse beating strongly in the hollow of his damp, tanned throat.

Agatha fought her arousal. There was no sanity in it. Nothing had changed since that disastrous episode on the Big Blue. Whenever he was near her, and he made certain those occasions were as infrequent as possible, the familiar barriers rose between them. It was that way now. The expression on his lean face changed instantly, becoming polite and distant.

Callie didn't notice the coolness between them when she joined them. "Lessons, I s'pose," she objected in disgust. "Do I have to?"

Agatha hated to end the pleasure the man and the child had been sharing, but she had promised Callie's mother that her daughter would have the education she had lacked. It was not an easy pledge. Callie was a reluctant pupil. She was grateful for Cooper's support.

"She's right, ol' son," he said solemnly. "Schooling comes first. We'll have another day when you beat me at golf."

Agatha watched him abruptly turn and stride away. The pattern, since that morning outside the soddy, was the same whenever he was threatened by some personal encounter with her. He always had a handy excuse. Scouting the trail ahead of them, riding off to hunt for fresh meat, grooming Bucephalus. She never questioned his absences. It was better this way, safer to limit the contact between them. It was also painful.

Callie was restless when they settled at the table, unable to concentrate on the heroism of Dolley Madison. She kept interrupting Agatha, who was trying to complete the daily entry in her journal.

"Know what? Cooper promised he'll teach me euchre. That's a game with playing cards."

"Your lesson, dear," Agatha reminded her gently.

Callie sighed and returned to her assignment. But a moment later her head was up again. "Know what else?" she chattered brightly. "We're gonna have us a spittin' contest to see who can spit cherry pits the farthest. Well, if we can get ahold of some cherries, that is. Bet Coop can spit real good."

Agatha regarded her young charge with a concern that had nothing to do with playing cards or spitting contests. Callie's welfare had become increasingly important to her. She was the daughter Agatha would never have, and she would do anything to keep her from being hurt. The time had come to speak plainly to the child.

"Callie, listen to me." Closing her journal, she leaned earnestly across the table. "I know how fond you are of Mr. Delaney, but there is something you must not forget. When the journey ends, he will leave us. He will ride off alone to California, and he will not come back. Do you understand what this means?"

Callie pulled at her hair and frowned. "You're sayin' he'll go away, and we won't see him again. But he won't. Coop wouldn't do that. He's my friend, and friends stick together."

"Callie—"

"No. I gotta read my lesson now."

She lowered her head, stubbornly refusing to accept the inevitable reality. Agatha hated to think of the heartache she would suffer when Cooper was no longer there, when . . .

Dear God, she thought, shocked by a sudden realization. Callie wouldn't be alone in experiencing the pain of separation. She, too, would miss Cooper Delaney when he stopped being a part of their lives.

Impossible. How could she be feeling such a thing? When had she started to feel it? It must have happened that night in the soddy. That night about which she was still so confused. Except for one clear memory that haunted her. Whatever his seductive purpose, he had been genuinely loving that evening. She was certain . . .

No! She was experiencing nothing more than the fanciful yearnings of an old maid. Yearnings that could never be realized. Hadn't Henry taught her that? There would be no man to cherish her, to give her children of her own. And to even remotely entertain Cooper Delaney in such a role was wildly unthinkable.

*A silly infatuation, Agatha. Your insular life never prepared you for a man like him. He is like no other you have ever known, so your fascination is understandable. The feeling is nothing more than that.*

157

How could it be otherwise when she didn't trust him, when their values and directions were as divergent as the earth's poles? Hopeless.

Then why must it persist, this nagging recollection of the sensual magic they had shared that long night on the Big Blue?

"They're back!" Callie shouted.

The girl had spotted the returning women with their baskets loaded with buffalo chips. Seizing any excuse to avoid her schoolwork, she fled from the table to inspect the haul. Agatha followed, and when she reached the scene, Callie had her head inside one of the baskets.

"All kinds of cow flops and buffalo bones out there on the trail," she declared in disgust, "but no herds. Shoot, I wanna see me a real live buffalo stampede."

Cooper appeared, dashing her hopes. "Sorry, urchin. You'll see plenty of buffalo, but you'd better forget about any exciting stampedes. They're a pretty rare sight, and be grateful they are."

If ever a man had to eat his words, Cooper thought grimly, this is probably the best damn example of it.

As luck would have it, those words were flavored with sand. He was choking on the gritty stuff, unable to avoid it in his mouth and nostrils as he stretched flat on the shaking earth.

No time to worry about his comfort, though. He was too busy firing into the charging herd from the point of the V they had hastily formed with the wagons when the stampede roared down on them without warning three days later.

He had never figured he would be grateful for Susan. The stern-faced woman was stationed on the ground beside him, feverishly helping him to fell buffalo. Only a wall of carcasses in front of them would keep the maddened herd from plowing into the wagons.

So far their effort was working. The charging sea of massive beasts was forced by the piled bodies into two streams that thundered past the flanks of the wagons.

He wondered if Callie was enjoying her stampede. But mostly he hoped she was safe. It was a dangerous situation, terrifying with the clouds of swirling dust, the shrieks of the women and the struggling brown mass of brawling buffalo that refused to be turned.

"Rifle!" Susan screamed. "Need the next rifle here!"

The women behind them, Agatha among them, were loading the rifles as rapidly as possible, passing them along the ranks to the two sharpshooters, who were striving to keep up a continual fire.

How did we get caught in this mess? Cooper wondered. Buffalo didn't stampede without reason, especially straight into a wagon train. It was not the moment for questioning it, though, particularly since he was experiencing his own delay in the chain that was serving him.

Cooper turned his head to find out what was holding up the next rifle. Rachel was crawling toward him with a fresh weapon. Her skirts were all bunched up, revealing the underside of her petticoat. He caught flashes of bright metal. Only a brief glimpse before Henrietta, who was waiting just behind them to retrieve his spent rifle, swiftly tugged Rachel's skirts over the petticoat.

That was all Cooper saw. All he needed to see. Surprise, surprise! Here they were pinned to the ground, a hell of noise and confusion on every side, and he managed to spot the thing he'd been searching for all these weeks.

His gold eagles were stitched inside a petticoat that, for all he knew, they had been wearing in turn in order to elude his suspicion. *Cunning, ladies. Real cunning. Wonder if it was all Aggie's idea.* It was another subject that would have to wait.

Minutes later it was ended. The last of the raging buffalo streamed away over a rise, leaving them to assess the damage. They had been lucky. No one, including the stock, had been injured. Only one overturned wagon was smashed beyond repair, its stores scattered and crushed.

"Why did it happen?" Agatha wondered aloud as she helped the women to collect what was usable from the strewn contents.

Cooper still wondered that himself. There had been no storms or prairie fires to spook the herd. They were in Pawnee country, not the friendliest tribe, but there'd been no evidence of Indian activity.

Callie was certain she had the answer. "Him!" she said, pointing at a low silhouette against the horizon. "Bad ol' critter's out there again."

Cooper followed the direction of her accusing finger, identifying the rogue dog that had appeared out of nowhere several days ago. The animal had been shadowing their train ever since.

"Roscoe doesn't like him," Callie said.

It was true that Roscoe wasn't happy with the newcomer, her hackles up as she growled a warning, but Cooper doubted that the wild dog was responsible for the stampede.

"Why's he following us?" Callie demanded.

"Probably a lost Indian dog looking for human contact."

He didn't think there was any danger in the presence of the animal. It made no efforts to approach them, always keeping a safe distance. Besides, he had something else to think about. His gold.

Why? Cooper asked himself repeatedly as the train pushed on through a terrain that turned rocky and increasingly bleak. Why did he do it? Why did he stay now that he knew the location of his gold pieces? Why didn't he do what he had threatened all along? Deliver his ultimatum. Either they turned back, or he would take his eagles and abandon them.

The trek was a madness. Had been from the start. He'd always known that. And what did it matter that, however harsh the conditions, the women continued to fight for each precious mile, growing tougher and wiser with every passing day? Or that, in spite of his exasperation, he had learned to admire, even respect their tenacity? None of this changed the outcome. They were bound to fail. The worst challenges were still ahead of them, a hostile country that had been known to defeat even the strongest men.

Worse, far worse, was his deepening involvement with the women on a personal level. He had fiercely resisted all knowledge of them as individuals. Had intended to keep them as faceless as possible. He had failed.

He knew them now, each and every one of them.

Yvonne, the little coquette from New Orleans who had been passed from man to man.

Grace, no brighter than a small child and whose family, when they weren't working her like an animal, had kept her hidden away.

Charlotte, raised in luxury on a plantation and after her father's death evicted by a stepmother who had learned she was the daughter of a mulatto.

And the rest of them. He had learned their identities and histories as well. Slowly, inexorably, he had been pulled into their lives. It angered him because, if he weren't careful, he might end up actually minding what happened to them.

All of which brought him back to his original dilemma. Why did he stay? Idiotic question, of course, because the answer had him by the throat.

Hell, face it, it was gripping him in a few other places, too, whenever he remembered how he'd had his tongue inside Agatha Pennington's mouth. And the memory was a frequent one, together with a perpetual longing to put his tongue in a few other places on that sweet body of hers.

His revenge had backfired on him. She was destroying him. He wanted her, and he couldn't have her. Didn't dare to try. Aggie was no quick tumble. She was a woman who would demand, and deserve, a commitment. Marriage. It was an institution that, with his dark memories, scared him into a cold sweat.

So there it was. Both of them consumed by dreams in direct conflict with each other. Aggie wanted Oregon, and his destiny waited for him in California. Frustrating. Impossible.

He had to keep away from her, maintain the barriers. If he couldn't bring himself to snatch his gold and get out, at least he could manage to keep the two of them from clashing. That was the sane, responsible solution to the situation. He was going to do it. He was going to be sensible.

What Cooper did do was to wait for the first opportunity to get her alone to himself. He found it at Courthouse Rock.

# Chapter Nine

The high, rugged plains of Nebraska, with their scorching sun and plagues of insects, were hard on both the women and their stock. But the wagons suffered more. A prolonged dryness since the crossing of the Big Blue shrank some of the wooden wheels, loosening the iron tires. The only solution was to remove them from their oak rims, shorten the metal bands and replace them on the felloes. It was a tedious process requiring a full day of repairs and the experience of a blacksmith.

Renata, the sturdy German immigrant, examined each of the tires in silence before pronouncing a stoic, ''Yah, this I can do.''

Agatha doubted neither her knowledge nor her strength. Renata's husband had been a blacksmith. She had worked at his side and would have gone on practicing the trade after his death, had anyone in the East been willing to patronize her. She had almost starved before joining the wagon train with her anvil, tongs and hammers.

They created a forge for Renata where they had stopped

below Courthouse Rock. Agatha was watching her at work, marveling at her skills, when Cooper appeared out of nowhere, muttering in her ear a terse, "Come with me."

Before she could question him he was gone, his rangy figure striding away from the ranks of women clustered around the makeshift forge. She hesitated, reluctant to be alone with him. But there had been a note of urgency in his command. She feared a new crisis.

He was waiting impatiently when she joined him outside the corral of wagons. There was a taut expression on his face that alarmed her.

"What is it? Is there trouble?"

He didn't answer her for a moment. He paced restlessly in the dust before rounding on her with a brusque, "The hell with this. We need to talk."

"I am listening."

"Not here. Up there where we can't be interrupted by some female with another emergency."

His thumb jerked in the direction of Courthouse Rock, a dramatic stone formation that freighters had named after the courthouses it roughly resembled back east. Agatha stared in disbelief at the outcropping, so massive it could be seen for miles on the flat plains. He might have been asking her to climb to the pinnacle of a mountain. A vertical-sided one at that.

"It's not as steep as it looks," he promised. "An easy climb really."

"I think not."

"Are you afraid of it, Aggie? Or are you afraid of me?"

She refused to be intimidated by his challenge. "What is so vital that it must be discussed in private?"

"Us, Aggie. We've been driving each other crazy since the Big Blue."

"I admit there have been . . . certain tensions."

"Tensions, hell. You could cook a flapjack on the heat that's been building between us. Time to smoke a peace pipe,

Aggie. We don't ease the strain, we threaten the progress of the trek.''

He used an argument she was unable to resist. She would do anything to protect the journey. "Very well, but is it necessary to go to the roof of the world to share our peace pipe?''

"Have my reasons,'' he insisted mysteriously.

"It involves a lengthy absence, and the women may need—''

"Damn it all,'' he growled, "they're adults. You don't need to be available to them every hour of every day.''

He had seized her by the hand and was drawing her across the plain.

"But we must let them—''

"They already know. I told Rebecca where we were going. Callie is with her. That doesn't leave you anyone to worry about. Unless you want to start stewing over Roscoe.''

Agatha offered no more objections. To her dismay, she found herself beside him minutes later scaling Courthouse Rock. He was right. It was not as formidable a climb as it appeared. The clay and soft sandstone composing the structure offered easy footholds, and the ascent Cooper chose was a gradual one.

But she was breathless when they reached the flat summit where grasses waved in the wind. She was also exhilarated. They were hundreds of feet above the plain, and the views that stretched in every direction were awesome. Far below was the trail that followed the North Platte River, and on the other side was Courthouse Rock's less impressive neighbor, Jail Rock.

"Magnificent,'' she murmured. "There is a poet inside you, after all, Cooper Delaney.''

"I didn't bring you up here for the damn scenery, Aggie.''

There was a wicked gleam in his eyes that worried her. Before she could prevent it, he drew her to the very brink of the lofty precipice.

"We're going to take care of those stresses, remember?"

Agatha looked down over the edge and nervously wondered if she had made a mistake in permitting him to lure her to this place. "If your remedy involves a leap into space," she warned him, "I am not in favor of it."

"Something much more effective than that," he promised her. "A technique this old trader once taught me for relieving the tensions of the trail. You go off on your own where no one can hear you, find the highest spot you can find open to the sky and then just let yourself go."

She gazed at him suspiciously, convinced he had taken leave of his senses. "And what, pray, does that mean?"

"Show you."

Head back, arms upraised like a warrior with an offering for the gods, he opened his mouth and began to yell to the vastness of the sky. Startling roars that issued from the depths of his being one after another.

He was a man who never ceased to surprise her, and this current example of Delaney philosophy, wild, unconventional, was no exception.

"All there is to it," he said, interrupting his demonstration. "You try it now."

"You are not serious?"

"I guarantee you'll feel better. Come on, together."

She had no intention of joining him, but that's exactly what she found herself doing. Within seconds she was screaming to the heavens, at first with reluctance and embarrassment and in the end with a joyful abandon that left her hoarse but strangely satisfied.

"It is relaxing," she admitted in wonder.

He grinned at her complacently. "Told you."

"But also very draining."

Exhausted by the rigorous activity, she settled herself on a patch of grass away from the edge. Cooper remained standing. There was a silence between them now, but it was a peaceful silence. He had scooped up a quantity of pebbles, and she watched him as he poured the pebbles back and forth from hand to hand.

Abruptly then, without preamble or invitation, he began to tell her about California.

"There's a ranch there that belongs to me. Or it will be mine when I get it back. It was my father's. Niceto Alvares. You wouldn't know it to look at me, but I'm half Spanish. My mother was Yankee. Irish Yankee."

"Your parents—"

"Both dead. Died when I was an infant."

He frowned, as if the subject confused him more than it pained him but was still something he couldn't bring himself to discuss. For a moment he stared off at the expansive view, his mind lost in thought.

Agatha prodded his memory gently. "Surely you were not left on your own after their deaths."

He seemed to remember then that she was there and waiting for him to continue. He began to fling the pebbles one by one over the bluff as he went on with his story. He told it simply and in a voice that was almost mechanical, but she detected a smoldering passion under his words.

"I was handed over to Luis, my father's older brother. His ranch adjoined ours. He raised me under his roof, saw to it that I had the essentials. Food, clothes and the education my mother wanted for me."

Agatha was quick to note an omission. "And love? Did he not also give you love?"

Cooper laughed derisively. "We didn't have the same kind of uncles, Aggie. Mine wanted as little to do with me as possible. Don't ask me why. That's just the way it was."

"Was there no one else? His wife, his own children?"

"No wife, no cousins. Just the local priest who was kept busy trying to save my devil of a soul. No one was allowed to interfere with that, not even Elena."

"Elena?"

"Maiden aunt who kept house for Luis. I hardly ever saw

her. I think she was ordered to stay away from me."

Agatha found it infinitely sad that there had been no woman in his life after his mother. No one to nurture him, to offer him any morsels of tenderness.

"Your uncle sounds . . . forgive me, a very cold man."

"Didn't matter. I had the future. It was all I lived for. I couldn't wait until I was old enough to get back to my ranch. But there was no future. Luis robbed me of the ranch when I was twelve, informed me he had done all he planned to do for me and kicked me out with no explanations or remorse."

"He could do that? Simply take your property?"

"It's California, Aggie. The law, what little there is of it, is in the hands of the land barons."

"But to be on your own, still a child . . ."

"I grew up fast. No choice. I had to survive because I promised myself that, whatever it took, I'd get my ranch back one day if I had to see my uncle in hell to do it."

"How did you exist?"

"Found work scraping hides." He smiled in memory. A bitter smile. "Not a pleasant job, Aggie. Hides stink to the heavens. I can still smell them. No money in it. And I had to have money. Enough money to pay for all the bribes that would be needed to win a case against my uncle."

"Your gold," she said remorsefully.

"That's just a part of it. Most of what I put together over the years is waiting for me safely in California. I got out when I was fifteen and old enough to learn something more profitable. I was using my mother's maiden name by then."

He didn't tell her why, but Agatha thought she could guess. The Alvares name must have become hateful to him.

"I went wherever there was money to be earned. Trapped furs in the wilderness until the demand for beaver started to decrease. Even tried mining. Then I turned to the trails and freighting. Nice profits there, especially the Santa Fe trade, providing you aren't murdered by bandits or fall off a mountain."

He had come to the last pebble in his hand. He considered it for a second, then pitched it far out into space, as if he were ridding himself of something he could no longer tolerate.

"But I didn't die," he said fiercely. "Couldn't. I had to keep sending gold back to California. Building the fund that's going to force Luis Alvares to surrender my ranch."

Agatha gazed at him standing there against the sky, looking harder than the rock under his feet. There was an intensity in his expression that frightened her. She could understand his determination to recover his land, but she sensed this wasn't the real need driving him. There was another emotion there. Vengeance. A vengeance that would ultimately be joyless. Recognizing it made her feel as if a hand were squeezing her heart.

Cooper, leaving the edge of the bluff, came and dropped beside her on the patch of grass.

"Why did you tell me all this?" she asked him.

"Didn't you want to know?"

She was aware of his provocative closeness, of his long body stretched out on the sun-warmed grass. A hard-muscled body that had been honed and toughened by his harsh youth.

"I . . ." She paused to clear her throat. "I suppose one cannot help a certain curiosity about fellow travelers."

She was babbling nonsense, and he knew it. He smiled a lazy smile, selected a long blade of grass and clamped it between his teeth. His mood had altered entirely now that he had purged himself of his history. His clear green eyes wore a look that was both teasing and sensual.

Why must she always be so conscious of his compelling masculinity? She forced herself to go on. "I assume, since California was your destination before we diverted you, that you now have sufficient funds to fight your claim."

"Good assumption," he drawled, no longer interested in the subject. Propped up on one elbow, he went on chewing on the stem. Went on watching her with that hot, intimate look.

Falling back on a familiar habit, Agatha began nervously tucking stray hairs into the heavy coil on the nape of her neck.

"Why do you do it?" he demanded.

Her busy hands went still. "What?"

"That." Tossing down the blade of grass, he swung himself into a sitting position. "What you're doing now. Hiding yourself behind a severe bun and an outfit like a nun's. What are you afraid of, Aggie? That there's a real woman under there, and you might not be able to control her if she gets out?"

"You are being absurd."

"Think so? Then why don't we conduct a little experiment?"

Scooting up against her, his hands went to her hair. She stiffened in alarm.

"What are you—"

"Easy, Aggie. It isn't going to hurt."

Before she could stop him, his clever fingers removed the pins securing her coil. Her thick chestnut hair was released and came tumbling down her back in a burnished cascade.

"That's more like it," he said, eyes gleaming with approval. His fingers sifted through the silky mass of her hair. Fingers that were suprisingly sensitive in their touch. The sensation was incredibly soothing.

"An interesting demonstration," she managed to tell him. "But as you see, being sober on this occasion, I am still in control of myself."

"That a challenge, Aggie? If so . . ." His fingers penetrated to her scalp, stroking downward in a long, slow caress that made her squirm with pleasure.

"I fail to see anything instructive in this experiment."

"You want schooling? I think we can manage some schooling."

"Regarding what area?" she whispered.

"Let's concentrate on something where your education is deficient. The subject of osculation comes to mind."

"Osculation. If I remember correctly, there is a more general term for the word."

"That would be kissing. Needs a knowledge of all its refinements, though, if you're going to practice it properly."

"Are you a qualified teacher?"

"Let's see if I am." His voice was husky, mesmerizing. He leaned into her until his mouth was a mere warm breath away from hers.

Wisdom told her not to permit what was going to happen. Hadn't she made this mistake before and regretted it? But the self-control she had boasted about seemed to have deserted her. Maybe his trusting her to know about his unhappy childhood had mellowed her, made her all the more vulnerable to him. Whatever the explanation, she was powerless to resist him.

"Pay attention now. First lesson." His lips brushed a light kiss on her cheek. "That's your greeting-type kiss."

"What one exchanges with family and dear friends, you mean?"

"That's right. But this one . . . this one is useful when the relationship is less casual." His lips made contact with the side of her mouth, deliberately missing the center. But it was a kiss more familiar, more lingering in its delivery.

"A kiss between loved ones?"

"You're showing real promise as a pupil, Aggie. Now we're going to move on to the advanced class."

"Are you certain I am ready for higher learning?"

"Oh, yeah." His fingers were wound in her hair again. "When a woman has a head of hair that drives a man crazy, she is definitely ready."

"Then, by all means, take me to the next level. Is it difficult to learn?"

"It's a serious-type kiss, Aggie. Used only when a man

171

wants to show a woman he really means business. Here's how it goes.''

This time, hand tightening against the back of her head, he drew her toward him. His mouth angled across hers in a slow, seductive kiss that deepened in agonizing degrees. He made her lightheaded with the skillful activity of his lips and tongue that stroked every contour of her parted mouth.

She was breathless when his mouth lifted from hers, barely able to croak, ''Is the lesson ended?''

''Hell, Aggie, we're just moving into the final stage.''

''More?''

''More.''

His mouth captured hers again in a hot, wet joining that demanded, and got, access to the inside of her mouth. With her defenses breached, his tongue embraced hers in a prolonged, intimate dance that sent flames licking along every nerve in her body.

Her lips felt swollen, ripe with his knowledge when he finally released her. ''You have the gift of a born teacher, Cooper Delaney,'' she confessed to him weakly. ''You make learning a pleasure.''

He grinned at her brazenly. ''That was just an introductory course, Aggie. But anytime you're ready for the full curriculum . . .''

She gazed at him thoughtfully. The meaningful, eager glint in his watchful eyes wilted under her scrutiny, changing along with his expression. He was suddenly wary.

''I don't think I like the way you're looking at me, Aggie.''

''How?''

''Like I might be a candidate for one of your lost souls you've decided needs caring for. Look like that makes a man real nervous.''

Agatha was quick to deny his dangerous charge, to herself as well as to him. ''Actually,'' she lied, ''I was looking at your eyebrow. Or, to be precise, the scar you carry there.

Might I assume it is a souvenir of one of your experiences in the wilderness?''

He shook his head and was brief with his answer. ''Always had it. Since I was little, anyway.''

''Result of a childhood accident, I suppose.''

She had thought the topic would be a safe, innocent one, but oddly it wasn't. He scowled and looked away. ''Maybe. I don't have any memory of it.''

There was something dark and unpleasant associated with the scar. He didn't want to talk about it, just as he hadn't wanted to discuss his parents.

''We'd better start down,'' he suggested, ''before we lose the light.''

It was true. The sun was beginning to settle toward the horizon. She had been so caught up in the emotions he aroused in her that she hadn't noticed the day was already fading. She began to quickly pin up her hair. Restless, he got to his feet and wandered to the edge of the precipice.

Agatha joined him there a moment later. They stood in silence, savoring the magnificence of a sunset that inflamed the western sky with banners of crimson and gold.

''Look down there.''

He pointed to a small, dark shape that had taken up a position within sight of the wagons where plumes of smoke rose from the cooking fires. Agatha recognized it as the rogue dog that had been shadowing them for days. Roscoe had also spotted her nemesis. She was barking in a frenzy from the edge of the encampment.

Cooper chuckled. ''Still with us and still driving poor Roscoe out of her mind.''

Agatha could sympathize with Roscoe. She had her own rogue who made her wild.

The warm glow Cooper had kindled within her on the summit of Courthouse Rock stayed with her through the evening. She couldn't expect it to last, not with a man as unpredictable as he was. He didn't fail her. Sometime after midnight the glow was rudely and abruptly extinguished.

Agatha was shaken out of a peaceful sleep by a very loud and insistent voice raised in familiar anger. She emerged from her tent, joining the other women awakened by the clamor and beginning to cluster around the scene in progress at the edge of the corral.

When Agatha arrived, pushing through the ranks, Cooper was harshly lecturing a contrite May, who had been on sentry duty.

"If you'd been alert, you would have challenged her when she left camp, not when she was sneaking back."

There was no question about the subject of his displeasure. A cowering Magpie stood backed against one of the wagons, her eyes wide and fearful in the gleam of a lantern hanging from the tail board. Agatha came immediately to her defense.

"This uproar is absurd. She is one of us, not an enemy."

Cooper rounded on her. "That so? Then ask her what she was doing out there on her own."

"I would assume," Agatha said coolly, "she was answering the call of nature."

"Yes, missis," Magpie murmured quickly, "this is so."

"She knows the orders. No one leaves camp alone after dark, not for any reason. You have to go out, you go in pairs, and you always inform the guard where you're going and why."

"I—I did not think," Magpie whispered. "My need was a desperate one."

Agatha slid a comforting arm around the girl, who was trembling visibly. "There, you see, her errand was perfectly innocent. You have frightened her for nothing."

Cooper stared at Magpie, his face hard with suspicion. "Maybe your little pet here was doing more than just peeing behind a bush."

"You talk as though she were guilty of some mischief. And must you be so crude, Mr. Delaney?"

Cooper's mouth curled in sarcasm. "Oh, we're back to *mister* again, are we, Aggie? All right, maybe I'm wrong. Maybe her trip out into the dark was harmless. All I know is that, since she joined the train, things have been happening. Things like lines breaking in river crossings and mysterious buffalo stampedes."

Agatha was incensed by his suggestion. "Those were accidents! Nothing more!"

"I guess that explanation will have to do. For now." The wide-eyed women parted for him as he turned and strode away.

Agatha, unable to bear his insolence, caught up with him halfway across the enclosure. "Would it have cost your male pride so dearly to have offered Magpie a small apology before you stormed away?"

He halted, swinging around on her so suddenly she almost smacked into him. "You just don't see it, do you, Aggie?"

"What?"

"The way you're always protecting them. You know what it is, don't you? You're existing for the women and not for yourself. They're more than just family to you. You've made them your whole world. You're living through them because maybe you're too scared to live for yourself."

His accusation wasn't true. Couldn't be true. All the same, it hurt. And so did the realization that the loving man she had shared Courthouse Rock with today was gone. This callous, infuriating one was back in his place.

"Yes, I care," she defended herself heatedly. "While you . . . *you* choose to see the worst in people."

"True," he admitted. "And most of the time they don't disappoint me."

He started to walk away from her again. Then he paused and turned. "Don't know if you noticed it," he said casually, "but the girl was fully dressed when she went out to relieve herself. Daytime wear, too. Now that's something for you to think about, Aggie."

*　　*　　*

Duke Salter was in a foul temper as he huddled in front of the campfire, staring sullenly into the flames. His moods were never easy ones under any circumstances, but his disposition had steadily worsened since the day Agatha Pennington and her women set a stubborn course for Oregon.

He'd laughed about them back in Independence. Considered them a pack of witless females representing no serious threat to his intention to keep settlers out of Oregon. He'd been convinced they would defeat themselves, even when they managed to actually put themselves on the trail.

Duke had waited, confident he would hear they had been turned back. It hadn't happened. The women had refused to abandon the trek no matter what obstacles were thrown at them. That was when Duke realized he couldn't rely on the scum hired to serve him. No choice in the matter. He'd have to ride out after the wagon train, personally direct this campaign on the scene itself.

Bull Bear had just delivered Magpie's latest report to Duke where he and his small band were camped miles behind the women. Still no results. Magpie was unreliable. What now?

Jack Salter watched his brother's scarred face as he sat there, brooding into the fire and absently digging his bowie knife into the soft earth beside him.

"Don't make sense," Jack complained. "Why don't we just wipe out this wagon train and be done with it?"

Duke shook his head. "Too risky, what with them bein' so well armed and Delaney always alert for trouble. Our force just ain't big enough to guarantee us a success."

Besides, he had to be careful not to involve Pacific Fur. His connection with the company was known, and if any of them on the train survived an attack like that and talked about it afterwards . . . No, he wouldn't chance it. Not a confrontation that could endanger all his hopes with Pacific Fur. Not before he absolutely had to.

"So what comes next?" Jack persisted.

# Thrill to the most sensual, adventure-filled Historical Romances on the market today...

## FROM 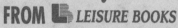 LEISURE BOOKS

As a home subscriber to Leisure Romance Book Club, you'll enjoy the best in today's BRAND-NEW Historical Romance fiction. For over twenty-five years, Leisure Books has brought you the award-winning, high-quality authors you know and love to read. Each Leisure Historical Romance will sweep you away to a world of high adventure...and intimate romance. Discover for yourself all the passion and excitement millions of readers thrill to each and every month.

## *Save $5.⁰⁰ Each Time You Buy!*

Each month, the Leisure Romance Book Club brings you four brand-new titles from Leisure Books, America's foremost publisher of Historical Romances. EACH PACKAGE WILL SAVE YOU $5.00 FROM THE BOOKSTORE PRICE! And you'll never miss a new title with our convenient home delivery service.

Here's how we do it. Each package will carry a FREE 10-DAY EXAMINATION privilege. At the end of that time, if you decide to keep your books, simply pay the low invoice price of $16.96, no shipping or handling charges added. HOME DELIVERY IS ALWAYS FREE. With today's top Historical Romance novels selling for $5.99 and higher, our price SAVES YOU $5.00 with each shipment.

## AND YOUR FIRST FOUR-BOOK SHIPMENT IS TOTALLY FREE!
### *IT'S A BARGAIN YOU CAN'T BEAT! A Super $21.96 Value!*

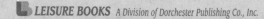

**LEISURE BOOKS** A Division of Dorchester Publishing Co., Inc.

# GET YOUR 4 FREE BOOKS NOW— A $21.96 Value!

*Mail the Free Book Certificate Today!*

# Get Four Books Totally FREE — A $21.96 Value!

▼ Tear Here and Mail Your FREE Book Card Today! ▼

PLEASE RUSH
MY FOUR FREE
BOOKS TO ME
RIGHT AWAY!

**Leisure Romance Book Club**
P.O. Box 6613
Edison, NJ 08818-6613

Duke didn't answer him. He went on thinking, went on gouging the earth with his knife. Minutes later, when he released the knife with a last savage thrust, Jack knew that his brother had made up his mind.

"Time I squeezed a little harder," Duke announced.

"Meaning?"

"I'm gonna add me another of my people to that wagon train. One I can count on this time."

"Who?"

"You, little brother."

# *Chapter Ten*

Ft. Laramie, Agatha thought. There wasn't a woman on the wagon train, herself included, who wasn't looking forward to their arrival at the trading post. It would mean a few days of rest and repair, an opportunity to refresh themselves at one of the few outposts in the wilderness. They all needed that. Even Cooper must want it, though she couldn't swear to that. He had been moody and difficult since Courthouse Rock. They avoided each other as much as possible.

But, yes, Ft. Laramie would be a relief. Meanwhile, they dealt with the grueling conditions of a trail that had become increasingly hostile. There was the long, exhausting pull up toward the high country of Wyoming, the endless, choking dust and the daily problems with strained wagons. Axles that broke, wheels that splintered, sore-footed oxen that cast their shoes.

Tempers were as stressed as the wagons, sometimes flaring uncontrollably. No one was immune, not even the animals, as Roscoe proved the afternoon they camped beside a dry arroyo near Scotts Bluff.

The rogue dog, as wild and gray as a wolf, had haunted them faithfully. None of them could bring themselves to shoot it, though Cooper threatened to when it boldly approached their camp each evening, a growing menace to Roscoe's nerves.

The dog had never ventured into the enclosure itself. But the odor of sizzling buffalo steaks on this occasion must have been irresistible. No one noticed the animal slinking toward a cooking fire. No one but an alert Roscoe, who went for the intruder like an avenging angel.

The serenity of the camp turned all at once into a howling pandemonium. From every direction shrieking women raced toward the tornado that was the two dogs locked in a snarling, savage combat.

Callie tried to rescue her pet and had her hand almost bitten before Agatha pulled her away.

The women screamed suggestions from every side.

Someone handed Agatha a bucket of water. She flung its contents over the dogs. The drenched animals showered the skirts of the closest spectators and continued to tear at each other furiously.

Susan produced her rifle and fired it over the heads of the dogs. No result. They raged on, a whirling blur of ginger and silver. Callie jumped up and down and bawled.

Agatha, searching around for a method to separate the dogs, spotted Cooper. He lounged against a nearby wagon, the only member of the company who watched the contest with placid detachment. She rushed to him in desperation.

"Stop them! Help me drag them apart!"

"And get my fingers chewed off? No, thanks."

"They will kill each other!"

"Doubt that. Hell, Aggie, they're just getting it out of their systems."

"That is an utterly primitive argument!"

"Yeah, that's the word for it. Nature taking its course. The character of the beast."

"And that is vile!"

"You got me all wrong, Aggie. I'm not talking any particular species here. I'm talking male versus female." He grinned at her lecherously. "Works the same, see, whatever the animal."

She could have smacked him. "It is a fight, not a courtship!"

"Have it your way. You want it ended, I'll end it."

Moving away from the wagon, he crossed the clearing in the direction of his horse. Agatha sped back to the battle that was still in progress. When Cooper reappeared seconds later, he had his bullwhip in hand.

"Move aside, ladies."

The women flew out of the way as, gripping the staff in both hands, he twirled the long lash of the whip over his head. Understanding his intention, and incensed by its casual cruelty, Agatha leaped toward him, meaning to snatch the whip out of his hand.

Too late. The lash cracked through the air like electricity, its sting delivered with the accuracy of an expert. The struggling mass of fur parted instantly. With a series of yips and yelps, the two dogs slunk off in opposite directions.

Long weeks of determined restraint had stretched Agatha's patience to its limit. Provoked by his action, as well as the scene that preceded it, her temper snapped. She was blazing with anger when she lit into him.

"That was brutal! Unnecessarily brutal!"

He began calmly winding his whip. "You wanted results, I gave you results."

"Not that way! You hurt them, you drew blood!"

"Hell, their teeth were doing a pretty good job of that. But that's all right, Aggie. You go on letting it all out. Just like Roscoe."

She did, blasting him with a bone-rattling, "You are a barbarian, Cooper Delaney! Worse than a barbarian!"

180

He chuckled. "Didn't think you could get much worse than that."

She knew what he was doing, the delight he was experiencing by deliberately inciting her loss of control. But her awareness didn't help. She was beyond any recovery of her composure, a storm venting its full fury.

"*You* can!" she insisted. "You can be what you are! A pigheaded, unscrupulous, lowdown son of a—a—"

"Come on," he urged. "Say it. You know you want to."

"Polecat!"

"Aw, Aggie, haven't I taught you anything? You can be more eloquent than that. Still, if you're feeling better now, that's what counts. By the way . . ."

"What?"

"They don't look to me like they're hurting." Gesturing with his whip, he drew her attention to a scene outside the circle of wagons.

Agatha turned, her mouth dropping open in dismay. The rogue had mounted Roscoe, apparently without her objection. Both dogs were quietly involved in an age-old ritual.

Cooper leaned forward, whispering, "See, Aggie, the mutts knew all along what it was about, even if you didn't."

He was laughing when he walked away from her.

"Eat," Susan urged, placing in front of Agatha a tin plate loaded with buffalo meat, corn bread and dried fruit.

Agatha shook her head. "Kind of you, but I could not manage a morsel."

Susan eyed her with concern as she joined her at the makeshift table. But she kept her opinion to herself and tucked into her own evening meal. The two women were alone at the table. There was a lengthy silence between them.

In the end, unable to bear her distress, Agatha leaned toward her friend and pleaded, with a plaintive, "Oh, Susan, what have I done?"

"Losin' your temper ain't the end of the world."

"But the situation did not deserve anger to that excessive degree. And the women . . . all the women right there, and Callie with them, witnessing my shameful loss of control. I cannot think what is the matter with me."

Susan knew exactly what was wrong with Agatha. There wasn't a woman on the wagon train who didn't understand it and who wasn't watching the whole thing with rapt interest.

"Under your skin real bad, ain't he?" Susan observed mildly.

Agatha saw no point in denying it. "Why do I let him provoke me? I have never permitted anyone to provoke me so, but *that man* . . ."

"Problem."

"Yes." She hesitated, then confided a wrenching, "There are moments, *actual* moments, when I feel, insane though it is, that he is tearing me apart piece by piece. The worst of it is, I do not see how I am going to bear this all the way to Oregon."

Susan couldn't bear it either. Couldn't stand by and watch her friend being emotionally destroyed. The matter needed settling. She knew what she had to do.

It was late, the rest of the camp asleep except for the nightly guard. Cooper knew he should turn in himself. Instead, he went on sitting there, gazing into the dwindling campfire. He didn't expect company and was surprised when Susan appeared. She was carrying a shabby-looking carpetbag.

"Talk to you?" she asked.

He couldn't imagine what she wanted at this hour. He preferred to be alone, but he nodded a silent assent. She settled on the ground beside him with a soft grunt.

On the other hand, Cooper thought, gazing at the determined jaw on the woman's stolid face, maybe he did know what was on her mind. "Let me guess. Agatha, right?"

Susan answered him with an unrelated question of her own. At least it seemed entirely unrelated. "Fort's only a few days away now, ain't it?"

"Providing there are no problems, yeah."

"And the trail from here to Laramie . . . easy to follow, right?"

"Easy enough."

"Will be some mountain men hanging around the post, won't there?"

"Probably."

"They know the trail as good as you, huh?"

There were two things about Susan that Cooper knew for certain. She had no use for small talk, and she sure as hell had no use for him. So why was she here asking him all these questions? "What's this all about?" he demanded.

She was a wily individual. Had probably needed to be in order to survive the harshness of her life. That was why she avoided a direct explanation. She wanted all the answers first. "You serious in any way about Agatha?"

Why did that question scare him? Maybe because he knew what was coming. "Looks like she is the subject we're discussing."

"For certain." Susan searched his face in the glow of the campfire. She was still looking for those answers. "Guess you aren't," she decided. "Leastways, not serious enough to count."

"What do you want, Susan?"

"You not hurtin' Agatha. And sure as anything, you hang on with us, you'll hurt her. Hurt her real bad. Don't aim to stand by and see that happen."

Cooper had never hit a woman in his life. But he could have hit this one—for being right.

He had known it all along. How vulnerable Agatha was under that formidable exterior. How easy it would be to hurt her. How close he was to doing just that. And how absolutely wrong they were for each other.

183

The expression on his face must have been all Susan needed. She reached for the carpetbag, opened it and removed the folded petticoat where his gold pieces had been concealed.

"Here's your gold back," she said. "Knew where it was since the stampede, didn't you? Only you never tried to take it and leave. Reckon that's all the more reason for you to take it now and go. We can make it on our own far as the fort, hire us a new guide when we get there. Leaves you free to head for California. What you always wanted, ain't it?"

She laid the petticoat beside him, got to her feet and melted into the darkness. Cooper went on sitting there, staring into what was left of the fire.

Damn it all to hell, she had left him with no choice. He could no longer make any excuses to himself for staying. Those excuses had run out with the return of his gold, confronting him with a cold reality. He and Agatha were never going to share anything more than a powerful lust. A lust she tried to deny and which had him battling daily with his perpetual arousal. They couldn't share more when they were consumed by opposing dreams.

Besides, she was one of those women who was not happy unless lavishing care on others, preferably a loving husband and children of her own. He could never give her that, not with the demons that haunted him.

Serious about her? Of course, he was serious. He just wasn't serious about commitment. Not when it involved vows and a preacher. And if he stayed . . . well, sooner or later he and Agatha would be intimate. Bound to happen when the temptation was so strong. He knew himself well enough to know it wouldn't matter, either, that he would be taking advantage of her. Better to go now before anyone got hurt. After all, California was waiting for him.

Cooper was feeling miserable about his decision when he rolled out of his blanket at the first hint of daybreak. Didn't matter. He had no intention of changing his mind. The camp had yet to stir when he collected his few belongings and saddled Bucephalus.

He'd leave the explanations to Susan. No good-byes either. Let Agatha think the worst about him. Maybe that way she wouldn't grieve over regrets.

Mounting the roan, he headed in the direction of Ft. Laramie and the California trail that was beyond it.

Agatha stared at her friend in disbelief. "Gone? It cannot be true. He cannot have left us."

Refusing to trust anything but her own eyes, she left Susan and rushed to the spot where Bucephalus had been staked for the night. The horse wasn't there. Nor, when she searched, was there any sign of Cooper around the camp. But it wasn't until she spoke to Emmie Jo, the last guard on the watch, that Agatha finally accepted Cooper's desertion.

"It's a fact, Miss Agatha. Loaded his saddlebags and rode out 'fore it was even light. Not a word outta him neither and never looked back."

Agatha was outside the circle of wagons, staring up the dusty trail, when Susan joined her a few moments later. There was no movement on the horizon, no glimpse to be had of a distant rider. She fought the longing that threatened to overwhelm her. Anger was a safer emotion. Anger and determination.

"We will manage without him. All of us. Even Callie must learn to manage without him."

Susan was relieved that she was handling it so well. Seconds later she wasn't so sure. Agatha's voice was edged with steel when she turned to her.

"I think," she confided softly, "it will be a long while before I ever trust any man again."

The stricken expression on Agatha's face made Susan wonder whether she had made a terrible mistake.

\* \* \*

"Where the hell did you come from?" Cooper demanded.

Twisting around in the saddle, he glared at the gray dog. The animal must have been behind him for miles, and he had just now discovered its presence.

"What are you doing following me? Why aren't you back with the wagons where you wanted to be? Get!"

The rogue sat back on its haunches and gazed at him foolishly, tongue lolling from the side of its mouth.

"You're a sorry-looking cur, you know that. Go on, I don't want any part of you."

Turning, he urged Bucephalus forward. When he looked again, the dog was there still, trotting faithfully at the roan's heels. Callie had already given it a name. Romeo. The reason had been obvious. But Cooper didn't want to think about Callie, or any of them on the wagon train.

He ignored the dog, confident it would soon give up and turn back. It didn't. It came loping along beside him now. Cooper lectured it, his tone severe.

"You oughta be ashamed of yourself. Running out on your girlfriend this way. You think she won't mind? Think she'll be just fine without you? It figures that a good-for-nothing bum like you wouldn't care."

The sun was hot now, the landscape bleak. Cooper rode on, trying to convince himself he was enjoying his freedom. No regrets, no remorse.

"Don't give me that," he defended himself to the dog. "They're not helpless on their own. They know how to operate now. Anyhow, I'm stopping at Ft. Laramie, aren't I? Planning to send a fresh guide out to meet them. Now that's fair."

Who was he trying to fool? He was concerned about the women back there on their own. Concerned about Agatha without him.

"Hey, close your mouth, mutt. I'm doing the right thing. I don't have anything to feel guilty about. *You're* the coward here, remember?"

They moved on. An antelope crossed their path. Romeo wasn't interested. He kept close to the horse.

No use, Cooper thought, furious with himself. He was trapped. Trapped by his own conscience. What had happened to him? He had never known the need before to feel responsible for anyone but himself and Bucephalus. And now . . . now he had this burden of a wagon train of women who had come to depend on him. Or at least he liked to think that they did.

Worse, far worse, he felt the emotional attachment for them that he had been fighting all these weeks to resist. And just when had that taken root?

Oh, hell!

Romeo stayed with him when he turned his mount and headed back. He cursed the dog, as though the silly mutt were to blame for his weakness.

"Stop grinning at me like that. This isn't permanent, you know. I'm just hanging around long enough to see them safely into Ft. Laramie. Then I'm pulling out for good. Got that?"

He was within a half mile of the wagon encampment when he heard the gunfire. Repeated gunfire. Something had happened in his absence. Something that he knew in his gut was bad. Sick with worry about Agatha and the rest of them, unable to forgive himself for not being there, he urged Bucephalus into a gallop.

Topping a rise, he found himself within sight of the wagons drawn into their tight formation. The camp was under attack. A band of Indians, firing into the defenders, howled around the circle on their swift ponies.

Cooper didn't hesitate. Flattening himself over the neck of the roan in order to make as poor a target as possible, he tore down the slope. Whatever the risk, he had to reach the women.

The Indians were too occupied to be aware of him charging up behind them. When they did notice, they were too late to catch him. Bucephalus didn't fail him. Flashing through the attackers, horse and rider sailed over a barricade and into the corral.

Cooper had barely flung himself from his mount before he had his Hawken whipped to his shoulder. The women were busy with their own rifles when he joined them.

The assault claimed his full attention in the next several minutes. But there were questions in the back of his mind as he knelt there in the dust and smoke and noise. They were in Dakota country now. He knew that Dakota warriors sometimes raided other tribes for women and horses, but he had never heard of them attacking a well-armed wagon train whose stock consisted almost entirely of oxen. The Indians weren't interested in oxen.

There was something else he wondered about. Hard to tell in all the frenzy, but he could swear there was a familiarity about some of the raiders out there. They reminded him of the renegade band the train had encountered back in Kansas.

None of it made real sense to him, including the suddenness with which it was all over. The band, after one final volley, lost interest in the fight, turned and rode off.

Cooper's immediate concern on the heels of the skirmish was casualties. Everyone seemed remarkably intact as he looked around. And then he saw them. The cluster of women on the far side of the corral. They were gathered tightly around something, or someone, on the ground. His heart dropped.

Agatha? No, couldn't be Aggie. He could see her tall figure head and shoulders above the others in the excited bunch. And then he realized that Callie was nowhere in sight. Sonofabitch.

Throwing down his rifle, he strode across the clearing. "Callie?" he demanded as he met Rachel in the center.

She shook her head. "S-safe inside a w-wagon."

"Then who—"

"Th-the m-man who came to warn us before the r-raid.

H-he was w-wounded in the f-fight.''

A man? What man was she talking about? Cooper didn't wait to ask. He headed for the gathering. The women registered no surprise over his return. Nor did they offer any greeting, silently moving aside as he slid through their ranks.

Faye, who had once worked for a doctor, was crouched down on the ground, blocking his view of the figure she was examining. "Reckon he'll do fine," she reported to Agatha, who was also hovering anxiously over the patient. "Lost some blood, but 'pears like a clean enough flesh wound. I'll dress it and fix him up a sling for the arm."

When Faye turned aside to reach for the medicine chest one of the women had fetched from the wagon, Cooper had his first look at the lean figure propped against a wagon wheel. His mouth tightened with recognition.

The other man, feeling his gaze, looked up. His suave, classically handsome face wore a lopsided grin. "Looks like your bad penny's come rolling back, Miss Agatha."

Agatha stiffened. "So I see," she said acidly, refusing to meet Cooper's steely gaze.

The man on the ground chuckled. "Don't seem to be gettin' a very warm reception here, Delaney. I'd say a friendly howdy myself and shake your hand, but don't look like my arm's up to it."

"Mr. Salter, you must not exert yourself," Agatha swiftly cautioned him. "We are grateful for your gallant action on our behalf but worried about you. How are you feeling now?"

She knelt down beside him, fussing over him. Cooper ground his teeth.

Cooper seized the first possible opportunity to corner an unwilling Agatha. "What the hell is Jack Salter doing here?"

She fixed a withering gaze on him. "It might be more interesting to know what *you* are doing here."

He supposed he deserved that. "Changed my mind," he

189

mumbled. "Decided I'd escort you into Ft. Laramie, see that you get a new pilot."

"Generous of you."

"All right, so I was wrong to run out on you. That doesn't make Salter right."

"He was here for us."

Meaning I wasn't, Cooper thought sourly.

"Mr. Salter arrived to inform us that an unfriendly-looking band of Indians was headed in our direction, giving us the opportunity to prepare for trouble."

"Real convenient."

"Yes, it was. He is a gentleman."

Cooper laughed at her innocence. "Jack Salter is a no-good drifter. Smooth as a snake when he's out to charm a victim and as pretty as his brother, Duke, is ugly. The both of them share the bad blood of a murdering father who was hanged in California. I know. I've had a few unpleasant encounters with the two of them in the past."

Agatha regarded him coldly. "You make the same mistake as those who unfairly judged the women back east, blackening their characters because of reputation or connection. Mr. Salter has already informed me of his unfortunate past and how much he regrets it. He has disassociated himself from his unsavory brother in Independence. Like us, he is on his way west determined to make a fresh, clean start."

"And I'm a choirboy."

"*I* believe him. Now if you will excuse me, I have a patient who needs looking after."


Magpie shivered as Jack leaned toward her, his face mere inches from her own. She wasn't deceived by his lazy smile. His nature wasn't as cunning and brutal as his brother's, but he was mean enough in his own right.

His low voice was deceptively silky when he spoke to her, stroking the words. "Duke's real disappointed in you, honey. Feels like you let him down."

"I have done what I could," she defended herself quickly.

"Don't look like that's enough, does it? This wagon train ain't turned back."

"It has been dangerous to try more. The Delaney man caught me returning from my last report to Bull Bear. Since then he watches me. I have had to be careful."

"Sure it's just that?"

"What else?"

"I dunno. Maybe your loyalty is shifting. Maybe these women and their friggin' dream are starting to appeal to you."

"No."

"Hope you mean that." His face was almost touching hers now, his dark eyes glittering dangerously. "Otherwise, Duke wouldn't be too happy. Might not want to give back what he's keeping for you."

The reminder of the weapon that Duke Salter cruelly held over her terrified Magpie. It was all that was needed to coerce her into a useful revelation.

"There is a strongbox on the wagon train," she informed Jack in a hurried whisper. "I heard one of the women say how the money and papers in it will allow them to settle in Oregon."

"That's more like it. Where is it?"

She shook her head. "It could be anywhere. I have not had time to search."

"Yeah, well, I'm here now. Between the two of us, we ought to be able to hunt down that box."

"But the Delaney man . . ."

"Too bad he decided to come back. Hell of a lot easier if he hadn't." He scowled, then shrugged. "Maybe we'll find us a way to eliminate Cooper Delaney along with the strongbox. Because without them, these women ain't goin' nowhere."

Magpie glanced around nervously, but no one in camp was eyeing them. They were all occupied with the evening meal.

Still, she had been with Jack long enough. She got to her feet, leaving the supper plate that had been her excuse to approach him.

"I must go before there is suspicion."

Cooper had decided years ago that justice in this world was a rare commodity. His conviction was reaffirmed as he straddled a trestle and picked at his plate of salt pork and beans.

Roscoe was flopped down nearby, happily licking her boyfriend's ear. Old Romeo had been welcomed back to camp without a hint of displeasure over his desertion. Whereas he, Cooper, had been treated like a contagious disease. Yep, no justice.

The women had been barely civil to him all day, Callie refused to speak to him at all, while Agatha . . . Well, Agatha was the coldest shoulder of all. She neither forgave him nor trusted him. All right, he was prepared to live with that. What he found intolerable was the way they all slopped over their hero, Salter.

Aggie was the worst. Playing nursemaid at every opportunity, fawning over him like he was a cherished invalid.

"Are you comfortable, Mr. Salter?"

"Is there still pain with the arm, Mr. Salter?"

*Can I kiss your rear end, Mr. Salter?*

Her exaggerated attention to the insufferable bastard continued as the wagon train rolled on toward Ft. Laramie. Cooper told himself he wasn't going to watch the two of them together. Wasn't even going to glance in their direction. But somehow he couldn't avoid the infuriating images.

Agatha spooning stew into Salter's mouth, as if both his arms had been amputated.

Agatha entertaining him with passages from her journal.

Agatha laughing over one of her patient's terribly witty observations, when everyone west of the Mississippi knew that the only wits in the Salter family belonged to Duke and not his brother.

Cooper wanted to think it was the sling on Jack Salter's arm that was the attraction. It had a way of making a man look dashing to a woman. There was something else. Salter was all sweet manners with Agatha, and she ate up every morsel of his counterfeit politeness. The two of them made him sick.

Jealous? The hell he was. He'd never been jealous in his life. Never sulked over a woman. The only thing that kept him glowering and grumbling was Agatha's blind faith in that reptile. He no more believed that Jack Salter was reformed than he believed in fairies. Which was exactly why he wasn't going to leave this wagon train. Not before Ft. Laramie, anyway. Somebody had to keep an eye on Salter. No, it had absolutely nothing to do with jealousy.

# Chapter Eleven

Their arrival at Ft. Laramie was a shock to Agatha and the other women on the wagon train. Long weeks on the trail had accustomed them to the isolation of the prairies and plains. They weren't prepared for the existence of this busy, crowded outpost, welcome though it was. It was like finding Philadelphia in the wilderness.

Ft. Laramie, of course, was nothing so ambitious as a city. But it was an impressive trading center established by the American Fur Company early in the last decade. Since then the log stockade had been replaced by a new structure situated on an eminence above Laramie Creek. As they forded the stream and climbed the ridge, Agatha admired the vastness of the fort above them with its high adobe walls and corner towers.

The lithe, handsome figures of the Ogala Sioux, whose lodges were pitched everywhere on the dry, grassy flats around the fort, came hurrying from all sides to inspect them. The wagon train was escorted by the curious braves on its final approach to the open gates below the massive blockhouse.

Agatha was startled by a loud whoop. A small, rotund man with luxuriant side whiskers charged from the open square inside the post. Obidiah Randolph, the factor of Ft. Laramie, had come out to greet them personally.

"If this don't beat all," he chortled, surveying the women. "Looks like you got yourself a regular harem here, Cooper J."

Cooper, dismounting from his horse, warmly shook the factor's chubby hand. "Wouldn't advise you to repeat that, you old cuss. They might take exception to it because what they are, with the trail having hardened them, is a petticoat brigade. Doesn't mean, though, that they aren't just spoiling to shop in your store."

Word of the women's presence had spread rapidly, and men were already swarming around the wagon train. Mostly French-Canadian trappers, they were a rough, tobbaco-spitting lot. But there was an irresistible exuberance about them.

"Fandango!" they cheered. "Fandango!"

Agatha pushed through their grinning ranks to reach the gate. "What are they shouting about?" she appealed to the factor.

It was Cooper who turned to her, answering her concern. "They haven't seen females from the East in months. They want a fandango tonight. A dance, Aggie. I'd figure on complying if I were you. Otherwise, you're going to see one hell of a riot."

It shouldn't have been there. It belonged in the salon of a fine modiste in New York or Charleston, not in a trading-post store catering almost exclusively to mountain men on the raw frontier. Agatha couldn't take her eyes off of it.

Blue-sprigged ivory silk. An ankle-length bell skirt. A high waistline with a boat-shaped neckline and full leg-of-mutton sleeves. Surely with those full skirts and that off-the-shoulder, low neckline it was intended to be a ball gown.

She decided it must have been hanging here in this corner undiscovered for some time. It was not in the latest of styles, but it was so lovely any woman would forgive that.

"I can offer you a good price on that, ma'am," Obidiah Randolph promised her.

Agatha turned her head, smiling at the factor, who had appeared at her elbow to tempt her. "I am sure it must be hideously expensive at any price. However did you come to acquire such a thing, Mr. Randolph?"

"Sad story, Miss Pennington. A freighter ordered it from back east for his bride. Was to be her wedding dress, but the wedding never happened, and I was left with the goods."

"Did she die, Mr. Randolph?"

He chuckled. "No. The freighter was very short, the lady tall like yourself. Decided she didn't care for that difference after she arrived. Ended up running off with a towering Cheyenne warrior. Why don't you try it on, ma'am? I'll wager, with a few adjustments, it will fit like it was made for you."

Agatha shook her head. "It is not the sort of apparel that suits me, Mr. Randolph."

Lettice called to him from the other side of the store, and he moved off to answer her question. The place was noisy with the babble of ecstatic women pawing over wares they hadn't seen since Independence. While they outfitted themselves for tonight's fandango, their wagons were in the post's workshops undergoing repairs and replacements for the second half of the trek.

Agatha's own purchases had been few and practical. There was no reason for her to linger in the store. But she went on eyeing the gown longingly, her hand unable to resist stroking the lustrous silk of the skirt.

Another voice whispered the wickedness of temptation at her shoulder. "Those blue sprigs are just the color of your eyes, Miss Agatha. You'd be a regular sensation in that dress at the fandango."

It was Kitty this time, and her sister, Polly, joined her with a persuasive, "Oh, do it, Miss Agatha. We could style your hair to match the dress."

Agatha laughed feebly. "I am not the raw material for such a conversion, ladies. I would look foolish. It is out of the question."

She was still objecting three hours later, though silently this time, as she perched on a stool in Obidiah Randolph's private quarters, which he had insisted the women use to ready themselves for the fandango.

Agatha had surrendered and bought the gown. She was now submitting to a treatment of combs and curling irons in the skillful hands of the twins, who were being directed by a bevy of women from every side. And she wasn't sure how any of it had happened. All she knew for certain was that she must be committing a terrible error.

"Done!" Kitty pronounced with satisfaction, making Agatha feel like a cake removed from a hot oven.

The women in their shawls and ribbons and evening bonnets, all the finery that had emerged from the depths of the wagons or been purchased that afternoon in the store, examined her with exclamations of approval.

"Come and look at yourself, Miss Agatha," Polly urged, indicating on the wall a gilt-framed, full-length mirror that was as much a surprise in this place as the silk dress that caressed Agatha's body.

She rose nervously from the stool, afraid to approach the mirror. Afraid she would see a six-foot disaster instead of the feminine radiance she yearned for. The wide silk skirts whispered around her as she moved slowly to the glass and looked.

Mavreen, just behind her, must have sensed her disbelief. " 'Tis yourself all right," she assured Agatha with a chuckle. "And a magnificent self it is."

The transformation wasn't real, Agatha thought. It had to be a trick of the candlelight gleaming on her unfamiliar chestnut hair, parted in the center and drawn into a topknot high on the back. Ringlets at the sides framed her face. But it was the gown that fulfilled her desire, its snug bodice emphasizing her small waist, its daring neckline exaggerating the provocative swell of her breasts.

Illusion or not, Agatha decided that for this one night she was prepared, like Cinderella, to be dazzled by the magic.

And then in a breathless rush came the uninvited thought: What would Cooper think of her?

Agatha swiftly pushed the question from her mind. It didn't matter in the least what Cooper Delaney thought. Tonight was something she was doing only to please herself.

"Fiddlers tuning up!" an excited Callie reported from the doorway.

Like butterflies, the women streamed out into the torch-lit square, whose hard-packed earth was the scene of the fandango.

It was Jack Salter who danced with her first, Jack who made her blush with pleasure when he gathered her into his arms and whispered into her ear, "You are a caution in that dress, Miss Agatha. Take a man's breath away."

"I value the compliment, Mr. Salter, but should you be dancing when the sling was removed only this morning?"

His teeth flashed whitely. "Arm's fine, ma'am, but I'd suffer another bullet in it before I missed this chance to step out with you."

"Nothing that extreme is necessary. I shall be happy to accommodate you with as many turns on the floor as you like."

"That promise is gonna be a mite hard for you to keep. There isn't a man here who doesn't have his eye on you. They're already shovin' each other for a chance with you."

"You exaggerate, Mr. Salter."

Agatha didn't know what it was to be surrounded by eager admirers. It wasn't possible. Not for her. But, incredibly, Jack was right. Partners claimed her without interruption.

She danced to a lively "The Blue-Tail Fly," to an even livelier "Turkey in the Straw," then to a slower, romantic "Loch Lomond."

She danced with mountain men who had slicked their hair with macassar oil, tough little trappers who had doused themselves with bay rum, lanky freighters who had added gaudy bandannas to their fringed buckskin shirts. She danced with a gangly bullwhacker who wore, of all things, a silk top hat and a frock coat with flaring tails. She danced with Obidiah Randolph and twice more with Jack Salter.

Susan brought her a punch cup and told her there was no reason why she should be surprised by her success. They had all known she would be. Callie waved to her from her perch on a ladder where she and a solemn Indian boy watched the fandango. Two French-Canadians argued in their patois over who was going to dance with her next.

Agatha was flushed with elation. The evening was perfect. Almost perfect, anyway. Cooper was its only flaw. He never approached her, but she couldn't help her awareness of him there on the sidelines. He lounged against a post, watching her with a stony expression as she glided by, silk skirts swirling around her.

She told herself she wasn't in the least disappointed that he didn't try to dance with her. That he didn't deserve her disappointment, or any other caring emotion, after the way he'd run out on them. She told herself it didn't matter when she glanced the next time in his direction and saw that he had disappeared.

Why then should she feel so ridiculously pleased when, minutes later, he was actually there in front of her and telling the bearded young fellow who had come to collect her for a waltz, "This one is mine"?

Cooper looked positively dangerous. The young man didn't object. Neither did Agatha when he captured her in his arms as the fiddlers began to play a poignant "Barbara Allen."

She was afraid to question her emotions as he held her far too intimately and swept her breathlessly around the floor. She'd had every intention of resisting all contact with him, even of politely refusing any request to dance, should it eventually occur. But Cooper hadn't asked. He had simply taken.

He didn't play by the rules. Every man here had made some effort to adorn himself for the fandango. Not Cooper. He wore one of his simple homespun shirts, drop-shouldered and open at the neck, the usual broad leather belt and cowhide boots. No color. Not even a bandanna. And he managed to be the most dynamic male in the square.

It was his size, Agatha thought. Everything was so big about him, so solid and forceful. She was even conscious of the breadth of his hand locked with hers, richly brown from the sun and with curling dark hairs on the back. His hand was appealing, strangely arousing. She was conscious, too, of the way he held her. Strongly, possessively, as if he had every right to hold her this way. But most of all she was conscious of her own feeling of recklessness as his cheek hugged her hair.

It was all wonderfully delirious. Until she was shaken rudely back to reality by his growled, "What do you think you're doing?"

Her head came back. She searched his face. It was grim. "May I assume there is some explanation for your demand?"

"You've got every lout in the place wild to get his hands on you. You can't play with these men. They don't understand it. They're used to the kind of women who expect to be ravished."

"Each and every one of my partners has been a perfect gentleman," she informed him sweetly. "Until now."

"Then you haven't been paying attention. Their eyes have been all over you like hot hands. And who can blame them when you're half naked in that damn dress."

But it was *his* lowered gaze that licked like a blaze over the swell of her breasts. Agatha, mystified and strangely exhilarated at the same time, struggled to maintain her composure. "There is nothing scandalous about my behavior or my dress. This is a perfectly respectable ball gown." She made the error of adding a gloating, "Mr. Salter was kind enough to *politely* admire it."

Cooper swore savagely. "I could break Salter's pretty neck for him." His hands tightened on her roughly as they swung around the earthen floor.

Agatha felt her face go hot. She didn't know how to deal with him in this puzzling state. Didn't understand a woman's power to inflame a man with her attractions. It was as alien to her as the feminine art of flirtation. She had never before been the object of a man's jealousy, so how could she recognize the condition in Cooper? Because whatever the transformation she had undergone this evening, Agatha remained innocently convinced that underneath it all she was still an unexciting spinster.

"You're enjoying this, aren't you?" he persisted. "You like it that they're lining up for you, Salter in particular."

"I *was* enjoying myself until you elected to spoil it with this primeval performance. What on earth has come over you?"

"You're right. I'm a damn fool."

The waltz ended. He released her, turned and abruptly walked away from her. She didn't expect him to return. But, following a spirited reel with Jack, he was back and claiming her for another waltz.

He ignored her reluctance and boldly appropriated her as the fiddlers struck up "Greensleeves." Again, Agatha failed to identify his mood. How could she? She'd never had experience with anything so elemental as a territorial male determined to stake his claim.

His closeness as they danced offered her what she thought was the explanation. This time she could smell whiskey on his breath. "You've been drinking," she accused him.

"Just about all evening," he admitted defiantly.

The situation worsened after that. He never lost the opportunity now to steal her away from any man who tried to dance with her, Jack in particular. It was a rivalry unknown to Agatha. It might have been flattering had she believed that anything but liquor was the cause for it.

She should have turned him away but didn't, afraid that in his volatile mood a nasty scene would result. Her judgment was a grave mistake. Cooper got his scene anyway.

The caller had announced a favorite quadrille after a brief interval. Cooper, who had vanished again, reappeared out of nowhere. He was prepared to seize her for the quadrille. This time Jack arrived to rescue her.

"You've had enough, Delaney. Of both the liquor and Miss Agatha."

Agatha caught her breath as Cooper turned slowly to face Jack Salter. There was an expression on his face that would have curled steel. His voice was low and lethal. "You challenging me, Salter?"

" 'Pears I am. Hell, I should have done it in the beginning,'stead of slinking off every time and letting you have her."

Cooper smiled at him. It was not a friendly smile. "Then it looks like maybe you and I have a difference here to settle."

"Yeah, looks like it."

"You ready to step outside the gates now and take care of it?"

"Let's do that."

"Good. And if that arm of yours isn't healed, I'll be happy to tie one hand behind me. Hell, I'll tie both hands behind me."

"Don't you worry none about my arm, Delaney. It's good enough to knock you flat on your ass."

Agatha had heard enough. "You will not fight over me,

gentlemen. I absolutely forbid it. Do you understand? *You will not fight over me.*"

She might have been addressing stone. They were already on their way to the gates.

The promise of a good fight was apparently more appealing to the crowd in the square than a quadrille. Once the word spread, and it did with the speed of an ugly rumor, there was a general stampede in the direction of the gates. Agatha found herself helplessly carried along in the surge of excited bodies.

Streaming from the enclosure into the open, the eager spectators surrounded the two men who were circling each other warily, like a pair of crouched apes.

Agatha couldn't stand it. She wanted to stop the fight before it got serious, before they ended up knocking each other senseless. Was *determined* to stop the fight. But how, when no one but herself was interested in anything but a bloody brawl? Hopeless. Until she felt a sharp tug on her crushed skirts.

She looked down to find Callie bearing in her arms a load she had fetched from the stables where Bucephalus was quartered. The quick, resourceful child was offering her a solution. Cooper's bullwhip.

"Take it, Miss Agatha," she urged. "Do what he did to break up Roscoe and Romeo. Serve 'ol Coop right for running out on us."

Agatha stared at her. On one level she was shocked by the little girl's vengeful glee. But on another level she admired her inspiration.

Agatha hesitated. Should she? *Could* she? No, it was unthinkable. But a shout from the crowd as the two men approached each other, fists ready to hammer vulnerable flesh, changed her mind. She seized the coiled whip.

Under ordinary circumstances, she could never have managed even a suggestion of accuracy with the heavy instrument, though she had often watched Cooper practice with it and knew how it worked. But, driven by desperation fueled with outrage, Agatha was prepared to deliver.

Gripping the staff in both hands, borrowing the technique of a master bullwhacker as she braced herself with feet spread wide, she swung the lash over her head. Once, twice, three times. Her performance must have been effective. Startled onlookers stumbled over each other in their rush to get out of the way of the whistling whip.

Cooper and Salter were lunging at each other when Agatha let it fly. The fifteen-foot lash snapped through the air like a rattlesnake on its way to sting an enemy. She must have connected, because the two men, howling in surprise, leaped apart.

"What the hell are you doing?" Cooper yelled, staring at her in astonishment. "Are you crazy?"

"Stay out of it, Miss Agatha," Jack warned her.

"He's right. We're going to finish this. Go back inside, Aggie, and take that damn whip with you."

They would have gone for each other again. Agatha, retracting the lash, had no intention of letting that happen. She had the feel of the thing now, and she used it with precision. Again, and again, she slashed out at them, her angry voice blistering the air along with the whip.

"You would like nothing better than that! Then you could slug it out with each other, like the two pagan brutes you are!"

"C'mon, Aggie, you disapprove of violence, remember?"

"Why, I am merely reasoning with you, Mr. Delaney! Since you will not listen to words, this must persuade you!"

"Ow, that hurt!"

"Good! You deserve it! The two of you are worse than children!"

"Miss Agatha, please—"

"Please, what? Let you go back to a man's business of pounding one another to jelly? You are as bad as he is, Mr. Salter! I suspect you, too, have been drinking! No, I would advise you not to grab for the whip again! Not unless you wish to wear stripes on your hands!''

By now, the two men were dancing around like grasshoppers on hot coals as they made frantic efforts to avoid the relentless slap of the lash. The crowd screamed with laughter.

Agatha laid into them repeatedly, only lowering the whip when both men finally raised their arms in surrender. ''Have I made a sufficient *impression* on you, gentlemen? Yes? Then I am satisfied.''

Throwing the whip to the ground, she smoothed her skirts and tucked a fallen ringlet back into place. Then, with as much dignity as she could summon, she turned and marched back into the fort, ignoring the gaping crowd who scrambled out of her way.

Agatha preserved her composure until she reached the factor's private quarters. Only when she was safely alone in a shadowy corner of the room, where they had earlier dressed, did her self-control fail her.

Feeling tears very close to the surface, she sank down heavily on a bench against the wall. She refused to cry. She *never* cried. But, of course, she did just that. She wept in disgust, wailed in frustration, bawled in anger. Then, afterwards, she sat there and made an effort to understand her uncharacteristic tears.

The explanation was not difficult. Cooper. Always Cooper. He had threatened her sanity on every level since Independence. This time he had driven her into a despicable action. The bullwhip. How could she have resorted to such a method? The very form of viciousness to which she had always objected, struggled to oppose.

No more, she fiercely promised herself. She could take no more of this destructive relationship. It had to end. Cooper Delaney had to go.

Gotta give it up, Cooper promised himself as he crawled into his blanket for the night. No more bouts with a bottle, either on the trail or off the trail. He was getting too old for that sort of nonsense. His body told him that. What didn't ache was tender and threatened to ache.

Couldn't blame it on the whip, either. Aggie might have looked like she was mangling flesh, but the truth was she hadn't hurt much. Except maybe for his suffering ego.

His head was the real problem, though. Would be sore as the devil by morning. Right now it was throbbing dully. Worse, it wasn't very clear about the events of the evening.

He did know one thing for certain. Aggie had fired his blood to the boiling point. Damn, but she had been exciting in that dress. Had been a magnificent sight, too, swinging his whip like that. The memory made him smile. Also made him painfully hard.

As for the rest of the evening . . . well, he just didn't know. Except for one thing. He had the distinct impression he'd made a terrible fool of himself. Aggie was probably steaming over his behavior. All right, so he'd apologize for his mistakes in the morning, even if he wasn't sure what those mistakes had been.

And then what? he wondered as he turned restlessly inside the blanket. An exchange of pleasant good-byes, right? They had reached Ft. Laramie as promised. Nothing to keep him now that he had his gold back. He could do what he had been longing to do all along, strike out on his own for California.

He told himself there was nothing more he owed them.

He told himself there were plenty of reliable men here at the fort and that one of them would agree to pilot the wagons to Oregon.

He told himself the women no longer needed him and that this time he could ride off without regret, carefree and whistling.

That's what Cooper told himself as he resolutely settled down for the night. He believed none of it. And there was one particular truth that he made every effort to avoid. A truth that was unexpected, unwanted and ultimately inescapable. He was falling in love with Agatha Pennington, and he was scared.

# Chapter Twelve

The morning was as bad as Cooper had expected. Worse. Each muscle in his body demanded a groan. That would have involved an effort, though, and his swollen tongue would have objected. Much better to lie here and hurt in silence.

Served him right. He could have begged a regular bed somewhere from Obidiah Randolph. Instead, he was out here in the open rolled in his blanket, which was no protection against a ground that felt as hard as the heart of a Santa Fe whore.

He found out a moment later that even his eyeballs were in pain when he tried to turn them in the direction of the fort's gates, which swung open with a god-awful screech. A figure emerged and briskly approached him. He wasn't capable of an immediate identification, not with the morning light stabbing him from every side.

It wasn't until Agatha stood directly over him that he recognized her. She was back to her practical, no-nonsense hair and clothes.

"Good morning," she greeted him.

Her tone was cheerful, friendly even. Maybe she was going to forgive him. "Morning," he managed in a voice like gravel. He tried to sit up, but when he started to move, some cruel demon began banging at his skull with a large rock.

She smiled and nodded in what he hoped was understanding. "Having experienced a similar regrettable condition," she said, referring to that morning at the soddy on the Big Blue, "I sympathize."

" 'Preciate it," he muttered, holding himself very still and thinking she didn't look sympathetic at all. Her bearing was too rigid. He was afraid she wasn't in a forgiving mood after all.

"In any case," she went on, "it is not necessary for you to stir, since my errand is a brief one. But I did think you would want to immediately know of the decision. You will be pleased to hear, Mr. Delaney, that you are released from your obligation."

"What're you talking about?"

"California, Mr. Delaney. You are free to leave for California. I have arranged for a new pilot to guide us to Oregon. He is willing and ready to lead us. Naturally," she blithely rattled on, "I am prepared to pay you for your services to us, though understandably it can only be half of the fee we originally agreed upon. When you are ready for the sum—"

"Who?" he demanded, struggling to lift his head and losing the battle.

"That should not concern you."

"*Who*?" he insisted.

"Mr. Salter is our choice, if you must know."

Cooper shot to a sitting position with such force that his head almost rolled off his shoulders. Ignoring his instant agony, he thundered in disbelief, "Jack Salter? *Jack Salter?* Of all the candidates available in the place, you go and pick that excuse for a—"

She cut him off with a crisp, "Mr. Salter assures us he is

perfectly familiar with the trail. I trust him.''

"You can't do it. Anyone but him.''

"It is already settled. Mr. Salter goes. I am confident we can depend on him."

Before he could stop her, before he could even *think* of how to stop her, she was gone. She had turned around and marched back through the gates. Cooper was left sitting there with a new part of him that hurt. His jaws ached from his clenched teeth. But his outrage was far stronger than the misery of his body.

His women in the care of Jack Salter? He'd sooner put away a keg of whiskey, now, feeling as he did, than see that lowlife ride off with . . .

Cooper broke off the thought, startled by its content. *His* women? Since when had they become *his* women? The truth exploded inside his head. Holy Lucifer, they *were* his women. The thing he had feared and resisted with every particle of his will had happened without his even knowing it. Somewhere along the trail, insidiously, relentlessly, they had wound their tendrils around his heart. And now he was bound to them and their goal, and not even the lure of California could alter that.

He was shaken by the realization. The women mattered to him, Agatha most of all. Face it. Wasn't that why he'd drunk himself stupid last night? Jealous. He'd been blindly jealous. But he didn't want to deal now with his personal feelings for Aggie. They were still too fearsome, too impossible for him to confront.

But he couldn't avoid his responsibility to the women. It was no longer a temporary responsibility, either. Whatever happened with Agatha and him, or didn't happen, he had to see the women all the way to Oregon before he concentrated again on California. So what was he going to do about Salter? How was he going to eliminate that reptile?

He couldn't think. Not with these pincers gripping his skull. Coffee. He needed bitter, scalding coffee to clear his brain. No help for it. Unless he wanted to crawl on his hands and knees all the way to the post's kitchen, he was going to have to climb to his feet.

He managed it in slow, punishing stages, but at last he was standing erect. He took a moment to steady himself, and then he began to shuffle toward the gates. Once he was inside the enclosure, the aroma of freshly brewed coffee guided him in the direction of the kitchen where breakfast was under way.

The cook was merciful and supplied him with a mug of coffee strong enough to raise the dead. Cooper carried the tin mug outside, perching with it on a bench under the arcade that fronted the buildings which framed the square on all sides. There were only a few people in the open square, and none of them paid any attention to him as he sat there swigging his coffee.

The stuff revived him, easing his worst aches. The world settled back into focus. He became aware of a small figure seated idly on the flat roof across the square. There was a glum expression on her face as she dangled her legs over the edge. She turned her face away when she noticed him watching her.

Callie. Along with the others, she had yet to forgive him for deserting them before the raid. Was probably even more resentful than the rest, considering her attachment to him.

His brain was functioning again, enabling him to figure out a way to get rid of Salter. But he knew he couldn't attack that vital problem until he had made his peace with Callie. He just wished he didn't have to climb up on a roof to do it. No choice. He'd have to go to her, because she'd never willingly come to him.

Leaving the empty mug on the bench, he made his way to one of the ladders that connected the square with the rooftops. His body objected as he scaled the rungs. He was grateful when he gained the level roofs, which served as a platform for the defense of the fort. He half expected Callie to scramble to her feet and take off in the opposite direction as he rounded the walkway and approached her. But she remained in place.

"Mind if I join you?"

She refused to look at him. Her thin shoulders lifted in a shrug. He lowered himself beside her, his own legs hanging over the edge.

"Guess I owe you an apology, urchin."

She scowled, was silent for a moment and then blurted, "That was a real rotten thing you did."

"Callie, be fair. I never promised you I'd always be there."

"But you weren't s'posed to leave us."

"No, not like that maybe. I guess I was wrong to leave like that."

"Sure were." She paused, then met his gaze. "Think it was because of me you rode off?"

"What are you talking about?"

"You know, my tryin' to be a feller for you so's you wouldn't be the only one. Maybe that didn't work so good. Seems like I'm stuck bein' a girl. Heck," she grumbled, "no one ever remembered to call me Cal like they was s'posed to."

Cooper felt a silly lump at the bottom of his throat. No wonder she was so upset, when she'd been convinced that she had failed him, blaming herself for his desertion. "Aw, ol' son, no, it was never your fault. Not for a minute." He tried to explain it to her, which wasn't easy considering he was confused about his own actions lately. Well, until this morning anyway.

He offered his hand when he was through. "Pals again?" She nodded and shook his hand. "And, look," he added, "don't worry about the boy stuff, huh, because I like you just fine as a girl."

She nodded happily. Obviously, she hadn't been told yet about his removal as their pilot. He hoped that wouldn't be necessary. But he still had to find a way to get rid of Salter.

He started to get to his feet when he noticed that Callie was suddenly wearing a sly, thoughtful look.

"What?" he asked her.

"You like Miss Agatha, too, don't ya, Coop? Like her a lot."

"Callie," he said warningly, prepared to avoid that subject.

"I was only thinkin'," she said quickly, "that if the real reason you left us was on account of you figurin' Miss Agatha didn't like you back and that since then she liked that ol' Mr. Salter better . . . well, I was only thinkin' you didn't have to worry none about him 'cause he's got someone else, and I'm glad 'cause I don't like him. Leastways, not for Miss Agatha."

Cooper stared at her, suddenly interested. "What's all this, Callie?"

She sighed impatiently. "I'm tryin' to tell ya. Mr. Salter likes Magpie, and she likes him. I know 'cause I heard them whispering together, an' he called her 'honey,' only in a sort of tough way maybe, but I figure that means they're real close else they wouldn't have been meetin' like that in secret. I guess they don't want anyone knowin' they's sweethearts."

"When did all this happen?"

"The last night we was on the trail. I couldn't sleep in the tent. Too hot in there, an' Dolly snores somethin' awful. I went an' bedded down inside one of the wagons. That's where I was when I heard the two of them just the other side of the canvas. Boy-howdy, did I ever keep quiet. Figured they'd be real mad if they was to know I was there."

"Callie, exactly what did they say to each other? Can you remember?"

"I dunno. I was sleepy. I just wanted them to go away so's I could sleep."

"They must have talked about something."

"Not much. He says, 'Did you find it yet?' An' she says back, 'No, not so far.' Guess they lost somethin'. Maybe the pledge of their love. I heard Yvonne say once that a real gent always gives a lady a pledge of his love. An' that's all I know."

"It's enough, Callie," Cooper assured her in a low voice that belied his excitement. "It's more than enough."

*He knew it.* He had sensed it all along down in his gut. All those accidents that hadn't been accidents. The line snapping without good reason during the crossing of the Big Blue, the mystifying buffalo stampede, Magpie sneaking out of the camp at night. He was certain the two of them had been responsible for every unexplained disaster, including the suspicious Indian raid that had so conveniently introduced Salter to the wagon train. Probably even the addition of Magpie to the train had been arranged by them with the help of those renegades back in Kansas. From the beginning, Jack Salter and the half-breed girl had been partners.

All right, so the evidence was thin, practically nonexistent in fact. Certainly nothing that Agatha would listen to. Didn't matter. Cooper knew it had to be the truth. They were partners. But for what purpose? Hell, the answer was as plain as the nose on his face. The strongbox, of course. They must have somehow learned about the existence of the strongbox on the train, maybe as long ago as Independence. Probably figured there was a fortune in it, at least enough to put them to a good deal of trouble. They were looking for the hidden strongbox. Had to be the explanation.

Cooper grinned in satisfaction. He had just found his method for disposing of Jack Salter. He was going to give the thieving bastard the opportunity to help himself to that strongbox.

"Where ya goin'?" Callie asked him as he swung to his feet.

"To lay a trap, and you're going to help me."

"I am?" Pleased, but puzzled, she trotted after him as his long legs carried him around the walkway.

The fifteen-foot-high adobe walls formed a parapet at the

outer edges of the continuous roofs. Cooper stopped at the back side of the square and peered through the palisade that surmounted the walls on all sides. He found himself looking down into the walled work yard attached to the rear of the fort.

The scene was what he had anticipated. Their wagons were assembled in the spacious yard, undergoing the repairs that would ready them for tomorrow's return to the trail. The crew of men was already busy, putting in an hour or so of work before the breakfast call in order to escape the blistering July sun at midday. And just as he had hoped, a swaggering Jack Salter was among them.

Cooper could tell from his gestures that the self-important reptile was already taking advantage of his new position. He was making a performance of supervising the labor and probably earning the resentment of the crew. But as long as they were present, Salter had no chance of searching the wagons.

"What?" Callie demanded impatiently, frustrated by her inability to see over the top of the wall. "What is it?"

Cooper scooped her into his arms, lifting her to the height of the palisade so that she, too, was able to look through a gap between the concealing pickets.

"All right," he whispered, "let's see how smart you are. Which wagon down there is Miss Agatha's?"

"Too easy," she scoffed. "That one over t'the side."

"Good. Here's another question. How fast can you hunt up your young Indian friend from last night?"

"Real fast. He's down where the horses are picketed. And his name is Panther."

"Think Panther would come with you if you promised to show him something?"

"Guess so. What am I gonna show him?"

"Nothing. You're just going to pretend to. I want you to take him into the work yard, now while the men are still there."

"Ol' Mr. Salter will have a fit if I show up down there

with Panther. Send us out for bein' in the way.''

"That's what I'm counting on. And that's when you tell him all you wanted to do was show Panther how the strongbox is hidden down inside that wood stove Miss Agatha is carrying to Oregon.''

Callie caught her breath, turning her head to stare at him. "I'll get skinned alive if I go an' say that. Not s'posed to mention that box ever t'no one.''

"Don't worry about it. I'll see to it that the strongbox is protected.'' He set her down. "Now, scoot. And, Callie?''

"What?''

"Don't argue with Salter. You leave as soon as he tells you to leave. You go off with Panther and forget all about it. Clear?''

"Uh-huh.'' Callie plainly understood none of it, but she was too pleased by her restored friendship with Cooper to question his intentions.

He watched her race toward the nearest ladder, her wild curls that had recovered their growth since Independence streaming behind her. He regretted the necessity of involving Callie at all. But there had been no choice about it. Anyway, he was going to remain right here, watching the scene to make sure she was safe.

Minutes later, Callie reappeared in the yard below. Panther was with her. Just as he had predicted, the officious Salter immediately intercepted the children. Cooper couldn't possibly hear any of the conversation that followed. He didn't have to. As Callie spoke, pointing in the direction of Agatha's wagon, Salter's head swiveled around. He could practically smell the reptile's sudden excitement.

Callie and Panther were ordered to leave the yard. The crew went on working, Salter moving among them. Cooper saw him glance longingly every now and again in the direction of Agatha's wagon. But he didn't dare go after the strongbox, not with the other men on the scene. Cooper knew just what Salter was waiting for.

A few minutes later the bell in the square clamored, calling the fort to breakfast. The yard crew laid down their tools and trooped off to the mess adjoining the kitchen. Salter accompanied them in order to avoid suspicion. But he would be back, and Cooper would be ready for him.

The yard was deserted when Cooper, familiar with the layout of the fort, slipped into the back tower and descended the ladder to the ground level, which doubled as a storage area. There were tools strewn across a work bench. He helped himself to a knife, tucking it in his belt. No time to go after his Colt or the Hawken. Not that a weapon was necessary since Salter, hardly expecting trouble, wasn't likely to be armed. Still, the knife was a smart precaution.

There were two doors at the bottom of the tower. One of them connected with the square. The other opened directly into the yard. Cooper cracked this one just wide enough to permit him a clear view of the area. The place was quiet, still. He stationed himself behind the door and waited.

Salter was too eager for any delay. It was only a matter of seconds before the gate in the far wall squeaked open. Sneaking into the yard, the reptile checked the area with a fast, sweeping glance and then made directly for Agatha's wagon. Cooper held himself until Salter had heaved himself over the tail board and disappeared under the canvas. Then he slipped into the yard.

He could hear the clang of metal against metal as he neared the wagon and knew that Salter was already burrowing into the bowels of the small stove. By the time he reached the rear of the wagon, Salter, his back to him, was raising the strongbox from the depths of the stove.

"Helping yourself to an early bonus?" Cooper inquired mildly. "I wouldn't bother, Salter. There's no way you can earn it, because you're not going to Oregon."

The crouched figure in the wagon whipped around, the strongbox in his hands sliding to the floor with a clatter. There was an expression of shock on his handsome devil's

217

face. There was also murderous rage.

"I don't have to answer to you, Delaney. You're history. I'm in charge now. And as for this here box and the stove . . . well, all I'm doin' is shiftin' the heavy stuff around a bit so's the load rides better."

"You don't say."

"Yeah, doin' my job." He smiled maliciously. "Or maybe it ain't been made clear to you yet that it's my wagon train now."

"Oh, it was made clear to me all right. The thing is, I've just decided to take it back."

"Think so?" Salter leaped down from the wagon. "Maybe it's time to see what Miss Agatha has to say on the subject."

When he started to move toward the gate, Cooper gripped him by the shoulder and pulled him around. "I don't think we'll bother Aggie. Think we can settle this real easy between the two of us. No, I wouldn't if I were you," he warned him as Jack started to swing at him. "See, I'm cold sober this morning, and if you try slugging it out with me I'll just end up beating you bloody. You're no match for me, Salter, and you know that this time, don't you?"

"You ain't got no right—"

"No right to catch a lying thief? That's what you are, Salter. From the start you and the girl planned to rob the strongbox. Don't bother denying it either or inventing some tale, because I wouldn't believe any of it."

Jack glared at him, his lean face tight with fury. "It's my word against yours."

Cooper chuckled. "You want to test that, Salter? Want to see what the boys here at the fort have to say when we compare stories? No, I didn't think so. You know damn well that, given the chance, they'd string you up. But I'm gonna go easy on you. This is what we're gonna do." His voice sharpened as he meaningfully fingered the knife in his belt. "I'm gonna walk you out of here, help you pick up your kit.

Then we're heading straight for your horse, no stops along the way, and you're riding out of here. Not in our direction either. Are we understanding each other?''

Salter was left without a choice. With most of the fort at breakfast, they met no one as Cooper escorted him out to the trail. The sullen Jack offered no argument until he mounted his horse.

''What about Magpie?'' he wanted to know.

''She stays with us. Let's call her a small guarantee against you sneaking back and trying something. And if you're a good boy, Salter, maybe you'll see her again. *After* we reach Oregon.''

He stood there and watched Jack Salter ride off in the direction of Independence. The man didn't look back, but Cooper knew that he wouldn't forget this humiliation, and if they ever met again . . .

But, hell, he had something much more real than that to worry about. He had Aggie to face. Was probably going to be a pretty rough scene, too. Unless . . . Yeah, there was only one way to handle it.

Then afterwards . . . after he had made plain to her just who was going to pilot the wagon train, and who wasn't, there was another little matter between them that needed settling. No more delays, no more denials. He wanted her, and she wanted him, whether she admitted it or not. He no longer cared what it involved.

With a decisive stride, he headed back inside the fort in search of Agatha.

She had done it. She had rid herself of Cooper Delaney, and she felt wretched about it.

The mess hall was noisy with the talk and laughter of the women who were sharing breakfast with the occupants of the post. Agatha paid little attention to the conversations around her. Nor had she any appetite for the hearty meal that had been placed in front of her.

219

Cooper. She couldn't stop thinking about Cooper. He was probably miles away by now, on the trail to California and celebrating his freedom with a bawdy rendition of "Comin' Thro' the Rye." He had what he'd wanted all along. And she had the willing guide now that she wanted. Both of them were supposed to be satisfied. Then why was she dealing with the pangs of regret?

Susan, seated beside her, nudged her with her elbow. "Reckon you're wanted."

Agatha looked up from her plate, following Susan's nod in the direction of the doorway. Just as though she had conjured him, Cooper stood there in the opening, waiting to catch her eye. For a brief moment she experienced an irrational joy. He was still here! And then she remembered. Of course. He had yet to be paid his promised sum. He had come for the money, no other reason. Her spirits plummeted.

When she met his gaze, he jerked his head in the direction of the square. She rose from the table as he turned and left the hall. He was waiting for her outside, an entirely different Cooper from that miserable one she had accosted in his blanket. His eyes were a stormy green, and there was steel in his long body as he faced her. Agatha started to tell him she would fetch his money, but he gave her no opportunity to speak.

"Thought you'd care to know," he informed her in an I-mean-business voice, "that I've just relieved your new pilot of his obligation."

He was serious. "What have you done with Mr. Salter?"

"What I should have done the first day he arrived in camp. I sent him packing in a direction that isn't Oregon. Now thank me nicely for that, Aggie, because I've done you a real favor." Before she could raise any objections, he told her about the strongbox. "Jack Salter was a little mistake in judgment, wasn't he, Aggie?"

"It would seem he was, Mr. Delaney. Unfortunate. That leaves us with the necessity of securing a replacement."

"Oh, I don't think so, Aggie. See, there's a small matter that neither one of us remembered about earlier."

"What is that, Mr. Delaney?"

"The contract you had me sign back in Independence. Makes me your pilot all the way to Oregon. You'd be violating it if you tried to replace me. Hell, it was *your* contract, Aggie. You insisted on it. Now you live with it."

"Yes, that is true." Her spirits soared again.

"No arguments then."

"Very well."

His gaze narrowed. He stared at her suspiciously. "Strikes me you're taking all this pretty calmly."

"You leave me no alternative, Mr. Delaney."

"Then why do I have the feeling that I've just been outwitted?"

"Your imagination, Mr. Delaney."

He grunted, nodded. "Uh-huh. Well, just as long as we understand each other."

"We do, Mr. Delaney."

"Good. Now I've got a letter to write. There's this friend of mine in California keeping my savings. Carlo Ramirez. Have to let Carlo know I won't be seeing him as soon as I thought I would. Sooner or later, someone will come through here bound for California, carry the letter for me. That's it then."

He started to turn away. Then he remembered something. Or pretended to. "Oh, yeah, there's this one other piece of business we have to take care of."

"Another small matter?"

"Not this time, Aggie. This one is major."

"What is it, Mr. Delaney?"

His gaze probed hers. Direct, meaningful and utterly potent. "I think you know."

She did. There was no mistaking his intention. She suddenly found it an effort to breathe. "Are you certain that I am what you—"

He cut her off forcefully. "New rule, Aggie. No more humility about your womanhood. If you can't judge it by now, then you let me judge it for you. Noon. The front gates. Be there, because if you're not I'll come and find you." He swung abruptly away from her, started off across the square, then stopped. Turning his head, he called back a simple, "Please."

It was that single, earnest word that left her completely defenseless. She knew that she would be where he wanted her and when he wanted her.

Agatha was in place when noon arrived, standing outside the gates of the fort and nervous with anticipation. She wondered what he planned for them and was astonished by her own recklessness, her desire to share with Cooper Delaney what promised to be a sensual adventure. She knew she could no longer deny what she had been longing for since Independence, and for once she refused to concern herself with the consequences.

Cooper appeared a moment later from around the corner of the fort, driving a small cart drawn by a sturdy pony. When he pulled up in front of her, she saw that there was a covered basket tucked behind the single seat.

"Just like Sunday in Philadelphia, Aggie," he informed her with a grin as he sprang down from his perch. "A drive through the park, then a lazy picnic under a friendly tree."

"Suitably romantic," she said, adding hastily, "In the pastoral sense, of course."

"Oh, of course," he agreed dryly.

Several Ogala children had gathered around, watching closely as he handed her into the curious two-wheeled cart. "They are fascinated by the conveyance," she observed.

"It's something I found shoved into the back of a shed, and don't ask me how it came to be here at the post." He joined her on the seat, taking up the lines. "Horses would have been a lot better where we're going, but I remembered how you feel about riding."

"Considerate of you."

"That's me, Aggie," he said cheerfully, directing the pony over the path that descended the slope. "Thoughtful to a fault."

Reaching Laramie Creek in the hollow, they turned onto a track that followed the stream away from the fort. Agatha looked forward to Cooper's version of a Philadelphia park as they bumped along through an arid landscape where the only vegetation was the thin, burned grasses. To their right stretched a range of desolate ridges baked dry by a blazing sun in a cloudless sky. None of it offered the promise of a sylvan picnic glade. It didn't matter. She wouldn't have felt anywhere near as exhilarated if this had been Fairmount Park itself. No point in denying it. The man close beside her was responsible for her silly smile.

She felt him eyeing her. "What?" she asked.

"Nothing. Just sort of hoped you'd turn up in that dress from last night. Not that what you're wearing isn't pretty enough," he mumbled, referring to her high-necked calico plaid.

Agatha laughed. "A silk ball gown is not appropriate for a midday picnic in the wilds."

"Yeah, but the neckline was damn interesting."

As was his own appearance at the moment, she thought. He had been an unappealing sight this morning with his bloodshot eyes, a stubble of beard and clothing that had suffered from a night on the ground. He had shaved and bathed since then, changing into a fresh shirt and trousers. Cooper Delaney cleaned up very well. Very well indeed. She was finding it difficult again to breathe.

The rough track along which the willing pony plodded narrowed to a footpath after another mile or so. It was necessary to leave the cart.

"We walk from here," Cooper said, freeing the pony from the cart.

Armed with the picnic basket and drawing the pony behind them, they ambled beside the sluggish creek for a short distance. Rounding an outcropping of rock, they arrived at their destination. Agatha was enchanted.

Nestled in a curve of the creek, in an isolated grove of ash and cottonwood trees fed by the waters of the stream, was a green meadow where wild roses sprawled in profusion, their fragrance heavy on the faint breeze.

"Your park is delightful," she assured him.

"I deliver," he said in a husky voice, standing close behind her as she admired the site. She knew he meant something other than the serenity of the grove.

"You do," she agreed softly, realizing that it was more than just the day that was beginning to heat up.

They stood there for a moment, neither touching nor gazing at each other but with an increasing awareness of their intimate situation, before Agatha gently reminded him, "I believe you promised me lunch in the park."

"Fuel for the fire," he agreed wickedly, thrusting the picnic basket into her hands and parting from her to turn the pony loose in the meadow. She hadn't missed his meaning.

Agatha spread the blanket that accompanied the basket in the shade of a crooked cottonwood on the grassy verge of the creek. She was in the process of unpacking the basket when Cooper dropped beside her on the blanket. He eagerly examined the contents as she removed them.

"Hope Cookie at the fort provided us with something tasty. I bribed him enough."

"We can have no complaint," she said, indicating a fare that included thick slices of fresh bread, jerked beef, a savory cheese, apples and the miracle of boiled eggs. There was even a jar of ginger beer which Cooper cooled in the stream.

There was silence after they had feasted on the meal, no sound but the sun-gilded waters burbling over stones and the lazy rustle of the gray-green cottonwood leaves overhead. It occurred to Agatha that this was the first truly peaceful interlude she'd experienced since leaving Independence. Or was it?

She was suddenly conscious of Cooper's searing gaze and of how he had edged close to her on the blanket. "You haven't had dessert," he said.

"I am much too full."

"Try it," he urged in a smoky drawl that made her insides flutter. "Just a bit."

She watched him break off a piece of the cake on his plate. He extended it toward her. She started to take it from him, but he shook his head. Before she could object, he brought his hand to her mouth and slowly fed the morsel to her. It was moist and rich, stuffed with sweet raisins. She could taste more than the cake. She could taste the tips of his fingers between her lips. They were warm and sticky, and her tongue lapped at them like a kitten's. It was an erotic delight, and she could scarcely believe her participation in the performance.

Cooper chuckled. "Good, huh?" He angled his head to one side, considering her. "Left some sugar crumbs on your mouth. No, don't," he said as she started to wipe them off. "Let me."

He dipped his head, his parted mouth closing on hers. The tip of his tongue slowly traced the shape of her lips, gently, carefully licking up the sweetness. She was trembling when he finally drew back.

"Much better than a napkin," she managed to compliment him. "Have you any other unique methods for cleaning the mouth?"

"Let's see if I do."

His mouth claimed hers again in a long, thorough kiss that was slow in its first stages, then quickened when his tongue eagerly met hers in a moist, restless contest that left her reeling with its depth.

## Jean Barrett

There was green fire in his eyes when he lifted his mouth from hers and a fierce accusation in his voice. "You've turned my life into a regular battleground, Agatha Pennington. I haven't known a minute's rest since you marched into my room uninvited at the Merchants Hotel. If it hasn't been runaway wagons, it's been stampedes or dog fights or the sting of a bullwhip. And, damn, if you aren't still giving me trouble."

"Is there no way I can provide you with peace, Mr. Delaney?"

"Believe we're about to find out," he growled softly.

"Yes, I believe we are," she whispered solemnly.

She was about to embark on a monumental journey, an adventure involving both the flesh and the spirit. Thrilling to contemplate and at the same time a little frightening. Not just because it was an unknown but because it was so wildly out of character for her. It was not too late to turn back. Should she? No! She longed for this. Longed to be like other women. She was ready and determined to experience the same wondrous, life-giving destination, and she wanted no one but Cooper to take her there.

Eyes locked with hers, he began to peel away his clothing. "Remember that night in the soddy, Aggie?" he asked as he tugged off his boots.

"Yes."

"I kind of introduced you to your own body that night, didn't I?" he said as he removed his belt.

"You did."

"Now let me introduce you to mine," he said, stripping off his shirt, then reaching for the fastenings on his jean trousers.

"It would be my pleasure."

Within seconds, he had rid himself of his last article of clothing. He knelt there on the blanket, inviting her to visually explore his unabashed nakedness. Cooper Delaney, sleek and muscled, glowing with vigor, was the largest man she had ever seen. In all ways. Agatha was riveted.

"Have you ever touched a man before, Aggie? Intimately touched him, I mean?"

She shook her head.

"Then I'll be your first," he said happily.

He stretched out on the blanket at her side, inviting her to examine him.

"Where shall I begin?" she asked, her voice hoarse with uncertainty.

"Wherever you like, Aggie. Hell, there isn't a spot I won't enjoy."

She leaned over him, frustrated with her inexperience but eager to please him. Her hands descended slowly until they rested against his shoulders. They felt warm and smooth and incredibly hard.

"You"—she paused to swallow, her mouth suddenly very dry—"must tell me what to do."

"Let your hands do the thinking for you, Aggie."

She obeyed him, watching in fascination as her hands, with a will of their own, began to investigate the contours of his superb body. Her fingers stirred through the thick, dark hair on his broad chest, trailed down to his flat stomach, then climbed again to his chest. She delighted in the sensation of his male flesh, in the sight of his eyes closed in satisfaction.

Her hands were shy at first, then grew bolder with confidence. They located his nipples, which they squeezed between thumbs and forefingers. Cooper inhaled deeply and shuddered.

"Have I caused you pain?" she asked him anxiously.

"Not the kind for you to worry about, Aggie. Keep going. This is getting better and better."

Her hands slid down his length, molding the thickness of his muscled, hair-roughened thighs. By then Agatha understood his intention. He was sensitizing her to his body, teaching her that she need not fear it when it joined with hers.

She found that very touching. He was, after all, an extraordinary man.

In more ways than one. She had inflamed him with her caresses, and the result was blatantly evident. Drawing a steadying breath, she gazed in wonder at the engorged shaft that demanded her attention. Did she dare?

"Do it," he urged, reading both her longing and her hesitation.

Her fingers closed around him, gently at first and then with increased pressure. She found the experience awesome, his rigid flesh hot and hard and satin smooth all at the same time. She would have stroked that amazing arousal, yearned to stroke it, but Cooper groaned aloud in what must be agony. She released him immediately.

"I have hurt you this time."

"You're killing me," he pleaded.

"Yes, I see." And she did now. "Then I must, in all fairness, give you the opportunity to punish me in return."

"I believe you should, Aggie."

Eyes glittering, he watched her as she sat back and began to slowly remove her clothing. Feeling awkward under his gaze, she lowered her eyes as she worked, shedding article after article until she was as naked as he was. Then, lifting her hands, she released the pins from her hair, permitting the chestnut mass to tumble down her back. Only then did she find the courage to raise her eyes and meet his probing gaze.

He had approved of her body that night in the soddy. But though he had touched every part of her, he hadn't been able to view her in the darkness. This was full daylight, the sun dappling her skin through the canopy of the cottonwood. Would he still find her pleasing? She waited nervously for his judgment.

"If I had any poetry in me," he said, voice husky with desire, "I could do justice to what I'm looking at. But all I can say is that you are one hell of a woman, Agatha Pennington."

And that was when she went to him. When he took her into his arms and held her. When he cherished her with his hands and mouth alike, stroking the fullness of her breasts, then suckling them until she was whimpering with need.

His mouth was everywhere, kissing her long and lovingly until, unbelievably, he was down between her thighs. Shocked, she started to object. But his bold tongue had already claimed its target. Agatha gasped as his mouth teased, tantalized and plundered.

What his skillful fingers had so effectively achieved that memorable night in the soddy was now the business of his clever tongue. Hands twisted in his thick, black hair, hips squirming as he gripped her tightly, Agatha cried out at the urgency that built inside her to an unbearable pinnacle. When his deeply buried tongue finally achieved its victory, she went wild with release.

Cooper, sliding up her length, watched the joy on her face and held her close as the tremors dwindled. He waited until she was quiet and then asked softly, "You all right?"

"Yes, splendid." She hesitated before whispering a self-conscious, "Is—is that all?"

He chuckled, nuzzling her ear. "No, sweetheart, there's more. Unless you don't want more."

"But I do," she assured him, aware of his pulsing arousal strained longingly against her flesh.

"That's good, because I'd be in a devil of a fix here if you didn't." He paused, his voice suddenly sobering. "Only there's one thing you have to understand before we go any further."

"Yes?"

His direct gaze sought and held hers. "I can't promise you any lifetime of tomorrows, Aggie. If you expect that, and you have every right to expect it, then you have to tell me now while I still have the will to hold back, because once we go all the way . . . well, it'll be too late to change your mind."

Hands on either side of his face, she drew his head down to her own and answered him with her mouth pressed to his in a moist, lingering kiss. The future should have mattered. It didn't. Not in this elemental moment with the scent of him in her nostrils, the taste of him on her tongue. She wanted nothing but the completion of their joining.

It was what she told him when she lifted her mouth from his. "Take me the rest of the way, Cooper Delaney."

And he did, his hands and mouth preparing her, swelling her to a renewed hunger. He was trembling with restraint when his raging body finally settled between her parted thighs.

Agatha could hear the struggle for self-control in his raspy voice. "I'll try not to hurt you, Aggie, but the first time can be a little painful for a woman."

"Then let us move beyond that," she encouraged him.

He was slow and gentle, careful to ease her acceptance of him. She could feel the pressure building as he filled her with his primal male heat. She caught her breath and held it, seized by a sharp, burning sensation when he penetrated a final barrier.

He rested then, permitting her to adjust to him. The rawness subsided, defeated by her wonder over the impact of their oneness.

"It—it is incredible," she murmured.

"That's just what it is," he rumbled.

There was a long moment of stillness in which Agatha savored the miraculous melding of their bodies. Cooper finally ended it with a frantic, "I know you've got to be feeling tender, but if you can bear it, I need to . . . I *really* need to . . . hell, I can't hold back any longer."

"Then, by all means, let us proceed."

With a grateful sigh, he began to stir inside her. His first thrusts were slow and measured, broken by rests intended to prolong their pleasure. The ache inside her intensified, but it was no longer related to the pain of his entry. This was an ache of joy.

Obeying her instincts, Agatha gathered him close, embracing him with her arms and legs. He lost his rigid control. His strokes became long and lusty, his body slick with sweat. He crooned words to her, blurred love words that she answered with feverish kisses.

There was nothing now but the two of them bound in a vortex of blinding rhythms. Then she felt herself being lifted. Higher, and still higher. Surging toward a fantastic completion.

When the first waves rocked her, Cooper paused to relish the sight of her in the throes of a powerful release. She twisted, heaved, her body gripping his manhood in her fury. It was her involuntary tightening that squeezed him over the edge. He went plunging after her with a shout.

Long, mellow moments later, Cooper, who had snuggled against her side, raised himself abruptly on one elbow to peer down at her suspiciously. "Are you crying? Oh, hell, you are crying. I've hurt you."

Agatha shook her head, smiled and wiped at the tears on her face. "There is a little soreness," she admitted, "but it is nothing."

"Then why . . . ?"

How could she tell him? How could she possibly make him understand that she was weeping in happiness, not pain? That his lovemaking had provided her with an awesome new confidence in her womanhood. That, because of him, she no longer had to consider herself an unwanted spinster.

She settled for an easier explanation. "These are merely tears of gratitude, Cooper. Because you made my first time . . . memorable."

He grinned at her. "Yeah?"

"Yes. Although . . ."

"What?"

"As delighted as I am, I am shocked by the wanton you have created."

That, too, pleased him.

There was something else she couldn't tell him. The recognition at last of her love for him. She was in love with Cooper Delaney, and she wanted him. But she dared not tell him, because she didn't trust that love, didn't trust him. He had warned her himself. He couldn't offer her the future. And, dear God, how was she supposed to live with that?

# *Chapter Thirteen*

Jack Salter stared at the snake and shuddered. It was writhing helplessly, pinned to the ground by the sharp bowie knife that Duke had driven through its head. Duke stood over the snake, watching its death agony with a satisfied smile on his narrow mouth.

Jack was uneasy when his brother was this nasty. It wasn't the deliberate cruelty he minded. It was Duke's loss of self-control. He'd been furious, on a real rampage, ever since Jack had arrived at the camp on the North Platte to report the latest failure. Every member of the band had suffered his wild rage, and most of them were grateful when he turned his viciousness on the trapped snake.

Jack had been lucky. Duke had raved at him, but he hadn't touched him. He knew, though, that by challenging him he risked a broken jaw. He couldn't help it. His brother's obsession with this wagon train was beginning to worry him.

"Look, Duke, maybe it's time to let 'em go. They got the hardest country comin' up, ain't they? Probably won't make it through, and if they do, so what? Don't mean other wagon

233

trains will be scramblin' to follow. You can explain that to Pacific Fur, can't you?''

Duke looked up from the snake and laughed. There was contempt in his laughter. "You got a serious problem, little brother. No brains. You think Pacific Fur is gonna forgive a defeat like that? I'd be out on my ass, and you along with me. 'Sides"—his gaze darkened dangerously—"it's more now than just haltin' that train or others like it. It's become personal. *Real* personal. I got me a score to settle with that bitch and her women, Delaney along with them.''

"Sure, I'd like to get even too, Duke, but that sounds like open war to me, and that ain't bein' careful. Ain't you said all along you got to be careful not to involve Pacific Fur, and if you personally—"

"Who said anything about involving Pacific Fur? How they gonna be involved if there's no one to talk about it? And I mean to see to it this time that nobody on that wagon train is left to carry a tale.''

Jack squirmed, disliking the savage gleam in Duke's eyes. It was a look that had him questioning his brother's sanity. "Well, yeah, but that means more than just turning 'em back. That means . . .''

He didn't finish. Duke's expression warned him that it wouldn't be smart of him to go on with his objections. But he feared that in his mania his brother was ignoring the reality that he, himself, had once argued. The women were well armed, Delaney experienced and alert, ready for trouble. Openly attacking and destroying that wagon train would require a sufficient force, and there were no more than a dozen in the band now.

Most of the renegades, including Bull Bear, had deserted after the raid that had wounded several of them. Already far from home, they had no interest in pursuing the women into the alien country beyond Ft. Laramie. The easy spoils that Duke had promised them had not been realized. They no longer trusted him.

The snake had stopped struggling. Duke regarded it with a sadistic snarl that convinced Jack his brother no longer cared about the consequences.

"Sooner or later, I'll catch up with those females, and when I do . . ."

His boot came down on the snake, crushing what was left of its head.

It was useless. No matter how often Agatha reminded herself that another session with Cooper like the one on the banks of Laramie Creek, magnificent though it had been, would ultimately result in heartache, and no matter how many arguments she used with herself to prevent further temptation, she was completely defenseless whenever he wanted her. And Cooper wanted her all the time.

The circumstances didn't seem to matter in the least. Not even the brutal conditions of the trail in those long weeks that followed Ft. Laramie kept him from seizing every shameless opportunity to provide them with pleasure.

"Come on, Aggie," he eagerly coaxed on that unforgettable afternoon he joined her on her wagon.

She gazed at him in disbelief, then glanced to the right and to the left. The barren country was so dry that the wagons were spread out laterally to avoid the caustic alkali dust raised by the rolling wheels. Here? Now? He couldn't be serious.

He grinned at her engagingly. "Why not? The oxen won't mind. They'll just go plodding along without us. And the women won't mind. Hell, there isn't a one of them doesn't know about us and isn't prepared to respect our privacy. Anyway, a little risk just makes it more exciting."

He was insatiable, dynamic, and she was powerless to refuse him. Somehow she found herself with him in the back of her rocking wagon where their stolen lovemaking consumed both of them.

Late July found them on the Continental Divide battling

the rigors of the South Pass where the air off the snow-capped Wind River range was so cold that ice formed in the water buckets at night. Agatha and Cooper clashed over the subject of her precious iron stove.

"It's got to go, Aggie. Thing's too heavy for a climb like this, and there's worse ahead of us. Anyway, it's a bad place to hide the strongbox."

It was no comfort to her when he created a false floor on the bed of her wagon to conceal the strongbox. The stove had been meant for the school she intended to build in Oregon. She mourned its abandonment at the side of the trail.

Agatha forgave him when he crawled into her tent late that night. She awoke on her side to find him squeezed up behind her, growling an urgent appeal just before his tongue found her ear. Within two minutes she was clinging to him as he buried himself in her, and she came alive in that exquisite way she could feel only when he was deep inside her.

She was shocked when she awakened in the morning. The muted light inside the tent revealed Cooper's naked back. It was striped with long scratches that her fingernails had put there last night. It was incredible to her that she was capable of such passionate abandon, but that's just how he affected her.

August came with a midday heat like a furnace and nights that were frigid. The oxen suffered so badly on the rough terrain that their hooves had to be wrapped with protective layers of buffalo hide. The women welcomed their arrival at Soda Springs where the California Road left the trail.

If Cooper had any longings for the southern route, he never disclosed them. He seemed far more interested in sneaking off with Agatha to one of the warm, bubbling springs away from camp. They bathed together in the soothing waters and afterwards made love. She stunned herself and delighted him when, at a crucial moment, she cupped him in a particularly electrifying way, producing a frenzied climax.

"Holy Lucifer, Aggie," he gasped afterwards, "where did you get an inspiration like that?"

"Several of the more experienced women aware of our activities," she confessed reluctantly, "have been instructing me in . . . uh, certain techniques."

He chuckled in approval. "They got any more lessons for you, you pay careful attention."

She sighed in his arms. "You will be my ruin, Cooper Delaney."

"That's the general idea, Aggie."

The first of September brought them to Three Island Crossing on the turbulent Snake River. It was a dangerous stream to ford with its foaming cataracts and roaring falls. The desolate badlands over which they traveled on the other side were far worse.

Day after day the wagons jolted across the endless sage flats where the heat was intense and the water holes undependable. Some of the oxen, weakened by the prolonged hardship and the scant grazing, lay down and refused to rise. But no matter how punishing the conditions, Cooper was never too exhausted to make love.

By now Agatha was a skillful, willing partner. She was far less confident where her emotions were involved. The prospect of losing Cooper was unbearable, but it was a threat she lived with daily. As much as she yearned for a shared future with him, she could never forget that he was still an untamed animal afraid to risk his heart, that his soul had been wounded by the darkness in his past. And one day, like a wild stallion, he would break away and vanish from her life.

That was why her passion was vital on a level much deeper than his. If she loved him hard enough, often enough, perhaps she could prove to him that powerful love, *honest* love, could surmount impossible barriers, could gentle even the wildest heart.

All well and good, but the problem was more complicated than that. Whatever her determination, Agatha couldn't ex-

# Jean Barrett

pect to win him unless the ultimate conflict of their goals was resolved. That outcome must wait for Oregon.

Rebecca's baby could not wait.

"Nonsense," Agatha declared. "We are fortunate. It is the perfect refuge."

She failed to understand Cooper's objections. He should be relieved by Rebecca's timing, not complaining about it. The harsh arid country was behind them. They had crossed the Boise River, gained the green foothills of the mighty Blues. And now, with thunder over the mountains threatening them with a storm, they had arrived at a trading post on the banks of a rushing stream.

Cooper shook his head and went on grumbling as he regarded the gaping gates of the fort's crumbling log stockade.

"Why must you be concerned?" she persisted. Hadn't he already carefully investigated the interior, making certain it was deserted? The post, too remote and difficult to supply, had been abandoned long ago.

"Never liked or trusted the place," he muttered. "It was one of Pacific Fur's, and it had a reputation for bad dealings."

"There is nothing sinister here now."

"Unless you count the ghosts, Aggie. Great spot for an ambush."

She refused to be alarmed. "It offers us a much needed shelter."

In any case, they hadn't much choice. Rebecca's delivery was imminent. She had been indicating signs since mid morning, with several of the experienced women reporting that she was already in the early stages of labor. Agatha had feared that the baby would be born out on the trail in a violent downpour with no other cover but the canvas on a wagon. She was grateful for the fort.

Cooper made his decision. "All right, ladies," he called

238

out to the company, "move 'em on in, but let's be vigilant about it."

The next half hour was a busy one. The wagons were driven into the compound and the stock secured while Rebecca was made comfortable for her lying-in. They prepared a bed for her in the largest of the crude log buildings at the rear of the enclosure.

Agatha, who was everywhere helping with the activities, found nothing menacing about the place except for the accumulated dirt and a nest of mice chased out of hiding by Romeo and Roscoe. Henrietta and Faye, serving as midwives and assisted by Dolly and May, shut themselves away with Rebecca. The others gathered in the long room next door. There was nothing to be done now but wait. Thunder continued to rumble over the mountains.

A chuckling Mavreen joined Agatha in front of the fire where she was setting a kettle of water to boil. "Lord love us," she murmured, drawing her attention to Cooper, "would ya just look at the man. Ya'd think he was the expectant father hisself, now wouldn't ya?"

Agatha had to agree that Cooper was in a bad way. Wearing a distracted expression, he paced the length of the cabin, pausing every few minutes to eye the closed door of the delivery room while tugging at his hair. His condition worsened when moans of pain reached them from the other side of the door.

"How long is this going to take?" he demanded.

"Babies do not come into the world easily," Agatha explained.

He resumed his pacing, clutching at himself in sympathetic agony when the moans became punctuated by shrieks.

"She's suffering," he complained. "Should she be suffering this bad?"

"Rebecca is a healthy young woman," Agatha assured him. "She will manage."

It was Cooper who wasn't managing. He groaned in misery as Rebecca's labor intensified.

"We ought to be doing something," he insisted. "Shouldn't we be doing something?"

Agatha decided he was right. It was time to do something. She had already sent Callie into the yard with the dogs. Now she had to get rid of Cooper before his nervous turmoil drove all of them into fits of hysteria.

"Wood," she said. "We need wood for the fire. We must keep the kettle boiling."

Cooper went after wood. When he returned, she sent him back for more. He fussed about it after the third load.

"That's a lot of wood. A lot of boiling water."

"Necessary," she maintained. "Births require a great deal of hot water. And we must have a dependable supply of dry firewood before it rains. Fresh water as well."

Out he went again to hunt for further wood and to bring water from the stream.

Mavreen giggled over her ruse. "Me soul t'God, he believes ya."

Agatha nodded. "Fortunately, there are occasions when men can be as innocent as babes." And as endearing, she thought wistfully as she glimpsed his rangy figure through the window heading with determination toward the gate.

Henrietta appeared from the delivery room to secure fresh towels. Her black face wore a look of concern when Agatha went to consult with her.

"The baby doesn't want to come," she admitted.

"Rebecca?"

"She's strong, but it's hard on her. We'll do our best."

Henrietta returned to the delivery room. Agatha turned around to find Magpie standing there. There was a solemn expression in her dark eyes.

"I heard, missis. This is a difficult birth."

"Yes."

"Rebecca needs help. I know of a way to ease her labor. A medicine used by my people. The inner bark of a fir tree

240

is mixed with tobacco leaves. The mother inhales the aroma from this without harm to her or the child, and it speeds the birth. I have seen this work myself many times.''

''What are you proposing, Magpie?''

''Emmie Jo has tobacco leaves. I have seen her chew them. We need only the bark of this certain fir tree. Let me go out there on the hill behind the fort, missis, and I will find it.''

Agatha considered the slim young woman, understanding her earnest appeal. Magpie had been a virtual outcast since Ft. Laramie, tolerated by the other women but no longer warmly befriended by them since her treachery with Jack Salter. She had never complained of her treatment or tried to leave them. Agatha, thinking sometimes that it had been a mistake forcing her to accompany them, had wondered why. Now she knew. Magpie didn't want Jack Salter. She wanted to be accepted by the women. She wanted to be one of them again, and going out on that hillside would demonstrate her loyalty.

Agatha made up her mind. ''Very well, Magpie, we will try your concoction, but do be careful out there.''

Magpie wasn't gone more than five minutes, basket in hand, when Agatha began to regret her decision. In her anxiety over Rebecca, she had forgotten one of Cooper's cardinal rules. No one was ever to leave camp without at least one companion. And though Magpie might be at home in the wilderness, there was a storm brewing in the mountains. The situation made her uneasy.

After a quick word with Susan, Agatha snatched up a shawl and left the cabin. It was already early September, and the air at this altitude was cool. Drawing the shawl around her shoulders, she crossed the compound. Callie was romping with the dogs just outside the gates.

''Callie, did you see which way Magpie went?''

''Yep, up there.'' She pointed to the slope studded with dark evergreens behind the fort.

## Jean Barrett

After sending the child back into the safety of the compound, Agatha started up the hill. Cooper was nowhere in sight, but she could hear him chopping wood down in the direction of the stream. Thunder still growled over the mountains where the sky had darkened like a purple bruise, but there was no rain as yet. The air was ominously still.

Agatha scanned the tall spires of the evergreens on the brow of the hill, but there was no sign yet of Magpie. She called to her as she climbed. No answer. She was worried long before she reached the first evergreens. Passing through their ranks, she neared a clearing in a shallow bowl on the side of the hill. Her heart stopped as she stepped into the open and saw the overturned basket lying in the thin grass, its contents scattered.

Agatha was reaching for the basket when a rough voice commanded, "Leave it where it is."

Startled, she straightened and looked across the clearing where two men had emerged from the trees. One of them was Jack Salter. The other, holding a terrified Magpie in front of him, was a chilling brute with a cheek slashed by a long, puckered scar. He had the blade of an ugly knife pressed to Magpie's throat.

Agatha was in no position to argue with them, but she did just that in an outraged voice. "How dare you! Release her at once!"

"Missis, no," Magpie started to warn her.

"Shut your mouth," her captor ordered, squeezing the knife until it drew a drop of blood at Magpie's throat.

Agatha gasped, hugging the shawl around her in cold fear. "It is not necessary to hurt her. Tell me what you want."

He grinned at her vilely. "That's better. I'll let her go. All you got to do is agree to a little trade."

The strongbox, Agatha thought. They wanted the strongbox, of course. It amazed her that Jack Salter and his companion would have pursued them all this distance for the sake of the box. They must have convinced themselves it contained a fortune, which it did not.

"What do you wish?" she asked them.

"You," he said, jolting her with his answer.

"But—"

"You don't have to understand it," he snarled. "It's either a deal, or it isn't."

"It isn't," came a voice like steel from off to the side.

The four occupants of the clearing swung their astonished gazes in that direction. Cooper stood above them on the rim of the bowl, his rifle raised to his shoulder. Agatha had never seen a more splendid sight.

"Don't try it," he drawled as Jack's hand started to inch toward the gun at his hip. "I'd have your head blown off your shoulders before you ever touched metal."

Jack looked helplessly at his brother. "Told you we shouldn't have left camp and sneaked all the way over here without the others."

"Don't be a damn fool! We've got the girl here as a shield, and he's only one gun, ain't he?"

"Wrong," came another hard voice, this time from the rim on the opposite side of the hollow. There was the click of a weapon being cocked as they turned in that direction to find Susan with her rifle trained on them.

"Hell, Salter," Cooper informed him, "she's even a better shot than I am. Face it, you're covered and without a choice. Now let the girl go and step back nice and easy, both of you."

Duke hesitated for a moment. Then, with a savage oath, he released Magpie and backed away slowly, Jack beside him.

"Far enough," Cooper ordered. "Magpie, get out of there."

The girl flew across the clearing to Agatha's side.

"Good," Cooper said. "Now let's move on to a little roundup and maybe a nice friendly chat."

He and Susan prepared to close in on the brothers. But

before they could descend into the hollow, the storm that had been gathering struck the hillside with a violent suddenness. The air that had been still in one second was in the next instant a wild wind sweeping down over the clearing, so powerful in its velocity that it raised a blizzard of dust.

For a moment Agatha was blinded. The rain came behind the dust, torrents of it. When she could see again through the slashing stuff, the opposite side of the clearing was empty. The Salter brothers had seized the opportunity to vanish into the trees.

Cooper was suddenly beside her, shouting an aggravated, "Lucky bastards got away! No sense in trying to go after them in this. Let's get ourselves back to the fort as fast as we can!"

The four of them scrambled down the hillside through the sheets of stinging rain. Once they reached the shelter of the stockade, Cooper lost no time in making the place safe. The gates were dragged shut and barred and women posted in the towers with rifles.

Then, with the light rapidly fading and the rain beating on the roof of the log structure, he confronted a shivering Magpie huddled in front of the snapping fire. "All right," he demanded, his tone severe, "it's time for a few particulars. What's Duke Salter doing here, and what's this really all about?"

Agatha tried to intervene. "She is drenched. Let her get dry first."

"We're all soaked. She can change afterwards. Right now we need the truth out of her." He thrust his face close to Magpie's. "Talk!"

She glanced nervously at the company of women gathered around the fireplace. They waited with suspicious expressions to hear her explanation. Agatha nodded encouragement when their gazes met. Magpie began to speak in a low, remorseful voice.

"Pacific Fur wishes to keep families out of Oregon. They

say if women and children come to settle, they will spoil the fur trade. The company has promised Duke much wealth if he can secretly stop the wagon trains like yours.''

She went on to tell them how she, and later Jack, had schemed their way into the train and of the efforts to turn the women back. Agatha understood now why this afternoon Duke Salter had tried to capture her. She would have made a much better hostage than the strongbox. He would have been in a position to demand the halt of the train.

''Why didn't I see it before?'' Cooper muttered. ''It's the explanation for everything that's been happening to us. Damn it all to hell, we've been fools, and I was the biggest one.''

''Please,'' Magpie whispered, appealing to the stunned and angry faces on all sides, ''I never wanted to hurt any of you, especially after you were kind to me, but I had no choice. Duke made me.''

''He ain't been around lately to make you do anything,'' Lettice observed tartly. ''You're so sorry, then why didn't you tell us all this weeks ago?''

Magpie shook her head. ''I dared not. Even speaking the truth now, when I can no longer help it, is very dangerous. If he learns I have told you . . .'' She closed her eyes and shuddered.

Agatha went to her, taking her hands and squeezing them reassuringly. ''He cannot touch you here, Magpie,'' she said gently. ''You are safe with us.''

The young woman opened her eyes and stared at her. ''You think I am afraid for myself?'' she whispered fiercely. ''You understand nothing. Never have I been afraid for myself.''

''Then why . . . ?''

Magpie turned her head to gaze at the others. They were all watching her expectantly. When she looked back, Agatha read anguish in her dark eyes. She had never seen an ache so wrenching.

# Jean Barrett

"Daniel," she said. "Everything I have done was for Daniel."

"Are you telling us . . . ?"

"He is my child. He is three years old, and Duke has him. He promises me Daniel is safe and with people who are caring for him, but he will not say where that is. If I obey Duke and do as he says, I can have Daniel back. If I do not, I will never see him again."

"Oh, dear God," Agatha murmured, expressing the shock and outrage felt by all of them.

"How did he ever get hold of the boy?" Cooper asked.

Magpie stared at him as if he should have already known a truth that was so simple. "He did not have to take what was already his. Daniel is his son."

Agatha couldn't bear it. Duke Salter was more than just a vicious brute. He was genuinely evil. She was still grasping Magpie's hands. Now she knelt down in front of her so that their faces were on the same level.

"Are you married to this man?"

"We are not husband and wife."

"Then he has no right to keep Daniel from you, even if he is his father. Listen to me, Magpie. Whatever it takes," she pledged earnestly, "I will see to it that you and Daniel are reunited. I will not give up until you are together again."

Magpie nodded slowly, but Agatha wasn't certain whether she completely understood or believed her promise. Before she could expand on it, Cooper caught her eye. With a slight nod of his head, he indicated his need to speak to her privately at the other end of the room.

"She tells a good story," he said in an undertone when Agatha joined him, "but how do we know we can trust her?"

"Are you forgetting how she looked when she first came to us? Those bruises were not an invention. She had been mistreated. Now I understand who and why."

"All right, Aggie, don't get all worked up because I don't happen to share your pure faith in every hard luck case that

246

comes down the trail. All I'm saying is, if Salter was so bad to her, why did she hang around him long enough to have his baby?''

She shook her head. ''There is never an easy explanation for women like Magpie. But this much I can tell you. Incredible though it seems, such women are convinced they deserve the abuse they receive from the men they are with and therefore tolerate it. I know. I met enough women like this through my efforts. Some I was able to help. Many I was not able to help. I am praying Magpie will be one of the fortunate ones.''

Cooper nodded. ''We believe her then. Which puts us in a tough position, with Salter after our necks. Way I figure it, he can't have much of a force with him or he would have wiped us out long before this. He's one mean animal, though, so sooner or later he's bound to try something else to stop us.''

''Then we shall exercise every precaution,'' she said urgently. ''We cannot let this devil defeat us. Not when we have come so far and sacrificed so much. We *must* get through.''

''Amen, Aggie.'' He cast a frustrated glance in the direction of the closed door to the room where Rebecca was still in labor. ''I just wish that baby would get born so we can leave this miserable place.''

But it wasn't until late evening that Rebecca delivered her child. Cooper was frantic by then, and when a tired Henrietta finally emerged from the borning room, he surged to his feet and asked anxiously, ''Is she . . . ?''

''It's all over,'' Henrietta reported. Then she beamed at them. ''She's exhausted, but both she and the baby will be fine. Rebecca has a healthy son.''

''A boy?'' Cooper looked gleeful. ''Well, hallelujah, I'm no longer the only male in this caravan.''

Callie, who had been napping with the dogs in the corner,

lifted her head with an accusing, "No fair. Romeo is a boy, ain't he?"

"You're right, urchin. I forgot that. Shall I apologize to him?"

"After you've seen Rebecca," Henrietta instructed.

"Me? What for?"

"She'll tell you. But you don't stay more than a minute, hear? That gal needs a long rest."

Mystified, he accompanied her into the adjoining room. The women crowded to the doorway behind him, eager for a glimpse of the baby nestled beside its mother. Agatha, watching Cooper crouch beside the narrow bed, could tell how clumsy he was suddenly feeling.

Rebecca smiled at him weakly from her pillow. "I want to name him after you, Mr. Delaney. I want to call him Cooper."

"Oh, Lord. Are you sure you want to do a thing like that to this poor mite?"

"Never surer 'bout anything. It's a good name, Mr. Delaney. You've showed us that all right."

"If he will tell you what the J represents, Rebecca," Agatha teased behind him, "then you will have a middle name for your son as well."

"I don't think so," he said with gruff haste. "It's enough to saddle him with Cooper."

"Wouldn't you like to hold your namesake?" Faye suggested as he rose to his feet.

Before he could object, Faye scooped up the bundled baby and placed him in Cooper's arms. Agatha experienced a tightening in her throat as she watched the big, rugged man gaze with awkward, tender wonder at the tiny sleeping child in his arms.

Fantasies were treacherous, yearnings positively dangerous. She couldn't help herself. The sight of Cooper Delaney with Rebecca's baby conjured up an image of him as a loving father. Worse, she had to go and imagine him as the father of *her* baby.

# *Chapter Fourteen*

Duke pressed the spyglass to his eye and searched for his prey. From the vantage point of the high ridge where he and Jack were stationed, he had a sweeping view of the broad valley that stretched out below them in the heart of the Blue Mountains. The trail curled across the floor of the valley as it approached the main pass through the higher peaks.

At first Duke couldn't locate his target, though he knew it had to be out there somewhere. He and his small band had been tracking the column of wagons for days now, maintaining a cautious distance since the episode at the abandoned fort but carefully observing the progress of the women.

Duke could read all the signs of their concern. They knew now that they had a serious enemy pursuing them. That there was no law in this wilderness to protect them and that they could rely on nothing but themselves. That was why they traveled with as much nervous haste as possible, Delaney constantly urging them forward and keeping every available woman armed night and day. There was never a moment when they weren't tensely vigilant.

But Duke had an ally in the weather. The nights were cold by now, and the aspens had already turned to a blaze of gold. Delaney had to be worried about this, and with good reason. The wagon train had lost precious time, and if there was any further delay they risked life-threatening snowfalls at this altitude. Duke was counting on all this to help him.

"Ain't you spotted 'em yet?" Jack asked impatiently.

"Have now," he grunted as the distant column emerged from behind a wooded rise. He watched hopefully as the wagons reached a fork in the trail. They paused momentarily while Duke waited anxiously. When they swung off finally into the left branch, he chuckled in satisfaction. He had anticipated correctly. Delaney had just handed him the opportunity he'd been waiting for.

"What?" Jack demanded.

"See for yourself." He passed the spyglass to his brother.

Jack looked, muttering derisively, "Delaney's crazy. He's taking 'em off the main trail. Hell, that's a murderous route to choose."

"Yeah, but it's the quickest way through the Blues, save 'em days over the other way around. And right now time is more important to Delaney than a tough trail. He's figurin' how he needs to get those women out of the mountains."

Jack lowered the glass and stared at his brother. "You're grinnin' about Delaney's decision. How come?"

"Because we're takin' our own shortcut, little brother. Delaney might know this country, but I know it even better. Gonna use a path even faster than theirs where wagons can't go, but our horses can. It'll mean some hard ridin', but I aim to get around and ahead of that train with time to spare."

"Then what?"

"Then we arrange a little surprise for when they arrive. Somethin' that's gonna separate Delaney from the others. Once he's out of the way, *permanently* out of the way, we can take those women. We'll need to go up to the Trelawney diggin's when we get there, but that's easy enough."

Duke swung his head, looking for his men who were waiting with the horses behind the ridge. "Where's that little Mex, Diego? Get 'im up here for me, Jack. With the experience that mole's had with black powder, he's gonna be mighty valuable to us today."

"He's back there in the trees with the others. Probably grumblin' with the rest 'cause we've come so far and there ain't been no rewards yet."

"Yeah? Well, a couple of 'em are gonna grumble even more when I leave 'em behind."

"Why's that?"

"Because that wagon train knows we're back here, and I want it to go on thinkin' that's just where *all* of us are keepin'. Smoke from a cooking fire should do the trick, and maybe showin' themselves a bit on their horses. All right, little brother, shake a leg. An' you can tell Diego and the others that by tonight there's gonna be rewards." He smiled in sadistic anticipation. "*Plenty* of rewards."

Jack, still puzzled by Duke's intention, hurried down the slope to summon Diego.

Agatha made every effort to maintain her faith in Cooper's decision as she carefully guided her oxen team along the narrow track. He knows what he is doing, she kept telling herself. This *is* the right choice.

Considering the hazardous passage they were negotiating, her confidence in him was undergoing a supreme test. Directly to the right rose the sheer, tremendous bulk of a lofty canyon wall. On the left was a sickening drop to a roaring stream far below.

Agatha knew the other women were as nervous about this route as she was. None of them spoke, making the silence in this closed, torturous place absolutely eerie. They had every right to be worried, knowing that Duke Salter and his band were somewhere behind them. If anything happened, they could be trapped in the canyon.

# Jean Barrett

Salter's presence was infuriating, she thought, making their struggle on the trail even more of an ordeal these last few weeks. Every hour of every day had demanded an uneasy vigilance. At any moment and from any direction he could strike. Worse, the viper had cost her dearly where Cooper was concerned.

There were no precious intervals of lovemaking for them now. Cooper was entirely focused on their safety. Agatha understood, but she missed him.

*Trust him*, she reminded herself. He is not the Cooper he was before Ft. Laramie. He is nearly as possessive and protective about the women now as you are. He would not risk us needlessly.

The formidable Blues were their last real barrier. Once these terrible mountains were behind them, their destination would be within easy reach. And then, she promised herself with a hopeful glow inside her, then . . .

Cooper's sudden shout from the front of the column reverberated through the canyon. "Hold 'em up back there . . . up back there . . . back there . . ."

Something is wrong, Agatha thought as his echo died away and the wagons came obediently to a stop. Mounted on Bucephalus, he had been scouting the trail ahead of them. Now he was back, and she wanted to know why.

Leaving her position in the middle of the train, she hurried forward. Several of the more curious women joined her. The others stayed back, guarding the wagons and teams.

"What is it?" she asked when she reached the head of the column where he was waiting for them on his big roan. "A problem?"

"Oh, yeah," he said, looking grim. "Come on, I'll show you."

Turning Bucephalus, he led them a short distance up the trail. They rounded a massive shoulder of rock where the cliff loomed above them. There was a gap in the steep wall on the other side. It opened out into a side canyon that was broad enough to support trees and grass and a pool of water.

It was beyond the gap, where the track curved again on its ledge, that the problem existed. There had been a recent landslide. A large mass of rock blocked the trail.

"No way around it, and no hope of movin' it," Tessa observed glumly.

"The side canyon," Agatha suggested.

"A dead end," Cooper reported, sliding from his horse.

"Regrettable, but at least it will permit us to turn the wagons. It seems we have no choice but to return to the main trail and the longer route through the mountains." It was a prospect she didn't relish, considering that Duke Salter and his band might be waiting for them when they emerged from the canyon.

"Always the alternative, of course," Cooper drawled.

"Is there one?"

"Think so. See how that pile is situated?" He indicated the landslide. "The ledge there is undercut, nothing more than a shelf of rock. We blow out that shelf from underneath, and the whole pile goes tumbling into the gorge."

"Splendid, except the trail at that point would be carried with it."

"So we lay a bridge over the break. There's enough timber in that side canyon and the oxen to drag the logs. It'll take some time and muscle, but nowhere near what it would cost us to cover the other route."

"Agreed. I see only one slight difficulty."

"What's that, Aggie?"

"How do we blast away your landslide? I believe such an effort requires explosives."

"Believe you're right, Aggie." He was looking exasperatingly sly again.

She nodded slowly. "And you are about to tell us exactly where to obtain explosives."

"Sure am. Remember that track that left this one about a half mile back?"

"I do. It winds up onto the mountain, does it not?"

"That's right."

"And how will that benefit us?"

"Because it leads to a gold-mining operation up there belonging to the Trelawney brothers. Couple of tough little Cornishmen who are crazy enough to think that, if they dig deep enough into that mountain, they're bound to strike a bonanza. Maybe they will. Point is, they keep a large supply of black powder."

"Excellent. Then let us acquire an amount sufficient for our purpose."

Within minutes the entire wagon train had swung into the side canyon and formed its protective circle. The women underwent the familiar ritual of establishing a camp, some of them turning the stock loose to water and graze, others swarming over the lightest of the wagons. Unloading its contents, they stripped the schooner down to the bare, open bed that would carry the kegs of black powder. Cooper, considering the oxen too slow for this purpose, selected a pair of horses from the few that traveled with them.

He had the animals hitched to the wagon and was prepared to clamber onto the seat when he noticed that Agatha was perched behind the lines.

"Where do you think you're going?"

"I am accompanying you, of course."

"I'm traveling alone on this one, Aggie. You forget how unfriendly the climate's become outside this canyon?"

"I have not forgotten. It is all the more reason why you should not be on your own. May I remind you of your own rigid rule? None of us is to leave camp without at least one companion."

"But that rule—"

"Applies to *all* of us. And we are wasting precious time with an argument I have no intention of surrendering."

"Aggie?"

"Yes?"

"You are going to make one hell of a teacher in that school you're planning to build in Oregon. There won't be an urchin who dares to cross you. Move over. I'll drive."

The strongest women were already busy cutting trees for the bridge when they left the camp. Susan and several others were mounting guard at the vulnerable mouth of the canyon. Agatha's last glimpse before they turned the corner was of Rebecca seated in the shade of a pine nursing her baby.

They were climbing the rutted mountain trail when Agatha remembered that Cooper had survived his early manhood with a number of occupations, including mining.

"Just how experienced are you with explosives?"

"Enough. Not that I'm anything like a seasoned miner. Too big for hard-rock mining. You have to be built like the Trelawneys to be at home in those shafts."

"I hope the brothers will agree to part with a load of their black powder."

Cooper chuckled. "They won't know anything about it, Aggie. They get out of there by the first of September. Winter's too hard on the mountain."

"Does this mean we will help ourselves to their supplies?"

"That's just what it means. Don't worry. They'll be at Ft. Vancouver, and we can settle up with them there."

Minutes later the wagon crested a rise and rolled into a flat clearing that was like an aerie clinging to the side of the mountain. The place was deserted. There was a curious stone platform off to one side of the clearing. Cooper noticed Agatha eyeing it as they descended from the wagon.

"An arrastra," he explained. "It's where the ore gets pulverized. And that's only the first stage of separating out any gold that might be in it. Dross gets shoved down there."

He indicated a gully where huge loads of the waste materials had been dumped. Agatha, following him as he headed toward a crude shack, was beginning to appreciate the enormous amounts of labor required to harvest precious minerals from the earth.

There was no sign of the kegs of black powder they needed when they entered the shack. Cooper registered her disappointment as he helped himself to a pair of mining lamps with tin reflectors from the clutter of supplies.

"The stuff is here," he assured her. "They would have moved it into one of the tunnels before they pulled out for the season. The snow on the mountain is heavy enough to collapse roofs, but in the mine the powder keeps safe and dry through the winter."

Armed with the lamps, Cooper led the way to the mouth of the mine in the vertical rock wall that rose from the side of the clearing. An ore car known as a giraffe was parked inside the opening.

"Too bad the Trelawneys took their burros with them," he said as he lighted the candles inside the lamps, which he placed in sockets on the giraffe. "Means hauling the loads by hand."

"We can manage the cart between us," she said.

"*Me*, Aggie, not you. You," he instructed, "will wait out here. And keep your gun handy. No reason for any trouble up here, but we'll take no chances, thank you."

He was less than two hundred feet along the main tunnel cut horizontally into the mountain, pushing the rumbling giraffe in front of him, when one of its wheels caught on something. Before he could investigate, a voice from the shadows was telling him coolly, "A chunk of rock, I think. Yes. Just let me remove it."

Cooper looked down to see Agatha shifting the stone away from the wheel. She had been right behind him the whole time.

"When are you going to follow orders?"

"When they make sense," she said. "My waiting outside did not make sense. I am much more useful in here. Now, which way to the black powder?"

Damn if she hadn't overridden him again. Now she was standing there calmly regarding the selection of passageways that, at this point, struck off in several directions from the main corridor.

"Like spokes radiating from a wheel, are they not?" she observed.

"It's called coyoting. And since you know best, you choose."

"That one, I think."

Leaving the giraffe, they took the lamps and investigated her choice. The tunnel ended in a blank wall about twenty-five yards into the mountain. Retracing their steps, they began exploring the other drifts. All of them were dead ends, and none of them yielded the black powder.

Agatha voiced no complaint as she followed Cooper, bending her head to avoid the shoring timbers, but she was not happy in the mine. The flickering light of the candles emphasized the somber, Hades-like atmosphere of the place. She had once read that rats were known to infest mines. The idea made her nervous, even though she detected no suspicious scurrying.

She distracted herself with the discovery of flecks of glittering material on a pillar of rock. "Gold?" she asked in awe.

"It's never that easy, Aggie. You're looking at yellow pyrite. Worthless in itself, but its presence does indicate the possibility of gold. It's why the Trelawneys are working this mountain. All right, this is the last tunnel. It *would* be the last one where the stuff is stowed."

He was so certain the black powder would be here. She hoped he was right.

The passageway turned, widened and ended in another blank wall. But this time, much to Agatha's joy, the tunnel was not empty. At its broad termination were stacked the kegs of black powder.

"Not as big a supply as I hoped," Cooper said, removing

a duck covering that had been placed on top of the stack to protect it from any possible moisture from the ceiling. "We'll have to take most of it and make it right with the Trelawneys before next spring."

Fetching the giraffe, they began shifting the kegs. They wheeled out two loads, transferring the casks to the wagon.

"One more should do it," Cooper said.

Agatha was relieved. She would be glad to put the mine with its perilous associations behind her. The wheels on the car were squeaking by the time they reached the diminished store of powder at the end of the tunnel.

"Better oil 'em up for the last load," Cooper said.

He was reaching for the grease bucket hooked on the lower end of the giraffe when thunder rumbled and the mountain shuddered. At least it sounded like the boom of thunder to the startled Agatha. Cooper knew better. With a shout of warning, he launched himself toward her, dragging her to the floor and covering her protectively with his body.

Seconds later, on the heels of grinding rock and shattered timber off in the distance, came a rush of violent air blasting through the tunnel. It was followed almost immediately by a thick, terrible stillness.

"You all right?" Cooper asked, lifting himself away from her.

The sound of his voice was intensified by the awful silence.

"Yes," she murmured, sitting up. "Was—was it a cave-in?"

He didn't answer her. There was a grim expression on his face. She watched him as he got to his feet and checked the lamps. One of them had been blown out. The other candle inside its glass screen continued to burn with a feeble, but welcome, glow.

"Let's hope it was in one of the other side tunnels," he said, seizing the lamp and heading toward the main corridor. Agatha followed close behind him, her heart beating with the hope that the outside entrance was not blocked.

Their worst fears were confirmed as they swung into what was left of the main passage. The air here was heavy with choking dust that had yet to settle. But even with the veil of dust and the weak gleam of the lamp, Agatha could see the obvious. Tons of rock had collapsed from the ceiling, sealing off the only entrance to the mine. There was not a glimmer of light from the outside.

Cooper handed the lamp to her and, without a word, scrambled up the slope of tumbled rocks. Praying that nothing else would give way, she anxiously watched him as he pressed himself against the ceiling, searching for a hint of daylight.

He was back in seconds. "Nothing. It's solid rock."

"Can we not dig through it?"

"I wish we could, Aggie, but I estimate there's at least a hundred feet of stone between here and the entrance."

He hadn't softened the truth, knowing she wouldn't have wanted that. But it was not easy to deal with the jolting realization that they were trapped in this oppressive place. Panic started to claw at her. She resisted it, struggling to remain calm.

"The women," she said. "They have tools and many hands. When we fail to return, they will not hesitate to . . ." She didn't finish. She started to cough on the drifting dust.

"Let's get out of here," Cooper urged, "before we strangle on the stuff or something else comes down."

He took the lamp from her and guided her back to the end of the side tunnel where they had left the giraffe. The air here was much cleaner, the walls and ceiling still safe. Agatha suddenly felt weak in the knees.

"Sit," he instructed her, spreading the duck covering on the floor.

She didn't argue with him. She settled gratefully on the cloth. Cooper, carefully returning the lamp to its socket on the car, dropped beside her. They were silent for several moments, each of them dealing with the bleakness of their situation. The fluttering glow from the single candle was so frail in the blackness that Agatha longed for the second lamp. But she didn't ask Cooper to relight it, knowing how precious it was now and that it must be saved for later.

He had his knees hugged up to his chest, arms clasped around them as he rocked slowly. She could almost hear his mind at work.

"I think I've been the biggest fool in the territory," he said abruptly.

"Why is that, my love?" she questioned him, her voice oddly gentle in the circumstances.

"Because I'm convinced that cave-in was no accident, Aggie. It was the result of a blast. A *deliberate* blast. Guess we both know who and why."

"Duke Salter?"

"Had to be. I should have realized the bastard was just waiting to make his move. He and his men must have somehow sneaked in here ahead of us and raided the powder supply, set the charges and then laid by for the right moment to trigger them. I've been careless, Aggie."

"You could not have known," she assured him.

"But I should have suspected something when we were blocked by the landslide."

She nodded, understanding it. "Yes, I see. The landslide was, of course, not a natural disaster either."

"All a trap, and I fell into it like a greenhorn. *Damn.*" He slapped his knee in frustration.

She placed a consoling hand on his arm, hating to see him berate himself for something that couldn't be helped. He put his own hand over hers, stroking her fingers.

"Our chances aren't too good, Aggie."

"I know, my love," she said softly.

He was telling her there was no escape for them. Duke Salter had been very thorough in his obliteration of the exit, burying them behind masses of debris. Even if the women did come, and were somehow able to remove the vast quantities of rock, there was little hope that they would reach them in time.

"Could not the remaining black powder here help us?" she wondered.

Cooper shook his head. "Not enough of it left in here to budge that much rock. The cave-in is far too deep. It would only bring down more ceiling."

"I thought as much, but it did seem to be a possibility."

Agatha was silent, her mind turning again to the women. They were entirely on their own now and at Duke Salter's mercy. She tried to tell herself that the canyon where they were camped was like a fortress and that they were capable of defending themselves. But she worried about them just the same, useless though it was.

Cooper must have sensed her deep concern, must have believed she was sick with alarm over their own plight. That was why he tried to help her with his own unique method of comfort. Why, hunching closer, he suddenly began to sing his familiar song to her in a low, soothing baritone.

" 'If a body meet a body, Comin' thro' the rye—If a body kiss a body, Need a body cry? Ev'ry laddie has his lassie . . . ' "

It was insane. They were trapped in the bowels of this mountain facing death, and Cooper Delaney was serenading her. It was insane, and she loved him for it.

She turned to him when he finished the song. "Thank you."

"Welcome."

There was a pause, and then she asked him gravely, "May I request another favor?"

"What's that, Aggie?"

"Will you hold me, please?"

"My pleasure."

His arms slid around her, drawing her against his solid chest. She cradled her head under his chin, savoring the

261

warmth and strength of him. The long minutes slid by, and she thought about this strangely peaceful and wonderful intimacy they were sharing while they waited for—No, she would not name it, not as long as there remained a vestige of hope.

Cooper had begun to softly whistle his song again. He went on for a moment. Then he abruptly stopped, and in a voice husky with need, he suggested an impulsive, "Let's make love."

Astonished, Agatha lifted her head from his chest and stared at him. He was serious. Death threatened them, and all the man could think about was sex.

He even had the effrontery to sound casual about it. "Come on, Aggie. Gotta pass the time somehow until we can figure a way out of here."

She didn't answer him. She searched his face, looking beyond the eager grin on his wide, sensual mouth. It was in his eyes, with their expression of urgency that he couldn't hide, where she read the truth. He wasn't fooling her now. He was convinced there was no way out of here. That was why he wanted her, and longed for her to want him, because all the odds were against them. Because this would be their last precious time together. She couldn't deny him, couldn't deny herself.

"The conditions," she teased, fearing a tearful emotion, "are scarcely appropriate."

"When have they ever been for us, Aggie?"

"True, my love." She lifted her hands to frame his rugged, appealing face. "Very true."

Drawing his face down to hers, she kissed him slowly, tantalizingly. His mouth, clinging to hers and impatient with her delay, deepened the kiss, his tongue seeking hers with a wet, searing desperation.

He groaned with both passion and complaint when his mouth finally parted from hers. "Been a long while, Aggie."

"A matter of a few weeks, I believe."

"No wonder this is killing me. Uh, will you be too cold if we—"

"Remove our clothes? I think not. I have every faith you will keep me warm."

"Count on it. And, Aggie?"

"Yes?"

"Could you please hurry?"

Rising, she obliged him with the swift removal of her garments. He shucked his own clothing with a speed that outmatched hers and was waiting for her, supporting himself on his parted knees, when she emerged from the last of her underthings.

Agatha gazed at him. She never ceased to marvel at the sight of his naked warrior's body with its brawny arms and legs, its broad chest darkened with a pelt of hair that arrowed to a flat belly and an arousal below it that was already thickly engorged. His hardness, wearing a provocative sheen in the golden glow of the single candle, made her weak.

"C'mere," he commanded, his voice raspy with desire.

And she went to him, permitting him to draw her down onto her own knees so that they were facing each other, flesh to raw flesh.

His arms went around her, clasping her to his robust length. He began to kiss her, long kisses that were lingering and reverent at first, interspaced with loving murmurs, and then became as sultry and demanding as his smoldering green eyes.

His head dipped lower, seeking the lushness of her breasts. "Like sweet cream," he whispered. And his mouth closed in turn over each of her breasts, his slick tongue tugging at her rigid peaks.

Mewing with pleasure, Agatha could no longer remain upright. She tipped over onto the cloth, drawing Cooper with her. He collapsed beside her, chuckling over her surrender.

"What happened to all that Pennington self-control?" he taunted her.

"Being male, *superior* male, you are, of course, immune to such torment. Is that what you are telling me, my love?"

"Try me."

"I accept the challenge." She lifted herself, hovering over him. "I believe this is the area under consideration."

Swooping down on his chest, the tip of her tongue found one of his flat nipples. She circled it slowly before drawing it into her mouth.

"Nothing, Aggie," he insisted, choking on the words.

"No? Then perhaps I should try here."

Her tongue moved lower, licking down across his belly through the whorls of hair, nuzzling and tasting his navel. He was emitting deep animal sounds now, but he refused to be conquered.

"Not—not a chance," he muttered, squeezing out each syllable with difficulty.

"How disappointing. I wonder then what this will produce."

Her hand traveled to the juncture of his thighs, gently fondling his thrusting shaft. Cooper, sucking in air, squirmed in misery.

"No effect there either?" she wondered.

He seized the hand that punished him, signaling her victory. "I just bet," he growled, "you were one of those sadistic little girls who tickled a victim until he howled for mercy."

"I was," she boasted.

"Then this is for all those poor urchins you cruelly abused."

Before she could stop him, he dragged her into a fierce embrace. His mouth and hands were all over her with hot caresses and plundering kisses. Agatha, unable to breathe under his assault, found herself trapped beneath his raging body, her hands pinned above her head.

A plea for release was on her lips when Cooper, levered

over her, suddenly went still. His laughter faded as his eyes, solemn now, searched hers.

"You know we're crazy, don't you?" he said. "Behaving like this when—"

"Does it matter?"

"No," he said slowly. "No, I guess it doesn't."

There was a moment of silence in which she was aware of his position. He was settled between her parted thighs. She could feel his swollen arousal poised for entry and knew that he, too, was conscious of their readiness.

His hardness began to stir, the head of his shaft teasing the sensitive petals at the mouth of her womanhood, opening her vessel but resisting the connection she yearned for. Agatha struggled to free her hands, needing to wrap her arms and legs around him, to strain him into a full joining. But Cooper refused to let her go.

She was wild with frustration when he finally accommodated her. With a swiftness that made her gasp, he buried himself inside her tight, wet sheath in one deep, blazing thrust.

"Oh, Aggie," he moaned. "No more games. I can't play any more games. I have to . . ."

His body told her the rest as he began to move inside her. Writhing beneath him, limbs free at last to hold him close, she responded with her own primordial rhythms. Slow and tender at first, rich with meaning. Then a tempo that mounted, demanding a fusion forged in a crucible of molten passion.

Relief from the frenzy came for them almost simultaneously in an awesome, blinding release that tumbled them into a sweet oblivion.

When the spasms had subsided, Agatha found herself savoring a union that had been almost spiritual in its intensity. Could lovemaking be like that? Actually bear a kind of healing power?

Cooper must have felt it, too. He was nestled beside her

now, having drawn her shawl across both of them. She could actually feel him struggling to express himself. He overwhelmed her with his declaration.

"I'm not sure I even know what it's supposed to be, Aggie. But this must be love I'm feeling. It has to be. I'm in love with you, and what a hell of a time for me to be telling you."

"No, there is never a bad time for that. I feel it, too, for you. The same love."

How could she tell him what his confession meant to her, that to have heard his words was almost worth dying for?

"That's good, Aggie," he whispered, his arms tightening around her. "Whatever comes, that's good . . ."

His voice trailed away. They were silent again. Agatha went on treasuring his admission, resenting the hateful little voice that asked: Did he mean those wonderful words? Or had he spoken them only to please her, because if they weren't going to survive this place it wouldn't matter what was said?

She didn't know. And she wanted desperately to know. Needed to learn whether it was possible that Cooper Delaney could actually be in love with the woman she had always thought undesirable to men. Agatha sighed. It was never easy to rid oneself of the harsh lessons of girlhood.

She was prepared to risk it and ask him. But her question would have to wait. Cooper was already asleep, exhausted from their long ordeal. She felt drained as well, unable to deal with their situation. Snug in his arms, she closed her eyes.

The candle, less than a stub now, sputtered out just as she drifted off.

# *Chapter Fifteen*

A crescent moon rode high in the night sky above the chasm, lighting a path for Magpie as she silently made her way to the back of the canyon. Unable to sleep, she welcomed her errand while regretting the necessity for it.

Yvonne, the pretty little coquette who talked so often of the New Orleans she was homesick for, was down with a fever. Henrietta and Faye, who were nursing her, had sent Magpie for a jug of fresh water to bathe their patient. They weren't seriously worried about Yvonne's illness, confident she would recover.

There was far more concern over Agatha and Cooper's failure to return to the canyon by sundown. The frantic women, trying to snatch a few hours of restless sleep, feared the worst. It had been decided that, if there was no sign of them by daybreak, a team would go out to search.

Magpie, leaving the silent camp behind her, prayed for the couple's safety. She was glad she had this reason to be occupied and even more grateful that the women trusted her now to be useful.

The sound of falling water carried her to the springs that trickled from the rear face of the looming canyon wall. It was this flow that fed the pool back in camp. But the stock had been drinking from the pool, and the water there was no longer clean.

Reaching the springs, she laid the loaded pistol she carried on a flat boulder. Susan, who was in charge now, insisted that all of them must be armed and alert. Magpie had complied, though failing to appreciate the need for precaution. The chasm walls were sheer and towering. If trouble came, it would occur at the mouth of the canyon where a constant guard was mounted behind stout barricades.

Within seconds of her arrival at the springs, Magpie found reason to be glad of Susan's order. Her hands now free, she started to fill the jug from the flow in the crevice. That was when she heard a suspicious scraping sound from the rim above her. Abandoning the jug, she snatched up the pistol and backed hurriedly into the deep, concealing shadow of a pine.

Just in time. The moonlight revealed a figure slithering down a line dropped from the top of the canyon. He came so swiftly that, before Magpie could decide on a course of action, he had reached the floor of the canyon only yards away from her.

Duke Salter. She could recognize him in the moonlight as he turned away from the rope to get his bearings. He had a rifle strapped to his shoulder, but he was alone. In a half crouch, he started to move in the direction of the camp. Magpie knew she had to stop him. Pistol leveled at his chest, she emerged from the darkness of the pine to confront him.

"No," she said as, recovering from his surprise, he started to swing the rifle from his shoulder. "You would be dead before you ever touched the trigger. Perhaps I will kill you just the same."

"Then you'd never learn where the brat is, would you?" he taunted her, referring to their son, Daniel. "Come on, be reasonable. All I want is the strongbox.''

Did he actually believe that would stop the women? He didn't know them. He didn't realize that, with or without funds, they would go on pursuing their dream.

"I will not betray the women," she promised him. "Not this time."

"Don't be a fool. You see to it that I get that strongbox, then no one gets hurt. I leave here quietly, and before I go I tell you where the boy is."

It was a tempting offer, but she knew better than to trust him. Her hand tightened on the pistol. She longed to kill him for all his past brutalities, but if she did that, he would carry the secret of Daniel with him. Besides, beast though he was, she couldn't forget that he was the father of her child.

"You are in no position to bargain," she informed him coldly.

"I believe he is," came a sudden whisper just behind her. And before she could turn or cry out, a hand clamped over her mouth in the same instant that another hand snatched the pistol from her grip.

Duke chuckled. "Good work, Jack. Figured if I kept her busy, you'd manage to get down on your own line an' sneak up on her. Now let's signal the others it's clear. An' keep a tight hold on that bitch, will you? I got special plans for her later."

Struggling against the arms that were squeezing her without mercy, Magpie watched in horror as Duke lifted his head and issued a soft whistle. Almost immediately other lines dropped from the rim, and a dozen silent shadows swarmed down the face of the canyon.

She had permitted herself to be tricked. If she had raised the alarm at the first sign of an invasion, none of this would be happening. She had failed the women again.

Agatha was disoriented for a moment, not knowing where she was or what had awakened her. The blackness around her was puzzling, unnerving. And then she understood. The mine! They had been swallowed by the mine!

What time was it? No way of knowing, but it had to be very late. She started to sit up. Then it came again, the startling noise that must have aroused her.

Cooper, she realized. It was Cooper close beside her. He was moaning in his sleep. Pitiful sounds. She had heard them before and in similar circumstances. It had happened that night they had been trapped together in the soddy back on the Big Blue. Cooper had experienced a terrible nightmare. Perhaps the same nightmare he was having now.

Unable to bear his anguish, her hands fumbled for him in the darkness. When she made contact with his shoulder, he came awake with a harsh cry and clutched at her like a frightened child. Her arms went around him, holding him close.

"A bad dream, my love," she murmured soothingly. "You were having a bad dream."

"Yeah," he muttered, face buried in her hair. "Sorry."

The shawl had slipped away from them. Her hands stroked his bare skin. He was covered with a sheen of perspiration.

"How long?" she asked him softly.

"What?"

"How long have you been having this nasty dream? It is the same one repeating itself, is it not?"

She could feel his sudden constraint. He freed himself from her embrace. He was ashamed of something he perceived as a weakness. A strapping mountain man wasn't supposed to be haunted by nightmares. But it was more than that. She sensed he was uneasy about the very nature of the dream.

"How long?" she persisted.

For a moment she thought he wouldn't answer her. But perhaps he decided the blackness around them guaranteed a kind of safety. "Don't know," he finally said with forced casualness. "Probably for as long as I can remember. It used to come a lot when I was little, then less often when I got older. Hardly ever happens now, maybe only when I'm in a stressed situation. Don't worry about it, Aggie. It doesn't mean anything.''

Agatha didn't think that was true. She suspected it meant a great deal. ''Perhaps,'' she urged, ''it would help if you described the dream.''

''Nothing to tell. Just something or someone after me, wanting to hurt me, and I can't get away. Can't help myself or see their faces. I just know they're out there.'' He hesitated before mumbling reluctantly, ''Probably all the result of what happened when my father died.''

''How did he die?''

''He was killed protecting my mother and me. We were on the road back from Monterey when bandits rode down on us.''

''How awful! Was your mother—''

''No. She died later, complications from a wound, I think.''

''Then that must be the explanation,'' Agatha decided. ''In your nightmare the bandits are still after you.''

''I suppose. Like I said, it isn't very clear.''

''How old were you when this happened?''

''Two, three years old. Too young to actually remember it, I guess. Which makes my demons nothing more than what I must have been told about it later. The thing is . . .''

''Yes?''

''There's more to it than just that.''

''What?''

He was silent again, battling with his resistance to open doors that he had kept tightly closed all his life. But if that life was destined to end here inside this mountain, there could no longer be any reason to hide secrets. There might even be a real need to purge himself of an old torment.

''I think, Aggie,'' he said slowly, ''that in some way I was responsible for my father's death.''

''How can that be? You told me—''

271

"I know. It doesn't make sense. It's all mixed up somehow with the bandits and the dream. Only it goes deeper than that. No one would ever talk to me about it, but I've always felt there was something wrong between my parents. Something bad, and I was to blame for it."

Here was the explanation for Cooper Delaney, she thought, sharing his pangs. A man who found love very difficult, and commitment even harder. Because if, in his hidden remorse, he had convinced himself that his parents' marriage was dark and troubled and he was the cause of the tragedy that resulted . . .

"Oh, love, no," she appealed to him. "You were no more than an innocent. There is no way you could have caused any of it."

Her hands moved toward him, reaching out to him both emotionally and physically, with a need to prove to him that love was not a disaster but a triumph. She wanted to touch him, stroke his cheeks with a gentle comfort. But in the darkness her fingers made contact with his forehead. She found her thumb tracing the slight roughness of that curious scar dividing his eyebrow.

He stiffened at once, drawing back from her touch.

"Cooper?"

He chuckled then and groped for her hand, raising it to his mouth and kissing her palm. As if to deny that anything was wrong. There was no mistaking his sudden intention to turn the mood in another direction. He told her as much with a quick, "Let's talk about mysteries that can be solved, Aggie."

He left her no choice. The subject of the scar was still a forbidden one. "And what would those be?"

"Middle names. If I'm gonna perish before either of us can come up with a way to get out of here, then I want to go knowing what that T stands for in Agatha T. Pennington."

She was astonished. "We are threatened with facing our

maker, and all you can think about is learning my middle name?''

''Well, yeah.''

She pretended to seriously consider his request. ''Very well, but only on condition that you reveal what the J represents in Cooper J. Delaney.''

''Guess that's only fair.''

There was a pause.

''Well?'' Cooper said.

''Well?'' Agatha asked.

They both laughed.

''Okay,'' he relented, ''I'll go first.'' He drew an exaggerated breath of courage. ''You ready for this?''

''Proceed.''

''Jehoshaphat,'' he muttered. ''It's Jehoshaphat.''

''Oh dear, that is a bit excessive, isn't it?''

''I know. What can I say? My mama must have loved her Bible. Your turn, Aggie.''

''Very well. Tacita. I am Agatha Tacita Pennington.'' She prayed he hadn't the knowledge to translate it.

''Tacita? Wait a minute. That's Latin, isn't it? And if I remember what the padre drilled into me in my school days . . . *To be silent*. That's what Tacita means. *To be silent*. Oh, Aggie, that's rich, and about as appropriate as Jehoshaphat.'' He was convulsed with laughter.

''*I* did not laugh.''

''You were laughing silently. I could feel it.''

''Are you satisfied?''

''I think I am, Aggie Tacita. Ready to rest in peace.'' She could hear him settling down again on the floor, his voice already drowsy. ''Bad choice of expression, huh? I just meant . . . need to sleep . . .''

He was snoring within seconds. Agatha curled up again beside him, re-covering them with the shawl. She was glad they had traded secrets, both the serious and the silly. There had been another secret, one not so trivial, that she might

273

have shared. But, unless they reached their destination, there would be no point in revealing her earnest ambition. Besides, withholding it was a small act of faith, a conviction that they had to escape this place so that she could tell Cooper afterwards all about her hidden wish.

"You cannot die here, Agatha," she whispered into the blackness, using her old technique of audible self-encouragement in a desperate situation. "You have far too many things to accomplish."

*Name them*, she commanded herself in silent urgency.

"There is your obligation to settle the women along the Willamette. Your promise to find Daniel for Magpie. Fulfilling that secret ambition. And Callie. There is Callie to love and mother."

*What else, Agatha?*

*Cooper*, she thought, and this time she didn't say it aloud. *There is Cooper, the love he expressed for you and your oh-so-important need to learn just how real that love is. And if it is genuine, to hold it tight, to cherish it and nurture it.*

Agatha awakened to a glow that seemed blinding after their long hours of inky blackness. Clutching the shawl to her, she sat up on the duck cloth. Cooper had relighted the second lamp on the giraffe. He was dressed and looked ready for action, though she couldn't imagine what that action might be.

He greeted her with a tense, "You finding the air stale, hard to breathe?"

She considered his unexpected question, then shook her head. "No, the air seems perfectly fresh."

"Yeah, that's what I thought. Come on, Aggie," he urged with sudden impatience, "get dressed."

She was barely into her clothes when he seized the lamp and started up the tunnel with an eager stride. "Where are we bound?" she demanded, trotting after him.

"To find the way out of here."

The fresh air, she thought. They were going to hunt for the source of the fresh air.

"How can that be?" she asked, striving to keep up with him. "We were in all of the tunnels, and there was no other exit."

"Think about it, Aggie. We never went to the very end of each tunnel, only as far it took for the lamps to show us that the tunnel stopped up ahead and that the black powder kegs weren't there."

"Then you believe . . . ?"

"We'll see, Aggie. We'll see."

She tried to share his hope, but she feared it might simply be an illusion. The mine was spacious enough that the oxygen supply would be sufficient yet. Nor had either of them glimpsed any sign of an opening or a glimmer of outside light at the backs of those tunnels, only blank walls. But he was right. They had to investigate, had to pursue any possibility, no matter how unlikely.

One by one they closely examined the branches radiating from the main passage. It was at the very rear of the fourth tunnel that Cooper, a few paces ahead of her, raised a shout of victory.

Agatha, crowding up beside him, looked where he indicated with the lifted lamp. There was a gap in the right wall just below the low ceiling. Less than a yard in diameter, the hole angled upward through the rock. She stretched on tiptoe, peering into the opening. Was it only imagination, or did she actually detect a faint gleam from above?

Cooper voiced his excitement over the discovery. "A winze! Bless the hearts of those two little Cornishmen for sinking it!"

"A winze being . . . ?"

"A shaft for ventilation and communication. I'd guess this one opens along the slope somewhere above the main entrance. I was dumb enough not to remember that miners like the Trelawneys wouldn't operate without one if they can help it. And thank God the Salters were as dumb as I was and overlooked it.''

Agatha's relief was tempered by caution. ''Can we possibly climb through it?''

''Gonna find out, Aggie.'' He placed the lamp on the floor. ''You wait here while I see if this has any chance of working.''

Heaving himself into the winze, he vanished from sight. Seconds went by. Then, alone there in the gloom, she made up her mind. It took her some effort to lift herself through the opening, but she managed it.

Agatha found herself in a wormhole that would have threatened a mole with claustrophobia. Refusing to think about that, she began to scale the shaft. It was difficult but not impossible. The passage was less than vertical, and there were enough knobs and crevices in the rough rock to permit support for her hands and feet. She could hear Cooper scrabbling up the incline ahead of her.

He must have been able to detect her own presence because he paused suddenly, calling down to her an aggravated, ''Didn't I tell you to wait?''

''I believe you did.''

''Are you ever going to listen to me?''

''I always listen to you, my love. Can you see daylight yet?''

His only response was a grumbled complaint. He began to climb again. She followed. They must have ascended another dozen yards when Agatha was gripped by excitement. There was no mistaking it now. Light, growing stronger with each foot, was seeping into the shaft.

Turning a kind of corner, she found her progress blocked by Cooper. He was clinging to one wall. Less than three feet above his head was the mouth of the winze. The low boughs of a juniper sprawled across the opening. It was the thickness of the evergreen that had prevented the outside light from being clearly visible on the floor of the mine.

"Why have you stopped when we are almost there?" she asked.

"Come up here with me and you'll see."

Lowering one hand, he raised her to the ledge where he was resting. The shaft was wide enough at this point to accommodate both of them. But, as she could tell once she was beside him, the situation just over his head presented a serious difficulty. The winze narrowed here like the neck of a bottle.

Agatha was dismayed. "Why?"

"Looks like the outside layer of rock is harder than the stuff down here. Must have been tough to hack through it, so they widened it only as much as they had to."

"But if the Trelawney brothers are able to squeeze through—"

"They're built like a couple of monkeys, Aggie. I can't fit where they can go. I've already tried it. My shoulders are too wide."

To be halted when they were this close to release was frustrating. And unacceptable. "Then *I* must push through," she decided. "I can bring tools from that shack, and together we will chip away the opening until it is wide enough to free you."

He nodded. "I don't like it, but it's all we've got."

Agatha eyed the gap overhead, measuring it against her own dimensions. "I have never been ashamed that I was not fashionably petite, but on this occasion . . ."

He grinned at her lewdly. "Don't worry, Aggie. You'll fit, but if there's any problem, I've got the solution. I'll just fetch that grease bucket from the giraffe, strip you down to the skin and lubricate you until you pop to the surface. Think I'd enjoy oiling your body for you."

"There is a word for you, Cooper Jehoshaphat Delaney."

"What's that, Aggie?"

"Licentious. Be so good as to provide me with a boost, will you?"

"With pleasure."

His big hands gripped her by the hips, a position that managed to be provocative even under these tense conditions. Agatha forced herself to concentrate on their escape and not on the tantalizing warmth of his hands against her soft flesh.

"Ready?" he asked.

"Ready."

With a grunt, he lifted her toward the light. With one twist of her shoulders, she was into the gap and thrusting through the scratchy juniper. A second later she was out in the open. She had made it!

For one breathless moment she sprawled there on the gravel, dazzled by the brilliance after the long darkness of the mine. The sun was newly risen, evidence that they had spent the whole night inside the mountain. There was a sharp autumn chill in the air. Loosening the shawl that she had knotted around her waist before climbing through the winze, she drew it over her shoulders.

"Hey," came a muffled voice, "remember me?"

Scooting around, Agatha leaned into the shaft. "Sorry, my love. It was just so sweet to be free again, which is exactly what we must achieve for you. I will try to be quick. Surely there are hammers and chisels in the shack."

He didn't answer her. She gazed down at his upturned face. Even in the dimness there was no mistaking his sober expression. It made her instantly alert. And fearful.

"What is it?" she demanded.

"It's no good, Aggie. The neck is too thick. We'd be all day chipping away the stuff, and even then we might not have it wide enough. We're going to have to blast it out."

"No! It is much too risky! What if it goes wrong, and you are . . ." She couldn't bring herself to say it.

"It's the only way. Don't worry. I plan to survive."

"But—"

"Aggie, don't fight me on this one. We can't afford the

delay, not if there's any chance left to us to help the women.''

It was the one argument she couldn't oppose. "Tell me what I must bring."

He named the essentials she had to fetch from the supply shack. "If the Salters took our wagon with them, I can always go back down into the tunnel for the black powder that's left there. It's enough for this size of a job, but the other stuff we need. And, Aggie?''

"Yes?"

"Be careful. I can't imagine that Salter or any of his boys are still hanging around, but don't take any chances.''

She assured him that she still had the pistol. She had tied it up in the folds of the shawl for safekeeping. Scooping it up from the ground where she had momentarily laid it, she clambered through the junipers down the steep, rocky slope.

A cautious check of the clearing when she reached it convinced her that the place was silent and deserted. To her relief, the wagon they had loaded with kegs was still there. Even the team of horses remained close to the watering trough where they had been able to drink and to nibble at the sparse grass on the banks.

Realizing how thirsty she was herself, Agatha helped herself to water. Food, if any was available, would have to wait, but she did find a battered canteen in the shed and filled it for Cooper. Then she set to work gathering the rest.

She was winded by the time she lugged the pair of heavy sacks in two trips up the mountainside, but pleased with the results. Kneeling at the mouth of the shaft, she reported her success to Cooper waiting below.

"I am coming down to join you," she insisted as she lowered the materials to him. "The process you described will require both of us."

"I could always single-jack the holes. But you're right,'' he admitted. "Double-jacking them will be a lot faster.''

Agatha shuddered over the necessity of squeezing back

into the cramped gloom, but she didn't let Cooper know that. Once she was beside him again, she expressed her determination with a firm, "Now, tell me exactly what I must do."

The team operation was simple to explain and difficult to execute, as she shortly learned. The solid rock had to be bored in several crucial places to contain the charges. It was Agatha's job to hold and turn the steel drill while Cooper hammered away at the head of the long bit with an eight-pound sledge.

It was punishing labor in the best of circumstances. But in their situation, balancing themselves on a ledge and with little space to swing the sledge, it was a brutal effort. The jarring, repeated blows left her hands and arms trembling with the stress. She was weak with relief when he finally lowered the sledge, wiping at his brow.

"Think we're ready to prepare the charges."

She watched him, helping where she could, as he measured out powder and wrapped it inside paper cartridges around the Bickford Safety fuses. The cartridges were inserted into the cavities they had cut, the long fuses dangling from the holes like the rattails they were called.

Cutting a length of fuse known as a spitter to fire the cartridges, Cooper faced her squarely. "Time for you to go back to the surface, Aggie."

"I will return to the floor of the mine and wait there until you join me."

Neither of them had mentioned the possibility that this action could fail. There was the risk that too much rock would collapse in the blast, sealing the shaft instead of widening it. And if Cooper was trapped at the bottom, to which he would have to swiftly retreat once he'd lighted the shots, she meant to be trapped with him.

"Aggie, be sensible. There's no purpose in your sliding down there only to have to climb all the way back out again." Then he used another argument, which again she was unable to oppose. "Besides, if this shouldn't work—and I'm not saying it won't—do you want to leave Callie without either of us?''

"Lift me through the opening, please," she requested softly.

Once on top again, she obeyed his last instruction, removing herself a safe distance from the mouth of the winze. Flattening herself behind a juniper, she waited, her heart beating rapidly as she pictured the sizzling fuses and Cooper scurrying to the tunnel below.

The explosion, when it came, was less dramatic than she'd anticipated. A smothered boom followed by dust belched from the hole. She didn't wait for the cloud to clear before she was hanging over the raw, jagged gap.

"Cooper!"

There was no answer to her frantic shout. Fighting despair, she tried again.

"Cooper Jehoshaphat, I will never forgive you if you have buried yourself down there!"

"Use that name again," came a wonderful growl from somewhere below, "and your sweet tongue won't be in any condition to pardon or condemn anybody for a long time to come. Knew I should never have told you that damn name."

Seconds later, pulling his way through the rubble, he was beside her on the ground, his dust-covered length submitting to her ferocious embrace.

He purred like a tomcat. "This has definite possibilities. Maybe even involving that tongue of yours. That is," he added regretfully, sitting up and drawing her with him, "if it weren't for—"

"The women!" she suddenly remembered. "We must get back to the women!"

"Right."

Getting to their feet, they hurried down the slope. They stopped only long enough at the shack to collect a few more stores before boarding the wagon and heading down the mountain.

They were nearing the side canyon when Agatha, with anxiety clawing at her insides, clutched his arm. "Look!"

He followed her fearful gaze. Above the mouth of the canyon, buzzards circled ominously in the sky.

# *Chapter Sixteen*

Agatha stared in dismay at the silent canyon that stretched in front of them. Gone. Women, wagons and stock had all vanished. The only evidence of yesterday's occupation was a dead ox that had been the target of the wheeling buzzards overhead.

Cooper, having inspected the animal, reported a gunshot wound in its head. They could only assume this was the accidental result of the fray that must have occurred when the women were seized. Thankfully, there was no sign of another body, animal or human.

"Guess we know who has them," Cooper said angrily, "even if we don't know how they were taken or where."

"We must find them," Agatha said, sick with worry over the plight of the women. She couldn't bear to imagine what they might be suffering, Callie in particular. Duke Salter was capable of anything.

"Won't help to search until we can decide on a direction," Cooper pointed out. "Let's see if any clue got left behind."

Leaving the wagon at the mouth of the canyon, they

moved cautiously along the perimeter. They had rounded a rocky corner when he suddenly halted, motioning her to silence. Agatha froze in bewildered alarm. Seconds later she understood his alertness.

Fine particles of sand were dribbling down on them from overhead. There was a ledge projecting from the wall just above them. Something, or someone, concealed up there was stirring, disturbing the grainy surface.

Cooper drew her protectively behind him and raised his Colt, issuing a sharp challenge. "You, up there! Show yourself! And no tricks about it, or you'll be wearing a bullet in your nose!"

There was a brief stillness and then a scrabbling sound. A small face, dirt-streaked and frightened, poked over the edge.

"Callie!" Agatha cried.

Mutual recognition triggered a noisy and joyful reunion. Callie, with Roscoe and Romeo bounding in front of her, scrambled down the sloping face of the cliff. The child and barking dogs threw themselves at the two adults, demanding fierce hugs.

Scant minutes later, settled on the edge of the pool, Callie breathlessly recounted last night's events.

"I wanted t'help make the camp safe from attack, but Susan said I kept gettin' in the way. So, after dark, she sent me to bed with my blanket. Well, I went to bed all right, only up there." She pointed to the ledge.

"I figgered, see, it made a good lookout, an' I could be the first t'spot trouble an' let the others know. Meant to stay awake an' keep watch right through the night. But I guess me and the dogs fell asleep. Next I know there was screams an' guns goin' off, an' when I peeped over the side those buzzards already had the women rounded up. Heard one of 'em brag as how they'd come down ropes at the back side of the canyon an' sneaked up on the camp from behind."

"Was anyone hurt?" Agatha asked.

Callie shook her head. "Didn't look like it, an' I could

see everything plain down here in the moonlight. Weren't easy, though, keepin' Roscoe and Romeo quiet. An' I was scared. *Real* scared. I thought they'd come lookin' for me sure. That ol' Jack Salter wanted to. Said as how I was missin' to his brother, an' he's sure a mean one. Just laughed an' said what difference did it make 'cause I wouldn't last out here on my own more'n a couple o'days anyways. Reckon he was too all-fired t'move on."

"They left then and there?" Cooper asked. "Didn't even wait for sunup?"

Callie nodded solemnly. "Pulled out with everything, right smack in the middle of night."

"Where to?" he questioned her. "Did you hear?"

"Uh-huh. One of 'em was makin' sport at the women. Tellin' how they was goin' t'California. An' they'd be sold there and taken on a ship all the way to China where they'd wind up in a—a—" Callie broke off, looking puzzled. "What's a brothel?"

"Dear God," Agatha whispered.

"A place we don't intend to let the woman go," Cooper answered Callie before swiftly meeting Agatha's worried gaze. "He's heading them back toward the California road."

"And they have a considerable start on us."

"Maybe, but you're forgetting the oxen are slower than our team of horses. We'll catch them, but we've got to move. Duke Salter," he promised savagely, "is going to give the women back to us before I send him to hell."

It was sundown before they overtook the captured wagon train. They could spot the telltale smoke from cooking fires rising from behind a wooded ridge and knew that the band must have made camp for the night.

Salter had no reason to fear pursuit, not when he must be convinced his enemy was still buried inside a distant mountain. But Cooper would take no chances on discovery. He had been careful all day to avoid any observation from the trail ahead of them. Now he insisted on full darkness before they reconnoitered the camp. They concealed themselves and their own wagon in a grove of aspen on their side of the ridge.

Agatha found the waiting unbearable and was relieved when Cooper, satisfied by the cloak of darkness, uttered a brief, "Time."

"I will accompany you," she informed him, "and there will be no resistance about it, please."

For once, he didn't argue with her. He must have realized how vital it was to her to learn firsthand how the women were being treated. They left instructions with Callie to remain in the grove and to keep horses and dogs restrained and quiet. Then they slipped away, creeping toward the head of the ridge.

The sky was overcast. There was no moonlight tonight to betray their presence. But they proceeded with every care, limiting their conversation to hurried whispers and pausing frequently to check for any possible patrols.

They were nearing the top of the ridge when Agatha heard it. The sound of drunken revelry from the camp down on the other side. Duke Salter and his band were celebrating. It was an infuriating situation with cruel implications for the women. On the other hand, she realized that liquor made their captors vulnerable.

Cooper dropped to his hands and knees when they reached the flat crown of the ridge. Agatha followed his example, crawling behind him through a concealing undergrowth. He was flat on the ground when he finally stopped. She squirmed up beside him and found herself looking into an open hollow below the ridge. The clearing was lit by several campfires whose writhing flames emphasized the lurid nature of the revolting scene in progress.

The women had been herded into a roped enclosure off to one side. Like frightened cattle in a pen. Magpie, her head lowered in shame, was crouched at Duke's feet out in the center of the clearing. He was controlling her by a line looped around her neck, as though she were a leashed dog forced to witness his sadistic performance.

Mounted on a box, Duke conducted a mock auction for the benefit of his men who were sprawled on the ground in front of him, slopping from the bottles they passed from hand to hand.

''Promised you rewards, didn't I, boys?'' he roared. ''Well, here's the first prize goin' to a lucky sonofabitch for a night o'real pleasure. What am I bid for this ravin' beauty?''

Agatha, watching, sucked in a breath of outrage. The massive figure of Dolly was on the block, her face hot with humiliation as she submitted to the ugly jeers and catcalls.

''Aw, wouldn't give a copper for that flabby baggage!'' one of them in the rollicking audience shouted.

''Hell, she should pay *me*!'' gibed another.

They hooted with laughter as Duke slapped Dolly on her backside. ''No takers, you ol' cow. Git back with the others. Hey, bring up something more interestin' from the pen, will ya, Jack?''

Agatha couldn't stand it. He was a monster. They were all of them vicious beasts. And whatever the parody of this sickening auction, she knew that the intended outcome was a night of debauchery with the women of their choice.

Cooper must have felt her tension. He closed a hand over her arm, warning her not to surrender to her fury. Not yet. He needed to concentrate on other important aspects of the scene. She watched him eye the two armed men who were guarding the women. Then he noticed that there was no sign of sentries around the camp. Duke Salter had been careless in his victory, which was definitely to their advantage.

Cooper put his mouth to her ear, hissing, ''Let's get out of here.''

Agatha started to object. Then, realizing the necessity of a temporary retreat, she held her silence. She followed him reluctantly back through the thicket.

Neither of them spoke again until they reached the grove where Callie was waiting with the wagon. There they conferred in low tones.

"Not gonna be easy," Cooper said. "Even with Salter's lowlife occupied as they are, we're outmatched. But we'll devise something."

"Outmatched?" Agatha scoffed at his observation. "The women are more in number than the men and helpless only because they are disarmed. Just give them the opportunity, and you will see how they turn on that rabble."

"Why not?" he agreed. "They've defeated just about every other obstacle in the book to get this far. All right, so all we have to do is provide a distraction and then watch the fireworks. What's it to be?"

"Fireworks! Of course! That is the very thing!"

"Aw, Aggie, no. Not our load of black powder. Because that's what you're thinking, isn't it?"

"But would it not be an effective distraction?"

"Oh, it'd be that all right. We ignite that wagon, and it'll blow like Vesuvius. But, yeah, maybe . . ."

"What, my love?" she urged him, face close to his.

"I was thinking how to make it more than just a distraction. If we muffle the wheels, I could drive the wagon right to the top of the ridge. There's enough cover there. And if I'm careful how I position it, time my fuses just right, there's no reason, once the horses are removed, that a little nudge wouldn't send the whole volcano straight down into that bunch. Trouble is, we could be risking the women."

"Not if they are forewarned. I can manage that while you deal with the wagon."

"How, without those guards knowing?"

She thought about it for a few seconds. "If I am very careful, I should be able to steal close enough to the back side of the enclosure to signal the attention of at least one of the women. Then the message can be conveyed with a few quick gestures.''

All less easily achieved than she'd promised, Agatha realized a brief time later as she found herself slithering through a tangle of thorny growth to gain the back side of the pen where the women were being held. While praying she encountered no creature prowling in the night, she trusted that Cooper was preparing the explosives on the ridge.

She knew he regretted the sacrifice of the black powder. Without the kegs to open the canyon trail behind them, their only choice was the longer trail with its threat of snow in the mountains. But it was a small price when measured against the freedom of the women.

Agatha crept as close to the pen as she dared. There was gravel on the ground. She armed herself with a handful of the stuff, intending to capture the levelheaded Susan's attention with a well-aimed pebble. She had to be careful not to alert one of the guards. That shouldn't prove too difficult, since the two men were more interested in Duke's latest offering than in covering the women with their rifles.

Much to Agatha's disgust, she could plainly hear and see Salter in the firelight. He was still mounted on his box out in the center of the clearing.

''Lookee what we got here, boys. A real trophy this time.'' Gloating, he displayed a pair of frilly drawers. ''Fresh removed from choice flesh.'' He held the drawers to his nostrils, sniffing them like an animal. ''Ah, still warm and smellin' of female.''

His drunken audience roared their approval. He held up a hand, silencing them. ''No biddin' on this one, boys. Comes from one o'those luscious twins back there. The first man who correctly guesses which of 'em this here belongs to gets both girls for the night. Now, how's that for a prize?''

Agatha, trying not to listen, concentrated on her target. But the pebbles she lobbed in Susan's direction failed to connect. She grew frantic. Unless she made immediate contact, it would be too late. Cooper would have lighted and released the wagon.

In the end, it was Rebecca, huddled on the ground with her baby, who spotted Agatha crouched off in the underbrush. Managing to conceal her astonishment, the young woman caught Susan's attention. To her relief, Agatha was able to mouth her message, which Susan furtively relayed to the others in the enclosure.

There was an uproar in the clearing by now. Duke, howling with laughter, had pitched the coveted drawers out into the crowd. The men had pounced on the garment, fighting over it like snarling, slobbering dogs. Jack Salter waded through the pack with a whip, lashing at them with bellowed curses. They never heard the clattering wagon descending on them. They were demons in their own hell, busy lusting after the fires that would consume them. Fires that Cooper obligingly provided.

Before any of them could scramble out of the way, the careening wagon was in their midst. The detonation that immediately followed was horrific, lighting the night sky with a hot, blinding blaze that numbed the senses. On the heels of the deafening blast came pandemonium.

The few survivors of the explosion staggered to their feet, grabbed their horses and escaped into the wilderness. A wounded Duke Salter was one of them. The two guards, running from the livid, swarming women, who had already snatched their weapons, joined the others in their flight.

"Magpie!" Agatha cried when the women had all assembled in the clearing and counted heads. "Magpie is missing!"

"She's with *him*," Lettice said, referring to Duke. "Saw them rush off together. Dunno whether it was by choice or whether he forced her to go."

"We must recover her."

Cooper, who, together with Callie and the dogs, had joined them from the ridge, vetoed her intention. "Sorry, Aggie, but there's no sense in our going after them. They could be anywhere out there in the dark. We'd never find them, and by morning, if they're smart, they'll be miles from here."

"But she is with that vicious cur."

"She knows how to survive him. She's done it before. And who knows? Maybe in the end she wants it this way. He's still the only connection she has to their child."

Agatha hoped he was right and that Magpie would somehow manage without them. But she mourned her disappearance. The young woman had been making such progress in their company that Agatha had entertained every hope for her future. Now, regrettably, this was lost. She could only pray that Magpie would one day recover her son.

Cooper slid a comforting arm around her waist. "I know, but look at it this way. We didn't lose anyone else, and none of our women was injured."

"True, and I trust that Duke Salter is in no condition to trouble us anymore."

"Probably not, only we've still got one hell of a mountain range to cross before we reach that magic valley of yours. But first things first. Ladies, break out the spades. There are bodies over there needing burial. I'm not sure the bastards deserve it, but we'll give them a decent departure anyway."

Duke, propped against the trunk of a ponderosa pine on the side of a dry gully, gritted his teeth against the pain in his leg. A shard of hot metal from the explosion had ripped open the flesh in his left thigh. Diego crouched over him, checking the binding on the wound. The little Mexican had remained faithful. Those other surviving yellow-bellies had deserted him, vanishing into the night.

"Hurt?" Diego asked, offering him the flask of whiskey.

Duke shook his head. He didn't want anything dulling his senses. He wanted to feel the pain, steep himself in all the wildness of his grief and rage.

Jack. They had killed Jack. Blown him to bits. The only

living being he had ever cared about.

It was his anguish over Jack that kept him going. Reminded him of what he had to do. California. He would go on to California as planned. There was a place there where he could heal. And once he was recovered . . .

No, it wasn't finished. Delaney and that Pennington bitch were wrong if they counted on his being through with them. They were going to pay for Jack. He would make sure it happened. Someday, somehow . . .

Magpie, waiting with the horses a few paces away in the pale light of daybreak, regarded Duke with contempt. He had dragged her off into the night, maybe as a hostage or maybe because she might prove useful to him again. Either way it didn't matter. She didn't want to be with him, but she had no other place to be. She had betrayed the women back in the canyon and was no longer worthy of them. So she would go to California with Duke because he was her one link to Daniel. And only Daniel mattered now.

# *Chapter Seventeen*

"Just hang on a little longer," Cooper called out to the women at the head of the caravan with as much encouragement in his voice as he could muster. "We're at the top of the pass now, and before long we'll start to descend. Once we reach a lower altitude, we'll be underneath this stuff."

He repeated the message to the others as he and Bucephalus worked their way back along the column of wagons, wading through shallow drifts that were beginning to accumulate along the sides of the trail. And it was what he earnestly hoped. But he couldn't guarantee his promise. It was October and the weather at this elevation unpredictable. It might be worse down on the other side. Even a raging blizzard, which would be fatal.

It was bad enough up here. The snow they had feared all along had become a reality, catching them in the pass. The evergreens were drooping under their loads of white, the air thick with swirling flakes that plastered the wagon covers and frosted the backs of the oxen, which struggled onward under the urging of their muffled drivers.

293

Cooper marveled at the heartening responses of the women as he progressed slowly along the column.

"Hey, Delaney, you interested in a snowball fight?"

"Better be warmer down on the other side. These nippy elements ain't helping my complexion none."

"One more stuck wheel, Cooper J., and I say we mount the wagons on sled runners and coast 'em down."

He had never been prouder of them. Even now, exhausted by conditions that might have defeated an army of hardened men, the women's fortitude never failed as they fought to bring the wagons through. Their strength was no longer a secret to him. It existed because of their nurturing support of one another. A reaching out that was sometimes emotional, other times spiritual and often physical as they helped each other, demonstrating the respect and affection that had overcome months of hardship. Hell, it was awesome.

Cooper reached the rear of the train as Agatha, bundled in her warmest clothes, emerged from the back of a wagon, easing herself to the ground. Dismounting, he walked beside her, the snow crunching under their booted feet.

"How is she?" he asked, referring to Yvonne who was lying on a feather bed inside the wagon.

"Weak and still feverish. Whatever it is, it does not seem to want to leave her."

"She'll improve once we get down to a milder elevation. You'll see."

He removed his hat, shaking off the snow that had collected on the wide brims. Aggie hadn't answered him. He turned his head to look at her and was startled by the expression on her face. There was more than just worry there. There was something he had never seen before, something he'd never expected to find in this woman. Doubt. Doubt and a kind of despair.

"What is it?" he demanded. "What's wrong?"

"I think perhaps," she confided softly, "that I have made a grave mistake. I should have left Yvonne in New Orleans where, if nothing else, she would have been safe. And the others, all the others . . . I had no right to bring them to this harsh place where we may all perish yet.''

''I don't believe what I'm hearing. Agatha Pennington with more grit than any female I've ever met, and she . . .'' He broke off, grabbed her by the arm and swung her around to face him. His face was hard, his voice tough. ''You listen to me. The women are here by choice, every last one of them, and that includes Yvonne. You didn't make any of them come on this trek. They wanted it, knowing all the risks, and you ought to remember better than anyone why they wanted it and why they still want it. All right, sure, we're all scared and miserable, but no one is going to die. I won't let that happen, and *you* won't let it happen. Enough?''

She nodded solemnly. ''I am ashamed of myself. Thank you for restoring what I should never have misplaced.''

''Welcome.'' He smiled. At the corners of his mouth was a trace of his old wickedness that tugged at her insides. ''Hell, Aggie, it's waiting down there for you, so close now you can practically touch it. The Willamette Valley, remember? We're going to get there, all of us. Believe it.''

They were interrupted by a shout from the front of the column.

''Holy Lucifer, another stuck wagon.''

She watched him, hat crammed back on his head, as his tall, solid figure plowed through a ridge of snow on his way to help the wagon. Ironic, she thought, that it should be Cooper who reaffirmed her confidence in an undertaking he had once so emphatically scorned. He had changed that much, his pure cynicism diluted by the power of love and faith and what that combination could achieve. She and the women had taught him that. But was it enough, she wondered longingly, to keep him with her when they reached their destination?

*    *    *

On a bright, mild day in late October, their wagons, carried on a flotilla of hired rafts made necessary by impassable bluffs upriver, approached Ft. Vancouver on the banks of the Columbia.

They were nearing the end of the Oregon Trail, and there was a hushed excitement among the women on the water-born caravan. Excitement and a nervous anticipation shared by all of them. They had been experiencing the wonder of their arrival all day. This was to be home for them now, this fertile country of towering firs and massive spruces so lushly green after the parched lands they had crossed that it almost hurt the eyes to behold them.

"Vancouver ahead!" called one of the boatmen.

Cooper stood beside Agatha as the settlement with its log stockade came into sight. Across the river from the fort, the Willamette merged with the Columbia.

"By God, Aggie," he said with genuine elation, "we did it!"

"Yes, my love, it seems we have."

The joy of victory shone in her eyes as she viewed the expansive fort, which was the major North American outpost for the Hudson's Bay Company. Its prosperity was already evident to her by the presence of ocean-bound sailing ships moored along the shore.

As the rafts moved toward the landing, she was able to appreciate how active and extensive the community was outside the fort. It was composed entirely of males, most of whom were swarming down to the riverbank to eagerly welcome the women. Word of their arrival had managed to precede them. Cooper recognized the Trelawney brothers and indicated them to her. Agatha was glad she would have the opportunity to repay the miners for the black powder they had used.

There was instant turmoil when the rafts touched shore. The men collected along the landing cheered the women. Roscoe and Romeo howled. Rebecca's baby wailed. A burly logger shouted, "You females actually hauled it on your own all the way from Independence?" And Lettice called back a sassy, "Sugar, you wouldn't believe what I went through just to come see you."

The men needed no further encouragement. Laughing and shoving, pleading to escort them into the fort, they mobbed around the women, who wore their best outfits for the occasion as they streamed ashore. Agatha noticed Yvonne, fully recovered now, flirting with a bearded trapper. There would be weddings, she thought. Perhaps even before they settled on their claims along the Willamette.

And what of herself? Agatha hardly dared to wonder. Was afraid to wonder as Cooper led her toward the stockade. There was no denying it, though. The triumph of their arrival was shadowed by her anxiety. Because whatever was between Cooper and her had to be resolved, perhaps within hours. She didn't know if the outcome would be one she could bear.

They were inside the enclosure now, an immense rectangle occupied by numerous buildings. Dr. John McLoughlin, a commanding figure with flowing white hair and the chief factor of Ft. Vancouver, was there to greet them.

"We heard you were coming, ladies. Your success in reaching us is nothing short of amazing. The facilities of the post are yours for as long as you need them. Cooper J., before I forget, there is a letter from California that has been waiting for you."

An agitated Cooper paced the dirt path along the river-bank, the letter from California clutched in his hand. His mind was seething over its contents, his gut on fire with the decision it required.

Out on the trail he hadn't let himself think about the possibilities of Aggie and the future. Hadn't been able to deal with the subject. Not with his history. He had known, though, in a deep corner of his mind that one day, feeling as he did about her, he would need to come to terms with the situation. But there had always seemed to be plenty of time for that.

That time no longer existed, he realized as he turned on the path to gaze at the trio of anchored ships. Circumstances demanded an immediate choice.

And he didn't know what that choice would be. Not until he spotted Callie on the other side of the ships. She was playing with the dogs, who were chasing gulls along the shore. He watched them for a minute, a lopsided grin on his mouth. And that was when he understood what he wanted. It was something that he still feared, wondering if he had what it took to make it work, but at least he was clear about his intention to go after it.

His stride purposeful now, he returned to the stockade. He went to the cabin where he had left Agatha meeting with the leader of the men who were holding the land along the Willamette on behalf of the women. He didn't let that stop him, but a sudden attack of nerves did call for a couple of deep breaths before his hand rapped on the door.

"Yes, come in."

He found her alone in the cabin, her visitor gone. She was standing by the hearth, wearing a frown. But he paid no attention to that. All he saw, *needed* to see, was the tall, regal figure that had given him so much pleasure and the bold-featured face that he'd come to cherish.

She turned her head then, smiled at him. As though just realizing who had entered the cabin. His heart seemed to expand inside his chest.

"Did your letter . . ."

She didn't finish. She seemed distracted. Never mind. He was focused enough for both of them. He crossed to her, took her by the hand and led her to a settle where they sat side by side.

"We're gonna talk about that letter, Aggie. At least I am. You're going to listen." He waved the letter under her nose before going on with an explanation of it. "From Carlo Ramirez. Remember? The friend in Monterey keeping my savings."

"Yes."

"Encouraging news, Aggie. *Real* encouraging. Carlo writes that Mexico is sending a new governor to California, one this time who won't be totally sympathetic to the arrogant land barons like my uncle. You know what that means? My chance now of recovering my ranch is stronger than ever. But Carlo says I need to get to California right away before the new governor arrives and is swamped with petitions."

"You are leaving," she said in a plaintive voice.

"One of the barks out there is sailing this afternoon for England with a load of furs. She's stopping at Monterey to add hides to the cargo. I have to be on that ship."

"I see."

He took her hand again, squeezing it. "No, you don't. I want you with me on that bark, Aggie. You and Callie and, yes, the damn dogs, too, if she can't bear to leave them."

She stared at him silently. She wasn't sharing his excitement. Why?

"Aggie, do you understand me? I'm asking you to share my life in California. We'll be a family, a real family. We can be married in Monterey or even on the ship if we decide not to wait."

Those vivid blue eyes went on gazing at him. They were troubled eyes. He could see that now.

"What's the matter?" he demanded. "Have I shocked you?"

She shook her head. "You move me with your proposal, Cooper Delaney, *deeply* move me, but . . ."

"You won't come," he said, his voice going flat.

"I *cannot* come."

"You didn't believe me back in the mine when I told you I loved you, did you? You thought it was something I just said because we were trapped there, and it looked like we'd never get out alive, so what difference did it make?" He couldn't help the bitterness that crept into his voice. He had risked his soul to give her those words. Had risked as much again now to ask her to be his wife, and she was throwing it all back in his face.

"Oh, my love, no. Your declaration meant everything to me."

"Then why?"

"There are difficulties that prevent it . . . so many difficulties that I . . ."

She couldn't go on. She removed her hand from his and lifted it to his face, intending to stroke his cheek. Cooper pushed it away. He didn't see, or want to see, the pain she was experiencing with her refusal. All he knew was his own anguish over her rejection. And his anger.

He got to his feet and began to pace. Then he rounded on her. "*Why?*" he demanded.

She remained on the settle, hands folded now in her lap. "There is trouble with the agent I met with," she said quietly. "A danger to our Willamette lands. He insists that his men signed contracts with Hiram, not us. And since Hiram is dead, he refuses to release the holdings to us, claiming the contracts are no longer valid. Even perhaps that females are not legally entitled to the properties. We shall win, of course, but my presence here is critical to the negotiations."

"Aggie, look at me and try to understand. It's over, done with. You brought the women to Oregon just as you promised. You don't have to fight for them anymore. They can fight for themselves now."

She shook her head stubbornly. "I have a responsibility to see the women settled on the land."

He laughed. Caustic laughter that made her flinch. He was hurting so much he didn't care what he said to her. "Things haven't changed, have they, Aggie? You still need them more than they need you. Why should you want a husband and family of your own when it's a lot safer to live your life through the women?"

"That is not true. I *do* want you. I had hoped, *prayed* . . ."

"What? What did you hope and pray for?"

"That you would stay, that together we could realize the rest of the dream. I have been longing all these weeks to tell you, but there was no point in discussing it until we proved we could bring the wagons through to the end of the trail. We have done just that."

"And it's time to let it go."

"No. There are other women and children back east who deserve the same opportunity."

He stared at her, understanding her secret ambition and appalled by it. "You want to bring more wagon trains out here, and you want me to help you do it."

"Yes."

"You're out of your mind. Have you forgotten what hell we suffered to get here?"

"It would be less difficult the next time."

"Oh, would it? And what did you envision for me after you'd satisfied yourself that I'd helped you bring enough needy women to your valley? Assuming, that is, I was still alive and functioning by then."

"That—that you would wish to stay on in Oregon." She glanced longingly through the window at the grandeur and promise of Mount Hood in the distance. "That we could settle and build a future together in this new land."

"What? As a dirt farmer?"

"I know that is not for you. You want cattle and a ranch. You can have that ranch here in Oregon."

"I already have a ranch waiting for me in California."

"And you may lose everything trying to recover it," she pleaded with him.

"But if I send for my gold and invest it here in Oregon . . ." He nodded, his voice harsh now. "Yeah, that's a pretty dream, Aggie. You got it all worked out for me. Only one thing wrong with it. It's *your* dream, not mine. Mine is still in California."

"And I can be no part of it."

"*Won't* be a part of it, you mean."

She stiffened on the settle, meeting his gaze. This time there was fire in her eyes. "You want the truth of it?" she said recklessly. "Here is the truth of it. I would sacrifice everything to be with you, go anywhere you asked if all you needed was the recovery of your ranch. But it is not the land that matters to you. What you really want is revenge against your uncle. You are driven by it, Cooper, and I cannot be there and watch you destroy yourself over it."

"Is that how you see it, Aggie? All these years that I've been slaving and waiting, and it amounts to nothing but a grudge?"

She should have known better, he thought resentfully. She should have understood that he needed the California ranch because it was all he had to offer Callie and her. That he wasn't ready to settle for what her damn inheritance could buy them here in Oregon. This was his prime reason now for reclaiming his ranch. Wasn't it? Sure it was. And if she couldn't see that on her own, he had too much pride to try to set her straight.

"You will not surrender it, will you?" she said in a small, forlorn voice.

No, he couldn't. How could he when, for most of his life, he had been fighting for this opportunity?

This was killing him. He hadn't trusted commitment. His belief in marriage was still fragile, but he had offered both to her. She would never know the courage that had cost him. Well, he was all out of courage now.

"There's no point in going on with this," he said. They were tearing each other apart, and he could no longer bear it. "I've got a ship to board."

"My love," she whispered. And that was all she said. All she needed to say, because there was the misery of a lifetime in those two words.

Cooper left the cabin without looking back. Once out in

the yard, he realized that he would have to find Callie. Telling her good-bye, and trying to make her understand why he had to go, would be the hardest thing he'd ever do. No, that wasn't true. The hardest thing had been walking out that door behind him.

Susan stood in the cabin doorway, the familiar stoic expression on her broad face as she watched Agatha drag a blackboard mounted in an upright frame across the plank floor.

"There," Agatha said when she'd satisfied herself that the blackboard was positioned at the precise angle she desired. "That should catch the light from the window just right. Now I think if I place the table and chairs here . . . yes, this will work nicely."

Susan didn't comment or offer to help as her friend went on fussing with the elaborate arrangement of her makeshift schoolroom. She knew that Agatha wouldn't have welcomed assistance of any kind.

"How fortunate Dr. McLoughlin was able to provide me with these essentials. A blackboard, no less! And to place this room at my disposal for as long as I need . . . he *is* kind."

She began briskly sorting through a stack of books and papers on the table, pausing briefly to consider the journal she had kept on the trail before discarding the volume in a drawer. "I think I may consider myself finished with this. So, where did I put the lessons I prepared last night? Ah, here they are."

Susan moved aside as Emmie Jo arrived on the scene. "Dug these slates outta the wagon for ya, Miss Agatha. Had t'go to China 'fore I found 'em. It's a fact."

"Thank you, Emmie Jo. If I may ask one more favor . . . would you find Callie and send her to me?"

Emmie Jo departed. Agatha continued with her preparations. "I have been shameful in my neglect of Callie's schoolwork these past few weeks. There must be regular sessions from now on . . .''

Her cheerful patter went on. Susan had been listening to it for almost two days. It had been accompanied by a ceaseless energy painful to watch. Susan decided she had seen and heard enough.

She approached the table with a gruff, ''Can't go on like this.''

Agatha looked up from her restless shuffling of the papers, an expression of warning in her eyes. Susan ignored it.

''Ain't foolin' no one,'' she said plainly. ''You been like this since Delaney sailed for California, an' we all know why.''

Agatha hesitated before admitting a stiff, reluctant, ''I do not deny it. I miss him, but I can and will go on without him.''

Susan's laugh was as blunt and abbreviated as her language. ''*Miss?* That what you call the ache that's got you hurtin' like you went an' lost a limb?''

''You exaggerate.''

''Grievin' somethin' terrible for him, an' all your bustlin' around ain't gonna change that. Like Emmie Jo's always sayin', it's a fact.''

Susan relentlessly held Agatha's gaze and was satisfied when some of the starch went out of her.

''I thought you did not approve of Cooper and me.''

''Didn't. Thought you was the most unlikely pair imaginable. Was wrong. Reckon you belong together.''

''It is too late for that.'' Susan watched her take a deep, steadying breath and knew that her heart was swelling with a love she had convinced herself would never be fulfilled. ''I thought that the love I had to offer him was enough to bind him to me, but I was mistaken.''

''Went and put the women first, didn't you? Shouldn't. Took care of us long enough. Can stand on our own now.

Win the land for ourselves, if it comes to that. Anyways, you're no good without him.''

"Susan, there is nothing I can do about it now. He is gone.''

"Go to him. Get yourself on the next boat and go to him. Enough said.''

"No.'' She shook her head with stubborn pride. "It is over. He made that very clear, and somehow I must live with that, even if he is the only man I will ever—''

Emmie Jo rushed into the cabin, her freckled face flushed with excitement. "Callie's gone! Filled a poke with her things an' went! Left this here on her bed!''

Agatha snatched the note that she waved at them. Since neither Susan nor Emmie Jo could read, Agatha read Callie's message aloud, struggling through the atrocious spelling.

"Dear Miss Agatha, you been as good as a ma to me, but I reckon that don't work so well without a pa to go with. I need the pa if we're gonna be the real family I been countin' on. Looks like the only way is for me to go and get Coop and bring him back. And that's what I'm set on doin'. Don't worry none. I figured it all out, and I will be all right. Only please look out for Roscoe and Romeo as I don't think they would be so happy on the ocean.''

There was a fearful, frantic expression on Agatha's face when she finished the note. "The ocean! Dear God, is it possible?''

"Must be,'' Susan said. "Got herself on that other bark sailed this mornin'. Heard it was puttin' into Monterey like the other one.''

"She was real friendly with the seamen on that boat,'' Emmie Jo remembered. "They showed her over the whole boat jest yesterday.''

"They would not have knowingly taken her with them. She must have sneaked on board and stowed away. Emmie Jo, are you certain that Callie—''

"Oh, she's gone sure enough, Miss Agatha. I asked around

on the way back here, and ain't nobody seen her since breakfast.''

"Then she *is* on that ship, and while we stand here she . . .''

Agatha put a hand to her mouth, looking, Susan thought, positively ill. "What you figure on doin'?''

Agatha straightened, recovering herself with an effort. "I must follow her. There is a sloop still at the landing. I will hire the sloop. Whatever it takes to bring her back safe.'' She met Susan's worried gaze, adding a wry, "It seems, after all, that I *will* be going to California.''

# Chapter Eighteen

"Durn!" Callie muttered to herself as she wandered the maze of streets. "Double durn and heck!"

None of it was working out as she planned. Leastways, not since she'd arrived in Monterey, because the voyage from Oregon hadn't been too bad. She'd made a cozy nest for herself behind tall bales of furs in the hold of the ship. No one had discovered her there, and she'd been sick only once when the ocean got really mean.

The trouble had started first thing this morning when the bark docked at the city's main wharf. Two of the crew, spotting her as she sneaked ashore, raised a cry. Callie had managed to get away and hide herself in the crowds along the busy waterfront, but she lost the satchel with all her belongings during her flight. Things had just gotten worse since then.

Monterey was too big for her. There were people everywhere on the streets. Merchants, government officials, soldiers, Indians, ladies wearing bright colors. Callie stopped as many of them as she could, asking over and over where she could find Cooper Delaney.

"*Yo no se*," they kept saying. "*Yo no se.*"

She never understood any of them. It was a strange place with a strange language. Even the buildings were different. Red-tiled roofs and white stucco walls with balconies that stuck out over the streets. Callie might have admired them against their setting of pine clad hills and an intensely blue bay if she hadn't been so worried. How was she supposed to locate Cooper if no one knew what she was talking about?

Didn't help that she was so hungry her stomach ached. The voyage had been much longer than she'd planned. She had eaten the last of the jerked beef and corn bread stuffed into her satchel early yesterday. Since then she'd had nothing but water, which was no problem because there were public fountains in the capital seaport.

Thinking about food, and how she had no money to buy any, was making it awfully hard for Callie to concentrate on her wonderful dream. It had seemed easy enough back in Oregon. Just a matter of bringing one half of the two people she cared about most in the world to the other half and watching the magic happen that would result in the family she craved. She just hadn't reckoned on so many complications.

Tired, hungry and discouraged, Callie found herself back on Alvarado Street where she had started. She kept on searching. Someone in this place must be able to tell her how to get to Cooper, if only she could make them pay attention to her. But no one was interested in a little girl who, after days as a stowaway, resembled a beggar. No one, that is, except the small, dark man who followed her at a cautious distance.

Diego Morrales wanted to be certain of Callie's identity before he risked approaching her. He had been on his way to seek the company of an accommodating woman when the child caught his attention. Not because he recognized her. He'd never seen her on the trail, though he knew of her existence through Magpie and Jack Salter. What had alerted him was what she'd been trying to ask an old woman when he passed them in the plaza.

Cooper Delaney! The girl wanted Cooper Delaney!

Excited by the possibilities of the situation, Diego forgot his need for a woman and trailed the child. If he had heard her correctly—and he meant to be sure of that—then Duke's enemy was somewhere nearby. Why Delaney and the girl were in Monterey didn't interest him. What mattered was how pleased Duke, hiding in that flea-infested *ramada* outside of town, would be if Diego could provide him with access to the man he had sworn to destroy.

Diego waited patiently and was rewarded when Callie stopped someone else outside the customhouse and again failed to make herself understood. There was no mistaking her request this time. She *was* looking for Delaney.

Diego didn't hesitate to intercept her as she turned away in disappointment from a mumbled Spanish she didn't comprehend. He had decided by now that she was the child from the wagon train, and that she couldn't possibly identify him. If she had been hiding close by that night in the canyon and managed to glimpse him when he and the others raided the camp . . . well, it had been dark and he'd gone unshaven on the trail. He was different now without his beard. He was safe.

"Deed I hear you right, leetle one?" he addressed her warmly as he stepped into her path. "You want Cooper?"

He smiled over the instant relief that lighted her small, dirty face. His was the first friendly face she'd met in this alien place. What's more, he spoke English. She was ready to trust him.

"You know Coop?" she asked him eagerly. "Where is he? Gotta see him!"

"Sure, you can see him. Only there ees a problem." He assumed a regretful expression. "He has gone to Yerba Buena and won't come back until after ees dark."

"Oh." Her face fell.

Jean Barrett

"Poor *pequeñita*. Theengs are not so good for you, eh?"

"Well, it's a real fix all right, an' I gotta say I'm awful hungry."

"Then, as a *compadre* of Cooper's, I weel help you. You like tortillas?"

"Dunno. Never had one."

No? Hokay, I take you to a *taverna* I know where you eat and tell me about this bad feex. Then I take you where Cooper weel be."

Callie experienced a momentary misgiving. Going off alone with a stranger was something she had been warned about since the cradle. But he had to be all right if he was a friend of Cooper's, and she just had to eat something.

"Guess that's the thing to do," she agreed.

But Callie didn't feel easy in the *taverna* several streets away. It was gloomy, and it smelled of smoke and grease. Besides, she had another serious problem.

"What?" her stocky companion questioned her as she stood there squirming.

She didn't know how to tell him. It was embarrassing. "Uh, I need to . . ."

He understood her. "Pee, eh? Here, I show you." He held aside a tattered curtain at the back of the low, raftered room and pointed toward a door on the other side of a cluttered kitchen. "Ees what you want out there."

He turned away and went over to the bar to wait for her. Callie timidly crossed the kitchen. It was occupied by a very fat woman who was dozing in a chair and paid no attention to her. She opened the door and found herself in a backyard. There was a privy at its far end. She started toward it and then stopped.

A large hound was lying in the yard, and when it saw her it rose to its feet and growled menacingly. Callie gazed longingly at the privy. Should she? No, the dog was too scary.

Fleeing back into the kitchen, she glanced hopefully in the direction of the woman. Her eyes were still closed, and Callie

310

didn't think she would appreciate being disturbed. Maybe her new friend in the bar would help her to get by the dog.

She moved to the connecting doorway to summon him. Through a gap in the curtain, she could see him at the bar. There was another man there, a Yankee seaman off a whaler. They were turned away from her, but she could hear them talking.

The young seaman chuckled and jerked his head in the direction of the backyard where he thought Callie was installed in the privy. "Like 'em just a bit young, don'tcha, *amigo*?"

Diego grinned amiably. "Not thees one," he boasted recklessly. "Thees one I have beeger plans for. She theenks she ees going to her Cooper, but she ees going to a gringo who weel pay me to use her to bait hees trap."

Callie wasn't sure what he was talking about, but she knew one thing. He wasn't her friend. She had made a bad mistake, and she had to get out of here and far away from him. The back door was no good. The dog was still out there and wouldn't let her escape by that route. She'd have to go through the bar and out the front.

She was tense with fear as she slipped through the curtain and began to edge toward the open door to the street. Praying they wouldn't turn around and discover her, she crept past a table and neared the exit. She would have made it if her gaze hadn't been pinned on their backs. She didn't see the chair until she banged into it. It turned over and clattered to the floor with a sound like gunfire.

The men at the bar whipped around. Someone shouted. Callie didn't learn who. She was too busy plunging into the street. She could hear her enemy behind her, cursing as he came after her. And she ran. Ran as she'd never run before, terrified that he would catch her.

It was after business hours. The streets had emptied. No one to help her, even if she could make them understand her desperation.

Rounding a corner, she flew up an alleyway, reached another street and then a second alleyway. She was hopelessly lost by now. Was he still back there, chasing her? She was afraid to look.

She went through somebody's garden, came to another narrow street. It was very quiet now. No sound of pounding footsteps behind her. Could she risk it? Breathing hard, she turned around to check. There was no one there. She kept searching the street as she backed away. Just beyond a pepper tree she came smack up against a pair of powerful legs.

Callie whirled with a yelp of alarm, her head snapping back as she gazed open-mouthed at the towering figure of the scowling man with whom she had collided.

"Holy Lucifer!" thundered a familiar voice. "What the—"

"Coop!" she shouted with joyful relief, grabbing what portions of him she could reach.

He squatted down in front of her, his face wearing a shocked expression. "Callie, is that you under all that grime?"

"Sure is."

"What are you doing in Monterey? How did you get here?"

Callie knew that she would be in serious trouble if she told him the truth. She was ready with her lie.

"Come on a ship. Miss Agatha and me."

She had figured it all out back at Ft. Vancouver. That note she'd left for Miss Agatha had said she was coming to get Cooper, but that had been another fib. Heck, she was no dope even if she was only eight years old. She had realized that Cooper wouldn't sail back to Oregon just because she pleaded for it. But something else *would* happen. Miss Agatha, being a grown-up, was bound to come after her. Probably on her way right now to recover the runaway. Callie was counting on it. 'Course, once Miss Agatha and Cooper got together they were sure to come up with the truth, but by then . . .

"Aggie? Here?"

Callie knew she had done the right thing when his green eyes, shining with excitement, searched the street over her shoulder. But this was the part she had to invent on the spot.

"Well, uh, she's not with me right now. That's 'cause she's off lookin' for you."

He regarded her with sudden suspicion. "This doesn't make sense, ol' son. What are you doing wandering the streets on your own?"

"Oh, see, I'm not s'pposed t'be. Miss Agatha, she rented rooms for us in this house when we got off the ship. Said I was to stay there until she went an' found where you lived 'cause we didn't know, an' it might take some time. Only I got real bored jest waitin' there so I come out explorin' a bit."

"You *look* like you've been exploring," he said dryly. "You're kind of a sad mess, urchin."

"I got lost. Couldn't find my way back. There was this man gonna help me. Only it turns out he wanted to sell me, or somethin'."

Cooper took her hands and looked fierce. "What man? What happened?"

Callie related a quick version of her encounter. "I was real scared, but I guess he gave up followin' me. Sure glad I ran into you." To her satisfaction, Cooper uttered a savage curse.

"I'd like to go after this scum and rearrange his face, whoever he was," he said, getting to his feet, "but right now we need to take care of you. Hell, Callie, what were you thinking? You know better than to trust any stranger that comes along. Where is this house you're staying, anyway? What's its name? We've got to get you back there. If Aggie's returned, she'll be calling out the garrison to hunt for you."

"Dunno. I can't remember."

"She must have left someone there in charge of you. Who was it?"

"Uh, jest a lady." She had to stall him until Miss Agatha had a chance to arrive in Monterey. She refused to believe that wouldn't happen. "Guess I'm so tired and hungry my brain ain't workin'." It was no effort to lean against him weakly.

"You do look on your last legs at that. All right, I'll take you to where I'm staying. Carlo's mother will be happy to spoil you with a meal and a bed."

And a privy, Callie hoped.

"I'll send Carlo back into town when we get there," Cooper added. "If anyone knows where to find a house that rents rooms, he will. His place isn't far. Think you can walk a little farther?" He glanced regretfully at the blacksmith's from which he had just emerged when she ran into him. "I'd ride you back on Bucephalus, but he's cast a shoe."

"I can walk," she assured him, happily linking her hand with his big one as they turned up the street.

They'd gone less than half a block when Cooper, looking down on her, asked eagerly, "Callie, why did Aggie come all this way looking for me? Did she say?"

It was late in the day when Agatha came ashore at Monterey. The lowering sun gilded the tiled rooftops of the substantial buildings clustered within the protective curve of the bay. The city, against a backdrop of the Santa Lucia Range to the east, was a serene, pleasing sight in the last amber glow of the afternoon. She might have taken a moment to admire the mellow scene if she hadn't been so anxious about Callie. The voyage from Oregon had seemed interminable.

The small crew of the sloop she had hired, which would wait as long as was necessary to return her to Ft. Vancouver, knew very little about Monterey. But they had suggested she begin her search by asking for assistance from the commandant at the presidio, which was within walking distance at the northern edge of town. Leaving her luggage on board, but armed with her familiar reticule, Agatha struck off in the direction of the post.

She was marching with determination up Alvarado Street when a smart gig drew alongside her. The man driving it called out to her, a note of gentle humor in his voice.

"Senorita Pennington, I think. I would know you anywhere."

Astonished, Agatha turned to stare at him. He had the black hair, classic features and ivory skin of a Spanish patrician, though there was nothing severe about his lean, well-dressed figure. He was smiling as he leaned from the gig, a teasing gleam in his dark eyes.

"Cooper described you thoroughly," he explained with an excellent English that bore only a slight accent. "Also, rather frequently since his return. Fortunately, I am a man of endurance. And you have no idea who I am."

Suddenly she did know who he was. "You must be his friend, Carlo Ramirez."

Hat in hand, he sprang down from the gig to acknowledge their meeting. "I hope your friend as well, senorita."

"You are already a blessing, sir. I know nothing of the town and would value your advice. I was on my way to hunt—"

"For the missing Callie, I believe. Consider her found. She is safe at my home."

"Oh, thank God. I have been imagining every horror. But how did you—"

"Cooper discovered her wandering on the streets. He is with her now. She was clinging to him like a burdock when I left."

"I must go to her!"

"Then permit me to drive you."

Seconds later, Agatha was beside him in the gig, and they were climbing a lane toward his home on a height at the southern fringes of the city.

She found Carlo easy to like but was surprised that he'd been so casual about encountering her on the street, almost as though he had already known she was in Monterey. She would have asked him about that, but now that Callie was accounted for, there was something more important she longed to know.

"How is Cooper?"

"Not fit to live with since he came home." He chuckled. "You have something to do with that, I believe. But also there is the delay over his ranchero."

"Then it is not settled. Has he not met with the new governor yet?"

"The governor has many excuses not to grant Cooper the audience he has been requesting. I think he is avoiding any confrontation that might make him unpopular with either side. People are beginning to be divided over this dispute."

Agatha didn't like the sound of that. "You mean it threatens to be more than just an issue between Cooper and his uncle?"

"Possibly. There are those who resent the monopoly of the land by a few men like Luis Alvares. They see Cooper's struggle as an opportunity to break the power of the privileged families who have controlled California for generations. And Cooper welcomes their support. But there could be trouble in that when a man is as frustrated as he is."

And as hotheaded, Agatha thought, worried about the simmering conflict.

"Welcome to Casa Ramirez, senorita," Carlo said as they arrived in front of a galleried adobe house softened by bougainvillea spilling over its walls.

Handing her down, he turned the gig over to a waiting youth and conducted her through a gate and up a pebbled path. Carlo's mother met them inside the front door. She spoke no English but greeted Agatha with a warm smile and showed her into a small bedroom where Callie was sleeping peacefully.

Carlo's mother whispered something, which her son translated. "She wants to assure you that Callie is perfectly well but so exhausted from her adventure that she isn't likely to stir before morning."

Careful not to disturb her, Agatha leaned tenderly over the child. That was when she saw what she was hugging in her arms, and she smiled. Any other little girl would have been cuddling a doll or a stuffed animal. Callie had her cheek resting contentedly against Cooper's coiled bullwhip.

There was no other evidence of Cooper's presence, but a glow from the window near the bed commanded Agatha's attention. Outside, barely discernible in the thickening twilight, was a patio that separated the main dwelling from a small guest house in a grove of pines. The glow was from one of its windows where an oil lamp revealed Cooper seated at a table, pen in hand.

Her pulse quickened at the sight of him.

She wasn't aware of Carlo joining her at the window until he spoke softly beside her. "He is writing a new letter of petition that he must have ready by the morning. One of his supporters close to the governor suggested it and will arrive tomorrow to try to bring both him and the letter to the attention of the governor."

"Then I cannot disturb him," she murmured.

The ache of disappointment must have been plain in her voice because Carlo assured her, "He would never forgive me if I allowed you not to disturb him. Go to him."

Agatha needed no further urging. There was a door in the passage just outside the bedroom. It opened onto the cobbled patio where she could hear the pleasant burbling of a fountain as she made her way through the gloaming.

It was a mild evening, and Cooper had left the door of his quarters open to the patio. Agatha stood there on the threshold, heart racing as she silently watched him hunched over the letter, his long, powerful legs sprawled under the table. He seemed out of place in this setting, his body too big and

317

rugged for the small house. He overwhelmed it, just as he had always overwhelmed her.

He must have sensed her presence. He looked up suddenly and discovered her there in the doorway. The slow, lopsided grin that lighted his wonderful face melted her insides.

"Come all this way looking for a new trail guide, lady?"

"Are you available?"

"Not for that, but I might accommodate you in other areas. You interested?"

"What will it cost me?"

Laughing in delight, he shoved back from the table and surged to his feet. "You're here, Aggie! You came after all!"

Nothing had changed, and she didn't want him misunderstanding her arrival in Monterey. "I had to come," she said quickly. "Because of Callie. It was unforgivable of her and dangerous to run off."

"Oh, that. Yeah, she told me everything."

He was so casual about it. "Yes, but you must know that I—"

"The hell with explanations," he growled, crossing to her with his swift stride. "We can save all that for later, because right now . . ."

"What?" she asked breathlessly, intoxicated by the musky heat of his body mere inches from her own.

"Right now," he muttered, his voice raspy with need, "I have to do this."

The inches between them vanished when his arms closed around her, dragging her up against his solid length.

"And this," he whispered.

His hands shifted, framing her face. He began to kiss her. Urgent kisses that targeted her eyes, cheeks, throat. Every portion of her face but her mouth.

"And plenty of this," he promised at last.

His open mouth settled then on hers. Moist, eager and demanding. Agatha didn't resist him. How could she resist him? She wanted his seductive tongue capturing and stroking hers, wanted his body molded so tightly against her flesh that she could detect the hard ridge of his arousal, wanted to hear the hoarse sounds of appeal low in his throat. Wanted everything that made her feel feminine and desirable. Only Cooper could give her all that, and he did until she was weak from his potent onslaught.

But it was a mistake when their differences hadn't been mended. When they had parted because of them and would be compelled to part again, even more agonizingly this time, if circumstances remained as impossible as they were. It was a mistake, and she tried to tell him so when his mouth finally lifted from hers.

"My love, we must not," she begged him. "You fail to realize—"

"I realize," he insisted roughly. "I realize I missed you so much I was like a wild animal and that you're with me now and nothing else counts. Not tonight, Aggie."

She had tried. There was nothing more she could do. Or, in truth, wanted to do. She was a willing participant when he kicked the door shut, blew out the lamp on the table, lifted her in his arms and carried her to the enormous bed.

Exchanging feverish kisses and murmurs of love, they shed their clothes with the haste of a long denial. Cooper's eager mouth found her breasts in the warm darkness, his tongue plundering her rigid nipples. Agatha whimpered with a spiraling need that he answered with his hand in her nest of curls.

His fingers squeezed and caressed. They parted, penetrated, withdrew, then repeated the tantalizing ritual until she was raw and quivering. She strained against him, pleading for release.

"You have punished me enough, my love," she gasped.

"And myself," he whispered, pressing his swollen shaft against the place where his hand had been as he mounted her.

She welcomed his inflamed body, clasping him with arms and legs. Hot bolts of desire licked through both of them when his flesh joined with hers.

He permitted her the barest moment to adjust to him, to savor their melding. Then he began to stir inside her, his rhythms slow and measured at first, then building to a driving frenzy. She was equal to his demands, riding the rapturous waves with him. Craving what he craved. Each giving to the other.

They crested together, the storm breaking over them almost simultaneously.

Husky endearments. She thought that afterwards there were husky endearments from Cooper as he cradled her securely. She couldn't be certain. She was already sinking into a sweet sleep.

Agatha was startled when she opened her eyes. Not by the blinding sunlight of morning streaming through the windows, although that in itself was unexpected. Her last memory had been of drifting off in Cooper's arms, but she hadn't planned to spend the whole night without once stirring.

The real surprise was the sight of him standing before a mirror across the room, adjusting a cravat on a fine linen shirt with a standup collar. She was used to the rough Cooper Delaney of the trail with his buckskins and boots, not this handsome vision in silk waistcoat and nankeen trousers. He took her breath away.

He must have heard her shifting on the bed. He swung away from the mirror, a sheepish grin on his wide mouth. "I was told the governor would receive a gentleman before a mountain man, and if you laugh you'll be punished."

His appointment! Agatha remembered then that Carlo had told her a supporter close to the governor would collect Cooper this morning, hopefully to secure him an audience.

"How?" she demanded.

He crossed to the bed, leaned down and planted a kiss at

the side of her mouth. "Like this."

"I am not suffering," she challenged him.

"I can get much more inventive than that. Care to try me?"

She shook her head regretfully and pushed him away. "There is no time for it."

He agreed reluctantly and moved to the table, checking over his letter of petition while she reached for her discarded clothes and began quickly to dress.

"I long for a change of my own," she said, "but my things are still on the sloop."

"Sloop?" he mumbled, frowning over some wording in the letter.

"Yes, where I left them when I arrived yesterday."

"Thought they'd be at that house where you rented rooms." He began folding the letter.

Agatha struggled with the last of her buttons. What on earth was he talking about? "There are no rooms. I was in a state to think about nothing but finding Callie when I came off the sloop. What made you suppose . . ."

She broke off as a sudden, fearful suspicion occurred to her. Cooper, too, must have realized that something was wrong. He was staring at her grimly.

"Exactly what," she asked him slowly, "did Callie tell you when you found her wandering on the street yesterday?"

He told her, and she understood now why Carlo, and then Cooper after him, had been so casual about her appearance in Monterey. Her face must have betrayed her, revealing some of the truth to Cooper.

"She lied, didn't she?" he said, a sudden edge of bitterness in his voice. "Callie lied about everything."

"I—I am afraid she did. It was in Oregon that she ran away."

"And you came to get her back. Nothing more than that."

"My love," she started to plead with him.

"Not now," he said, a sharp bite to his words that tore at

her. He reached for his dress coat and slipped into it. The coat had wide lapels and a nipped waist that emphasized the breadth of his shoulders. "We'll talk about it later. Providing there is anything left to talk about. At this point, I'd say there isn't."

He had been made to believe that she and Callie had arrived in Monterey together for the express purpose of being reunited with him. The reality hurt and angered him, and he was unwilling to listen to her as he headed for the door, hat in hand.

Agatha followed him from the guest house, calling to him, "Cooper, please."

He refused to answer her. Without looking back, he strode across the patio and down the path leading to the street. She went as far as the corner of the main house, and there she stopped, dismayed by the sight of Cooper warmly greeting the occupant of the open landau that had come to bring him to the offices of the governor.

The last thing she'd expected was that Cooper's supporter would be a woman. A striking woman with a cloud of black hair and an eager smile that she flashed at him as he joined her in the landau. Agatha couldn't help the jealousy that stabbed at her as she watched the two of them, looking far too intimate, ride off together in the carriage.

"Don't be alarmed, senorita," said a deep voice behind her. "While it may be true that Bianca Sanchez has eyes for Cooper, he can see only you."

Agatha turned around to find Carlo standing there looking slightly amused. "It's true," he assured her.

She shook her head. "I am afraid that this morning he refuses to look at me at all." She explained their discovery of Callie's elaborate lie and how Cooper had reacted.

Carlo nodded understandingly. "Yes, that must have been a blow to him when he thought you had come to Monterey for no other reason than to join him."

"It is all so hopeless."

"Give him time," Carlo advised gently. "And in the meanwhile, don't concern yourself about Bianca Sanchez. She is useful to Cooper because she has the ear of Governor Diaz. When he is in the mood. She also has the governor's bed," he added dryly, "and for that I understand he is always in the mood. So, my mother and Callie are at breakfast, and I've been sent to invite you to join them."

"Kind, but I want nothing just now, thank you."

"Then keep me company over my own breakfast." He produced an orange. Seating himself on a bench under a cypress tree, he began to peel it.

Agatha went on standing there, too distraught to settle beside him. Or to appreciate the pleasant setting with the fountain playing softly and the sunlight dappling the colorful Mexican tiles that decorated its coping.

"I should get back to the sloop," she said. "They will be wondering about me. Also, my things are there, and I do need fresh clothes."

"You'll stay then?"

"I am no longer certain what I should do. I must decide."

"Until you do, the gig is at your disposal. Julio will be pleased to drive you wherever you wish to go. He even speaks English. Of a sort."

She assumed Julio was the hired youth who had met them at the gate last evening. "That is good of you, but will you not need the gig yourself?" She noticed that he was dressed for the city in sober black.

"I can walk to my bank. It's no great distance."

"You are a banker then?"

"Yes, handed down to me from my father." He offered her a slice of the orange. Agatha shook her head. "I can see that Cooper never told you this was how we met. I wasn't much more than a boy learning the business, and he was no older when he came looking for a safe place to keep those first meager savings. And that's how it was through the years, Cooper sending us whatever he could when he could."

"That part he did share with me," Agatha said. "How it was necessary for him to build a considerable fund before he could fight for the recovery of his ranch."

Carlo shrugged. "Bribing officials is a costly affair. Sadly, that's how our corrupt government has operated for too many years. Let us hope Governor Diaz will be an improvement."

"And if he is not, Cooper may spend everything he has slaved for and still not win his ranch."

"It is vital to him, senorita."

"But why? Because the land means everything? I could appreciate that, join him in his battle. But I have sensed from the beginning it is not the land itself that matters to him. It is this fierce need for revenge against the uncle who robbed him of his birthright. It is not worthy of a man like Cooper."

"Are you so certain that is his motive, senorita?"

"You think I am wrong then?"

"What I think," he said slowly, "is that you are right in your feeling the rancho alone is of secondary importance to him. But I believe you're mistaken about the other. It isn't revenge Cooper longs for. It's what the rancho represents."

Agatha stared at him, waking to the truth he wanted her to understand. To *belong*. This was what Cooper's struggle was all about, even if in his pride he was unable to acknowledge it. Why, it was as simple as that. He wanted to belong, to regain the world that had so cruelly and mysteriously uprooted him and cast him adrift. A world symbolized by the ranch taken from him. That's what Carlo was trying to tell her.

*My love*, she appealed silently to Cooper, *I have been a fool.*

Well, it was time to correct that. She would help him. Whatever the outcome of their own relationship, she would help him to recover his ranch. He was the man she loved, and she owed him that now that she knew his real need. But how, when she refused to be a party to an open conflict that threatened to end in violence and bloodshed? There must be a more peaceful solution. Perhaps . . .

"Senor Ramirez," she said decisively, "would you object if Julio drove me to the ranch of Luis Alvares?"

"You intend to speak to his uncle?"

"It is presumptuous of me, I know, but I must make the effort. If this desperate situation could be settled reasonably . . ."

"Anything is possible, of course. Julio will take you."

"Thank you. There is something else. You have been Cooper's friend for many years. Can you tell me how he received the scar above his eye?"

Carlo must have thought her request surprising and odd, though he didn't say so. Agatha didn't offer to explain that she was convinced the scar and the nightmares Cooper suffered were connected and that they had their origins in his dark, unhappy childhood. A childhood that might hold the answer to the loss of his ranch.

Carlo shook his head. "I've no knowledge of that." He paused, then went on solemnly, "I wish you success with your intention, senorita, but Cooper may not thank you for visiting his uncle."

"Yes, I know. But it is a risk I am prepared to undertake. Would you not do the same for someone who meant everything to you?"

# *Chapter Nineteen*

Magpie, crouched on a stool with her mending, cast a furtive glance in the direction of the daybed. Duke was stretched on its length with pillows piled behind his head, resting the leg that had been wounded on the overland trail. It had failed to heal properly, and much of the time he couldn't walk on it for the pain. She knew by the amount of grog he'd consumed that he was suffering with it this morning.

Good, she thought, relishing his torment. It was the one small satisfaction she had. That, and whenever it was safe to do so, staring at him with contempt, as she was doing now. He was too occupied to be aware of her scornful gaze. Re-reading the letter that had somehow managed to reach him in this awful place.

Magpie was familiar with its contents. Duke had been ranting about them since its arrival. Pacific Fur had written to inform him that he should consider his services terminated. The dictates of fashion made fur trapping no longer profitable to them, and the company was turning to other interests.

That was the polite language of the letter. But, in effect,

they were telling him he had been defeated in his efforts to prevent the women from reaching Oregon, and they no longer wished to be associated with him.

Pacific Fur's dismissal fed Duke's hatred for Agatha Pennington and Cooper Delaney. They had cost him his brother and now his dream, and nothing but their deaths would satisfy him. Magpie knew that was why he kept reading the letter, brooding over it hour after hour. His hunger for revenge obsessed him, a poison worse than the festering leg that unpleasant doctor had finally lanced.

Duke caught her looking at him. "What are you gaping at?" he snarled. She knew he would have struck her if she had been within reach. Drunk or sober, he was abusive.

When she made no reply, he flung the empty mug in her direction. "Make yourself useful. Go out there and get this refilled. Gotta kill this pain."

Magpie set aside her mending. Without comment, she rescued the mug and left the cluttered back room they were occupying at the *ramada*.

Duke frightened her when he was in these black moods. They were evidence of a deepening dementia. She was equally insane to stay on with him. No other choice, of course. He, alone, knew where their son was hidden. She had made repeated efforts to pry Daniel's whereabouts out of him. He never told her. He was evasive and cunning, promising her that she could have Daniel back when he was finished with Agatha and Cooper. Magpie felt helpless, caught in a trap that was racing toward ruin and tragedy. What could she do? Daniel was everything.

The barroom was noisy with drinkers and gamblers. Magpie eyed the crowd in distaste as she waited for the nefarious landlord to refill the mug. His place was a filthy hole frequented by thieves and lowlifes. She wasn't surprised that Duke considered it a suitable hideout.

The mug, slopping over with grog, was shoved at her with a lewd comment she ignored. She left the bar and returned to the back room. Duke was no longer alone. Diego Morrales, who had gone into Monterey yesterday to spend the night with a woman, was with him. He had news. News that excited Duke and made Magpie's heart sink.

"Both of 'em? You sure?"

"*Sí*, here in Monterey close by." Diego went on to tell his story of how he had encountered Callie on the street and then lost her. But he had persisted with his search, asking careful questions around the town. It wasn't until this morning that he had finally learned that Delaney and the child were staying at the Casa Ramirez. What's more, the Pennington woman had joined them.

Duke was overjoyed that his enemies were within reach. "Go back there, *amigo*. Watch the place, see who comes and goes. I gotta figure out how to lay a trap that'll catch both of 'em. Don't want no errors this time."

Diego, like an obedient dog, hurried off as he was instructed.

Duke sat up on the daybed, both feet on the floor. He waved away the mug of grog in Magpie's hand. "Need to clear my head." Then he laughed viciously. " 'Sides, my leg already feels better. Gonna feel really good when I can smash my boot into Delaney's face."

Magpie shuddered. She hated to think of his getting his hands on Agatha and Cooper. She wished she had the nerve to try to warn them, but there was still Daniel. She didn't dare risk it.

Agatha tried not to be anxious as she sat in the gig bearing her toward the sprawling ranch of Luis Alvares. She hoped this visit wasn't a mistake and that Cooper would forgive her intervention. Most of all, she hoped for an encouraging outcome.

At least she was dressed appropriately. She had managed to recover her luggage from the sloop and was wearing a fitted blue merino dress with cream collar and cuffs and a simple straw bonnet. Nor did she have to worry about Callie while she was gone. The child was safely in the care of Carlo's mother, who had been introducing her to a litter of new kittens in the Ramirez kitchen when Agatha left.

The journey itself helped to distract her from concern over her errand. They were traveling the highway known as El Camino Real south of Monterey. It offered a pleasing landscape of golden hills studded with oaks where the wild range cattle browsed under the warm California sun.

Her cheerful young driver, Julio, played guide for her in his peculiar English. He named the immense ranchos they passed, their rambling haciendas, some with private chapels and bull rings, connected to the main road by wide *avenidas*. Agatha caught glimpses of the mounted *vaqueros* tending the cattle which provided the hides and tallow that made all this wealth possible.

They were nearing their destination when Julio slowed the gig, gesturing with his whip in the direction of a smaller hacienda situated against a hillside.

"She ees the rancho that Senor Delaney wants back. She ees—I do not know the English word—*vacante* now."

Agatha knew he was trying to tell her that the low adobe structure was not currently occupied. She could see that for herself. Even from here the house had the forlorn look of desertion. She tried to associate the place with Cooper, to remember that he had probably been born here and that he was fighting to return to what he considered his rightful home. But it all seemed alien to the Cooper Delaney she knew.

The gig continued on its way, reaching the adjoining rancho of Luis Alvares with its vast acres and enormous herds. Agatha had an impression of carefully tended olive trees and wide verandahs as they arrived in front of the hacienda.

"The *patrón* eesself," Julio murmured, nodding in the direction of two men at the side of the house. There was no mistaking which of them was Luis Alvares. He was a tall, gaunt figure dressed in a short-jacketed dark suit with silver braid and a crimson sash.

Julio remained with the gig. She would not need him to translate. Carlo had assured her that Cooper's uncle spoke excellent English.

Steeling herself for the meeting, Agatha made her way along a pebbled path. Neither of the men was aware of her approach. They were engaged in the merits of a spirited black thoroughbred wearing a silver-mounted saddle. She'd been told that fine horses were a passion with Californios.

It wasn't until she reached them, stopping outside a window with a lovely iron grille, that they noticed her. Don Luis's dark, probing gaze registered surprise over her exceptional height, as most men did when meeting her. Otherwise, there was no emotion in his expression.

"*Madama*?" he inquired. His tone was courteous, but his lined face was austere. The haughty face of an aristocrat. She searched it for a resemblance to Cooper and found none.

"I am Miss Agatha Pennington," she introduced herself, "and I have driven from Monterey to speak to you about an urgent matter."

Don Luis dismissed the *vaquero* with a nod. The man walked away, taking the thoroughbred with him. "Now, senorita," he said suspicously, "what is this grave subject you wish to discuss?"

Drawing a steadying breath, Agatha explained her connection with Cooper and asked to be forgiven for her presumptuousness. Cooper, of course, had no knowledge of her errand and probably wouldn't approve of it. But Don Luis must see how worried she was about the situation.

She appealed to him. Yes, she could appreciate that both Don Luis and Cooper were proud men. Perhaps, however, the uncle was less stubborn than the nephew. Perhaps he could recognize his nephew's claim, even if he did oppose it. Would he not at least be willing to meet with his nephew, or his representative, to examine the issue amicably? Otherwise, Agatha pleaded earnestly, she feared that the conflict would escalate into a serious crisis. Surely Don Luis did not wish for this to happen.

He listened to her. Listened in stony silence. When she was finished, drained of all polite arguments, he said to her coldly, "You were wrong to come here, senorita. Cooper Delaney has all that he is going to get from me, and that was more than enough." He bowed to her stiffly, turned on his heel and strode off in the direction of his stables.

Agatha stared after him, aching for Cooper in the realization that he had been raised under the authority of the heartless Luis Alvares. It was a miracle that his capacity for love, however battered, had managed to survive this environment.

It had been foolish of her to come out here. She saw that now. How could she have been so naive?

Discouraged, Agatha was returning to the gig when an elderly woman in the garb of a servant appeared on the front verandah and signaled to her. She didn't understand what the woman was trying to tell her in a hurried whisper.

Julio, who had been waiting to hand Agatha into the carriage, translated. "She ees asking you into the hacienda, senorita. Her lady begs a word with you."

Mystified, Agatha followed the servant into the house and along a broad passage with heavy, elaborately carved chests. They came to a room at the side of the house. Its door was open. A frail-looking woman stood there waiting for them, an anxious expression on her face. She was soberly dressed except for a Chinese silk rebozo around her thin shoulders. Its colors glowed like jewels.

"Thank you for coming, senorita. I am Dona Elena."

The *patrón's* sister and Cooper's aunt, Agatha realized. She started to introduce herself, but the woman stopped her.

"I know who you are, senorita," she said with quiet dignity. Dismissing her servant, she stood aside in the doorway, indicating that she wished her guest to enter.

331

Still puzzled, Agatha obliged her. She found herself in the bed-sitting room of a woman who was obviously a devout Catholic. The carved and painted images of saints were everywhere, and a crucifix was mounted in a prominent position above a prie-dieu.

"Please," Dona Elena said, inviting her to take a massive Spanish chair. When Agatha was settled, she seated herself facing her. There was a decanter of fine Montecito wine on the table beside her, and she started to offer it.

Agatha shook her head. "What is it you wish?"

"I will be direct then," Dona Elena said. "You are perhaps a woman of influence, senorita. At least where Cooper is concerned. And if you are armed with the truth, it is possible you can persuade him to give up this fight before it ends in blood. I think, like me, this is a matter of the deepest concern to you."

Astonished, Agatha leaned forward in the chair. "But how did you . . ."

She broke off in sudden understanding. The deep window in the thick wall directly behind Dona Elena was open. There was an ornate iron grille covering it from the outside. The same grille Agatha had admired earlier when she had stood there with Don Luis. His sister had overheard their exchange.

"I will tell you something, senorita," Dona Elena continued solemnly, "and, like everything else I am going to trust you to know, it is the absolute truth. My brother may be an unfeeling man, but he is not an unjust one. Honor is everything to a family like ours, so believe me when I say that if Cooper were entitled to the rancho that was Niceto's, Luis would never withhold it from him."

"But as Niceto's son—"

Dona Elena lifted her hand, interrupting Agatha's argument. "There is more, much more."

She would have to be patient, Agatha thought. That's what the woman was telling her. She would have to listen to the whole story in order to understand.

"It is Niceto you must hear about first," Dona Elena continued. "He was young when our parents died. Luis and I raised him. He was a beautiful child but also much spoiled. Luis adored him and denied him nothing. Even the girl he demanded for his wife when he was barely a man. She was the daughter of a Yankee sea captain who carried our hides and tallow to New England."

"Cooper's mother."

"Yes, Kathleen Delaney. She was a beautiful flower, senorita, but it was not a suitable match. Luis argued against it, but Niceto would not listen. In the end Luis surrendered, promised Niceto the rancho next to ours and arranged for the marriage with Kathleen's greedy father."

"And it was a mistake," Agatha said, remembering what Cooper had confided to her when they had been trapped in the mine. That his parents' marriage had been a troubled one.

"It *was* a mistake. The girl never wanted Niceto. I think she did try, though Luis was unwilling to credit her with that. But, yes, it was a mistake because Niceto was possessive and expected her complete devotion."

"And Kathleen was unable to provide that."

"She was unhappy, senorita. Only her son gave her joy."

"And did her husband share that joy?"

Dona Elena shook her head. "Cooper made no difference to Niceto. He cared only for Kathleen, brooded about her. And, though it pains me to say it, drank far too much. I think he must have been out of his mind with drink the night he died. It is the only explanation."

Agatha was slightly confused. "You mean if he had been sober the bandits could not have killed him?"

Dona Elena stared at her. "Bandits? What are you saying?"

"Cooper told me that when he was a child of three or four, they were returning from Monterey and bandits rode down on them out of the hills. His father was killed protecting them."

"But this is nonsense," the woman scoffed. "There were never any bandits. They were at home in their own hacienda."

"Then just how, Dona Elena, *did* your brother die?"

"Niceto, may God forgive him," she whispered, "took his own life."

"What a terrible thing," Agatha murmured, leaning toward her sympathetically. "But then why did Cooper . . ."

"This I can't tell you. I don't know about the invention of the bandits. Nor do I know exactly what happened that awful night in that house. But Cooper was there and somewhere in his mind must know the truth. He was not a child of three or four. He was a full six years old."

Old enough to remember, Agatha thought. Which meant he had shut out the actual event, turned instead to a fanciful explanation for his father's death. Why? Would she or, for that matter, Cooper himself ever know?

"But there was Kathleen. Surely she had an explanation for her husband's suicide."

Dona Elena spread her hands in a gesture of helplessness. "She was hysterical that wild night she rushed to us with the boy in her arms. She could do nothing but wail how Niceto had been drunk and raving." She shuddered in memory. "Both she and the child were covered in blood. Horrible."

"Oh, Lord."

"Yes. Kathleen had been wounded in her struggle to prevent Niceto from shooting himself. The boy also had been hurt, though not so seriously."

Was this the explanation for the mysterious scar Cooper carried? Agatha wondered. She didn't have the opportunity or the heart to ask. Dona Elena, deeply distressed by now, wanted to rid herself of the rest of her painful story.

"Luis was not satisfied," she said. "He wanted to know more, but Kathleen was in no condition to be questioned. She was ill from the injury. And Cooper . . . well, he was only a child and very frightened. Very confused. He could tell us nothing.''

''Kathleen never recovered, did she?'' Agatha said, remembering Cooper's version of his mother's passing.

''No, the wound became infected and she grew worse. In the end there was nothing to be done but to call for the priest. She was just strong enough to ask him to hear her confession and to grant her absolution. And then . . . then, senorita, my brother did an unforgivable thing.''

Dona Elena paused, pulling fretfully on the fringe of the rebozo. Agatha could see just how difficult this part was for her.

''I do not excuse Luis, senorita, but understand that to commit suicide in our faith is a mortal sin. He could never accept it of his beloved Niceto and was determined to know the truth. That is why he concealed himself close enough to listen to Kathleen's last confession.''

''But what did he expect to hear?'' Agatha asked, half afraid to know.

''That Niceto did not take his own life. That it was Kathleen who had killed him. But,'' she went on after taking a deep breath, ''this is not what Luis learned. What he learned was something just as shocking and perhaps a reason why Niceto shot himself.''

Dona Elena got up from her chair, lifted the crucifix from the wall and sat down again with it in her hands. ''I swear on this cross so that you know I speak the truth when I tell you that Cooper Delaney has no Alvares blood in him. He is not Niceto's son. He was fathered by an officer his mother loved on Captain Delaney's ship, a man who died at sea just before she wed Niceto. This, senorita, was Kathleen's confession.''

Agatha stared at the woman, shaken by her revelation. There was no doubting her assertion. It had the ring of absolute truth to it. Besides, it made sense on other levels. Like Cooper having no look at all of a Californio about him. And his persistent feeling that in some manner he'd been responsible for his parents' bad marriage. Perhaps in some dark recess of his mind he had always sensed the worst but refused to recognize it.

"If, then," Agatha speculated softly, "Niceto learned of his wife's infidelity that night and was unable to bear it . . ."

"Yes, perhaps," Dona Elena conceded. "Niceto *was* of a passionate nature, and with the drink in him . . . but suicide is so extreme. We can't know, though. Luis was able to hear no more of Kathleen's confession after that. The priest caught him listening and was outraged."

Agatha understood. "He had committed a violation of the sacred confessional."

"Yes, senorita, and his penance was a harsh one. The padre swore him to an eternal silence, which he faithfully kept except for one weak moment when he confided in me. On pain of damnation he was never to disclose the boy's illegitimacy. And he was to honor Kathleen's dying wish, that Cooper be raised and educated by him."

"He fulfilled his penance then," Agatha murmured.

"As much as he had to, and then he could endure no more and cut Cooper loose. Cruel, but he never forgave him for Niceto. It has not been easy, senorita. For any of us. For my part, I have wished many times that Luis never shared these things with me, since knowing them made me also guilty. But I, too, kept my silence all these years." She crossed herself quickly. "May God forgive me the need for having spoken now."

She sat back in her chair, looking tired and old but relieved as well. Agatha knew why. Dona Elena had passed on to her a burden she no longer had the strength to carry. She was trusting Agatha with it now, expecting her to convince Cooper that he must surrender his fight for something he had no right to claim. And Agatha didn't know whether she had the courage to perform that duty. Her sorrow for Cooper was almost more than she could bear.

*Oh, my love, I wish there were a way to spare you this suffering.*

Agatha was alarmed when she returned to Casa Ramirez. A meeting had been held during her absence and was just breaking up as she approached the guest house. A dozen or so men emerged from the small building and streamed across the patio on their way to their horses. She couldn't understand the rapid Spanish they exchanged as they passed her, but the fiery tone of their conversation was unmistakable. They were aroused and spoiling for a fight.

The last to appear was Cooper. He was accompanied by Bianca Sanchez. Feeling helpless, Agatha watched them part from each other in a flow of warm Spanish. Then Bianca, ignoring Agatha after a single, indifferent glance, swept by her on her way to her landau.

Cooper joined Agatha where she waited by the fountain. He looked pleased to see her, but there was a tautness around his mouth that worried her.

"Just a few friends," he said, explaining the gathering in the guest house. "Most of them from the old days. We were discussing strategy in the event that . . ."

He didn't finish. He didn't have to. She knew that those so-called friends were the interested supporters Carlo had mentioned and that their meeting had amounted to a council of war. This couldn't go on.

"Your audience with the governor," she said anxiously. "Was it not successful?"

He smiled wryly. "The governor was pleased to receive my newest letter of petition, not me. I was kept waiting and then sent away. He's afraid to see me, afraid to make a decision, and I'm getting tired of all the delays." He changed the subject abruptly. "Where have you been all day?"

He no longer seemed angry with her about this morning. Perhaps she could risk giving him the truth. She *had* to risk it. There was no choice now.

"I was paying a visit." She took him by the hand and drew him down on the rustic bench beside her. Then she turned to him with an earnest, "I went to see your uncle."

He stared at her, and there was a dangerous gleam in those compelling green eyes. "You did *what*?" he said softly.

She grasped his other hand, holding both of them tightly as she pleaded with him. "I had to go. This thing is tearing you apart. I thought that if I—But that's no matter now. My love, it is going to be hard for you to hear what I learned, but you must listen to it."

And she told him. Told him as gently as she could how Luis had turned her away and what Elena had shared with her afterwards. Told him everything about his mother and Niceto and the harsh truth of his parentage.

Cooper asked no questions, offered no response, but when she was finished there was such a wounded, betrayed look in his eyes that she could have wept for him.

"I know," she murmured. "I know what it will cost you to give up the dream you struggled for so long, but you must see that you no longer have a right to it."

Still he said nothing. She went on appealing to him. "They are not important, love. Neither California nor Oregon. I understood that when Callie ran away. The three of us being together is all that matters. Please tell me you can see that, too, and I will live with you anywhere. Please . . ."

"You believed her," he said, his tone rigid with accusation. "Because my aunt is this pious woman who sings her rosary beads all day long, you went and believed her."

She should have known he wouldn't simply accept it, that he would go on resisting the truth with all the fierce effort he could command. "Think, my love," she tried to reason with him. "It all makes sense if you will but let yourself see it."

"Lies," he said, blind to her argument. "All lies calculated to defeat me. If they can't win with the truth, then maybe they can win with lies. Only it won't work. Luis Alvares is going to find that out.''

She had never seen him so livid, and she had never been so afraid. ''Look at you!'' she said, squeezing his hands as if to compel him into a state of reason. ''You are burning for a fight, and that rabble with you!''

He snatched his hands away and shoved to his feet. ''Yes, if that's what it takes in the end, with the law in this place worth next to nothing.''

''It is madness!'' He gave her no choice. She couldn't stand the thought of parting from him again, but he gave her no choice. He was a man she no longer knew in his fearful obsession. ''It is madness, and I cannot stand by and watch you do this to yourself.''

He understood what she was telling him, but to her anguish it made no difference to him. His face was hard as he looked down on her, his voice even harder. ''You do what you have to do, Aggie. I know I'm going to.'' He started to move away from her.

''Cooper—''

''It's all been said, and I've got to collect Bucephalus from the smithy.''

She watched his commanding figure stride away in the direction of the street. He was walking out on her. That was what was happening. He had made his decision and was walking out on her, as he had walked out on her in Oregon. Only this time there was a finality to it. He had told her as much himself. *It's all been said.*

She had done her best to win him, and she had lost. She loved him, would love him forever, but there was nothing left for her to do except take Callie and go. She had no illusions about what this would cost her emotionally, both now and in the years ahead. Her heart already felt as if it were being consumed, but if she stayed, the rest of her would be destroyed while she helplessly watched him fight a battle he couldn't hope to win.

\* \* \*

Callie was heartbroken as they boarded the gig with their things. "Doesn't Coop want us?"

Agatha tried again to explain it to her. "I am afraid we do not come first with him, love, and that would be the only way we could stay."

She knew that Callie wasn't ready to accept this, but the child made no further objection as Julio drove them in the direction of the waiting sloop.

Agatha planned to stop briefly at Carlo's bank when they reached the commercial center of town. She wanted to say good-bye and thank him for his hospitality. She also intended to ask him to watch over Cooper.

Cooper hadn't returned before they left Casa Ramirez. Just as well, she thought. This leaving was already wrenching enough. She was dealing with the pain of that when the gig turned a corner and came to a sudden halt.

Agatha was startled to see their way blocked by a closed carriage angled across the street. Its driver was sprawled in the dust of the roadway, his sombrero tilted over his face as if struck from his head by a hard impact.

"*Madre de Dios,*" Julio muttered.

An accident, Agatha thought. The driver must have been pitched from his box and was unconscious. She didn't like the way his arm was twisted under his body. It might be broken.

"He needs help," she said.

She started to descend from the gig, but Julio placed a restraining hand on her arm. "No, senorita. I look first."

Agatha waited with Callie in the open gig while the youth went forward to investigate. Though there was no other vehicle in sight, she wondered if there had been a collision and whether there might be injured occupants inside the carriage.

Julio was starting to kneel beside the driver when the stocky figure moved like lightning. The twisted arm came whipping up into sight, bearing a revolver that was shoved into the young man's astonished face. At the same time, the sombrero slid away to reveal a swarthy, grinning face.

Callie issued a gasp of recognition. "The man who chased me!"

That hideous grin was vaguely familiar to Agatha as well, but she had yet to identify him. Convinced that they had been tricked into a robbery, she started to reach for the whip that Julio had left behind. Before her fingers could close around the weapon, there was a sharp, warning click just behind her head. It was the unmistakable sound of a gun being cocked for readiness.

"Behave yourself," growled a voice at her ear, "and no one gets hurt."

The figure who had sneaked up behind them came limping around the side of the gig, wielding his own revolver and chuckling with satisfaction. Agatha found herself looking into the scarred face of Duke Salter, his eyes blazing with hate.

"Never know who you're gonna run into all outta the blue, do ya?" he taunted her, pleased by her shocked expression. "Now git down from there, you and the brat. You're goin' with us in our own rig."

There was nothing to be done but obey him. Julio, held at gun point while the transfer was made, was powerless to interfere. Nor was there any outside help available. The spot for the ambush had been wisely chosen. There were no houses here. It was a lonely corner with high, concealing shrubbery on both sides of the lane.

Duke opened the door of the carriage and waved them inside. There was another surprise waiting in the gloomy interior where the shades had been lowered. Magpie was huddled in a corner, her frightened eyes pleading for silent forgiveness as Agatha and Callie settled on the shabby seat.

"All right, Diego," Duke instructed his accomplice before joining them in the carriage, "give that pup there the note for Delaney and tell 'im what'll happen to 'im if he tries anything before we're gone."

Seconds later, with Duke inside and Diego mounted on the box, the carriage raced away from the scene of the kidnapping, leaving a distraught Julio standing in the roadway.

Agatha put her arm around Callie and held her close. ''Where are you taking us?'' she demanded.

Duke, from his position on the seat facing them, kept the revolver leveled at them. ''Wait and see,'' he snarled. ''In the meantime, do the smart thing an' keep your mouth shut.''

A moment later Callie, squeezed beside her, dared to whisper, ''Coop'll rescue us. You wait an' see if he don't.''

Agatha silently hugged her and wished that she shared her easy confidence. But she just didn't know. Cooper had become a stranger.

# Chapter Twenty

Bianca Sanchez stood in the open doorway of the guest house at Casa Ramirez, her dark eyes glowing with satisfaction over the exciting news she had just delivered. Cooper stared at her in disbelief.

"Why? What made the governor change his mind when only hours ago he wouldn't see me?"

"A letter arrived from your uncle. Luis Alvares demanded that Diaz refuse to meet with you and to order his officials to accept no fees from you. Diaz was furious over his arrogance and immediately sent me to fetch you." She tipped her head to one side, regarding him with disappointment. "But, *caro*, are you not pleased?"

Pleased? Of course, he was pleased. Why wouldn't he be? This was the moment he had been waiting for. And if he wasn't shouting with elation over this first sign of victory . . . well, that was Aggie's fault, damn her.

He wished Aggie had never come to California. Wished Callie had not arrived here looking for him. Now he had it to do all over again, learn to live with the impossible ache of separation. He had found them gone when he returned with Bucephalus. Aggie had fled, taking Callie with her.

Bianca expressed her impatience over his delay. "Why do you stand there? Put on your coat and come with me before he changes his mind again."

She was right, Cooper thought, angry with himself over his hesitation. Angry with Aggie for her failure to believe in him and for her desertion just when he was so close to getting everything he'd always wanted.

"You have the landau?" he asked, reaching for his dress coat.

"Waiting for us out front," Bianca assured him.

No, he wasn't going to let Aggie spoil his victory. "Let's go," he said decisively.

They were leaving the guest house when Carlo hurried across the patio to intercept them. Julio was at his heels. Cooper knew immediately that something was wrong. There was a grim expression on his friend's face.

"What?" Cooper demanded.

"Julio should have gone to you at once, but he was frightened and confused and came for me at the bank. Julio, tell him what happened, and do it quickly."

The youth stammered an account of the kidnapping while Cooper listened. Salter here in Monterey? He heard the rest, and his insides tightened with a sick fear. Jesus, the bastard had them! He had grabbed Agatha and Callie!

"There is a note," Carlo said when Julio was finished. "Directed to you."

He produced the note and handed it to Cooper, who read it rapidly. "The mission at Navidad. He's holding them at the old mission at Navidad."

Carlo nodded. "I know it. It is remote. And, of course, abandoned like all the missions since they were secularized years ago. No one goes there anymore."

"Which makes it the perfect spot for a showdown,"

Cooper said, his face like flint. "That's just why Salter chose it."

"You must let the soldiers from the presidio rescue them," Bianca urged him. "They will know how to deal with this. We will alert the commandant on our way."

She actually expected him to go on to the governor's. She didn't understand. "It's *me* Salter wants, Bianca. And if he doesn't get me, he'll kill them."

"You mustn't go there," she appealed to him. "Think, *caro*. Diaz is waiting for you. I know him. If you fail to appear, he will not forgive you. There will be no meeting with him then, and you may forever lose the chance to recover your rancho."

Cooper realized that this was the decision of a lifetime. Except there really was no decision to make. He had understood that the moment he'd learned his family was in danger and needed him. *His* family? And that was when he knew. Aggie and Callie *were* his family. They meant everything to him, and if he lost them . . .

"I'll risk that," he informed Bianca fiercely. "What I won't risk are the two people who make the dream not worth a damn without them."

"You are a fool," she said bitterly. "Sacrificing everything to run off to what could be your death."

He ignored her. He was busy arming himself with his Colt.

"I am riding with you," Carlo insisted.

"Salter wants me on my own, *amigo*."

"Which would be committing suicide. I won't permit this. He will have to accept both of us."

Cooper had no time to argue with him. He was already on his way out the door to saddle Bucephalus.

The church at Navidad, like the rest of the mission complex, had been stripped of its essentials and was approaching a ruinous state. But the baroque beauty of its massive walls, though stained and peeling, was still evident as the two men rode toward it through the overgrown orchards and vine-yards.

There was no way to exercise caution, no way to plan any strategy as they neared the looming structure. Salter was in control of the situation, and unless they showed themselves, he would fail to reveal himself or his hostages. They were prepared for the risk as they dismounted in the weedy yard and crept toward the ornate main portal, hands on their weapons.

A sadistic laugh from somewhere overhead had Cooper freezing in his tracks. His gaze lifted to a chilling, infuriating sight. There was a squat belfry at the front corner of the church. Aggie was up there beneath its dome. He could see her clearly through the broad, open arches. Her upraised arms had been bound and lashed to the crosspiece that had once supported the bell. A gag was over her mouth to prevent her from screaming any warnings. Salter was with his captive in the belfry.

Carlo nudged his friend, drawing his attention to a matching belfry on the other corner. Callie, also bound and gagged, was mounted there with Diego Morrales standing guard over her. Magpie was there too, looking dazed and powerless.

Cooper felt the fires of rage begin to burn in his belly. "Salter!" he shouted.

Duke, still cackling, leaned out from the arch. "Come to pay your respects, Delaney, before I sacrifice them on the altar?"

"You've got what belongs to me," Cooper informed him savagely, "and no one hurts what's mine. You either let them go, or before I'm through with you you'll be begging to roast in hell."

"You want 'em," Duke challenged him, "then come up here and get 'em. Stairway's in a tower over there at the side. Only leave your partner behind. You was supposed to come out here alone."

"It's a duel, isn't it? Consider him my second. I see you

got one,'' he said, referring to Diego.

"Yeah, and he's gonna make sure your second stays put.''

"I'm on my way, Salter.''

"I'll be waitin' for ya. Been waitin' since Jack died. Gonna enjoy paying you back for Jack.''

Carlo stopped his friend with a swift, whispered warning. "If you use that stairway to the roof, he'll be waiting for you at the top. You'll be walking right into his gunfire.''

"I know, but if I don't go—''

"There is another way. A door inside the bottom of the stair tower opens into the nave. You can slip into the church without his knowing and out again through a rear exit from the sacristy. There are iron rungs fixed to the outside wall of the apse climbing to the roof.''

Cooper understood him. It was a chance to surprise Duke from the back end of the roof. "I'll manage it.''

"And I will try to keep the other one diverted,'' Carlo promised.

From her outlook in the belfry, a helpless Agatha watched Cooper race toward the stair tower. His vow to Duke Salter was still throbbing in her head. *You've got what belongs to me, and no one hurts what's mine.* Even in her horror over the situation, she was thrilled by his words. She was also terrified for him.

The rope that secured her to the bell rafter allowed her to twist in every direction. Hearing movement behind her, she swung in that direction to see Duke scrambling from the belfry onto the roof just below. His revolver already drawn, he headed across the broken tiles toward the door at the head of the tower. When Cooper emerged, he would be stationed there. Cooper would be an easy target, and the filthy bandanna muffling her made any warning to him impossible.

Catching another movement, this time in her peripheral vision, she whipped around until she was facing the other belfry where poor Callie was also restrained by a line fixed to a rafter. Magpie, who was with her, had objected to their

347

brutal treatment of the child and been slapped into a cowering silence. Callie, resisting submission, was still struggling against her bindings.

But it wasn't her wild squirming that had alerted Agatha. It was the sight of Diego dropping from that belfry. He was on his way to join Duke. Two against one. Cooper wouldn't stand a chance.

Moaning in frustration behind her gag, Agatha began to tug furiously against the rope wrapped around the crosspiece above her. There was some give in the old, weathered beam. If she could just manage to snap it, free herself in time . . .

Diego, on the low ridge of the roof now, suddenly stopped and looked down over the front of the church. Something had captured his attention. Agatha turned slowly in order to follow his gaze.

Carlo. Carlo was stealing along the yard, trying to work his way toward the stair tower. He meant to join his friend. While Agatha watched in alarm, a grinning Diego raised his weapon and fired. The bullet bit into the dust, barely missing its mark.

Giggling now, Diego went after him again. Carlo, unable to return the fire for fear of hitting one of the captives in the belfries, dodged the shots. But he was an easy target from the height of the roof, and in the end he was struck. Agatha, groaning behind her gag, watched him go down beside the stone wellhead.

Crowing with victory, Diego climbed onto the stone coping of the facade. It was a position that would permit him to finish off his victim without a mistake. But Carlo was already motionless on the ground, and Agatha feared the worst. Until Diego leaned out from the coping to gain himself the best angle. In that instant, Carlo's gun flashed from the shadow of the wellhead.

She heard Diego's scream, saw him pitch from the facade. Then he lay sprawled in the yard below, no longer a threat. Carlo, supporting himself with the rim of the well, tried to lift himself to his feet. In the end, he sank down again on the ground, unable to stand. Agatha could see the blood soaking through the trouser of his lower left leg and knew that Cooper was on his own now.

*But where are you, my love?* she asked silently as she turned inward again to face the tower. He should have appeared on the roof by now. Duke, cursing over the loss of his accomplice, was down there by the door, waiting for him impatiently.

From the corner of her eye, she spotted activity in the other belfry. With Diego gone, Magpie dared to free Callie from her painful bindings. But she was not prepared to risk releasing her from the belfry. She clung tightly to the struggling child, crooning to her softly, promising that she would keep her safe.

Agatha, willing Magpie to meet her gaze, begged her with her eyes to help Cooper, to somehow prevent the ambush. But Magpie appeared to have retreated from reality and ignored her mute appeal.

Why didn't Cooper come? What had happened to him?

Agatha began to drag frantically again at the rope. The crosspiece wobbled and creaked, but it refused to liberate her. A second later she froze, hope swelling inside her.

There at the far back end of the roof! Cooper's head and shoulders had come into view! He had found another way up! Duke, his gaze fastened on the tower door, was unaware of his arrival. Agatha held her breath as Cooper, swinging himself fully onto the roof, crouched there with his gun in hand. He began to inch his way along the tiles, trying to reach a position that would keep the belfries out of range of his fire.

Magpie had seen him too, and she gasped. Duke heard and whirled around. Both revolvers barked at once as Agatha sobbed behind her gag. A gun, shot from a hand, went skidding along the tiles out of reach. Agatha sagged on her rope in relief. Neither man had been hit, and Cooper still had his weapon. It was Duke who was defenseless, standing there in a howling rage as Cooper closed on him murderously.

"I'm gonna put you in a grave where you belong, Salter, but I'm damned if I do it this way. Hell, I'm gonna kill you with my bare fists."

And then the man she loved did a valiant but very foolish thing. He tossed his gun into space and launched himself like a missile from a catapult. Agatha watched Duke reel under the repeated blows that were landed on him, heard Cooper's biting accompaniment to each punch he delivered.

"String up my woman, bastard!"

"Touch my little girl!"

"Try it! Just try going for that dirty knife of yours again, and I'll break your arm!"

The telltale white scar dividing Cooper's eyebrow positively glowed with his fury. As before, his action thrilled Agatha, but the violence of his assault worried her. Not because of what Duke Salter might be suffering. It was the roof on which they fought. Low-pitched though it was, it was rough and unsafe. Tiles were missing, and where the timbers below were exposed and unprotected, punished by years of harsh weather . . .

Dear God! The fear had no sooner occurred to her than it was realized. Having abandoned all caution in their wild battle, neither man was aware of a section of rotted planking until it collapsed without warning under their feet. One of them went down like a stone. In one second he was there. In the next he was dangling above the floor of the nave fifty feet below, nothing to prevent his certain death but his hands locked on a rafter that was still solid.

Cooper. It was Cooper who was suspended in that awful cavity. Duke had clawed his way to safety. Scrambling to his feet, his bruised and bloodied face contorted with an ugly triumph, he approached the edge of the jagged gap. For a moment he savored the sight of Cooper hanging there. But as Cooper made an effort to raise himself from the hole,

Duke's boot came down over his fingers gripping the support. He began to exert a slow, crushing pressure.

Agatha went out of her mind. With all the desperate strength she could command, she heaved and jerked at the rope that held her, heedless of the cord biting into her wrists. Cooper needed her. She had to reach him.

There was a cry of outrage from the other belfry, followed by a blur of movement. It was Callie. She had twisted out of Magpie's grasp, clambered like a monkey through the arch and down onto the roof. She was on her way to Cooper.

Agatha screamed to her silently: *No, Callie! No!*

But the child ignored any threat of danger and raced on across the roof, caring only about the man she couldn't bear to lose. Duke's head turned at the sound of her feet scrabbling on the tiles. For a second he was surprised. And then he laughed. An excited, demented laugh.

He caught Callie without effort as she charged toward the hole. She squirmed and kicked and yelled as he lifted her off her feet. And then she went very still when Duke's bowie knife suddenly appeared against her throat.

One arm like a steel band around her waist, the other bearing the knife, he held Callie above the hole like a trophy. "See her, Delaney?" he gloated. "I'm gonna kill her while you watch. It's gonna be the last sight you see."

Agatha, witnessing the horror from the elevation of the belfry, felt herself dying inside. She could see the spittle at the corners of Duke Salter's twisted mouth. Like the foam of a rabid animal. Could see Callie's white, frightened face. She could even see the helpless rage on Cooper's face along with a strange, stunned expression she didn't understand.

And all the while she dragged at the line that was restraining her, knowing that no matter how strong Cooper was he couldn't hang on much longer. Not with Duke's booted feet still pinning down his hands that were barely clinging to the rafter.

The bowie knife moved toward Callie's face. And then

something else moved. A figure behind Duke. A slim figure that had approached him swiftly and soundlessly. She was bearing one of the revolvers that she had recovered from a corner of the roof.

Magpie, Agatha realized with a surge of renewed hope. Magpie who had endured Duke's every vicious insanity for the sake of her son. But not this time. This time she would not stand by and watch the destruction of an innocent child.

Agatha watched with unbearable tension as the young woman reached Duke and placed the barrel of the gun at the side of his head. "Put her down," she ordered him. He backed away from the hole, still clutching Callie. Then he spun like lightning, flinging Callie at Magpie.

There was the bark of the gun, a spurt of blood, and Duke sank to the tiles. With all the strength she could summon, Agatha yanked at the line holding her to the beam. This time there was the sound of splitting wood as the half-rotted rafter finally caved in two. She was free!

Though her hands were still bound at the wrists, she was able to tear the gag from her mouth. Without pausing to gulp fresh air, she managed to crawl through the arch and lower herself to the roof. Callie and Magpie, unhurt, were already on their knees and clutching at Cooper when she reached the gap. Dropping between them, she added her own effort to the rescue.

They grasped what portions of him they could reach and began to haul at him. Cooper, straining every weakened muscle, fought the battle with them. Slowly, slowly he rose through the opening until he was at last able to lift himself the few remaining inches to the solid roof. He was safe, and Agatha was overjoyed. But there was no time for celebration. There were matters that still demanded their attention.

"My love, if you can manage it, Carlo is wounded down by the well and needs you."

Cooper didn't stir. He went on crouching there on the tiles with a faraway look on his face. What was wrong with him?

"My love, are you hurt?"

He shook his head silently. There was an urgent cry just behind her, and Agatha shoved around on her knees. Callie? she wondered in alarm. No, the child was all right. It was Magpie. She was leaning over Duke sprawled on his back.

"Tell me!" she begged the dying man. "Tell me where to find Daniel!"

Agatha added her own appeal as she bent over him. "For the sake of your soul, let her know where your son is before you go. Do that much, Duke Salter."

His eyes were still open. They fixed on her face. Then he smiled. An evil smile. Blood bubbled from the corner of his mouth, and his gaze went blank. He was gone, taking the secret with him.

Magpie began to wail in heartrending despair. Agatha went to her, taking Callie with her away from the edge of the hole. While Callie picked at the knots of the cord that still pinned her wrists together, Agatha tried to comfort the anguished young woman.

"Remember my promise on the trail? It is still my pledge to you. We will find Daniel. We will not give up until we do. Whatever it takes, Magpie, we *will* bring him back to you."

Once Callie's nimble fingers were able to free her hands, Agatha put her arms around the huddled, sobbing woman and rocked her consolingly. When Magpie was finally quiet, she remembered Cooper and looked around. He was gone.

"Where is he?" she demanded. "Did he—"

"Dunno," Callie said, her eyes wide with concern. "He just got hisself up and left. He looked all funny."

Carlo, Agatha thought. He must have gone to Carlo. "Everything will be fine, Callie. Stay here with Magpie while I look."

She could hear a sudden commotion in the yard as she got to her feet and made her careful way to the edge of the roof where she looked down over the facade. A squad of mounted soldiers had arrived on the scene. One of them was already working on Carlo's wounded leg.

Cooper, who had been hunkered down beside his friend, left him in the care of the uniformed surgeon and started across the yard to his horse. Agatha shouted to him from the roof. There was no way he could have failed to hear her, but he never reacted. Like a somnambulist, he moved on without pause, mounted Bucephalus and rode toward the highway. Not once did he look back.

Frightened by his strange departure, Agatha hurried toward the stair tower. The door burst open just as she reached it. A flushed and excited Julio emerged from the tower accompanied by an officer. The youth breathlessly explained that Carlo's alarmed mother had sent him to bring the soldiers from the presidio.

Agatha instructed the boy with a swift, "Julio, see to it that Callie and Magpie get safely down from the roof and watch over them for me."

Without another word of explanation, she flew down the spiraling stairs and across the yard. Reaching Carlo, she knelt beside him where he was seated on the ground, his back propped against the stone wellhead. The surgeon had cut away his trouser and was dressing the leg.

"It will mend," Carlo assured Agatha with a grave little smile and then asked her anxiously, "What happened up there on the roof?"

"Cooper did not tell you?"

He shook his head. "Nothing. He made certain I was being looked after, and then he left. What's wrong with him? The little girl—"

"No, we all survived. Cooper nearly lost his life, but that would not have shaken him like this. It is something else, something awful that must have happened inside him when he was hanging from that rafter."

Agatha sank back on her heels, searching her mind for an explanation. "Yes," she murmured finally, "that must be it.

I have been a fool not to realize immediately.''

"What?" Carlo demanded.

She shook her head. "I think I can guess where he has gone. I must go to him at once. If I am right, there is every reason to believe he will need me.''

Carlo didn't press her for details. "Follow him then. Take my mare and follow him.''

Understanding what he was urging, Agatha stared at him, overcome by her old terror of horses.

"What now?" he wondered.

"Horses," she said. "I have never been able to ride a horse, and on my own . . .''

"Dulce is the most gentle of creatures," he promised her. "She will carry you safely. Trust her.''

He was right. She couldn't let her silly fear stop her. The time had come to conquer that particular demon. "Thank you," she told Carlo, getting to her feet. "I will manage.''

Strength lay in determination, she reminded herself as she hurried decisively toward the place where Dulce waited. She had been saving battered women. Now it was time to save the scarred soul of the man she loved. It wouldn't be a horse that would stop her either. The ghosts of the past were another matter. They would be the real enemy she would have to confront and defeat if Cooper were ever to be hers.

Agatha's old tactic of maintaining her courage by talking aloud to herself in a difficult situation had never been more essential.

"You can do this, Agatha Pennington," she ordered herself as she clung nervously to the animal's back, the unfamiliar reins clutched in her unsteady hands. "You *are* doing it.''

The little mare was much too polite to actively object to her exclusion from this audible self-encouragement, but she did nicker a soft disapproval as she trotted toward the highway. Agatha, much to her surprise, understood and corrected the matter.

"Sorry, Dulce. *We* can do this, you and I together."

Dulce registered her appreciation by gathering speed as they turned onto El Camino Real. She could sense how inexperienced her rider was, how clumsy she was with the reins, but Dulce handled the journey safely and smoothly.

Skirts bunched under her, striving to find a rhythm that kept eluding her as she bounced in the saddle, Agatha strained her gaze along the road ahead.

"No sign of them, Dulce. Of course, they did have a start on us, and Bucephalus is very powerful. But you are clever, and we will reach them yet."

They continued flying southward.

"Amazing, Dulce. I am still here, thanks largely to you. I do apologize for my awkwardness, though I believe I am improving."

After another mile or so, Agatha offered a further reassurance.

"Not far now, Dulce. I am sure the turning is just ahead."

It was. Agatha remembered the low adobe hacienda cradled against the hillside. Leaving the highway, they followed the weedy lane to the front door. The place looked sad and neglected, inhabited by nothing but memories that were better left undisturbed.

Obviously, however, Cooper had chosen to resurrect them. Bucephalus was there, fastened to a post of the sagging porch. Sliding from the saddle, Agatha secured Dulce to another post. Stiff and sore though she was, she was grateful for her accomplishment. She expressed as much to Dulce, stroking her nose and whispering her thanks. "I am ashamed I was ever afraid of you, and I do apologize."

Then, facing the open door of the hacienda, she squared her shoulders and moved forward to meet the challenge that she knew was waiting inside.

\* \* \*

The place had been stripped of its furnishings long ago. The rooms were hollow with their bare tiled floors and stark whitewashed walls. It was strange to think that Cooper had been born in this house, had spent his first years here.

Agatha found him in the sitting room. He had opened the shutters, disclosing a view of the expansive grazing lands rolling to the mountains behind the hacienda. But it wasn't this scene that commanded his attention. His rangy figure stood near the corner fireplace where he gazed at the cold hearth, a man lost in a trance.

She went to him, touched him on the arm. Drawing a deep breath, he glanced at her with an awareness that relieved her. He didn't seem surprised by her appearance. He acted as though he had been expecting her.

"This is where it happened," he said. "Here in this room."

"What, my love?" she prompted him softly, knowing the answer but feeling she had to ask him anyway. It was important that he purge himself of the hideous tragedy.

Cooper began to describe the fatal event. "There was a wind blowing that night. One of those wild, dry winds that come down from the hills. I don't know whether that woke me up or whether it was the sound of their arguing. They were always arguing, but it was worse that night."

"Enough to bring you here to the sitting room," Agatha guessed.

Cooper nodded. "He'd been drinking more than usual, and he was in a dirty mood."

"Niceto, you mean?"

"That's right, my . . . yeah, Niceto. He was giving my mother hell here in front of the fireplace. They didn't know I was standing over there in the doorway hearing what he was shouting at her."

"Do you remember what he said?"

"I think so, though I'm not sure I understood it back then. Probably because I didn't want to understand it. But it was

357

always there in his eyes, the way he would stare at me with that black expression. He must have been watching me as I got older and changed, seeing that I didn't look in any way like him. That I didn't resemble an Alvares and what he'd always suspected must be true.''

''You were not his son.''

''That's what he was after her to admit. He was threatening her, slapping her. I don't know what was worse, the howling wind or his curses. I must have wanted to stop him from hurting my mother. I think I charged him, and he grabbed me. He had a knife.''

Cooper frowned, struggling with the unwanted memory. ''Luis had given him that knife when he was a boy. He was never without it. He had the knife, and he . . .''

He couldn't say it. Agatha, understanding, said it for him. ''And he cut you there,'' she whispered, her finger gently tracing his scarred eyebrow. He didn't object to her touching him in that sensitive place. Not this time.

''He wanted my mother to know he meant business, that he'd kill me if she didn't tell him who had fathered me.''

''Like Duke Salter tormenting you with Callie.''

''Yes, Aggie, just like that. When that bastard had his knife to Callie, it triggered everything I'd buried. It all came rushing back to me, every detail of that rotten scene in this house. But you knew that, didn't you? That's why you followed me out here.''

''I guessed as much, yes.''

''Sorry I ran out on you that way, but I had to come here. I had to be sure my mind wasn't playing tricks on me.''

''I know,'' she murmured.

And she did know. Or at least enough to be able to piece together the explanation of what amounted to a self-imposed memory loss. He had been a six-year-old child living with the fearful guilt that he might not be who he was expected to be, of feeling in some mysterious way responsible for the disaster of his parents' marriage.

Then that night . . . that cruel night the little boy with a stricken conscience had been traumatized by the man who was supposed to love and protect him. The same man who suddenly wanted to viciously destroy him. So he had painted over the reality, inventing a much kinder tale involving bandits and a caring father who had lost his life saving him. It was his way of escaping the demons.

But if Cooper was ever going to survive the past and begin all over again—and she prayed for that—then the rest of the truth, every bit of it, had to be dragged out of the darkness and confronted.

"Niceto," she urged him. "How did he die?"

"I got away from him. I think that's right. I got away from him, and he came after me again. He was out of control with the liquor and that hot wind that makes a man crazy."

"He did not kill himself, did he?"

"No, it wasn't suicide. He kept a loaded pistol in a cabinet here. My mother got the pistol. She wanted to hold him off, keep him from hurting me. There was a struggle. I don't think she meant to kill him. I think it was all an accident. She must have told me what to say afterwards. I don't remember. I was already living with my own lie and believing it." He laughed cynically. "It must have been a damn good lie, Aggie. There wasn't a crack in it. Until today."

She watched him as he moved away from the fireplace. He left her and crossed to the open window where he gazed out at the sweeping acres.

"It's all true," he said, his voice numb. "Everything you learned from Elena. Everything I refused to accept when you tried to tell me back at the guest house. It's all true."

"Yes, love."

He nodded. "I don't have a right to any of that out there. I'll have to let it all go, give up the fight. Because I don't belong here. Never did. I belong . . ."

He didn't finish. He began to rock slowly on the balls of his feet as he stared out the window, began to softly whistle a lifeless version of "Comin' Thro' the Rye."

Seeing him like this, Agatha felt as if her heart were bleeding. She knew how much he had to be suffering inside. In one shattering moment he had lost both his identity and his vital, lifelong dream. Now he didn't know who he was. But *she* did.

For the past several years she had been fighting to convince women battered by life that their origins didn't matter in the least, that their worth was to be measured not by their old errors but by their new directions and the strengths within themselves. Now she had to take that fight to Cooper, because if he failed to rise above this defeat, she would lose him forever.

She crossed the room swiftly and stood by his side, trembling with the urgency of her need to reach him. "It means nothing," she insisted fiercely. "None of this."

For a fearful moment she thought he wouldn't respond. Then he turned his head and looked down at her, his expression bemused. "Damn it, Aggie, don't you understand? I don't have a ranch to offer you. I don't have anything."

She faced him angrily. "If I have to tell you, Cooper Delaney, just where you do belong and all that you do have to offer me, then you are not the man I want after all."

He was silent for a time that seemed forever. Then, to her vast relief, he grinned at her slowly. "It's just me now, Aggie. That's all there is. You think it's enough?"

He was going to be all right!

"It always has been," she assured him. "However . . ."

"What?"

"A small demonstration of your value would be appreciated."

"Guess I can manage that," he drawled.

And he did, superbly in fact as his arms slid around her, gathering her against his rugged length. His mouth captured hers in a deep, compelling kiss that involved the heat of his skillful tongue and the hardness of his robust body. The prolonged kiss awakened memories of the pleasures they had shared, memories so tantalizing that she felt lightheaded when his mouth finally lifted from hers.

"That satisfactory?" he challenged her.

"For the moment."

He regarded her suspiciously. "Don't know that I care for that brisk tone in your voice. Whenever I hear it, it means trouble for me. What is it this time?"

"I was only thinking . . . well, there is so much to be accomplished, and you and I together . . ."

"Aw, Aggie, no. Not that scheme of yours to bring more wagons to Oregon."

"There is that, of course. But also we must find Magpie's son for her, and I have every confidence we will. And a school. I did promise to build a school. Then a ranch for us, along with Callie's future to plan . . ."

Cooper groaned.

"But it can be done, my love. The two of us can manage all of it. And," she continued enthusiastically, "you must teach me to be a proper horsewoman. Did you know I rode Carlo's mare out here all on my own? Well, I did, and with your support I am certain that in time I can be a credible . . ."

He was not groaning now. He was laughing. Whooping with laughter.

"What are you laughing at, Mr. Delaney?"

"You. Never let any grass grow under your feet, do you?"

"Not when there are so many needs to be answered."

"Guess that's one reason, along with a few others, why I love you."

"Good, because I love you, but I am not finished."

"There's more?"

"One last thing." She caught her breath, wondering if his wild heart had been tamed enough to give her the miracle she had never dared to dream was possible until now.

"Let's hear it."

"I am greedy, my love. A husband is not enough. I also

361

want," she said hopefully, "a child of my own."

"A baby?"

"*Your* baby."

"H'm." There was a tense pause while he considered it. "Now that one I find damn appealing."

Agatha was delighted. No, more than delighted. Delirious. "How so?"

"Because, Aggie," he growled, his hands tightening on her waist, "we are going to have such a good time making that baby."

She could hardly wait.

## SEVEN BRIDES
## LILY

### BY LEIGH GREENWOOD

**Seven Brothers Who Won the West—
And the Women Who Tamed Their Hearts.**

The way Zac Randolph sees it, he is the luckiest man on earth. The handsome devil even owns his own Little Corner of Heaven, the best saloon in California. And with every temptress on the Barbary Coast yearning to take him to paradise, he certainly has no plans to be trapped by the so-called wedded bliss that has already claimed his six brothers.

Refusing to bet her future happiness on an arranged marriage, Lily Goodwin flees from her old Virginia home to the streets of San Francisco. Trusting and naive, she vows to help the needy, and despite Zac Randolph's wealth, she considers him the neediest man in town. When the scoundrel refuses Lily's kindness, she takes the biggest gamble of her life. And if she wins, she'll become the last—and luckiest—of the Randolph brides.

_4070-0                            $5.99 US/$6.99 CAN

# LEIGH GREENWOOD'S
## SEVEN BRIDES
### Laurel

Although Hen Randolph is the perfect choice for a sheriff in the Arizona Territory, he is no one's idea of a model husband. After the trail-weary cowboy breaks free from his six rough-and-ready brothers, he isn't about to start a family of his own. Then a beauty with a tarnished reputation catches his eye and the thought of taking a wife arouses him as never before.

But Laurel Blackthorne has been hurt too often to trust any man—least of all one she considers a ruthless, coldhearted gunslinger. Not until Hen proves that drawing quickly and shooting true aren't his only assets will she give him her heart and take her place as the newest bride to tame a Randolph's heart.

_3744-0                                    $5.99 US/$6.99 CAN

# LEIGH GREENWOOD

**"Leigh Greenwood is a dynamo of a storyteller!"**
*—Los Angeles Times*

Jefferson Randolph has never forgotten all he lost in the War Between The States—or forgiven those he has fought. Long after most of his six brothers find wedded bliss, the former Rebel soldier keeps himself buried in work, only dreaming of one day marrying a true daughter of the South. Then a run-in with a Yankee schoolteacher teaches him that he has a lot to learn about passion.

Violet Goodwin is too refined and genteel for an ornery bachelor like Jeff. Yet before he knows it, his disdain for Violet is blossoming into desire. But Jeff fears that love alone isn't enough to help him put his past behind him—or to convince a proper lady that she can find happiness as the newest bride in the rowdy Randolph clan.

_3995-8                                        $5.99 US/$7.99 CAN

# Midnight Rose

## Robin Lee Hatcher

### *Romantic Times'* Storyteller of the Year!

**Diego**—Although he travels to California to honor his father's pledge to an old friend, he doesn't intend to make good on a marriage contract written before his birth. But then, he doesn't expect to find violet-eyed Leona awaiting him—or to find himself desiring a mysterious masked bandolera.

**La Rosa**—Into a valley torn asunder by greed, she rides with a small band of trusted men to bring justice to her people. To protect them all, she has sworn never to reveal her identity, not even to Diego, the man who has stolen her heart.

_3347-X                                $4.99 US/$5.99 CAN